CRITICAL ACCLAIM FOR
JJ STONER & THE KILLING SISTERS

'A fast-paced, high-powered thriller featuring a Jack Reacher with balls of added steel character who was once a contract killer for the army and rides a mighty motorcycle and plays a mean blues on his guitar.'
Maxim Jakubowski, lovereading.co.uk

'There is a hint of Derek Raymond in the more visceral physical descriptions and the sense that we are looking at a dark and dystopian oil painting. Stoner's final speech, when he realises how he has been played, is almost Shakespearean in its bitterness and helpless anger.' **Crime Thriller Lover**

'A compelling read with plenty of "didn't see that coming" moments. Great writing by any standards, but sheer brilliance as a debut novel.' **Colin Barnett, T&D magazine**

'An intriguing debut novel that combines the best of crime fiction: a gritty hero, a weaving plot, and constant suspense.'
Raeden Zen, author

Serial killings and strange sisters, hard as nails hit men and shady superiors, sleazy blues and sometimes seedy sex . . . it mixes grim and dark crime scene action with sticky-floored music venue philosophising in a way that shouldn't work but does. **Redleg Interactive Media**

'Gritty story-telling at its best, with graphic (but well-written) sex and a plot that fires from the hip.' **Amazon.co.uk**

'Compelling crime fiction, packed with twists and turns and colourful characters.' **Dan Sager**

'Guns, girls, guitars and scenes of gruesome violence, all shot through with a wit sharp enough to draw blood. With terse and brilliant prose, Westworth delivers a plot that drags you along relentlessly. Loved it, unconditionally.'

R J Ellory, award-winning author

'Rich and ambitious, this violent tale plays out with memorable scenes interspersed with writing to savour. A feast of poetic prose wrapped in noir.' **Crime Thriller Hound**

'A truly unique reading experience. The author injects style, pace and energy into a witty, thrilling, and sometimes sickening story. The cool, often emotionless Stoner takes you on a roller coaster of a ride right until the very end.'

Simon Duke, crime author

'There are some sequences which are as satisfyingly testosterone-soaked as any Jack Reacher adventure, and then some which are as bleakly subtle as über-nuanced Japanese noir. For every alpha male with a gun and a hard-on, there's an equal, often opposing feminine force: frequently just as effective and half as smart again. The writing is clever, the plotting is convoluted and the outcome is so utterly unexpected that it caught me completely off guard.' **Goodreads.com**

'A punchy and compelling tale of an ice-cold assassin, more nuanced than your average hired killer. The writing is sparse and crisp, the dialogue frequently laced with sardonic British edge.' **Amazon.co.uk**

ALSO BY FRANK WESTWORTH

THE CORRUPTION OF CHASTITY

Killing Sisters

Book II

Frank Westworth

Book Guild Publishing
Sussex, England

First published in Great Britain in 2015 by
The Book Guild Ltd
The Werks
45 Church Road
Hove, BN3 2BE

Typesetting in Cambria by Ellipsis Digital Ltd, Glasgow

Printed and bound in Great Britain by CPI Group (UK) Ltd, Croydon, CR0 4YY

A catalogue record for this book is available from
The British Library.

ISBN 978 1 910508 68 8

ACKNOWLEDGEMENTS

A remarkable number of friends contributed to this, the second of the *Killing Sisters* series. There's no space to credit everyone, but it would be feeble not to thank R.J. Ellory for continuing support, encouragement and suggestions, Ieish Gamah for more ballistic understanding than any single person should possess, arch-editor Jonathan Ingoldby for finding so very many inaccuracies and inconsistencies, and the several friends who read the various drafts along the way. Thank you all, humbly. The Special Tolerance Award must go to Rowena Hoseason, without whose relentless input, carrots and sticks there would be no book, and without whom life would be so very, very . . . less.

1

HIS ROD AND HIS STAFF

'Where's the fun in killing by gun?' The lone gunwoman wriggled for comfort as the desert sun bleached the land. She was alone. The best audience; that audience of one. The solo performance. She was talking again. To herself. Again.

'It's so remote. No involvement. No sense of association. It's like bombing someone from a long distance. Clean. Civilised. How can anyone make killing civilised? Being killed is never civilised. It's always crappy for the target.' She was heating to her theme. The sun scorched, relentless. Nothing else moved. The road in her sights rippled through the haze, but no vehicle moved along it. She swung her viewpoint left, then right, then back to the tight, slow curve where she had set up her point of focus.

It's not easy to maintain your cool when the ground is acting like your own oven, baking through the clothes. The camo-netting above her provided some shade, reflected back some of the heat and the blinding bright, but although the listless breeze moved it, the air beneath was as heated as the air above; probably more so.

Deserts are only lively places in the visions of TV documentaries. Life is rarely time-lapse. Killers must be patient. Patience may be their only virtue. She wiped sweat from the ridge above her eyes, wiped her eyebrows. Good job she had eyebrows again. Shaving them is stupid; sweat like smoke gets in your eyes. Eyebrows deflect the drips.

The rifle stood without concern upon its tripod. Rifles are machines. Dead already. It had no views on anything. Not its target. Not its shooter. Not the weather. The heat was a mechanical inconvenience, but it was set and cleaned and oiled and ready. It shot straight and had been zeroed, trued in the heat. It didn't care. Of course it didn't. Rifles are machines.

She didn't care either. Not much. She anticipated that the rifle would shoot straight and that her aim was good, that her measurement of the distance downrange had been exact and that the ammunition was good. She had placed a head-sized watermelon on the road at the target spot and put four rounds through it before it was reduced to mush. Dead mush. By the time she'd walked down to the road to retrieve her pet melon, desert things had appeared, removed it, and disappeared. Nothing moves in a desert. Despite what they say on TV documentaries.

She was talking again. 'Where's the joy in this?' No one would hear her, because there was no one there. No one for miles. Many miles. The wind, consistent in its strength and direction at this time of day, her hide chosen to take advantage of the sun and the wind at the appointed time, brought her no sound of mechanical movement along the desert road. If talking to yourself is a sign of madness, then so be it. Madness is not a problem when a soul lies prostrate, baking in the early afternoon rage of a desert, staring through a long sight, down a long barrel, across a long slice of sand. So long as the madness did not interfere with the higher brain functions involved in aiming and firing. Focus, not distraction, was required. But there are limits on how long even a most experienced killer can retain focus. An army sniper she was not. Army trained, and occasionally army employed, indirectly, but a soldier she was not.

The rifle lay inert, like her, in the shade. The camo-net

covered them both. Netting makes you invisible from a satellite, she'd been advised. How nice. She could imagine no reason why anyone would ever aim a satellite at a patch of desert where nothing moved, nothing interesting lived, in the off-chance that they might see the shadow of a rifle barrel. Not a chance. Not a hope. Satellites cost a whole load of money. Masses of it. They looked for important things, like missiles, troop movements, mighty ships prowling the oceans. Possibly also topless girls on beaches, depending on their focal length and the quality of the staff operating them.

That's distraction, she decided, and forced away the half-smile. She was developing an itch in the small of her back. Maybe it was the sweat pooling and boiling, producing her own personal miniature salt lake. Maybe it was imaginary. Maybe it was a deadly scorpion and she was about to die in convulsions, all alone in the light.

The vehicle appeared, exactly on time. It entered her field of vision from her left and turned through maybe thirty degrees until it was facing her. It was clear and plain in the sight. The cross-hairs lined perfectly on the passenger side of the front windscreen. The rifle fired, she reloaded. The rifle fired again. The windscreen was crazed. She shifted her aim tidily to the driver side and fired twice more. Then she lifted the sight a minute amount and placed two further rounds as high up through the screen as she could safely achieve, in case of rear seat passengers. Repeated the exercise again on the passenger side.

The vehicle continued in its straight track.

Second vehicle; a repeat of the exercise. Six more rounds. The rear vehicle ran remorselessly into the back of the first. The dead driver of the lead vehicle had ceased to pressure the throttle pedal some small time before the dead driver of the vehicle following. Collision was inevitable. Both vehicles ran together for a while, and then, like a scorpion stinging itself, they piled broken-backed from the road and crabbed into the roadside ditch, the rear vehicle pushing the front until, quite suddenly, the front vehicle slewed radically sideways, reared up on two wheels and rolled onto its back. All this in near silence and an ever-increasing cloud of dusty sand.

They stopped. All stopped. There was a murmur; at least one engine was still running. Automatic transmission, probably. A wonder of civilisation. The sand settled, followed by the lazy, light dust. She reloaded. Took aim again. Placed a full magazine's worth of shells through the windows of the lead vehicle. No movement. Repeated the exercise for the other. No movement. Reloaded. Watched. Lying still in the heat while the haze increased. No movement. Job done.

The rocket entered her field of vision from her right. It travelled with deceptive laziness before her surprised, wide eyes, landing in the lead vehicle and destroying itself and both vehicles. The selflessness of a machine. Body motionless, she tracked her eyes to the right, towards the source of the missile. Nothing. Nothing but sand. Mile upon mile upon mile of sand. The rocket's exhaust trail whisped through transparency to invisibility on the desert thermals. She could see no source. No shadows on the sand, no long barrels. No movement. Nothing. A missile from nowhere, from no one. Killing those already dead.

The dead vehicles burned. A funeral pyre billowing the remains of anything organic into the overheated desert skies. A boiling black beacon. Exactly what she had aimed to avoid. She could have used an RPG or any number of explosive devices. She could have sent up her own smoke signals. Here I am, they said. Here be dragons. Here lies death.

Time to leave.

She rolled onto her left side and lifted binoculars; scanned the sand again. Endless sand. Dunes, pebbles. No shadow. No movement. Nothing. No human stain on the purity of the desert.

Her intention had been to remain for a half hour, to watch

for movement, survivors. No more. No time. No need. She drank a full litre of warm, clean water, scrubbed the bottle clean of prints. Scoured all the surfaces of the rifle, wiping them down with the rag soaked in gun oil she had earlier used to clean its mechanism. Returned the weapon to its carrier, rolled out from under the camo-net. Rolled the gun, the redundant tripod, the spent rounds, the empty water bottles into the camo-net, scraped a shallow grave into the sand, buried everything and kicked sand in after it all. The night's wind would do the rest.

She stood still, an easy target. Waiting for the shot, for a clean death. The inevitable betrayal. None came. Gentle breeze. Outstanding heat. Sun. Silence. Miles of sand. No further projectile surprises.

The silence could not last. The targets would have been in contact with their base; a signal which would have been cut off, quite suddenly. They would soon be late at their destination, too.

Time to leave.

She fanned her face with her bush hat, wiped her brow with it, checked around herself, and walked over the skyline and down to where she'd left the Land Rover.

Which was exactly *where* she'd left it. But not exactly *as* she'd left it. The flat tyres – stolen valves; nothing so crude or so onerous as slashing the things or putting a bullet through them – would have been an effective delaying tactic on their own. Not fatal, not on desert sand, not on a Land Rover, but progress on four flats would have been so painfully slow that capture would have felt like rescue after an hour or two in the heat, and no one, but no one, not even on a dark desert highway, carries four spare wheels in case they might meet a comprehensively deflated Land Rover. No, the deciding factor was the disappearance of the battery. Both batteries. She was no stranger to desert driving, and had packed a spare. Gone. Unlike her water reserve. She drank some. Was it poisoned?

Why would anyone do that? The mysterious Land Rover disabler wanted her caught and blamed.

There was a symmetry to this. She had taken the shot, clipped the tickets of the occupants of both vehicles. Justice, then. She was a murderer. No doubt. And whoever had converted her Land Rover from a means of transport into an angular desert decoration had probably also lumped the rocket into the wreckage on the road, the pillar of smoke by day as good a beacon now as in biblical times.

Pause for thought. She had plenty of time, suddenly. Fried priorities. An invisible departure was only possible in a reliable vehicle. On foot, this deep into desert and only personal power to propel her, she needed to attract a saviour; a guardian, angelic or otherwise. No panic. Panic is purposeless. Panic is for employees, not freelance professionals. They survive only by fast footwork and fast thinking. Improvisation. Employees can call for evac and hang the consequences. She had no backup, no support structure. Just a little curiosity about what was happening around her, a desire to lie for a year or two in a deep bath, and the compulsive challenge of an unexpected problem. Problems were always entertaining – at least, devising their solutions was entertaining. The unwelcome pillar of smoke was now her very own rescue beacon. Well then, she would see what turned up to render assistance. Or the exact opposite; assistance out of her current physical incarnation. In the regional faith, martyrs graduated to heaven and the company of a fleet of virgins following their demise in a holy cause. She wondered whether adding a couple of dozen virgins to her long bath would improve it. Probably not, depending.

She drank more water. Loaded the remaining few litres about her person, ensured that she was adequately armed for any potential close-quarter scuffling, and set off. Back to the road. The immobile Land Rover and the redundant long gun she left abandoned. Her cell phone had no signal. Time to hike. It was a beautiful day.

In less than a half hour, she had reached the road and was heading north, the smoke cloud behind her. It hung and it grew. Vehicle fires could burn for a long time once they reached a decent temperature.

In under another half hour, she detected the movement of a vehicle approaching from behind. It was travelling steadily; neither particularly fast nor particularly slowly. She wondered, just for a second or two, whether the mysterious rocketeer was the driver, decided that it mattered not at all, and stuck out a thumb, as though hitchhiking in the remote middle of the remotest nowhere was a perfectly natural thing to do.

Which it might well have been. The car slowed, pulled to the crown of the road so its driver could take a good look at her, crawled past her, then stopped. She approached it. Late model Asian car – Japanese, Chinese, Korean, who could tell? And who cared? – it idled with mechanical contentment, unfazed by the heat. A window powered smoothly down. She leaned through it. The driver leaned in her direction.

'Were you in the wreck?' He sounded more concerned and curious than anything else. No suspicion. He was speaking English.

'No.'

'But you saw it, right?' Still no evident agenda. Simple curiosity.

'Yeah. No one lived through that. What happened?' The driver was male; he knew everything about everything concerning cars. She was female; she knew nothing. He would be confident. He was.

'Head-on, by the looks of it. Really hard.' His English was excellent, his accent Israeli, slight American highlights here and there. No surprise; few inhabitants of the Palestinian camps and townships drove cars like this one, a large luxury

4x4 of some nameless bulky variety. 'You need a lift, hey?' She heard the passenger doors unlock. She opened the front one, reversed her rump onto the seat, swung her legs in behind her. Pulled the door closed. Its closure was smooth, silent, no clang nor bang. The window rose without any help from her and cold air exhaled around them both. No similarities to her Land Rover.

'Thanks.'

'Hot out there, huh?' The car accelerated away, changed its own gears as it felt like it, the driver more helmsman than engineer. 'How come you're out here on your own? Oh, sorry. I'm Simeon. Simeon Guest.'

'Chas,' she replied without hesitation. No reason to lie. 'Man trouble. He'll be looking for me now, I guess.'

'Chas? Short for Charlene, Charlotte, Champagne?' And what? An argument? He left you out here? Damn, that's hard.'

'No loss, plainly.' She drank from a flask. 'You OK?' Offering him a drink. He shook his head.

'Must have been one hell of a fight to just leave you.' He was plainly, genuinely surprised.

'Not the first,' she leaned back and shivered slightly as the sweat evaporated from her clothes. 'But the last. He would have come back.' She looked over to the driver, smiled; 'Men always do. Chas; short for Chastity. Y'know?'

He grinned broadly at that. 'I bet. Where're you headed?'

She smiled at him. Already he was her friend. 'Anywhere with a bath, a bank and an airport. Maybe a decent hotel . . . a hotel with a bar. And a phone signal. Palm trees and a swimming pool. Is that a lot for a girl to ask?'

He smiled some more. Smiling suited him. She liked him. It was important that she liked someone after killing once more. She found herself drifting, just for a moment. Women and children in the cars? She hoped not. But the flash of caring concern flickered away as abruptly as it had arrived. Here was here, and now was now. All the past lies behind, and the future waits for no woman. She floated a grin over to the driver, who caught it as his gaze returned from mirror to the road ahead.

'Where are you going? Does it have a pool?'

'Ashdod. On the coast. About two hours if there are no hold-ups.' A military convoy, lights ablaze and bristling with intent, weapons and aerials, was heading towards them, on the crown of the road, travelling very fast. Simeon pulled the car to the side, gave them room to pass. 'They've seen the smoke, then.'

He pulled the vehicle back onto the crown, king of its road once more. 'You don't have a hotel? Kit to collect? I can take you anywhere that's on my way – or nearby. Glad to have company.' He had avoided flattering and flirting; she was pleased about that.

'He'll be waiting.' She stuck to her completely fictitious tale. 'Don't want to see him. Ever again. No loss,' she added, dropping her voice to a theatrical sigh. A helicopter rattled overhead, overtaking them, swivelled and flew backwards, matching their speed. They slowed, the copter slowed likewise but made no move to land. It lifted, turned, accelerated away.

'Like in a bar,' he said. 'They took one look at us and left.'

'OK if I sleep?' Chas had no wish to talk more. The fewer lies she told, the fewer lies she'd need to remember.

He nodded. 'Music? Radio?'

'Music. Anything soothing. Don't need angst right now.' She dropped the back of her seat, slapped her bush hat over her face; her sweat on it had chilled in the aircon. Dance, trance, rhythmic motion music glittered, tumbling from several speakers. 'That's fine . . .'

She woke from a calm quiet place when the vehicle's ride shifted into the chops and changes of the suburbs, unmistakeable after the steady rolling of the desert road. Outside was late afternoon bustle and clamour, reduced to a genteel murmur by the car's quality.

'I know what this sounds like, Ms Chas, but do you have any thoughts on where you might want to go?' Simeon looked ahead, concentrating on the road, driving steadily, expecting pedestrians to get out of his way. As if by magic . . . they did. 'I have a hotel booking in the centre . . .' A thought surfaced, almost audibly. 'Should I find you a bank?'

She stretched, a curiously unfeminine motion, and rolled her shoulders. Despite the comfort of the car, she was more tired than she'd been before her half-sleep, as is often the way. She reached over into the back seat, wincing a little, and retrieved her bag. Pulled it onto the broad seat beside her, and began to rummage.

'You OK?' His voice was quiet concern, nothing more than that.

She aimed a small laugh at him, raised her eyebrows when their eyes met and smiled. 'I'm stiff as a board. I need a hot bath. And my hotel – nothing grand about it – is in Haifa. But the bozo will be waiting for me there. If not already, certainly by the time I can catch a bus, a train, a camel, whatever.' She flapped her bag closed. 'Hey. Don't think I'm hitting on you, but does your central hotel boast a bath? I could really do with a little soaking and thinking time. I'll buy you dinner, drinks, something like that. I'm pretty beat, very dry and just knackered . . .'

He pounced.

'Knackered? You're a Brit, then? Only Brits say knackered.' He laughed. 'Great language. Love it. It's like talking in code.'

'You got it.' She laughed, coughing at the same time; dry throat, despite the luxury aircon. Or maybe because of it. 'Yep, Brit through and through. You?'

'What's your guess?' He was watching the way ahead.

'You sound American. Maybe Oz. Mid-Pacific. Something like that?'

'Nothing like that. Halfbreed, me. Simeon the halfbreed; half-Brit and half-Jew. I should say Israeli, but I prefer Jew. It's more honest. Two passports. It's how I get about and scratch a living. If you've got an Israeli passport, getting into any of the Arab states can be a real hassle; Brits are OK. No idea why; Brits are as dishonest as Israelis. Maybe more so. Not so much history.'

'Simeon the halfbreed.' She rolled her eyes, gazed blankly through the windows. 'I like that. That's cool. You married, Simeon the halfbreed? Little lady waiting at your hotel? You can tell me; I can always go get a bath at another hotel; I appear to have most of my money and most of my cards. Don't want to cause grief for my good Samaritan.'

'Married? Yeah. Twice.' He paused.

'One Brit and one Jew? One of each to match the passports?' She squirmed to find comfort in the deep seat. She really did ache. 'You got anything drinkable? There's some water in my bag, but I don't fancy it much.'

'Excuse . . .' he pressed a button, some unimaginable technology opened a flap in the sleek structure dividing their seats, and he reached inside to unclip a second cover. 'It's a chiller.' She smiled her thanks, dug out two cans of Red Bull – caffeine and calories; just what she needed – offered him one.

'Drink them both. There's probably more in there somewhere. Rentals are good like that.'

'Brilliant.' She drained the first can slowly and steadily, concentrating on rinsing her mouth with every mouthful. 'A killer chiller. Don't you love the Japanese?'

'Germans,' he smiled. 'The car's a Krautvagen. Love the Germans. Always buy German, I do business in Germany. Friends. Spend a lot of time there.'

'Stone me; you have a German half as well? What next? Venezuelan grandparents? Martian uncles?' She drained the second can rapidly, produced a heroic belch and apologised for it. He just laughed.

'You're OK, Chas. You're OK. Come to my handsome hotel with me and have a bath, make some calls, get yourself sorted. I can't do dinner tonight, but business should be done quite early. Get yourself a meal in the hotel if you like; the company can pick up for it.'

'You're not offering to scrub my back for me, then?' She looked at him with deceptive focus. His eyes followed the road ahead; a decent level of his own focus, aimed elsewhere.

'If you like. I'll need a shower before I meet the clients. There's always time to scrub a lady's back, though. This is the point at which you reveal to a shocked world that you're no lady, and you can speak in a deep movie seductress voice, too. Also that you'd never share a bath with a man – much less a twice-married halfbreed!'

'Still married? This is the point where you reveal that you're twice divorced and that you can tell lies as well as the next married man, halfbreed or no.'

'Yep. Still married. Wife's in the States. Wonderful woman.'

'What? No complaints? No justifications?'

'Nope. She's a mixture of Mother Theresa and Angelina Jolie. Or something. She's great.'

'You sound like you even like her! This must be something special.'

'Here we go.' He swung the car through an entrance so tight she almost expected the door mirrors to be wiped out. Pulled up in a surprising courtyard; circular drive, fountain and servants. The latter descended upon the car, opened doors, bowed and gestured towards the main doorway.

Simeon handed some paper money to the uniformed character holding the driver's door, pointed at the car's ignition. 'Driven one of these before?' The uniformed young man, handsome in a remarkable way, nodded. Spoke in flawless accented English.

'Of course. I'll send up your baggage . . .' he looked at Chas, 'while you check in.'

They made an unlikely couple, a study in role reversal. She, grimy, visibly dusted and sun-dried; he, pale skinned, neat, spotless, a man in a half suit with the other half slung over a single shoulder.

Chas inspected the deep russet tan of her hands.'We make an unlikely couple.'

'The only sort. I'll check in while you powder your nails, polish your nose, or reassure your friends, family, fan club about your well-being.' He nodded to a cluster of desktop computers, each and every one of them offering free internet services for honoured guests. 'Don't know how much access they have, but you must be able to do email. Maybe Skype.' He strode suddenly straight-backed across the lobby to the check-in desk, a vast solid wood edifice more suited to a Victorian movie set than to a modern hotel, extracting papers and a wallet from sundry pockets as he walked.

She walked to a terminal with its screen facing away from the mighty desk, her back to the wall, her fingers agile on the black, wireless keyboard. The prompt was instant, demanding a room number. She leaned back, clasped her hands behind her head, raised her eyes from the screen and turned to see Simeon looking her way. He raised four fingers, then four, then two. She tapped the numbers onto the keypad, followed by Simeon's name when it asked for hers; the screens opened before her; worldwide access at her service if you please. She looked up, saluted Simeon's back, and opened up Facebook, entering a name which was not her own along with the appropriate password. Access was slower than she'd hoped, quicker than she'd expected.

She scrolled through the waves of nonsense, looking for clues to her predicament. Her mother had posted some holiday snaps taken in what appeared to be Istanbul. This was at least a little remarkable, given that her mother had been dead for over a decade, and the selection of shots of mosques, a bazaar and an outdoor cafe were plainly intended to convey some kind of message . . . but probably not for her. They meant nothing to her.

Chas clicked her liking of a couple of the amateurish images, added suitably inane comments, then posted a message to her late mother's Timeline announcing her arrival at the resort, remarking that it was a lot hotter than she'd expected, but that there were a load of interesting-looking men around, and despite some trouble with the travel arrangements (aren't there always when dealing with foreigners?), she was booked into a grand hotel and looking forward to a hot bath. All the exercise in all this heat . . . well, enough said. She closed with a screenload of pleasant platitudes, asked after her little sister, hoping that all was well and wondering whether anyone had missed her or been asking after her. 'Time for a bath,' she typed, and logged out. Looked up. The lobby bustled with random activity, as is the way of all lobbies. Of Simeon there was no sign.

Two banks of four elevators with a similar number of queues. A broad staircase, entirely unoccupied. There were cameras over each elevator door; she could see none staring at the stairs.

'Four flights. Four flights of stairs.' She strode through the door to 442, which turned out to be a decently large and decently furnished suite of at least three rooms. 'If you were aiming to wear a girl out, you could have gone to the tenth floor at least. I'm exhausted. I may need a lie-down.' She appeared to be breathing normally and moved like the athlete she was.

'A shower to cool down, at the very least.' Chastity appeared cool as well as calm. But her perfect performance had no audience. The door had been ajar, propped against a complimentary hotel slipper, but the visible rooms of the suite were unoccupied so far as she could see. She checked that the door was fully closed behind her. It was. She locked it. Neither surprises nor service required. She retrieved the slipper and, slapping it gently against her palm, walked through the rooms. Big rooms and well furnished. Comfortable. They matched the lifestyle suggested by the car; luxurious and at the same time functional.

Bathroom. Had Simeon elevated to the suite, stripped off and dived into the bath, waiting for her, ready for the reward for his generosity in rescuing her from the desert? He hadn't seemed to be the type. But many men were deceptive. She tapped on the door, listening for a response or for the splash of expensive water. No reply. The door was unlocked, and the room was empty. She turned slowly, and returned to the main room, slipper still slapping against her open palm. Her host was standing in the centre of the room, watching her.

'A neat trick; you hid in the light fitting,' she said admiringly, with no interrogatory inflection. Simeon heard a question anyway.

'Balcony. I was outside. On the balcony.'

'OK. Admiring the view?'

'Checking for snipers.' He smiled. She returned the smile with the ease of long deceit.

'Oh? An occupational hazard? Everywhere you go, mysterious strangers take a pot at you?' Her tone was relaxed, easy, light-hearted. His also.

'Not usually. I always reckon that if anyone out there wishes me harm then I should present them with a clear target so they can kill me cleanly and save all the skulking about.'

'That isn't normal tourist behaviour, Simeon. There's a story behind it. Care to share it? Do strangers often shoot at you? Do I need a bulletproof vest while we eat dinner?'

'The food here's more likely to do you damage than bullets.' He smiled. 'Dinner? Feels like I've not eaten all day. Fasting is for fools. Also the religious. Restaurant or room service? How private do you need to be? You'll be dining *toute seule*, I'm afraid.' His smile had not slipped at all, he was asking a simple question. Which answered at least one of her own.

'Private? Do I need to be private?'

'I'd say so.' His smile remained unslipped. 'You've business with your . . . boyfriend, and I'd not want to intrude on that. Or did you sort that out in the lobby? Can't see that blasting off a fierce email is likely to worry the type of guy you're going to attract, or who'd strand you in a desert, but all things are possible. Anyway, whatever, I'm out for the evening so you can do whatever you want to do in peace and quiet.'

'And I can stay here?' She looked directly and spoke directly; eye to eye, mind to mind. No misunderstanding.

'Yep. Here comes the twist. The sofa makes into a divan. You should sleep on that. I'll be quiet when I come back. If you're asleep.'

'You'll have company? A wife in America and a girl in every state?'

He returned her smile. 'Something like that. You know how it is, I'm sure. Nothing is certain in this life.'

'If I'm snoring, then it's deliberate and I'm awake and being considerate.'

'I'd expect nothing less from a Brit.'

'Do I need to be gone before breakfast? Before the great awakenings?'

'Nope. Not on my behalf. Be here or not; all the same to me.' He reached for the belt at his waist. 'But I need a shower, I need it now, and then I need to get going.' The room telephone rang. They both turned and stared at it. Both moved as one and checked their cell phones. The room phone stopped. They paused like actors losing their place in a script.

Simeon shrugged. Kicked off his pants, landing them neatly on a chair, Chastity applauded. And with a smile, Guest peeled away the second silk skin of his shirt, dropped it into the same chair and was gone into the bathroom. His smile returned around the doorframe.

16

'Steam sets off the smoke alarms.' And the door closed behind him.

Strange city by night. Strange culture. Strange sounds. Strange lights. Strange sights, conflicting sights. The muddled east. Extreme wealth and extreme poverty. Smirks and scowls. Designer stubble vying with the simply unshaven; the eyes identify. Always the eyes.

Chastity covered her bright hair, half of her fair-skinned face, big sunglasses hid her reddened eyes. She was lost in the noise. The art of being unobtrusive is the reverse of every woman's ability to be seen when she wants to be seen. No formally Muslim country this, but plenty of veils on the streets. The poor wear black. Chastity haggled a long bright scarf from a street stall, wore it like one of the faithful. Metal threads in the weave glittered under the street lighting; she was invisible behind it.

Internet cafe, the refuge of the anonymous lost. Facebook, where her several mothers, all of them deceased, shared make-believe lives with their friends, real and otherwise. Chastity visited one mother's Timeline, discovered that her mother shared her enthusiasm for hot baths and had wondered how long her errant daughter was likely to stay in Israel, whether she fancied some company, whether her funds were holding out, and wishing her well on her well-deserved holiday. Mothers are like that, even imaginary dead mothers.

'A bit lonely, to be honest,' wrote Chastity, providing a sanitised account of her predicament for the benefit of any eyes that might intercept their conversation. 'Company would be really sweet', mostly because she was 'a little bit alone in a big strange place', but also because her car 'had been stolen and her travel arrangements were way out of kilter as a result'. A good word, kilter. Worth remembering.

Mother's reply was instantaneous and arrived as a message, just to her, the beautiful, dutiful daughter. It was filled with sympathy, understanding, perhaps a little steel in the suggestion that Chas may have bitten off a little more than had been wise. But all would be well, of that there was no doubt. Did she have enough money for a few quiet days of sightseeing, bathing, maybe a little light reading? Had she acquired a new cell phone yet? She should, her brother was a little bit concerned and would like to talk. Real talk. Voice stuff. Just to reassure her mother that everything really was all right while she and her brother arranged a visit.

Chastity transmitted reassurances, smiley-faces and promises to sort out a phone, ever the dutiful daughter, she. And as soon as she left the net cafe, she searched for, found and purchased for cash a pre-paid cell phone, strolled with studied innocence until she found a dusty park with a petrified wooden bench which was possibly biblical in its antiquity, sat and dialled a faraway number.

'Hello mother,' she spoke conversationally as soon as the device connected. 'Is brother Chas on his way yet?'

A delay. A reply. A laughing woman's voice. 'We thought we'd lost you!' Tone of voice intended to sound amused, entertained more than alarmed, but concerned too, perhaps. A perfect tone for the mother of a wayward daughter, a wayward western daughter. 'Are you OK for money? Got somewhere to stay?'

'I met a man . . .'

'Why am I not surprised. You always do. I don't know where you get it from. Is he nice? Would I like him?'

'He's a rich American with a big German car and a bigger suite in a smart hotel, that's what he's like.'

'Sounds good.'

'Oh it is, mother, it's great, but I don't know how long he'll be around, and I'm not sure what to do next. It would be great to see brother Chas again. Really.'

The connection hummed and muttered to itself in some

faraway space of its own. Maybe it was offering sympathy. Maybe it was simply eavesdropping. These things are never easy. Mother's voice faded in, clipping a little.

'Could be a week. Maybe two.'

'You serious?'

'Afraid so. All the obvious options are . . . fully booked. And it's terrible timing for you to be unavailable. Balloons are going up. Seems like you're a popular girl, and likely to get even more popular soon enough. Just the one party invite so far, but there's another on the way, so the twins say. Gosh. Just got a message from them; already two parties for you to go to. I'll tell them you've got a headache or need to do your nails or something.' Mother sounded entirely entertained. 'Make like you're royalty, just play hard to get. I would. Call if you need me. Glad you're safe and well. A mother always worries.' And she was gone.

Chastity closed the phone. Gazed at it in silence. Finger-nailed open the back, picked out the SIM card and battery, put the latter into a pocket and snapped the former into two pieces, then flicked them into a desiccated thorn bush. Anonymous rodents scuttled their confused protest. Chastity felt, for a single elusive instant, sympathy for them.

She remained where she was, seated on her petrified wooden bench for some time. Ashdod, an alien city, shared its conflicts with her. Israeli troops, armed with youth and rapid firepower, chewed gum and watched while the evening call to prayer summoned the faithful to worship their own prophet in the studied calm of the many mosques. Several of the soldiers looked her over, but only in a sexually speculative way, none of the gazes threatened and she reacted not at all. There was no sign of any other interest. None she could see, nor even feel. She was shattered. Exhausted. The uncertainty and inaction were like the hangover of a serious drunk; instead of relaxation they sucked her towards sleep. Willpower only works so far. After that determination will hold off the demanding embrace of unconsciousness, but not for long. And after that, drugs, hard action or . . . sleep.

She rose to her feet, stretched, attracting more speculative and appreciative glances from the soldiers, and walked briskly back to the big hotel, to Simeon's big comfortable suite, the silent room. She folded down the sofa into a decently wide, decently long, decently comfortable divan, kicked off everything she was wearing bar the T-shirt, lay down and . . .

. . . morning. Another call to prayer and a craving for coffee, the taste of it calling from her mouth's memory, wailing like the muezzin. The dawning awareness of her situation, her surroundings, and that there were at least two other people within her field of awareness. She could hear quiet voices and movement. The sounds, the unmistakeable unmissable sounds of sex. A twinge. A momentary amusing twinge of jealousy, not for Simeon in particular, but for the sharing of sex, of closeness to an almost-stranger. Someone to abandon, creatively, and with the twist of delight that brings. She felt quite suddenly alone. Time for coffee.

It was too early for theatrical clatterings, she felt, although there was plenty of brightness. She did the usual things involving filter papers and pre-ground coffee, nodded a silent thanks to the east, or wherever the dark bitter gods of caffeine lived their lives of stress and tension, tension and strain. Bottled water boiled and bubbled; she showered herself while the dim machine built the reviving drink; dressed in yesterday's clothes after beating the dust from them over the dry bath.

'And hey, here comes the early bird.' Simeon was lining up three small morning cups in a shallow triangle. He would no doubt place his own central and above the others; Chastity smiled only with her mind. 'Black? To counter the morning light?' He was smiling at her, the self-confident, easy smile of the sexually relaxed male. She smiled back, nodded.

20

He filled the three cups, lifted the centre cup in both hands and offered it to her. 'Sugar? Or are you civilised, too?'

'As it comes. As it is.' She sat, her shower dampness vanishing into the air conditioning. Simeon placed the cup before her on the low table, placed the others by two chairs facing her, and nodded towards her unmade, makeshift bed.

'Sleep OK? You were long gone into slumber when we returned. Motionless. A disciplined sleeper. Rare. Except in soldiers.' He drank the nearest coffee in a single silent draining, rolled his eyes and closed them. Picked up the second cup, fingers reaching for it with entire accuracy while his eyes remained closed, and drank it in another slower, more luxuriating movement, a complex enjoyment involving holding the brew in his mouth while exhaling through his nostrils. His eyes flicked open. He stood, the movement as fluid as the drinking ritual.

'Another? Breakfast? Here or downstairs?' He poured three more cups, placed them as before, but this time added a little cream to two of them, not waiting for a reply.

'Your guest, Mr Guest?' Chastity raised an eyebrow towards the bedroom. Simeon flickered small amusement across his features.

'Gone now. The demands of the city life. No time for sentiment, the city. Never sleeps, so they say. The call of commerce.' He drank the first of the second duo of cups, slowly, without ritual or affectation, eyes watching her steadily, openly. 'What's your plan? Have you got hold of friends, family? Your missing man? If you need to make calls from the room, feel free.' He was quite suddenly entirely serious. 'I'm here for two more days after today, maybe three. I'll be out of here during the day. Back this evening. You should probably be out of here during the day too. We can dine tonight, if you wish, Chastity.' He stared at her, contemplative eyes, expecting a reply.

'I'll buy some clothes and sort some . . . things. Find out how long . . . how long I'll be here.'

21

'Can't just stroll off to the airport and catch a plane to the homeland? That just too easy?'

'Too easy. Too . . . simple.'

'OK.' His smile had been packed away for the moment, replaced by a confident calm. 'It's complicated?'

'Isn't everything?'

'Not everything.' The smile returned, amused at something. 'I can't pry . . . don't want to pry. I don't need life to be more complicated than it already is.' He reached a decision. 'You're leaving no trace. In my country we call that tradecraft. If you have a beef with me, this is the time to tell me.'

'No beef.'

'Honest injun?'

'Honest injun. Hands on hearts; up school, up school; crossed hockey sticks, whatever you like. I . . . OK, I would prefer to be invisible for a little while. If you have . . . a beef with that, just say.'

'Nope. That's fine. Let room service search the room in their own time, make up the divan like you didn't intend to sleep on it. We're foreigners; they watch us. It's just a habit, like saccharine. Means nothing.'

'But they'll know already that you had a friend staying . . .'

'So I had two friends staying. We can leave together if you like. Hug on the sidewalk.'

'Not leave in the car together?'

'Being collected. I'm being important for a couple of days.'

She smiled broadly. 'The hotel won't think it a little . . . un-British that you had two friends staying?'

'I stay here quite often. They're used to it. They'll probably leave an extra bathrobe, maybe some more slippers.' He smiled again, more easily. 'But they'll log keystrokes on the lobby terminals and record the phones. They sell the stuff to the Yanks. The mighty dollar rides again. You in serious shit, Chastity? Do you need heavy help?'

She shook her head. 'There's a misunderstanding. There's

always a misunderstanding. Some lies, too. Always some lies.'

'Ain't that the truth. You OK for cash? Local currency?'

'Not really. Dollars and cards. I'm a tourist, remember? I do dollars.'

Guest conjured a fat roll of New Shekels from nowhere, stood it on the table. 'Go haggle for clothes. Shout loudly and slowly in English. Play like a traveller, not a tourist. Time to go.' He stood up, headed for the bathroom. The door chimed. Chastity stepped into the bedroom, moving with ease and speed. Simeon grinned at her. 'It's just my suits.' And indeed it was, three of them, pressed and shouting the international language of solid money, a powerful voice the whole world over.

2

FLOATING WHIRLS

'No. In fact, I believe that an instrumentalist should concentrate on the instrument.' A long man, not young, solidly smiling, relaxed into a long drink and met the eyes of his interrogator. She smiled back, closing as far as she was able the whole world of the wide and busy bar into a private flirtation chamber for the two of them. The table they shared space with had been designed for around six occupants, but was coping with an attendance of maybe three times that number. The two performers, one expert musician, the other opinionated audience, had an audience of their own supplying moral support or something like that for the relaxed and protracted seduction which was being enacted before them.

The bar was busy, loud, shifting its 500 feet to a shared if unheard rhythm. A group memory of the last number of the last act, maybe, or something more tribal, natural for groups of excited, gregarious creatures engaged in a permanent if mostly unrequited mating dance. As they shuffled in strange orbits attempting to collide with future maybe-mates, they welcomed the opportunity to share a focus, a conversation in which they could share without contribution; they could pretend familiarity with the conversation enacted before them. Even though they knew nothing of the musical matter under debate, they knew what they liked and were sufficiently well into the evening's drinking to feel relaxed about their obvious ignorance, because no one in their shared group could reveal that ignorance for what it was.

'You should sing,' the young woman announced to the older man. She was tense, he completely relaxed. She shared the air of someone who recognised where the evening was heading, of the nature of the night which should follow. The growing group around the table nodded, support and encouragement in equal measure. Of course he should sing. His smile was expanding into a wider appreciation of their collective flattery. He drained the glass, which was as if by magic replaced at once; a uniformed waiter shaking his head with a smile as he avoided any acquisitive glances.

'You do sing sometimes, so why not more? Why not tonight?' She was as persistent as she was pretty, then, and she was certainly pretty enough to support her evening enterprise. She glanced around the widening circle of good-natured swarming barflies, looking for support. Which she found, along with encouragement from the rest of the audience from which she was bent upon separating herself.

'And will you play some jazz? Proper jazz?' Again the noisy ripple of consensus; jazz was suddenly popular in one bar at least. She was warming a little to her theme, persuading herself that it was less a request, more the beginning of a beautiful and certainly meaningful friendship. Maybe a partnership.

'Guitar players should stick to playing the guitar. They usually lose it when they start to believe they can sing songs rather than just playing tunes.' He paused, but not long enough for a reply. 'And when they start to write their own songs and sing them . . . well, then they stop being guitar players and become entertainers. Stars. Something like that.'

'You don't want to be a star?' The woman sounded genuinely surprised. Plainly she felt that everyone wanted to be a star. 'Doesn't everyone want to be a star? Or . . .' her voice trailed as an idea landed, lost and lonely perhaps. 'Have you *been* a star? Were you a star when . . . when you were younger?' She suddenly looked a little embarrassed.

He smiled. 'Star? All they do is fall. They sparkle a bit, but they always either fall or fade away. Who needs it.' Not a question, the last remark. He picked up the larger of his self-filling glasses, the one with the beer, and gazed through it at a light in the ceiling. The ceiling shone with a thousand tiny bright lights, dimming and brightening in a pattern known only to themselves. He leaned towards his companion, held the glass before her.

'Look up. See the stars?' She stared through the glass at the sparkling ceiling. The surrounding crowd stared at her and fell suddenly silent. She breathed out, plainly a great moment of revelation. Maybe she'd never looked at a light through a beer glass before. Some people lead lives of mystery and imagination.

He whirled the glass, swirling the contents. The small sudsy head drifted like clouds across the surface.

'And now they're gone. Just like stars. Who needs them? What are they for?' He smiled again, leaned back and rocked his chair up on its two hind legs. Drained the glass. 'You want light, switch one on. You want music, grab a musician. You want a star? Go outside and catch one. They always fall.'

A hand fell on his shoulder. A flicker of tension phased over his features, was immediately replaced by the same briefly interrupted smile. He reached his left hand to cover the new hand on his right shoulder. 'Hey?' He did not turn around.

'Would you take a walk?' Another female voice, as attractive and interesting as most female voices are to men who appreciate music. The woman across the table, the star-gazer, glared over his head. She could see what he could not. He imagined from the glare that the sight would please him as much as it displeased his admirer. 'Maybe wave at a star or two?'

'Wouldn't that be nice?' He squeezed the resting hand. 'If you meant it, babe.'

'I do. I do. Just after the next set, hey?'

'OK! Lead me to it.' He rose. Leaned across the table into the world of his frustrated admirer. 'You'll still be here? For that walk with the stars?'

She nodded, eyes suddenly wide.

'Well? Were you?' His new companion paced him across the lounge to the small stage.

'Was I what?'

'A star? You're a star here, John, right enough.' She caught his arm, pulled him to face her.

Evening gown. Jewellery. Sculptured hair. Perfume. Faintly straining smile.

'You think? They're all on holiday. It's a world of make-believe, fake. Fake everything. Fake stars, too. Here they dress like retired bouncers, pretend wealth, style, charm and education. They tell lies, get laid, get drunk, tell themselves they're having the time of their lives. Then they go back to reality, to the friends they despise, the jobs they hate and the lives they waste. They watch stars on the TV and they listen to all the lies, the bullshit about how stars are just like them only lucky somehow and . . .' He stopped. Pasted the smile back across his face. 'Let's assume the position.' He turned back to face the stage. She pulled him back.

'Hey, don't be bitter. No need. You don't need to play. You're a guest here like they are. A passenger.' She looked suddenly embarrassed. 'That sounds rubbish. I'm sorry.'

His smile improved to a point at which it might even have been genuine, sincere. 'No need. Thanks for letting me sit in with your act. You're the star. You *are* the star, Ace. I'm just the help. The amateur. Do me a favour?' They stepped together onto the low stage. Scattered applause.

'What?' She beamed out at the crowd.

'Let's not play "Girl From Ipanema" again? I really hate that.'

'But you're so good at it. Hello again!' She spoke into the microphone and spread her arms to embrace the audience. 'We'd like to welcome you to the Starlight Lounge for an hour of the most gentle jazz to see us through our nights. And again, back by popular demand, joining us, your own Starlight Trio, for the rest of the evening, John Hand. Let's have a hand for John; the smoothest guitar player around!'

Of course the audience applauded. Of course he bowed. Of course they broke into the set with 'Girl From Ipanema' . . .

'The trouble with twenty-four hour bars is twenty-four hour drinking.' Musician, vocalist and a reduced fan club of just three were well into the second hour after midnight.

'What's the trouble with that?'

'No one can handle it.' The long-limbed lady vocalist warmed to a tuneless theme. The long-suffering lacquer was losing its grip on her hair. 'You get past . . . oh I dunno . . . twenty-five, you can't take it. You start falling asleep. You start suffering really badly from hangovers. Guys can't get it up – or they can't get it to stay up – girls forget everything they learned in high school about values and dignity.'

'Easy! Easy, lovely lady. You'll have us all in tears any minute. Can't be doing with that. We're on holiday. Holiday is a different reality. Real rules don't apply here.'

'You're on holiday, John. You're on holiday. Not me. You . . .' she gestured all-inclusively. 'You're all on holiday. I'm working. I am that working girl.' She appeared genuinely mournful for several silent seconds . . . and then burst out laughing. The long guitar player laughed with her, quietly.

'Yeah. We have to pay to listen to you having a good time. Being a star.' He laughed again, quietly again. 'And it gets worse.' He lowered his voice in a conspiratorial way. His co-conspirators leaned closer to catch the whispered punchline. 'I have to pay to play for you!' Gentle laughter, shared by all.

'That is so sad.' A new voice. A tall voice, carrying itself along before its speaker hove into view, the speed of sound being more rapid than the fleetest of feet. 'The least we can do is stand you a glass of something.' The voice appeared, tall, uniformed and bearing a bottle.

'All rise. Officer on deck.' Muttered disappointment from a female portion of the small audience. No one stood. The bottle berthed itself centrally on the table, followed by a nautical cap. 'Does anyone need a fresh glass? John?'

'John? First name terms? You're off duty then?' John Hand's smile expanded to include and to welcome the newest recruit to the small band. 'Calm waters ahead? Shark-free and blood-warm?'

'You should write the ads for the cruises as well as sailing on them. First officer, no longer officer of the watch nor the watcher of the officers. Off duty. Ladies.' She produced a small glass from nowhere, cracked the whisky and poured. 'And gentleman.' She raised the glass. 'Happy birthday!' A broad smile to the company. No other glasses raised. Everyone looked around at everyone else.

'Happy birthday John. No need to be bashful. Or embar-rassed. You're doing well. You look a lot younger than the age on your passport.' She beamed. Leaned across the table and poured expensive whisky into his almost empty glass. He smiled back.

'Do you know.' He paused. 'I'd quite forgotten. I must be getting old . . .'

'The company discourages fraternising.' The officer's nautical cap sat on a table, in between a basket of weary fruit and an allegedly personalised invitation for John Hand to share drinks with the captain. The remainder of her uniform was hanging neatly and comfortably alongside his own clothes in the large walk-in wardrobe.

'We should attend this event together.' He waved the invitation at her, before dropping it back onto the small oval table and refilling her glass. 'You should go as you are. You do look good in underwear. You'd be the talk of the evening. And I'm running light on buckshee bubbly – last bottle, this.'

'Are you going? To the bash with the captain? Didn't think that was your style at all.'

He smiled. 'Right again. Horrible. "Well, Mister . . . ah . . . Hand,"' he mimed an appalling Italian accent. '"Welcome to my sheep. I thank you for screwing my own first officer. This is above the call of duty. I will refund the cost of the cruise. You have saved me a lot of work . . ."' She threw a cushion at him and rolled over on the sofa.

'Asshole. He's very proper. No one's caught him out yet, not with crew nor passengers. He spends a lot of time in the gym. Works out.'

'I bet he does. Needs muscles to fight off all those rich widows. Occupational hazards every one of them. I couldn't do it. Well . . . I expect I could steer a ship, but deal with the passengers? Nah. You're all saints, every one of you. I mean, you have to go to these drinkies sessions, you have to smile all the time and pretend interest in all the social workers from Sussex, weird welders from Wigan, time-expired teachers from Tewkesbury . . . and that's just those in the posh cabins. What the hell do you say to the trogs who infest the cheap seats? Those windowless halls of hell in the middle of the ship. How does the skipper of a technological miracle like this damn great ship pretend any interest at all in the world view of some retired part-time primary school teacher whose idea of a great adventure – prior to this particular great adventure of course – has been an annual excursion to watch Widow Twankie at the Tunbridge Wells Christmas panto? "Oh really, Madam? You feel so deeply about the environment that you oppose windmills but go sailing on a great big ship adding to Mediterranean pollution as you go? How fascinating."'

'I've no idea how you do it. Really. Max respect!' He raised another toast. She just laughed at him.

'What do you talk about with them, Miss First Officer?'

'Mrs, if you please. I am a happily married first officer.'

'You are? I see no ring.'

'There's a sort-of tradition that we don't wear them at work.'

'I see that. Might put off the eligible millionaire widowers. Do you get many of those?'

'None so far. Would it put you off, Mr Hand?'

'Not so far.'

'You married, John?'

'Not so far. Go on, what do you talk about with the trogs – passengers like me?'

'I ask what they do when they're at home. Get them to talk about themselves. They always find themselves interesting. I can yawn and smile at the same time. Takes a little practice but you get the hang after a year or two. What do you do when you're at home, John? Oh I forgot . . . you don't talk about it. I bet you're a nice respectable husband really, with a nice respectable wifey and a rich mistress with a red dog.'

'A red dog? Why a red dog? I'm a musician. And I drive a van.'

A long stretching silence.

'Hello? Is grim reality so shocking? I don't actually know anyone with a red dog. You still here?'

She reached out a hand and squeezed his thigh. Slid the hand up the thigh, looked down and smiled. 'Let's go to bed now.'

'Vans turn you on? It's a big van. Black . . .'

'Fool. That's the first personal thing you've told me. Thank you.'

'Oh gods, sentiment. You'll be asking me to undress you slowly next.'

'Undress me, sailor. That's an order.'

'Ladies first. You undress me. I deserve it. I've been entertaining your passengers while you idled away the evening with cocktails and the captain.'

She pushed him onto his back, undid his belt, the trousers, slid down the zip, slipped her hand inside. 'Oh. My. Underpants. You're dressing formally tonight. Expecting royalty?' She slapped his cock free of the clothes, pulled them down and stood over him, excellent in underwear. Stood to one side and kicked away her panties, stood over him again. He watched her opening up above him. Said nothing.

'Happy birthday, John. I mean that. Hope you're happy to spend it with me, rather than little miss hots in the bar?' Her voice rose gently, slightly, into an interrogative. 'Was that why the pants? Expecting someone more refined? Cultured?'

He folded his hands behind his head, stared up at her sex. Then into her eyes. She smiled. He did not.

'Is it really my birthday?' She nodded, squatted so that the lips of her sex rested on the shaft of his. Both shone with intent and purpose.

'You'd forgotten? You don't know when your birthday is?'

'I know perfectly well. But I have no idea what day it is. Or where I am. Or what I'm doing here.' She moved above him; his cock bulged obligingly. She reached down to load it into her. He shook his head gently. 'No hands.' He pulled his own from behind his head, clasped her shoulders and moved her body higher up his, slid her back and slipped inside. She leaned onto his arms and closed her eyes.

'You've done this before. You've done this a lot.' She smiled, easing into a slow rhythm with him; he moved in perfect harmony. 'Lots, John. How lots is lots? Or shouldn't I ask?'

'Ask away, babe.' His eyes were closed now, lost in the music of the moment.

'And you'll tell me the truth? How lots is lots?'

'Hmmm . . .'

'How lots?'

'No idea. They all merge into one after a while.' Their rhythm picked up a little pace.

'But lots. Lots.' She was breathing hard. 'Lots . . .' She pushed all the weight of her body and all the strength of her arms into sharp focus, scraping her clit against the coarseness of his body hair, harder and harder until her moment arrived. 'Come with me John, come on, come with me.' And come she did, squeezing and soaking him with her pleasure. Rhythm lost, she sat back, sat upright, opened her eyes and gazed at him with slowly returning focus. He remained hard, fat inside her. Replaced his hands behind his head, said nothing.

'OK.' She restarted her rhythm, eyes languid, and reached down between them. He caught her hand, raised it to his mouth and kissed it.

'No hands.'

'Birthday treat, birthday boy?'

'If you like.'

'Your birthday. What do you like? Special pleasures? A surprise?'

'There are no more surprises, babe. None. Not at my age.' His smile balanced the words. 'But this is fine. This . . . I could do this forever.'

'Nothing lasts forever.' She increased her movements, rolling herself along and over him, rising above him to the point of disconnection and then sliding hard down him once more, banging herself against him with increasing abandon until, sweating hard, she came again. And stopped, panting. He remained hard, fat inside her.

'You OK?'

'I'm good. You're looking great.' He caught her eyes and smiled into them. And suddenly gripped her hips, lifted her above him, caught his cock as it fell from her, slid it through the swamp of her sex, past it to the damp puckered ring behind it and slipped into her once more, this time with sudden force and no gentleness at all until he was entirely inside her again. She was panting, eyes wide, staring at him. He pushed her shoulders away from him, raising himself to do so, until she was leaning away from him, her empty, soaking sex gaping while the dry muscles of her arse spasmed hard around his cock.

He stroked her belly with his left hand while she leaned back on both of hers, reached beneath his pillow and produced a slim vibrator.

'Shhh . . .' He moved gently beneath her. She breathed out slowly, moving only a little. In some discomfort, if not outright honest pain.

With contrasting gentleness, he lifted the vibrator to her sex and slid it slowly inside her, loading it inwards until she shook her head. Then he twisted its engine into life, closed his eyes and lay back. 'Shhh . . .'

Later still, she lay across him, head on his chest, her closed eyes gazing through their lids at his closed eyes, safe behind lids of their own.

'I hurt.'

'Hmmm . . .'

'I mean it. Feels like I'm bleeding.'

'Have a bath if you like.'

'I don't want to move.'

'Then you're not bleeding.'

'John?'

'Hmmm . . . ?'

'How lots is lots? Really lots?'

'Hmmm . . . Shut up and go to sleep. I'm a very old man. You're a young woman. You need beauty sleep. I don't. We can tell each other lies in the morning.'

'It is morning. I'm on duty in about two hours.'

'Then you need to shut up and go to sleep. The lies can wait. They'll keep. Lies always do.'

'John?'

'Hmmm?'

'We're in Malta the day after tomorrow.'

'Yes.'

'If I pull double shifts tomorrow – today – I'll be free after the noon bells. Fancy going ashore?'

'I don't usually.'

'I know that.'

'I like the ship when she's empty.'

'You said that before.'

'So.'

'So you won't go ashore with me?'

'You askin'?'

'I'm askin'.'

'I'm dancin'.'

'What?'

'OK then.'

'OK?'

'OK. Now shut up and sleep, unless you want an encore. You'd need to work for that. Age is a terrible thing.'

'Youthful vigour overcomes all.'

'Keep the lies 'til morning.'

'John.'

'Hmmm?'

'I love you.'

'No you don't. Keep the lies 'til morning.'

'You are one smartarse bastard, John Hand.'

'Truth at last. How's your arse?'

'Bleeding. Hurts like fuck.'

'Swearing is unbecoming in an officer and a lady.'

'You just don't care, do you?'

'Shut up and go to sleep.'

'You don't though, do you?'

'Shut up and go to sleep or I'll smother you with the duvet.'

3

SERIAL ENCORES

A barkeep known as the Chimp and a pianist called Stretch leaned on the bar kept by the former. The latter gestured with his glass, half-filled or half-emptied, depending upon your perspective, towards the stage. Nothing appeared to be happening on that stage, although tell-tale lights were lit on most of the half-dozen amplifiers, which suggested the imminence of music. Amplified noise, at any rate.

A short speech joined the gestured glass: 'Not a sight you see every day.' The pianist, a beefy, bald but bearded, mountainous black man, beneath whose fingers a piano's ivories seemed lost without trace, drained a measured more from his glass.

'Hmmm.' Barkeepers are often chatty, professionally garrulous even, but this one was plainly still warming up for the evening ahead. He leaned against his bar and laid his gaze towards the stage. 'Indeed not.' That seemed to be the limit of his views.

'Goths in a jazz bar. Not one but a pair of them. In full dress, too. A sight of wonder, even in these days of miracles and wonders.' The pianist emptied his glass, passed it to the barkeep for the purpose of fulfilment. The Chimp obliged, and stared stagewards again. He warmed to his theme.

'Hmmm.' He wiped the counter top with a towel intended

for the sanitary cleaning of glasses. 'A wonder.' His sigh, so profound that continents could have been moved by it, was largely lost among the racketing arrival of customers. 'Customers,' he announced grimly. 'More customers. Always customers. Bringing us money and demanding drink and entertainment in return. Hard to handle, isn't it?'

Stretch the pianist was unmoved by the latest arrivals and ignored them, as a musician should. 'Wonder what they're here to hear? Don't they go for punk rock or something?'

'Do you play that? Isn't that all about smashing instruments?' The Chimp aimed his flat stare at his pianist friend. 'It often sounds as though you're trying to wreck the old joanna, rather than, y'know, extract music from it. Punk jazz, is that?' His expression was entirely innocent, his voice devoid of inflection. Stretch, a very large man whose very large hands concealed very large talent and delicacy combined, smiled at him indulgently.

'We'll soon know, at a guess. Bili knows them.' A diminutive woman had appeared from somewhere and had sat down with the two men in black. Both barkeep and pianist had assumed that their black-clad guests were male, but it wasn't easy to be sure. A certain large coat shapelessness concealed many things, but the powder-white faces, dark eye make-up and thin red lips were strangely asexual. Although the tables were filling as the evening grew, the goths were isolated, on an island. Plainly the audience was insufficiently lubricated to venture near their strangeness. Bili, accomplished bassist and nonchalant beauty, laughed and slapped the table, then stood, walked slowly to the bar, nodding here, shaking a hand there, laughing with faces less unfamiliar than most until she joined the drinking pair. The Chimp nodded, smiled and moved off to provide refreshment for the audience, whose appetite for alcohol would build from this point, reach a crescendo after the first couple of sets, peak after the third set and fade as evening folded into night and the music closed down into the blues, the blues which would always bring down the curtain in this jazz club. Not that there was in fact a curtain to bring down, but the spirit was willing.

'Bili.' A statement as well as a greeting.

'Stretch.' A greeting and an acknowledgement.

'Nice friends,' he nodded towards the pair of black-robed, white-faced characters. 'They new? Not seen them before. Don't think so. Would have remembered.'

'They know Stoner.' Bili waggled fingers to attract a drink. Regular inhabitants of the Blue Cube rallied at once, spoke with the Chimp, and a tall glass filled with froth and a virulent red fluid materialised before her. She stared at it with wide eyes. 'And what the fuck is this?' She shook her head; curls flew; she tamed them back behind her ears, looked around until a pair of adoring audience eyes found hers, smiled her thanks and took a draw from the glass.

'Fuck.' She was plainly in a mood for descriptive comment. Took another mouthful. 'Fuck.'

'Drain cleaner?' offered Stretch, smiling a worried smile.

'Could be.' She drained the glass, froth, fruit and everything. Slid the empty across the counter top. 'Another. Fuck yes. What a girl needs, to play her through the night.' The same audience rallied around with the funds and the same glass was refilled from the same cocktail shaker; the Chimp knew his stuff.

'Stoner?' Stretch touched his lips to the beer in his glass. 'He back? He coming back?' His eyes fell towards the stage, to where an elderly Fender guitar slouched in its stand. Every evening, whoever of the band arrived first set the Stratocaster on its stand and switched the Marshall amplifier to standby, before they did the same for the rest of the amps. Every evening. Every evening for over a month. Over a month since the old instrument had been played. Bili tuned it, every evening, before each set. And every evening the audience – the regular audience – applauded her tuning as though she had played the world's finest-ever piece of axe music upon it.

'No idea.' She sipped at the bright-red drink. 'The goths aren't saying. But they are saying that they're meeting someone here who might know something. They even asked if they could sit somewhere private. Somewhere away from the music. Noise, they called it. Noise.'

'You said no?'

'I said no. I don't know them. Who the fuck are they? Any fucker can announce that they know Stoner. Maybe they do, and maybe they don't. All the same to me.'

Stretch placed his large black hand over her small white hand. 'Hey, Bili, babe, we all miss the guy.' She reversed their hands; hers on top of his.

'Yeah.'

'You steamed enough to do playing? Or should I get the house band to do warm-up? They need the practice.'

'One more drink.' She emptied the second red cocktail, chased it down with a half bottle of Bud, followed Stretch to the stage, hopped up the steps and collected her big bright-red Rickenbacker bass from its resting place against the battered cloth of its amplifier's speaker cabinet. Bowed to the audience. Then bowed to Stretch, walked to the microphone. Looked once more at the pianist; 'Hit those white keys, black man . . .'

And he did. And they played a fine opening set, just acoustic piano and long-scale electric bass guitar, and Bili sang, and Stretch joined her for weight and for chorus.

'Once I lived the life of a millionaire. Spent all my money, did not have one care. Took all my friends out to have a good time; bootleg whiskey, champagne and wine . . .'

After thirty minutes or so – who was counting? – the duo ended their set, the audience applauded as audiences do, and Bili walked down to sit once again with the goths, who had been joined by a hard-faced man. A face she almost recognised.

She'd seen that face before. But not necessarily in the club. She nodded to him. 'Bili,' she said.

'So you are. Shard.'

'You a friend of the stone man? You come to tell me when he's coming back? Where he is, even? You come to tell me where I can reach him? I call him. I call him every day. He's not there. I don't get no satisfaction from the voicemail.' She smiled as the audience supplied her with another beer, explained to the supplicant that she needed to be alone with the guys at her table, and she was sure he understood . . .

Shard spoke again. He looked tired. 'These guys know where he is.' He corrected himself. 'They *say* they know where he is.' He looked more tired than a moment before, somehow. 'But they can't contact him. And neither can I. Even if I knew where he was. Which I do not.' Frustration, Bili decided. He wasn't so much tired as frustrated.

One of the goths spoke. 'We know where Stoner is. Approximately. But we can't contact him directly.'

'And you are?' Bili's voice was suddenly harsh. 'And your connection with Stoner is? What? Are you friends?'

'Colleagues only. But colleagues for a long time.'

'But he's told you where he is? Is he OK?'

'No idea *how* he is. And no, he didn't tell us anything. We looked for him and we found him. One of the things we do is find people.'

Shard spat into the conversation. 'And then you sell that information. To whoever pays best. Info whores. Reliable as the bedroom backstreet varieties.' He did not look happy. He did look violent.

The first goth shrugged, a study in unconcern. His companion looked through Shard as though he wasn't even there. As though his chair was empty. No interest. Not a flicker.

'We sell information, Mr Harding. We choose to whom we sell it, and we choose whether to sell it at all. Often we discover people, places, and the places where people are . . .

hiding. Or not hiding. It is a fascination. A remarkable number of people remove themselves from view, for many reasons. Mostly they simply prefer to be somewhere else, away from everything. And sometimes, depending on who the missing person is, sometimes we prefer to keep that information to ourselves. As in this case, in fact.'

Shard shrugged. 'You found Stoner because you were tasked to find him. You've found him, you say?'

The talkative goth nodded.

'Who asked you to find him?'

'The better question. Right now, we're not answering that. There's an ethics issue here. A good, long-time customer asked us to find Stoner, and we're not in the business of betraying good, reliable, long-time customers. That's an easy way to die young. Or to lose customers. They go together.'

'So why are you here?' Bili's attention was evidently unclouded by the alcohol. 'If you're not telling us anything and you're not telling your good and oh-so-very-valuable important customers anything, then what the fuck is your point? Excuse my mouth. I've been having a bad time, what with the beauty, the adoration, the loneliness, the free booze and dope. It's not easy.'

The goth answered Bili, but presented the answer to Shard. Directed it at him.

'We've told our customer that we have located Stoner.' A pause. 'But not where he is. Simply that we believe that we know where he is and that we have no reasons to believe that he is other than completely fit and well.'

'Then you are a pair of sly fuckers and should just fuck off.' Bili waved her emptied bottle of Bud at the bar. 'Unreliable and untrustworthy, hey? They – your precious customers – have asked you to find Stoner and you're here telling us but not them. Are we supposed to put up a better bid or something?'

'Our customer didn't ask where he is. They asked us to find him.'

'Semantics. Pedantics. Some fucking antics or other. Hair splitting. Twats. You probably listen to death fucking metal.' She rose to her feet.

'Tell her to sit down and listen.' Once again the white-faced man in black spoke to Shard. 'If she'd shut up and listen, we could get on. That way we can leave you to your desperately weary attempts at music.' Bili sat, distracted, waved another admirer away.

'Our customer wants us to contact Stoner on their behalf. To make physical contact, talk face-to-face, recruit his assistance. He is not in this country, and although of course anyone anywhere is contactable, there is a time constraint and in any case our customer needs to deliver some items to him so that he can carry out the job they need doing.'

Shard spoke. 'Will he do it? Is it a job he'd want?' He appeared less stressed than earlier. He could recognise where the trail was leading.

'Yes. He would be happy, I think.'

'So what's the catch?' Shard was focused, Bili nonplussed.

'We would prefer to send both you and this . . . this lady musician to meet Stoner. It will involve some flying and it needs to be agreed now. Here. Preparations need to be established.'

Bili was looking more interested. 'Both of us? Why both?' She whispered 'coffee' into the air and mimed a letter 'C' towards the bar.

The goth addressed Bili directly for the first time. His black-eyed focus pulled in her attention completely. 'Several reasons. He trusts you. He may not welcome . . . ah . . . Shard's appearance in his current environment, and could even react badly. But if you're there, he'll be reassured. And you can maybe help with the job, too.'

'The job being what?' Shard's voice was neutral.

'The job? The hardest part of it is believing that we can trust you to carry it out. Stoner we know well and trust

42

without any doubts at all. If he agrees then he'll succeed. You're another matter. You are a concern. Not so much to us personally, but it's likely that our customer would decline your services. And of course we cannot simply ask them. Not without compromising the security.

'So. We need to trust you, Mr Harding. Bili here is only a risk because of her relationship with Stoner and her addictions. Our customer will be prepared to trust our judgement, and our judgement is that the two of you can provide back-up.' He nodded to Shard. 'And support.' A nod to Bili.

Bili leaned across the table. 'When do we leave?' She slapped Shard on the wrist; he nodded slowly. 'And where are we going?'

The goths rose to their feet with perfect synchronisation. 'Very soon. Inside twenty hours. Somewhere hot. Pack light. Trust us.' And they left.

Bili turned to Shard, her expression comically questioning. 'What? What was that about? Who are they, Tweedledumb and Tweedledumber? Are they for real?' She flagged for the coffee – again.

'They're . . . it's not easy to explain. They're data hunters. At one point – back in Stoner's active career – they got nick-named the techno prisoners, mainly because they inhabit no reality known to mortal man; they live inside computers. Really. Uber-geeks.'

'Techno . . . as in take no prisoners?' Bili watched the approach of her long-awaited coffee as the Chimp threaded a complex path towards her through the shifting topography of the club's tables and chairs. She smiled. 'One of JJ's little jokes?'

'No idea. Everyone goes through phases when they think puns are for grown-ups. The prisoners, though, are very good. They know everyone; everyone in the business knows them. They're . . .'

Bili interrupted him. 'The business? What business?

Exactly?' Her coffee finally arrived. She nodded her thanks to the Chimp and asked him for another coffee and a full litre of sparkling water. When he could spare the time. In this lifetime, preferably.

Shard was fully focused on the blonde bassist. 'Business? Stoner's business. It's not for me to discuss that. If he wanted you to know his business then you'd already know it. If you don't . . . then ask him. Not me.'

'He finds people.' Bili's tone was dead flat. No inflection at all, although her eyes were sharp; a real razor gaze. 'That's what he's always told us. If it's not true, then tell me now, and you can go on those idiots' magical mystery tour all on your own.'

'It's true enough. That's what he does. Finds people. Good way to put it. Makes it sound respectable. Yep. That is what he does.'

'Then where's the catch? I can hear the catch – a deaf girl could hear the catch. He finds people; lost kids, straying husbands, that kind of people?' She sipped her cooling coffee, waved acknowledgement and dismissal to the Chimp, who returned to his increasingly busy and noisy bar.

'You don't need to be suspicious, small lady. And you don't need to worry about JJ – about Jean-Jacques, Father John as we called him in the regiment.'

'You've known him that long then?'

'Yep. He's always a good guy to know. Always an education.'

'Stop dodging the issue. You were going to tell me the catch. Stoner finds people and what? Sells their secrets to the newspapers? To their wives? Blackmails them? How much of a shit is he really? Is he a shit? Is that what you're not saying?'

'Mainly he finds people who don't want to be found. A lot of the guys he uncovers have good reasons to stay hidden. Some of them can get quite . . . forceful about it.'

'You do the same thing?'

'Basically, yes.'

44

'But isn't that what those goths do? They say they've found JJ.'

'You miss the point, miss. Think about it.'

'Fuck off. You tell me about it. I'll think about it later.'

'The prisoners can tell you where someone is . . . usually, and usually accurately. That's why they're who they are. But Stoner will go and . . . contact the missing person. Make contact. Walk up and say hello stranger. That kinda thing.'

'What's the difference? You . . . JJ too, pay those guys to find lost souls and then you . . . what? Take the credit? Charge more? I'm missing something else, aren't I?'

Shard shook his head and half-smiled at her earnest expression. Bili started on the water the Chimp had left for her.

'It's very risky. It's not all Doctor Livingstone, I presume. All too often Doctor Livingstone has a deep grudge, and a real, deep reason for not wanting to be found and a great big gun or great big guys with great big guns to protect his privacy.'

'Oh. Fuck.'

'You got it.'

'You're like . . . bounty hunters?'

'Nope. We're private contractors who find people.'

'Don't the plods do that?'

'Only if they want to. But that's not the right question. The police look for criminals, and they often find them. Guys like me and JJ find people who might not be crims.'

'So you work for crims then?'

'Define criminal for me.' Shard reached into a pocket and extracted a cell phone. Flicked it open, read a message. 'Hang on.' He returned the call. Said nothing, until, 'Got it.' Turned back to Bili. 'The job's a good one . . . if you're up for it. That was Mallis, the more talkative of the prisoners. Arrangements arranged. If you're on – and you need to decide sort of . . . now – then we fly to Malta in the morning. Early. In about an hour.'

'JJ's in Malta?' She was incredulous. 'Why?'

'No idea. That doesn't matter. If we find him, if he'll talk to us, then you can ask him.'

'Why wouldn't he talk to us? What happened? Why'd he vanish?'

'Can't say. Ask him.'

'You must know.'

'Perhaps. But if he wants you to know, he'll tell you. If not . . .'

'I've no idea whether my passport's up to date. Or where it is. Fuck.'

'No problem. You'll be flying as someone else. Better that way.'

'What? What the fuck are you on about? Fly as someone else? Who?'

'No idea. It doesn't matter – really doesn't matter, lady. Can't you get your head around this? It's really easy. You get picked up, driven to Heathrow. We meet there, sit in the top-class lounge staying extremely sober and straight and carrying nothing we might regret, and then we sit in an aeroplane until it gets where it's going and then we get off and . . . ah . . . await further instructions. But you need to tell me that you're in. Now.'

'Yeah, I'm in. God's rot, yes, but flying as who? How does this work? Do I need to pack stuff? How much money – what money do they use in Malta? This is seriously crazy.'

'I'll have the travel docs for you when we meet at the airport. You don't need money; they'll provide some cards and maybe some cash, though you'll not need much. Leave all your own ID at home. Do you have a safe? If not, go now, get your ID and store it somewhere secure. JJ'll have a safe here, betcha.'

'Yeah. He does. But I've no idea how to open it.'

The bartender will, I'm sure of that. Or the pianist.'

'You know the Chimp? Stretch? That well? Fuck's sake, how much of this . . .'

'No. Don't know them. But if they work with Stoner then they'll know some secure storage places. Ask on your way out.'

'I can't just leave. Got music to make.'

'Suit yourself. It would be helpful if you could keep schtum about this. Say nothing, just that you'll not be around for . . . oh . . . a week. If it's not sorted inside a week, ten days max, then it won't get sorted.'

'What time? When will you pick me up?'

'No idea. Your phone switched on?'

'Yeah, but . . .'

'Just hold on.' Shard thumbed a message into his phone, sent it. Bili pulled her own cell phone from her small bag. It played a happy tune.

'See you in the morning.' Shard stood, smoothly silent and fluid too. Tapped the tabletop twice and headed for the exit. Bili answered her phone.

'Hello . . .'

4

A BLUE DREAM

'Sometimes I just want to lie down and die in the darkness. My very own darkness.' The man who was, temporarily at least, known as John Hand, smiled. He stood by the desk, by the overflowing desk with its detritus and its paraphernalia and its snapshots into everyday, floating life. He stood there, pretending interest, and he smiled, though the smile was mostly on the outside. Mostly.

'What's all this stuff for, anyway?' His evening companion was talking to herself. Not to him. Not really. He answered, anyway.

'It's . . . it allows you to pretend that where you live is in fact your home. I bet you carry all this . . . all these prized possessions around with you from ship to ship, so you can make your cabin your home. So it's familiar. Easy. Relaxing. I can see that.'

'But you wouldn't do it, would you?' She looked across the cabin at him. 'And you were going to say "junk" or "rubbish", not "prized possessions" or whatever you said. You travel very light, John. Lighter than any other top-suite passenger I've seen. They usually have mountains of luggage. Mountains.'

'But why? What's it all for? This is a ship. It's a small town, or a huge hotel, I'm not sure which. Take your pick. It's got everything I need. Food to eat, drink to drink, music of a sort, movies. And it's quiet. It's always leaving somewhere, always heading off to somewhere else. There's never any real purpose to it. It just goes where it goes, parks up for a few hours then goes somewhere else. I like that. Suits me.' He paused, looked into the eyes of his companion, and smiled again. 'Why are you showing me your cabin, anyway? Why am I here?' He smiled again, aiming to ease the edge from his words. To soften them, at least a little. He quite suddenly believed that all smiles were deceits.

'I thought you might like to see where I live. Thought you might be interested.'

'I get that. I'm not completely stupid. But you don't live here. You live at home, with your husband, kids, dogs and cats.' He waved a hand at the photos of at least three cats. 'You have at least three cats. No pics of kids or proud hubby, though. Do you leave them at home? Leave them behind you when you step into the telephone box and become Super First Officer Woman?' Another self-confusing, self-deluding smile.

'Coo! You almost sound like you're interested, maybe even care a little. Do you?'

'Do I what? Care a little? What sort of question is that? Of course I care a bit. I wouldn't be here if I didn't, but don't get carried away with the romance of it all. I'll be off the ship in a few weeks and you'll hook up with some other jolly roger.' He paused once again. 'Oh. OK. I see.' His smile vanished. 'The you when you're afloat really is a different you to the you ashore. Got it. Two lives. I can relate to that. Not a problem.'

'You too?' She spoke gently, not meeting his eye.

'I'm sorry. Me too what?'

'You have two lives? Parallel lives?'

'No. Not really.'

'You don't have a home? You must do. Everybody has a home. Friends, family, a cat. Lots of cats. Why don't you talk about yourself, John? You just . . . don't. Most men . . .'

49

'Do they? Talk about themselves? Are they interesting, most men? Do they tell you about their jobs, their businesses, their kids, dogs, parrots and the big imaginary Mercedes-Benz they drive in their dreams? I'd have thought you'd be bored senseless by all that mundane crap. I drive a van. A Volkswagen. It's black and it's a van. A VW. Are your fires ignited by this? In any case, I told you before, this is a stupid conversation for 05:37, five hundred and something miles from Malta, in the middle of the Med. And your shift starts . . . sorry, your watch starts in, oh, twenty-two minutes.' He stopped, leaned against a cabin wall and clapped his hands together, gently and almost silently. 'Sorry, babe. Y'see, if I get going I just don't shut up. Why have you put on that armoured bra? Your tits look a lot better without it. Speaking as an interested observer. A connoisseur, as it were.' He smiled again, defusing any insult.

'Company regs, John. Regs. Rules. It's more like four hundred. Miles to Malta. I wanted you to see my place. So you can know me better. But you don't care, you really don't. Amazing.' She had pinned up her hair and was positioning her uniform hat.

'I don't . . . That was going to sound terrible. What I could care about is you. Not a cabin you sleep in when you're on a ship. Even with some pics of some cats. I do like cats, as it happens, but not usually their owners. Tell you what. Let's get wrecked after dinner and we can do a bit of that cuddly couple stuff, if that's what you like. Walk around the decks and sneak into the gaps between the worlds for a quick snog and a grope. Make like kids making out. I don't have anywhere to go. I'm on holiday, me. What time do you get off? You're allowed to dine with the plebs, the passengers? Are you?'

'Yes. You're a VIP, a suite passenger, so I could dine with you in public. I should probably tell the purser and maybe the captain. They know who you are.'

He laughed quietly. 'I doubt that. I do doubt that. You're going to be late.'

'I'm never late. I'll be at your suite at 18:00, so I can get you properly dressed.'

'Say what? Properly dressed? Dressed for what? I don't do the penguin suit crap, don't do the formal dinners. Don't even have a suit.'

'Buy one. A dark one. It's the captain's invitation cocktail hour, followed by dinner tonight. You have an invite to eat with the skipper, the purser and I'm first officer, so I can be your own invite. That should wind them all up, get their clock-work working.'

'This is a joke, right? I truly, truly do not do formal dinners. Jesus H and all his Apostles. A fate much worse than death . . . and far more frightening. Sorry, chick, Ms First Officer. Not my scene at all.'

'Buy the suit. Or rent one. No. Buy it. I, me, I will give you an evening you will never forget. Promise. Gotta run.'

'Me too. Best time to run the decks is now. Do I get a fond kiss? A fond farewell?' He grinned, one hundred percent genuine, suddenly taken by her conspiracy. She punched his left shoulder, turned to the door.

'Buy the suit. See you at six.' And was gone.

At 18:00 on the dot the door to his cabin, his suite, opened quietly and without ceremony. Or indeed a knock. The first officer entered, hat in her hand, smile on her face. He rose to greet her.

'You have a key to my suite?' A simple question, no dispute, plainly.

'Of course I have a key. I'm the first officer. I can go any-where. I'm allowed. The company trusts me.'

'Handy. Do you do it often? Breaking and entering without the actual breaking?'

'No. Not really. Passengers get sick. They die sometimes, but not often.'

'Not often enough?' He smiled, took her hat and stood it on the standard lamp. Lit the lamp. The hat glowed, possibly with delight. It's not easy to tell with a hat.

'I didn't say that, John. There are lots of little deaths on big ships, but few of the terminal variety, despite the idiotic amounts of food some passengers put away.'

'Also drink. And speaking of which . . .' he gestured towards a chilling, beefy bottle of champagne, cooling in a bucket of ice.

'No time. Get your clothes off.' She slipped from her jacket, hung it. Then the skirt, then the up'n'thrust bra. And turned to him, wearing only her tan. 'You might like to speed up. We are in something of a minor hurry. Did you get the suit?'

'Yep. Hanging in the closet like a dumb waiter. All my clothes? If we're in a rush we can't have time for much in the way of meaningful sex, surely?' He stripped rapidly and with efficiency.

'Indeed. But you're having a shower.'

'I've had a shower. Two. This morning after my run and about a quarter hour ago. I am fairly clean. For a man.' She ignored him, propelled him towards the shower, rummaged in her bag, and produced like a magician from a hat a mitten constructed from some naturally abrasive fibrous material.

'Shut up and just enjoy a little exfoliation.' She soaped the glove and went to work. He glowed, water flowed. She scrubbed with vigour and obvious enthusiasm, finally taking his cock into her gloved hand and working up a good lather.

'Lots, did you say, John? Lots like me? Girls. Ladies.'

'What? I can't say. Not just at the minute. Mind is else-where.' If he was not in fact the happiest man on the ship, someone somewhere was enjoying a profoundly excellent time.

'I can see exactly where your mind is. Not for too long.' She

52

worked him with efficiency and impressive dexterity, while he leaned against the wall of the shower, closed his eyes and let nature take over. Which it did, rapidly enough, and in the traditionally messy way, washing away as the shower water sluiced him clean.

'That was truly excellent, babe, but I can't see what it's got to do with the captain's cocktails and my wearing a penguin suit and talking bollocks with idiots.'

She inserted the glove's thumb, with her thumb inside it, up his arse. He jumped and went silent. 'Got to get you clean and pure, inside as well as outside,' she observed, a grim smile with the words. 'Lots like me are there?'

'Getting fewer by the second. There's a reason for the special delight? Revenge?'

'It's a sharing thing. Lie on your back. On the towel. Have to think of housekeeping. Tongues will wag.' He did as he was bid. She spread his legs, and replaced her gloved thumb with something smooth and lubricated. It slid inside. He closed behind it, involuntarily.

'An egg?'

'As you say.' She threw him a pair of sport shorts.

'I'm going to meet the captain with a battery egg up my arse? It does have batteries, I suppose?'

'Right both times. The switch is here.' She slapped his bottom, like he was a baby. 'I'll turn it on when we get there.'

'Hence the hand job. OK. A pre-emptive jack.'

'Smart boy. Lots? Lots like me?'

'I think we're heading towards a very select group now, first officer. You do know what's going to happen?' He seemed to be less than unhappy, more amused.

'Oh yes. And how is limp willy?' She lifted his cock from his shorts, pulled a hair band from her ponytail and snapped it around the base of his shaft, then slid him back into his shorts. 'Not too tight? Not too loose?'

'Not . . . yet.'

'Dress up. I'll tie your tie. You did get a tie? A dicky bow?'

'Had to be. Had to be. This does feel . . . strange. Walking tall is going to be a challenge.'

'We'll take the lift. How many times will you come before you start to beg?'

'Two. Maybe three. Then my seas will be all dried up, as the song goes. You've done this before, then?'

'Lots. Come along and meet the captain. He's looking forward to it. He's heard about your musicianship and I've told him you're a great conversationalist.'

'Lots?'

'Lots. Then there's the purser. You're really in luck. His wife's aboard and will be joining us. She's a stunner. Tits like you would not believe and a great believer in showing them off and putting her hand on a diner's thigh for a little emphasis, I believe. Hard yet? Blood still flowing in? Band's not too tight? Don't want it going black and dropping off.'

'This is going to be messy.'

They walked into the salon to meet the senior officers. She reached behind him and pressed the small pink switch under his jacket.

'Captain, may I introduce Mr John Hand? He's been with us in the Bangkok Suite for . . . oh . . . almost a month now. And will be staying aboard until we return to Southampton, and then on to St Petersburg. I think that's correct. John?'

'Malta has a lot of history. Germans, Italians, knights, crusaders, the George Cross and cool ice cream.' The first officer observed the busy dockside, leaned professionally on a deck rail and privately against her companion. 'Mooring protocols all complete. We have permission to be here. I am officially off duty, off watch. Where would you like to go?'

'Bed.' His reply was instant, if not original.

'You're feeling tired? You need a lie-down? A bit of a nap?'

'You truly truly are something else, Jenny. And why did the

54

captain keep calling you Jimmy? If you're really a bloke you're hiding it very well.'

'Jimmy the One. It's some ancient Royal Navy thing. First officer. Surprised you can remember. Impressed. You did very well. Did you actually come when the purser's cow wife was squeezing your thigh? You were very pink under the tan. I almost felt sorry for you. Might even have switched off the egg if I could have reached it.'

'Tried to come, I think. Hard to tell by that point. Certainly twitched a little in a gruff and manly way, but it was all over by then. Bloody amazing experience. Never knew formal dinners were such fun. Been missing out all my life. Must do more. Trousers have gone in the trash. Ruined. Also the bloody socks. Shoes. Didn't know I had so much in me. Amazing dinner. Never ever had one like it.' He wrapped a long brown arm around her. She pulled away.

'Wait 'til I'm out of the whites.' She kissed him on the nose, pulled away a little.

He slapped her backside, not ungently. 'Did I actually make any sense? Do all your crew think you're dating a drooling incontinent idiot? And why didn't you mention that you were back on duty after the dinner? That was a cruel trick. Really. Sleeping was a trial. Christ, I hurt. Your bloody hair band cut a mean trench. Thought it was circumcising me. Bloody thing. And I must have smelled pretty awful.'

'I was . . . too cross.'

'With me?'

'A gentleman asks for permission before fucking his lady up the ass, John. I bled like a pig.'

'You could have said no. At any time. I respect that. Always. Rules of engagement.' A pause. Then, 'Do you want to do it again?'

'Absolutely. But not here.' Her radio called her. A short conversation.

'You're back on duty?'

'Nope. Passengers embarking. Number two will handle that.'

'It's OK to get aboard mid-trip? I never knew that.'

'Oh yeah, lots do it, but not usually at Malta. Not a problem; we've got plenty of room. Two women, travelling together. Both suites. Your kind of girls. Hey! Let me get out of my whites and we can go ashore, do tourist stuff. I can show you around. Been here loads. We sail at 18:00 – six – so we can do dinner – my treat, you choose where – and I'd really like it if we can go up to the Crow's Nest and I can watch you play guitar a bit.'

'Won't get you in trouble? Fraternising?'

'Nope. The captain likes you. Thinks you'll be good for me.'

'Jesus H. The only time I've spoken to him I had a vibrating egg up my arse and had just come in my shorts. Again. He has low standards. And no keen sense of smell.'

'You should meet more of the passengers. Then you'd understand. Most of them are more dead than alive, the ones he meets. The lively ones live in the cheap seats and he never sees them. Come on . . .'

'Like the beard, JJ. Suits you.' Jenny had left their table at the Crow's Nest, heading off to snag drinks for two at the busy midnight bar. A small woman overloaded with a storm of wild blonde curls had claimed the seat.

'Bili.' A simple statement. Flat. 'The name is John. While I'm here. Why are you here? And how are you here? Who are you with?'

'You take the fucking biscuit. You vanish like a bad con-juring trick, you say nothing to anyone and you give me a hard time for tracking you down and flying halfway round the fucking world to find you. For fuck's sake, JJ, that is fucking appalling, even for you.'

'The name is John. You didn't find me. You don't know how, and I'm not lost. Who did the finding and who're you with?'

The first officer hove into the conversation, a drink in each hand. 'A new friend, John?' She smiled, comfortable with the authority of her rank. 'May I have my seat?'

Bili picked up the nearer glass, drained it, picked up the second glass, looked up. 'Not really. It would help if you could just fuck off out of it.' She emptied the second glass. 'What piss is this?'

'Is this the wife you don't have, John?' She sounded calm, considering. Professionally calm.

He stood. Towering. Dark. 'No. Jenny, meet Bili. Bili is probably the nearest thing I have to a best friend. Bili, meet Jenny. Jenny is first officer of this fine vessel and if you piss her off she can probably have you keelhauled or something worse. She does a great line in something worse. Jenny, Bili is probably the best bass player you'll ever meet, and can get a little gabby. We play in a band together sometimes – a lot of time and for a long time. I left . . . I left without saying goodbye.

'And that's quite enough of the pleasant conversation shit. Bili, who've you come with? You came aboard today? In Malta? Sorry, Jenny, I need to know what's happening here.'

'Is it a problem? Can I do something to help?' Suddenly and totally efficient, the first officer ignored the smaller woman, looked unsmiling into the tall man's eyes. 'Do you need to be alone? If so, take it to your stateroom.' No smiles at all.

Bili stood. 'Grab your seat. I'll get another. Sorry for the bad start. I've been worried, is all. I'll find a seat.'

'No need. A lady knows when to leave.' The first officer was entirely calm.

'Give me an hour?' He caught her hand. 'See you in Bangkok?'
'OK.' She left.

'Christ, JJ. What is this? You're . . . soft on her? That's cool. You ran away to sea to make out with a sailor? That is so cool. You could have fucking told me. Hello? You still here? Hello? JJ? Are you listening? Oh. Hi, Charley.'

Another, taller, woman had joined them, squeezing into the booth and standing relaxed beside Bili.

'Is the hair entirely natural? Charley?' He smiled with glittering nails-hard insincerity at the vivid gloss blue highlights in the newcomer's otherwise flat black hair. 'I like it. Suits you. Did you borrow it from a friend? You lost a bet?'

'Good to see you too, Mr Stoner. The beard suits you. Is it yours?'

Stoner put a hand on Bili's arm. 'On here they know me as John. Please. Let's not make with too much confusion. Spooks the horses.'

The tidy woman with the blue hair nodded and stitched together a decently convincing smile. 'Yes. Bili, meet John Hand, mysterious millionaire and reclusive musician on this quaint cruise ship. Thanks for making the intro easier than it could have been if I'd had to do it on my own.'

'What's she on about? Can I get a drink? Aren't these things just floating gin palaces? Gin sounds good. How do I order some?'

'Flag down a waiter and give him your little plastic card. The one you got when you came aboard. Show me?' Stoner reached out a hand; Bili placed a card in it. 'Belinda? Yay! Belinda Notyournameatall? We're all incognito here. Excellent. Like the scarlet pumpernickel or something. Charley? What gives? You here to take me out, or what?' If there was humour in the question, it quite suddenly wasn't obvious. Bili shook out her curls; three handsome, young, slim waiters and an optimistic or possibly confused waitress appeared at her side.

The woman with the blue hair leaned towards Stoner, held his gaze and laid both hands on the table. Palms up. 'I need your help. That's why we had you found, and why I'm here. Bili is simply concerned for you. You should marry her, settle down and raise a lovely family together.'

Stoner's gaze was flat. His eyes as flat and empty as a

shark's. 'You used her as bait. I could kill you for that.'

'You could. You could certainly try. But that's for another day. Chas is below ground in Israel and I need to help her get out. I would appreciate – in more ways than you can imagine – your help in this. Bili knows only that I want you to help me help my sister. That's all. I've no angle with her . . . or with you. You know that.'

'I did know that. Maybe. But things change. I'm retired. How did you find me?'

'Mallis.'

'OK.'

'The twins. They took some persuading. They found you fast enough, but wouldn't tell me where to find you. Only that they knew where you were. They said they knew approximately, which was a first.' She smiled, an easy confidence.

'But you persuaded them?' A deceptively complicated question.

'Nope. Not a chance. We extracted the information from Harding, your friend Shard. They intended to send him with Bili to talk you into helping us. I thought that would take far too long. Chas is in the crap and we need her out of there. Fast. With or without you, although your help would hurry things along.'

'Shard sold me out? That's unexpected.'

'Not as such.'

'Explain?'

'I caught up with him. He met the twins in your club.'

'You followed him? Impressive.'

'I can be efficient when I need to be, Mr Stoner. And that need is upon me at the moment. Nothing subtle. I just swamped him with followers . . .'

'And you persuaded him to give up his seat on the good ship *Lollipop*?'

'A lot of ordnance does this. A lot of visible unsurvivable ordnance. Even then, I had to explain that I wished you no harm, and that in any case I thought you would agree to help. You've met Chas . . . Chastity. She spoke highly of you.'

'Wouldn't that be nice? If it were true.' He laughed, mainly for effect. For punctuation.

'Oh. She did. You took her completely seriously, she thought, which allowed her to . . . to solve the problem she had in the exact way it needed solving.'

'She put bombs in my club. Don't be telling me I should like her.'

'And she removed them. No harm done. To anyone.'

'She did?'

'She did.'

'And now she's stuck in Israel? How come? Oh hi Bili.' The diminutive stack of curls had drifted into view, balancing two long vivid drinks with excellent precision.

'You guys got stuff, haven't you? I'll take a walk and crash out with my friend the bottle.' Bili's entire being sagged with exhaustion. 'Charley; you bang on my door in the morning? JJ, ignore this blue woman and go find your navy lady. She looked dead fierce. Bet she's dominant! Perfect for you. You need a good slap, the stunts you pull on me.' The ship moved a little; she staggered a little. Two young men in waiter uniforms appeared instantly at her side. Balance restored, she drifted away, the centre of a small flotilla.

'She's a star, that one. Really is. Loves you to bits, too.'

'Yeah yeah yeah. She's a hell of a bass player.'

'Don't play games. She talked about you a lot on the flight. Was worried witless about you. Seems you just vanished completely without telling her at all. That is so, so sweet.'

'Don't take the piss. You're playing your own game. You have a plan? Of course you have a plan. Tell me. Be quick. The two minute version.'

'You go ashore and you bring Chas back on board with you. She gets off again once we're back in the EU but long before we sidle up to Southampton. You really going on to Russia aboard this tub? Seems extreme. Who're you hiding from? I'll owe you . . . we'll owe you after this. We always repay a kindness.'

Stoner let his eyes drift away from Charity, away to a horizon visible only to himself. A near horizon, because the journey there and back took very little time.

'Say I agree.' He paused.

Charity smiled at him. 'No no. You say "I agree". I say "Oh great" and then we make out like best mates and the sun shines forever. Do you agree? You going to help us? Even though Chas . . . Chastity shot out your headlights? I can see how that would . . . diminish a man. Enlimpen him.'

'Do what to him? You made that up.'

'Correct. Laugh a minute with me. And?'

'It's an OK, Charity. Charley. Whatever you're calling yourself. OK. But listen. Listen up good and loud. This is not a gig. Not a contract. No fee. No boss, no Ts and no Cs. It's a favour. A favour for a friend. After it . . .' He paused and latched his gaze onto hers, steady. 'After it you leave me alone. I want nothing back but that. I'll play at friends, we can make like allies, but we share no agenda but this one; this single one. I'll do my boy scout shit with Chastity and then I'm gone. And you leave me and mine alone. That includes Bili. Me. Bili.'

'Lissa, your black blonde top girl at home? The woman who lives in your house back home? What about her? She wants to find you, so she says.'

Stoner was unshifting, unblinking. No emotion evident. 'She's dead to me. Nothing. She can't locate me even if she wants. And you're not helping her. Got that?'

'Yeah. I don't care either way. But yeah, that's fine. I'll even tell Mallis.'

'Why? Why would you . . . Oh forget it. We have a deal.'

She smiled, almost sadly. 'Your Navy lady is going to be a problem, though. So . . .' she stood. 'You go below and make up some big stories for her. How senior is she?'

'First officer. Number two on the ship after the captain. She is excellent, smart. Can't just spin her a yarn. And you can't just bring extra people on board without passports, tickets and the like. But you're right. There are ways to work this. See you tomorrow. My cabin's . . .'

'Bangkok Suite. Inevitably. I'll find it.' She smiled. It may have been genuine. He stood . . .

. . . and was propelled back into his seat by a pair of beefy hands landing on his shoulders. A beefy body was attached to the hands, and a beefy head to the body. The head sweated into view, glaring like a cartoon villain. It spoke in a beefy regional accent; unintelligible nonsense.

Stoner freed himself from the hands, instantly, smoothly; Charley stood, flicked her chair onto its side, jammed its back into the backs of the knees of the intruder, who staggered and grabbed for Stoner again, more for support than from violent intent. A woman appeared at the beefy man's side, pointing at Stoner with venom and accusation. Words flew; he heard not a single one, but he recognised the woman from late night music and drinks sessions. An untouched woman. Untouched by him, at any rate, which was presumably the root of the problem. Playing the rejection boogie at max volume, then. The beefy man swung at him, feeling better balanced, maybe, and everyone in the lounge scattered to a safe distance. A waiter hung onto a telephone.

Stoner easily caught the flying arm, twisted it around under its own momentum, applying immutable physical principles to the man's mass, pulled his trapped hand up behind him and muttered fondly and quietly into his ear. 'Outside, big boy. Hope you've got insurance.'

A stream of incomprehensible invective was the reward for his patience and restraint. Both men headed fast for the exit, one in comfortable control of the other, the other unaware of the status quo, despite the restraints on his freedom of movement. He bellowed, enraged, and pulled an arm free. Stoner stepped back. Beefy man swung again, maximum force, minimum effect; his woman friend appeared, adding vocal support until Charley appeared at her side and caught her hand and whispered into her ear, whereupon she fell into sudden and complete silence.

Stoner ducked the wild swing, stepped close to the beefy man, and, conscious that three crewmen, including an officer in whites, had appeared and were striding towards the melee, he leaned inside the beefy man's range and tapped him sharply with a set of tight-folded knuckles once on each temple, then delivered two stiff fingers to his throat. Beefy man tottered on the spot, rocking on his feet, silent, arms loose, eyes wandering, consciousness ebbing and flowing. Stoner stood back, arms held out, hands in plain view, while the crew arrived. The officer recognised Stoner, looked surprised and not a little worried.

'Mr Hand? You all right? What happened here? Should I call Jenny? I'm sorry, the first officer? She's not on watch, but . . .' he trailed into silence. Stoner held out both hands, palms uppermost, and smiled.

'I think our friend here has enjoyed one drink too many. Not a problem. I just helped him outside for a little fresh air. He'll be fine in the morning. I'd suggest keeping someone with him for a while in case he throws up while asleep. That's always a worry. The lady here with my friend got a little carried away with it all. No harm done.' He radiated reassurance and calm kindness. Two crewman supported the beefy man and helped him away. He was coughing a lot, trying to speak. Nothing sensible emerged. Stoner managed a serious expression and clapped a hand onto the young officer's shoulder.

'Please tell him – once he's sober – that if he tries a stunt like that again I will put him into the infirmary. It is just so embarrassing. Imagine how Jenny . . . how the first officer would have felt. Doesn't bear thinking about.' He smiled.

'How I would have felt about what? John?' The young

officer nodded formally to his senior as she arrived.

'This passenger,' he waved towards to beefy man, whose progress along the deck was steady enough, if less than rapid, 'attacked Mr Hand in the bar. Mr Hand subdued him and brought him outside, then held him here for us to . . . umm . . . to return to his cabin.'

'And the woman?' Jenny nodded towards the weeping lady, wreckage on legs as she contemplated the unexpected ending of her ambitious evening. Of Charley and her bright blue hair there was no sign.

'I think she was a little jealous of the first officer.' Stoner looked suitably, comically contrite. 'The big guy was some sort of knight errant. Maybe.'

The weeping woman squeezed out the words, 'She said she'd slice my face,' and collapsed into tears once more. The first officer raised a quizzical eyebrow at Stoner.

'John?'

'I think she mis-heard.'

The first officer called over a female bar steward and tasked her with returning the weeping woman to her cabin. Then turned to Stoner. 'Can we talk a little? Is there space in your social whirl for a chat?'

'Your place or mine?'

'Neutral ground.' She smiled gently, cautiously. 'It's a beautiful night, let's grab a table on the top deck. They'll serve us as long as we're drinking.' He offered an arm, she took it, squeezed it. 'Does fighting turn you on? My husband's like that. Just look at those stars.'

Her cap, her officer's cap, sat on the tabletop between them. She kicked off her shoes and untied her hair, released her tie and freed the top button of her blouse. 'I think you have a few things to tell me. John. Like . . . you are actually called John Hand?'

'That's what it says on my passport.'

'And that is not what I asked. You're not really a van driver, then? It never seemed very likely.' There was a smile in her words and a matching smile in her eyes. 'No shit, John. Not for me. I've met too many warriors like your blue-haired friend. The husband's real Navy. He has friends like that. Girls and boys. No jokes. You active military? No. Too old for that. Is it something very illegal, then? Dirty? Something I need to worry about? Professionally? Doubt you'd shock me . . . personally.' She sighed. 'Please tell me it's not running guns. Or drugs. Your little miss lover, she's true rock 'n' roll, that one. An odd mix. You look very serious. Am I breaking all your rules here? I can't make you answer, but I think . . . I think we work very well together and . . . you still on board until St Petersburg?'

Stoner's expression was flat, almost grim. No smile at all.

'I am a van driver.' He held her gaze. 'I have a small company. It's called the Transportation Station. It has a small fleet of Transporters, VWs, like I told you. Mostly black ones. That's it.'

She shook her head angrily. 'Horseshit.'

'You sound like Bili.' He smiled a little. 'But only a little. She'd tell me to "Fuck right off, JJ." Always brilliant, Bili. Belinda on her passport. I'll talk to you assuming that you'll need to report to someone. In my world . . . in my wider world, everyone reports to someone. If I tell you a story, and if you treat it as only a story, nothing more, then you'll be fine. I'll sail on to Petrograd if you want me to, or I'll get off before that if you want me to.'

'You'll tell me the truth, the whole truth and nothing but the truth?' Jenny matched him, smile for strained smile.

'No. I'll tell you the truth. Nothing like the whole of it.'

'Why not? Am I too thick or unreliable?'

'Nope. You're a serious officer lady and I take you seriously.'

'You do?'

'I do.'

'Fuck.'

'That too. Should we get down and do it right now? Would it make you feel better? More secure?'

'Out here in public? On deck? On the table?'

'Get you in trouble?'

'Discharged. For certain.'

'Best not then. Ask away. My terms. No lies but you don't need to know what you don't need to know.'

'No shit?'

'Now you do sound like Bili. Though you should throw in a fuck or two.'

'I like Bili. More and more. You a serious item?'

'Have been. May be again. Once and future, maybe. That sort of thing. Like her lots.'

'Love her?'

'They say that if you say you don't know then you mean no, don't they?'

'No, then.'

'No idea. That's the truth. She's great. I think she'll die young.'

'Mr Cheerful. Hit me with it. You some kind of drug smuggler? Arms dealer? One of those security contractors we hear so much about in the Middle East?'

'Have been. For a long time in a lot of places. Retired now. Drive vans and play guitar and lay about on cruise ships. That is the future.'

'Bili?'

'Plays bass. Drinks. Destroys herself.'

'Why?'

'Ask her.'

'Charley?'

'Charley what?'

'Is that her name? Fucking hell, John, this is like extracting teeth without a paddle.'

'No. Mmmm . . . Don't actually know. It might be but I doubt it. I know her better as Charity.'

'Charity what?'

'Don't know. Never formally introduced. My wider world is like that. I'd like to say that what you don't know can't hurt you, but that's not true at all. What you don't know can't hurt the guys you don't know it about. I have no idea what her real name is. Her birth name.'

'She reliable?'

'As what? As a Volkswagen? In some senses. She always starts in the morning. She's not entirely what she seems.'

'No shit! The blue hair isn't natural?'

'I made that joke already. She didn't laugh. Not at all.'

'She didn't seem keen to talk to you for too long, either.'

'No need. And she's not the kind of girl I want to spend much time with. Not her and not her sisters. They're . . . unpredictable. Charity in particular. And we're far from being friends.'

'But she's not here to do you harm?'

'If she was then I'd be harmed. As badly as she wanted me to be.'

'Kidding, right?'

'Nope.'

'What's your real name. Is it John?'

'Jean. Jean-Jacques, in the full unexpurgated version.'

'OK. Hence the JJ stuff from Bili?'

'Uh-huh.'

'JJ what?'

'It . . . might be better you don't know. At the moment. If we carry on ashore, I'll take you to the club and tell you then. All aboard . . . I am John Hand.'

'The club?'

'I play . . . Bili and I play music together in a jazz club.'

'You running away? Hiding from someone?'

'I am running down a bit in the patience department, Jen. Let's ease up on the Spanish Inquisition routine soon, huh? But . . . Sort of. Everyone needs to get away for a bit when things go south. And they did. Go south. All the way. Polar.' Stoner rose smoothly, walked very slowly indeed to the closest steel wall and banged his head on it. More theatrical gesture than an attempt at suicide, and when he turned and returned it was with the air of a man preparing to unload something unpleasant.

'Your husband's Navy.' He smiled. 'That's cool. One of my closer . . . acquaintances back home is ex-Navy. A good guy. Navy guys are like soldiers. Trust no one except your buddies, your friends, your comrades. You easy with that? The idea of total trust in whichever part of your whole life – your complete life – they occupy?'

'Your life is in compartments, then, John?' A quiet question. She was carefully non-committal.

'They all are.' He grinned, suddenly. 'They tell me that marriages aren't like that, like married guys share everything. I've never been married, but I've screwed a lot of loving wives.'

She nodded, eyes never leaving his. Said nothing.

'Right. Insult complete. I just lost the two guys who were closest to me. One a lady, closer than I'd believed possible, and . . .'

She interrupted. 'Closer than me? Closer than Bili?'

'Oh. Yes. Close enough to retire for. To go straight, if that was what we wanted to do together.'

'The other? A guy?'

'Yeah. My boss, if you like. The man who placed . . . contracts my way. Commissioned almost all the work I've handled for the last ten, twelve years.'

'Illegal stuff?'

'Mostly. But . . . also not. And I'm sorry with the hesitations, the contradictions, the vague shit. It's not easy to define. He worked for the government and I worked for him. Like your husband but without a ship. Or a uniform to protect me.'

'OK. What did he do? What did they do? Oh . . . They did it together? That kind of betrayal?'

He nodded. She shook her head and smiled at him. 'But John, that's what we're doing here, you and me, here and now. Betrayals. I don't understand you.'

'No. No you don't. In my world betraying a trust like that... like those, well, it's a fatal betrayal. Work and pleasure is a deadly combination, in that world you want me to tell you about.'

'Fatal?' her eyes were wide and her voice very low. 'For whom?'

'For . . . I was the target. I always defend myself. And I always one hundred percent defend the few people I trust. Defending yourself against someone you trust one hundred percent is always going to be fatal. For one of the parties. It's not easy, and I don't want to talk about it. It's done, it's dusted and it's behind me now.' He spread his hands wide, then laid them palms up before her. 'No more, no less. I never run away. Never could. But I can stay away from a warzone, now.'

'But . . .' Her voice was lower, more quiet. 'Fatal? You killed them?'

'No.'

She reached for his hand, took it and squeezed. Firmly. He squeezed back, less firmly. Jenny flagged down a weary waiter and ordered coffees, big and black and strong. They arrived pronto. She leaned against the rail.

'Just look at that moon.' It hung huge above them, stars crisp glitter in the Mediterranean midnight. Faraway lights on the sea. The ship slid with easy grace towards the Middle East. The decks were empty, brightly lit for the never-ending cruise party. Which was currently elsewhere. 'It never loses its appeal. Pulls me to it.'

'You're a romantic, Jenny.'

'I need to be. Here comes the big one, John. JJ. Whatever. Your pal Charley, your pal Bili and your pal you are all here under fake names. You're going to do some dubious job or

69

other. I should – really should – have you all put ashore. Should I do that, John?'

'You can't persuade yourself that the ladies are here simply to locate me, their long-lost pal?'

'Not easily. Are they?'

'No. Well. Bili is. Charley wants me to help her find someone else. No risk to anyone else. That person is ashore and needs a little help.'

'Muscle?'

'No. Reassurance and back-up, I think.'

'Where's the friend?'

'Ashdod.'

'There's a coincidence. Not.'

'There are no coincidences. But my presence on the ship is exactly that. A convenient coincidence. So far as I can tell, that's true. It won't have been easy to find me. Or cheap. I didn't choose to go to Israel and I'd certainly no plans to get off there. I don't like getting off much. You know that.'

'The ship isn't going to Ashdod.'

'Day after tomorrow. It's on the itinerary.'

'It's not any more. Gaza rocketeers are having another of their fireworks displays; security has canned the port call. You didn't know?'

'Obviously not. Not going to Israel at all?'

'Haifa. Day after tomorrow. Just missing out Ashdod. You bothered?'

'Nope. It's none of my business. I can't alter that. If Charley's pissed off then she can be pissed off, huh? Makes my life easier, if anything. Two days in Haifa, then? I should tell her, though. Do you know her cabin number?'

'You don't?'

'Nope.'

'Thought you were good at finding people.'

'Used to be. Retired. I'm old.'

'Fake identities, John.'

'What?'

'How do you fake identities? Passports. Credit cards. How do you do that?'

'No idea. The IDs are genuine. The passports are real. So are the cards. It's all legit kit.'

'It can't be.'

'You've led a sheltered life for one so travelled. Information technology is a wonderful thing. Governments only worry about what they call identity theft because they thieve identities all the time. I mean . . . how do I know you're even an officer? Because you wear a funny hat?'

'Sod off. Is there more about you I should know?'

'How would I know that? I am what I am, you are what you are. I think you're great. We get on good, no? Can we keep it like that? For the duration?'

'Is it so easy?'

'Yep.'

'OK. No more questions. Not 'til we get back to the UK. Then . . . then there may be some more. OK?'

'OK.'

'OK. I've asked, you've answered. Your turn.'

'How do you mean?'

'Your turn to ask me questions.'

'I have no questions. Why would I have questions about you?'

'You don't care?'

'About what?'

'About me!'

'Of course I do. Come back to the cabin and I'll show you how much I care.' He attempted a smile, reached for both of her hands. She pulled back from him.

'You don't, do you? You don't care at all. I'm just a holiday lay.'

'Fuck's sake, Jenny. Don't make things difficult, huh? You're . . . oh I don't know. Top stuff. Head girl. I'm knocked out by you, and your company has made this, this trip, utterly out-standing. I don't need to know any more about you to know that. I take things . . . people . . . as I find them. I make a judge-ment. If I'm wrong about them, then I'm wrong. But I'm not often wrong.'

'You're not, huh?'

'No.'

'Work stuff?'

'No. Human stuff. People stuff.'

'So I could be a married mother of five with a passion for killing my lovers and you wouldn't care?'

'You are married. I doubt you're a mother. There are ways to tell these things.' He rolled his eyes theatrically. 'If you murder me in my sleep . . . you might be doing both of us a favour, frankly.'

'How do you know I'm married?'

'You told me.'

'I might have lied.'

'Why would you do that?'

'To make you feel safe.'

'God's sake. I do feel safe. With you. Although I'm starting to doubt my sanity. And yours. Why would you lie to me?'

'You lied to me.'

'Gods.'

'Do you really not care enough to want to know anything about me? Where I come from, where I'm going in this great life? What my plans are?'

'Not really. The past is the past. I can't do anything about it. Nothing you did before we met matters to me . . . to us. Here and now is all I care about. There are no plans. The future will be what it will be.'

'You're secretly a miserable bastard.'

'Nothing secret about it.'

'Don't you have plans?'

'Yep. I want to lure you into bed and see where that goes.'

'You really truly don't think further than that?'

'What's the point? This morning I was sharing a great affair with the most stunning first officer afloat, heading for romance and passion at every possible moment and in creative, unusual and deeply enjoyable ways, and tonight I'm all at fucking sea, surrounded by fucking Charley and Bili, one a madwoman and the other . . . a madwoman. No plan in the world would have planned for that. What simple plans I might have had, involving this ship, this brilliant woman – that's you, by the way – have all been screwed up. So there was no point in having them – the plans. Once I've helped Charley out, I want make you my friend again, I want you to fuck me senseless and I want to baffle the blue-rinses in the Crow's Nest bar at every midnight with the endless soppy love songs I can play about lost love, making you chuckle because they'll all be about the first officer and no one but you and me will know that. Then the cruise will end, Bili and Charley can fuck off out of it and we can consider the next step. If you want to.'

'And if I don't?'

'Then you don't. I can't change that.'

'You think that's true?'

'Yes. Absolutely.'

'They'll leave at Southampton?'

'Can't see why not.'

'And you'll stay on til St Petersburg?'

'Unless you want me off, in which case I'll get off at Southampton too.'

'You make it all sound simple.'

'It is simple. Why people need to complicate everything, I have no idea. None at all. Never have. Dishonesty lies in pointless complication. A straight line is a straight line. No deceptive bends.'

'Are you being straight with me?'

'Yes.'

'What's your real name? All of it? Tell me and I'll trust you and you'll be John Hand all the time you're on this ship.'

'Jean-Jacques Stoner.'

'Is that like Bond, James Bond?'

'If it turns you on, then yes.'

'You know what? I'm turned on.'

'Oh fuck.'

'My thoughts exactly. Should we go fuck or would you prefer to go and see Charley and talk about Ashdod?'

'Don't be silly, Jen.'

'I'm not. I want to know.'

'Your cabin or mine?'

'Mine. Charley already knows where yours is.'

'Of course she does.' Stoner smiled, took her arm and started to walk.

'She can also pick the lock?'

'Probably. I'd count on that. She won't pick it; she'll have a keycard. Betcha.'

'Bloody bloody bloody hell.'

5

WALKING IN JERUSALEM

Ashdod. An Israeli city, a coastal Israeli city, a city filled with dark Arabs and otherwise, and a smaller, much smaller, number of white European types. Languages all over the place. Threats in everyone and in everything, in every place. The screamed shouts of threat, clouds of smoke, cooking smoke, the sharp tang of hashish and thousands upon thousands of staring eyes. Eyes staring at her. All of them. This was the place of a thousand paranoid nightmares. Chastity had never felt paranoia, rarely felt fear or worse, but she recognised with an immersive understanding that this Israeli city was no friend to her, no refuge. She was entirely alien, and she felt the stares. This was a rich European sector of the city, many of the polyglot voices were American-accented and some street signs were in scripts she could read. It was still alien. Still intense.

A hand touched her arm, gently. She stopped. Stood. Still. The hand tugged at her sleeve. No urgency, little intrusion. A woman. Small and round, and offering a string of shining postcards with a wide smile. The smile gleamed like a trophy from inside the completely black clothing, a false offering to match the postcards displaying another city in another country – Cairo, photographed in the 1970s, judging by the cars, and labelled in English as Ashdod. Chastity stared unblinking into the all-black eyes and held that gaze as she shook her head, slowly, gently. No trace of an answering smile. Simple negativity.

'American woman.' A flat statement. 'Rich American woman.' Two men, small, dark-eyed and nervous, stood behind the woman, observing, nothing more. But close.

Chastity grinned, laughed out loud and clapped her hands together loud as twin pistol shots.

'Great!' she yelled. 'You speak English!' Her American accent would have fooled anyone. 'Can you tell me where I can grab a coffee? A real, live honest-to-goodness Italian coffee?' She magicked a pair of local bills into view. 'Can you, y'know, show me where to get coffee?'

The two men moved on as other eyes turned to the noisy foreigner. The small woman's smile returned, the postcards disappeared into a large bag and she held out her hand, a neat, spotlessly clean brown hand with perfectly trimmed fingernails gleaming like pink teeth, and nodded. 'Coffee. American coffee. Yes.'

'American?' Chastity's smile brimmed with joy, delight and friendship. 'Can't you show me Italian coffee? Y'know, Star-bucks?' She folded the flamboyant notes into the smaller woman's hand and followed her through the crowd. Just two blocks and into the outdoor seating of an Italian restaurant, complete with model ice-cream cones the size of small adults and photographs of food, food labelled in many languages. The small woman nodded towards a table.

'Coffee. Italian. Thank you.' She turned to go. It was Chastity's turn to catch her sleeve. In her turn the smaller woman stood stock-still. Then turned, a calm question across her features.

Chastity clattered into a loud metal chair, kicked out another for her new companion. 'How's your English? Have a coffee with me. Soda? Ice cream?' She flapped a hand in true tourist imperialist manner and a waiter, possibly an Italian waiter and possibly not, headed towards them. Chastity kicked the seat further away from the table, gestured towards it. 'Go on. My treat.'

The smaller, darker woman stayed standing, standing still. She looked down at Chastity and shook her head, retaining eye contact. 'You do not understand, American. American woman.' And she left, eyes lowered.

'You trying to corrupt her immortal soul?' A new woman slid into the unoccupied seat. She beamed at Chastity, whose inner improviser beamed right back with extra smiling sunshine, sensing the arrival of another unexpected opportunity. 'If the offer of a coffee stands, then I'd be delighted to accept it.' Chastity flapped her hand at the bemused waiter, whose Italian descent remained uncertain, and raised two right hand fingers while the thumb and forefinger of her left hand conspired together to produce a letter C, the universal symbol for coffee. At least, it's universal where it's recognised, as is the case with so many symbols. And sometimes it is also the request for the check, but that's too much sophistry for a hot morning in Israel, or so Chastity reasoned, briefly.

She spoke to her new unannounced best friend. 'Feel free. And you are?'

The woman threw a small wall of black hair from her face, revealing features which may or may not have owed their origins to eastern European bloodlines, and laughed, aiming out a hand for Chastity to shake. Or merely grip, if restraint was important here. It wasn't. Chastity shook the offered hand.

'Josephone.' A flat statement. An introduction.

'Excuse me?' Chastity performed mild bemusement like a professional. 'Josephine?'

'Nope. You heard. Josephone. Pronounced like Persephone. My dad was either feeling classically lyrical or he was smashed. One or the other. Either way, call me Jo. I'm Jo. I'd drink your coffee with delight. It's good to hear a familiar accent.' Chastity waited while the waiter waited on them, somehow translating her finger signals into two slices of chocolate cake and two shots of the meanest, darkest coffee she had ever seen.

'Would you just look at that?' Chastity dipped an experimental finger into the coffee. She felt noticeable resistance. 'I can feel my brain reeling in advance. This is Israeli coffee? And what's with the cake?'

'The cake hardens the arteries, the coffee sweats them back to normal. It's unsafe to do the one without the other.' Jo scooped a small portion of chocolate cream from a cake with a single long pinkie fingernail, lifted it to her nose as though it were the finest cocaine, and sniffed it. And sighed.

Chastity was still staring at both cake and companion.'You going to eat that or snort it?'

'You from New York?' Jo licked the finger clean, forked a generous portion of cake into her mouth and followed it with a sip of the coffee. Chewed. Waiting. No reply. Chastity poked at her own cake with a fork. Experimentally. With suspicion.

'Only a New Yorker could suggest snorting chocolate cake. Maybe someone from LA, but you sound more East Coast.'

'Boston. Near Boston. Massachusetts.' Chastity resigned herself to her portion of dark indulgence, mixing the sweet cake with the bitter coffee and surprising herself with the result. 'You?' A polite enquiry. Politeness is often its own reward.

'Everywhere and nowhere, really. Here, there and everywhere, as they say.' Jo's portions, both solid and liquid, had vanished as if by magic. She caught the eye of a willing waiter, spat at him in an unfamiliar glottal language. He vanished and returned with impressive speed, two more less intense coffees, cream and a wide, ingratiating smile.

'You sound more Anglo than American, though.' Jo waved her cup as though to catch condensing coffee from some celestial fountain. 'More, you know, Brit.'

Chastity smiled back. 'A lot of people say that. It may be

true. Lots of early Bostonians came from England, so they say. English think I sound American, Americans think I sound English. It's all part of being from Boston. You get used to it.'

'Is it a bad thing? Confusing?'

'Not really. Brits think I sound interesting and rich; Americans think I sound interesting and impoverished. They both pay for everything somehow. It makes them happy.'

'Who's right, though? You rich or poor?'

'Neither. Entirely average. Not even interesting!'

'Oh come along. American blonde, here in Ashdod? Not a haunt for the usual tourista, is it? You here on holiday? Working?'

'Just waiting to go home. Man trouble.' Chastity shook her head, made sympathetic eye contact.

'Oh crap. You ditched him here? In Ashdod?'

'Other way around, mainly.' Chastity sipped at her coffee. 'He just . . . vanished. Left me stuck.'

'What an asshole!' The outrage was blistering. 'He left you here? You OK? You need anything? Where's he gone? Back to Boston? You got enough money?'

'I'm OK. Thanks. Don't know where he is. Don't know if I even care. Expect he's looking for me now, made his point, put me in my place, now wants to rescue me. You know how it goes. He'll be looking for me. I'll be looking to avoid him. Get home . . . then I'll find him. He will regret that day.'

Jo regarded her with approval. Maybe more than that. 'I'll bet. You military?'

'Was. A while ago.'

'But you never lose it, right?'

Chastity nodded, grim-faced.

Jo spread her hands wide. ' Hey! Here we are, jabbering like long-lost old friends and I don't even know your name. I'm sorry. I should have asked,'

'Chas. Friends call me Chas.'

'Charley?'

'Chas. Chas is fine.'

'Is that short for Charley? Charlaine?'

'Not really. Chas is fine. Call that and I come running. Woof.'

Jo grinned at her. 'Woof? No dogs here!' She laughed along with her new friend. 'How're you getting along? Got a place to stay? Friends here? Am I intruding? Tell me to shut up if you want.'

'I met this guy . . .'

She got no further. Jo erupted into a wide laugh and waved once more at the willing waiter. 'Oh I so love you. You get ditched, thousands of kilometres from Boston. You just . . . like . . . meet some guy in the middle of some foreign city? Magic. Superb. What a woman.'

'Met him . . . in the desert. Good Samaritan.' Chastity did her best to look modest, shy almost.

'In the desert? Asshole boyfriend ditched you in the desert? Prince Charming found you there and carried you off on his white charger? What exactly is a charger, anyway? I never met one yet.'

'Some kind of horse. No. Not a horse, some big German car. With industrial aircon. Also a fridge.'

'Cool. Cold beer in the desert? How could you resist?'

'Exactly.'

'And he carried you here in his big German charger car? And you're living happily ever after and you're going to have a hundred kids together and then you'll meet his mother? Is he Jewish? German?'

Chastity raised her hands in mock surrender. 'My head hurts!'

Jo leaned across the table, laid her hand on Chastity's. Smiled. 'I'm sorry. We only just met. Can I help is what I mean to say? Do you need anything?'

'What're you offering? Who are you anyway!' Both woman laughed.

'Why am I always saying I'm sorry? I'm sorry! I'm a soldier.

A serving soldier. If you're in any way stuck here, I can help. Seriously.'

'Oh gods, I knew it. I've found another military force. You don't look much like a soldier.'

'Neither do you, baby.' Jo leered in the best impression of a bull dyke Chastity had seen . . . except on the chops of genuine bull dykes. 'You look all woman to me.' The leer had vanished, replaced by a more gentle, friendly face. 'I'm in intelligence. You want to find your guy? I can do that. It's easy in Israel. No one can hide, especially not foreigners. Just say.'

'Thanks. Thank you. Sincerely. I'll find the fucker in the States. Best that way. I wouldn't want to be in trouble over-seas, even in a friendly state. I will find him and he will suffer. Believe me.'

'I do. I so do that.'

'There is a tiny thing, though.'

'There always is with men. They think it's a big thing, like enormous, but it's a tiny thing. Which tiny thing is this?'

'My guy's going to be looking for me. I don't want him to find me. Not at all. That wouldn't be cool. If he finds me before I get home . . . oh I don't know. He's . . . I don't know why I'm telling you this. But I'd rather have our tearful reunion in the USA than here. When things have cooled down. Let him sweat for the time being.'

'OK. OK. I got that. Fuck all men, hey?'

'Them and the horses they rode in on.'

'Amen. What do you need?'

'I just need to be out of his way 'til I go home.'

'I get this. You're not serving military?'

'No.'

'You're here legit?'

'Yep.'

'I can check that.' A statement. A flat statement. No banter there; no humour.

'You can. I have a passport and entry papers.'

'Tourist visa?'

'Yes.'

'OK.'

'You flew in? You'll fly out?'

'Yes and yes. I just need to be off the radar until I stand on American soil again.'

'I can do that for you here. Easy enough. But the minute you book a flight the embassy will know.'

'Yeah. Figured that. Any thoughts?'

'You're from Boston?'

'Mostly. Why?'

'And you truly are here on holiday?'

'Me? Yes. Absolutely.'

'Your ex?'

'Can't say. Why?'

'Nothing. Not really. He left you in the desert?'

'Yes.'

'Do you hate him?'

'What? Why?'

'Why do we trust each other, huh?'

'Jo, you've lost me.'

'Do you trust me?'

'I don't know you. We just met. You're cool . . . but I don't know you at all.'

'Is the correct answer. Is your name really Chas?'

'It is.'

'And you're from Boston?'

'What is this shit? Yes. Boston. Home of Harvard and history. What the fuck?'

'I might be able to show you a way out. What's your guy's name?'

'I'm worrying now, Jo. What's the score with this?'

'You give me his name, I can harass him enough for long enough for you to get a plane home. To Boston.'

'Get out of here. Get right out of this place. How can you do that? And why would you anyway? He's done nothing against the law. We're on holiday. Fuck's sake, Jo. We just met and you want to get my guy banged up? Can you even do that?'

'Which desert?'

'Pardon me?'

'Which desert did he abandon you in?'

'I don't know. I wasn't driving. I didn't even look at a map. What is this?'

'I'm here with a team looking for someone.'

'Well aren't we all? Who? It won't be my guy, Liam.'

'Were you driving a Land Rover? A big Brit SUV?'

'How did you know that?'

'Humour me. Were you?'

Chastity sat grim-faced, almost sullen. 'Yes. But so what?'

'Humour me. A white Land Rover?'

'Yes. Long wheelbase. A Defender. Noisy diesel thing. Seats harder than hell. Brits love them. Why?'

'Because they're strange and they live only for pain. Give me your guy's full name and I'll pull him in.'

'What? What for?'

'There was an incident – a murder – in the southern desert a couple of days ago. Some big hitter Palestinian got himself hit big. Him and his family, top ten wives, pet goat, that sort of thing. We're looking for whoever did it. Stupid, because the guys who did the deed should be our new best friends and get the Happy Israeli Medal of Mass Appreciation, but that ain't the way politics works. No no. We have to hunt them down and make a big media show of the whole thing. My entire unit has been hiked out of Jerusalem and parked in hotels in this concrete shithole so we can pretend to hunt down this crack team of international terrorists and bring them to justice. We won't find them, of course, because they'll be back in Tehran or wherever by now, but we have to make a show of it. And we found an abandoned Land Rover, white, long wheelbase, more seats than a jumbo jet and an engine fit only for a tractor, right by the scene of the crime. Alleged crime.

'So, give me your asshole boyfriend's details and we'll pull him in. He'll get treated like some kind of hero and then we'll let him go again, probably even pull his SUV back to civilisation for him. Hell, if he confessed to even thinking about offing this Arab asshole they'd probably service his Land Rover and polish it for him . . . or swap it for a Humvee or something worth driving.

'What,' Jo leaned right into Chastity's airspace, 'do you think of that for a plan?'

Chastity leaned towards her. 'Why, Jo? We just met. Why would you do this?'

Jo leaned further, kissed her softly on the tip of her nose. 'That's why. OK?'

Chastity's reply was to stand, to reach across the table, to take Jo's shoulders in her hands, to pull her face towards her own face, to pull her lips onto her own lips and to kiss her. It took a while. The restaurant held its breath, breathing again only when the two women breathed again, followed by a collective looking away with a mixture of shock and some smugness.

Chastity leaned back. 'OK. Nothing like sharing a little saliva to raise a lot of interest. You Israelis really are liberated, then? I'd never have thought it.'

'The fundamentalist thought police are probably on their way right now.' Jo shone in the sun, somehow like a teenager. 'What's this asshole's name and a rough description?'

Chastity paused, held up a hand, a parody of deep and sudden thought. 'I have a better idea.'

'You do?'

'I do. Call your office, unit, whatever it is you do here in the hellish hotlands, and tell them you're following up a lead. A hot tip. Can you do that? You senior enough? What rank are you, anyway? Can't be fraternising with the lower orders. Get you into trouble in the mighty US Army.' She smiled, no sting in her words. 'I have a plan.'

'You do? I'm a sergeant, a senior sergeant. I can do pretty much what I want unless and until ordered otherwise. What's this great and mysterious plan?'

'Oh. Simple enough, sergeant. You get some time, some freedom for manoeuvre, and we'll go find him together, my sweet Liam.'

'Liam. What sort of name is that? He from Boston too?'

'He's Irish. Irish American. The worst sort.'

'Redeeming features?'

'Many. Tell you later. Which is the other part of the plan.'

'Which is?'

'I could do with freshening up a little. Do you have any-where nearby where a lady might wash off the dust of this parched land?'

Jo smiled, signalled for the check. 'It so happens that my employers, strapped for space at the nearby barracks, have booked me into an almost decent hotel. Nearby. Fact is, we're sitting outside it right now. You need to shower?'

'Do you provide room service?'

'Everything is negotiable. Chas. But there's a question first.' She dropped colourful notes onto the check.

'Shoot.' Chastity stood, arms folded, eye to eye with the other woman.

'You're straight. You have a guy. A man.'

Chastity rounded the table, caught Jo from behind and pulled them together, Jo's back to her own front. Bumped up against ordnance.

'Christ, you're carrying!'

'We do. I do. Always.' Jo's words faltered when Chastity's hands caught the belt of her cargo pants. All other diners looked away, in a way. Sort of. The better to overhear these remarkable women, fodder for some eventual gossip and chatter.

'When you meet someone and you click, you know? When it's just obvious that it's going to happen. Why fight it? My best lovers have been women. Women know what women like. Men know what men like. I'm not . . . ah . . . gay, but I know what I like. And . . . you I like. I like men too. Everything in its proper place at the proper time. We cool? Or do you prefer lies?'

'Girlfriend. Let's walk inside, where it's cooler.' They walked out of the forecourt cafe into the foyer of the hotel itself. 'My room's upstairs. You can shower and clean up and I can provide back-scrubbing services, and I'll call my unit and tell them I'm following up a lead. Do you mean that? Do you really want to come hunt your guy with me? Will you want to after . . . well. Anything?'

'For the look on his face? Oh yes.'

Jo's room was round back and on the third floor. Comfortable, so long as no occupants needed to spend much time there. Chastity followed her host in. 'Cool. Aircon, even. What I need. A bath?'

'Wetroom. Big shower only.' Jo stopped by the small, closed window, suddenly losing confidence, it seemed. Chastity opened the door to the wetroom, turned to her companion and smiled broadly.

'Better yet. Easy room for two.' With no attempt at artifice or overt seduction she kicked off her boots, unhitched her jeans and stepped from them, reaching over her head in a single fluid movement and removing both shorts and bra as one. It took longer for Jo to say 'Wow' than it did for Chastity to get naked.

'Wow.' Jo said it again. 'That's fit. You sure you're really ex-military?'

'I'm sure. No need to fall apart when you leave the ranks.' She snapped her bare heels together and ripped off a salute. 'Private on parade. OK, cut the shit, where's the shower?'

'Let me show you. It's too easy to become lost, disoriented

in these palatial lodgings.' Jo was nude in almost exactly the same time as Chastity, pausing only momentarily to slip her holstered pistol into a drawer, and to remove the sheathed knife from her boot, at which point she took her new companion by the hand and led her into the wetroom, where they dodged like teenagers while the water reached an acceptable temperature.

'You always armed?' Chastity's question sounded entirely casual.

'It's the law here. Every citizen is expected to put in military service of one kind or another. You don't carry?'

'No reason to. I have no enemies!' Chastity laughed easily. 'Just no-good unreliable shit boyfriends. And speaking of shit ex-boyfriends, did you call in to get time off? I fancy going on a bad man hunt. After maybe a little lie-down first, of course.'

'Good thinking.' Jo ran back into the bedroom, extracted a cell phone from its hiding place, keyed in a rapid-dial number and waited. Spoke. Waited some more. Spoke some more. Hung up. Tossed phone onto the bed. 'All done.'

'Things are that relaxed in your army?' Charity's voice sounded as surprised as she actually was. She dripped fetchingly onto the carpet.

'I'm near the end of my tour, I'm a sergeant, this investigation is stonewalled, no assignments after this one, really, so, yes. Guess so.'

'You can just wander off? I don't speak Yiddish, so I've got no idea what you said.' She laughed, suddenly, a blonde beauty, naked and alone with an Israeli soldier, a femme fighter at that. A ridiculous situation for almost anyone.

Jo grinned. 'Forty-eight hours, and the use of a vehicle if I want.' She reached over to her new best friend, took one of Chastity's hands in both of hers and lifted it to her left breast, where it rested, a tiny pale orphan on a hill of dark, one finger and the thumb encircling a hard dark peak of a nipple. Finger and thumb closed slowly, squeezing so, so gently, rolling the nipple between them.

A sudden moment of tension, maybe of doubt. Jo whispered; 'Are you really ready?'

Chastity walked backwards into the wetroom. 'I feel . . . I feel like a little adventure.' She paused. 'Hey now, what's with the nerves, girlfriend? Throw me the soap, I'm gritty where a girl does not need to be gritty.' Jo under-armed a bottle of shower gel, Chastity emptied about one third of it into her cupped hand, dropped the bottle and soaped a monster lather over herself, under her arms, over her breasts, pausing as her hands soaped their way over her belly and to the borders of her immaculately bald sex. Jo stared, almost trembling. Chastity looked slyly up to her companion, opposed thumbs and forefingers halted in the act of parting her lips. 'You got more soap? You got some soap for a lady in need?'

Jo awoke from whichever nirvana she'd been drifting towards and threw the bottle across the room. Chastity caught it one-handed, emptied it into her hands and gestured. Where she pointed, Jo followed. Chastity worked up a second lather, this time on the body of her friend, who now seemed entirely lacking in the self-confidence she'd shown before, allowing herself to be pulled towards and finally against Chastity, body to body, soaped skin on soaped skin. Chastity backed up against a corner of the room, moved her shining skin against the dark, darker skin of the other woman, the soap foam and its scent filling all the spaces between them. Chastity pushed Jo away just enough to allow her to descend, for her face to travel slowly southward, wiping her cheeks, nose and lips against Jo's breasts and belly as they passed by. Jo stood stationary. Stock still, panting slightly as her companion's tongue and teeth penetrated the considerable hair of her pussy, her breath ceasing completely as teeth nipped and tongue teased.

Chastity rose to her full height, stretched her arms as wide as they would reach and stood as on an invisible cross. 'Kiss me. Do it now. Close your eyes, think of whichever god is your god and kiss me like you've never kissed anyone before.'

Jo obeyed, slowly parting her companion's lips with her tongue. She moaned, a deep, warm, soulful delight, shuddering to silence as both Chastity's hands, clenched into folded fists, met her temples simultaneously, once, twice, her tongue gripped tightly by Chastity's teeth, then as suddenly released. Chastity stepped to her right, swept Jo's feet from under her with her right foot, balancing herself with a shoulder against the wall as the same right foot kicked again, this time behind Jo's left knee, tilting the stunned, stricken woman. Chastity, securely balanced once more on both feet, swung Jo's left arm up and away from the hard tiled floor as she fell, and as she fell, Chastity's right hand, still soapy, warm and fragrant, gripped Jo's forehead, accelerating it further, fast towards the unavoidable impact.

Which came, shocking loud, car-crash loud in the small, steaming, soapy fragrant place.

Chastity knelt, no smiles remaining, no humanity, and searched Jo's neck for a pulse. Found none. Lifted her head from the tiles and smacked it down again. A sound, a sickening sound of broken shells, grinding and loose. A thin trickle of blood from the ear she could not see, the ear on the floor tiles.

Chastity left her nearly-lover where she lay, left the water running, washing away the tiny blood flow from the corpse. She walked into the main room, dried herself by standing in the sunlight brightening through the window and padded nude around the room, collecting all of Jo's ID, money, weapons and phone, finally dressing in Jo's combat clothes, folding her own into a bag. And, mainly out of habit, she wiped down any surfaces she might have touched; no reason to leave obvious traces. Finally, she stepped into Jo's boots, offering a silent thanks that they were just one size too large, mostly manageable with an extra pair of military green socks. And she paused at the door to the wetroom, her last would-be lover's resting place.

'So. Onward, Sergeant Jo, Josephone, rhymes with Persephone. Fight on in another life, sweet soldier.' And she departed, leaving the room key inside the room.

Early afternoon. She needed to become familiar and comfortable in her new identity, and she needed to check in with 'mother' to learn the details of her extraction. Hairdresser first. Easy, just stroll into the first clipper she found with signs in English as well as Hebrew and Arabic and ask for a military. Back from leave, the clipper-girl wondered, and Chastity confirmed this sad fact in her very richest Boston drawl. Had she been to the States, the clipper wondered, and Chastity agreed that she had and that it would be great to say she was glad to be back, but really, this heat, the dust, really? They laughed in agreement, and a military-cropped bright blonde soldier left the salon, swinging her military baggage with her. She needed to be brunette too, but that was best left for somewhere private.

Another internet cafe, another appointment with Facebook. The social network worked its usual slow magic, pictures of imaginary friends doing imaginary things flashed up before her. She sent a daughterly enquiry about her mother's health out into the ethers and surfed innocently around, watching the Facebook window for a reply.

Which came, soon enough. Mother, tragically, had been called away and was unable to provide personal reassurance to her stranded daughter. However, she was invited to join a couple of other friends for coffee, or maybe lunch on the following day. In Haifa.

'Haifa? WTF?' she wondered, acidly, via the keyboard. In bloody Starbucks, no doubt, main street Starbucks? The reply was positive. Noon, her time. If there was a real problem with this then she knew the number to call, but it would be better not calling it. Of course it would. And it would be good to post a new cell phone number in case her friends needed to contact her. Could she do that? Of course she could do that. She was in control once more, tooled up and ready for flight.

Chastity logged off. Haifa. Up the coast a way. Back online to check trains, car hire, coaches between Ashdod and Haifa. There were many, many ways, and it was about eighty miles to travel along the busy coast road.

Time to return to Simeon's hotel room, to tidy up any ends left loose there and to become brunette. Chastity had been many things and being brunette was just another of those things. She adjusted her cap and flagged a cab. No need for the military to march everywhere. In any case, it was far too hot for marching.

Simeon's suite was cleaned, immaculately and expensively. Nothing out of place. It was bright and it was airy and the air conditioning was unobtrusively excellent. It was spacious enough to call home, if your ambition was to live in a hotel. The furnishings were tasteful, discreet as well as functionally comfortable. Chastity closed the door quietly behind her, the habit of a lifetime's stealth being hard to break, and stood still, stock still, taking stock. She was not alone in the suite, of that she was certain.

The military footwear was not made for sneaking in silence, so she peeled it from her feet. Socks slide, so they followed the shoes. The jacket with its hard-earned merit badges and labels dropped behind a large chair, joining the bag with Chastity's civilian identity. She stood still once more, then moved to check the balcony. An earlier lesson learned. Empty.

She eased the bedroom door. Two dark heads, sound asleep. Or maybe dead, given the day she was having, but sleep seemed the more likely. A slow satiated sigh provided confirmation. She eased the door closed again and took her hair dye with her into the bathroom, where she followed the instructions as quietly as possible, hoping that the hotel's ambient drone would drown the sound of the shower. Which it did. When Simeon Guest emerged from the bedroom, he was presented with the unexpected sight of a woman with very short, very dark hair, where he could have been forgiven for anticipating a shoulder-length blonde.

'Hi, Simeon. You're back early. Do you like it?' Chastity rose from her drying chair and did a twirl, showing off the hotel's fluffy white bathrobe to its best advantage. The only man in her audience of one gave every appearance of being perplexed.

'Chas.' A statement. He had identified the change and recognised the target, then. 'Hello. The new look? Do I like that? No idea. Give me a moment. I'm mainly asleep.' He raked his fingernails through his hair, shook his head and yawned spectacularly. 'Yep. You look good. Very good. You'd look like a man if you didn't look so much like a woman. You could pass for a soldier, though.' He grinned suddenly, fully awake and readjusted.

'Can I get you something, Simeon? Two somethings? Do I get to meet the very lucky lady?' Chastity could flirt with the best of them, and her smile shone from the pale tan of her face. The bedroom door opened again behind Simeon.

'Chas. Meet Khalil. Khalil, Chas. She's mostly British. It explains everything.'

The slender dark-skinned man bowed. '*Enchanté, mademoiselle.* This is the waif you saved from the desert storms, Simeon?' Neither man appeared even faintly embarrassed by their shared nakedness.

'The same. Worth rescuing, no? Although she was a blonde beauty at the time.' He turned the focus of his wide smile away from Khalil, the smile reacquired her as its target. 'Coffees would be splendid. Both black, I think. Strong. They need to be strong.'

Khalil slapped his lover on the shoulder, bowed an excuse-me to Chastity and walked into the bathroom, snapping the door closed behind him. Simeon returned to the bedroom and re-emerged fitting himself into another of the hotel's fluffy bathrobes. He grinned again at Chastity, who was battling once again with the coffee construction kit offered by such places.

'Are you enjoying an interesting day, young lady? The sights and sounds of the big Israeli city providing food for thought . . . as well as a radical change in appearance. You certainly are a surprising lady.'

Chastity laughed, mocking gently. 'Surprises, Simeon? I think you've got me beaten in that department.' She spread her hands in a gesture intended to be welcoming. 'Thanks for all you've done.' Aquatic sounds drifted from the bathroom. 'But . . . two wives? And a . . . a man in every port? That makes a change. Even in this day of endless events, this stands out.'

'You bothered?'

'Not one bit. When in Greece . . .' They shared quiet laughter. 'It is certainly a strange day so far. Odd parallels . . .'

Simeon interrupted her. 'Before Kahlil emerges like a butterfly, what's with the transformation? More tradecraft, as I might say were I suspicious, which I am, or worried, which I'm not.'

'A little. The lady vanishes a little. Sometimes it pays to be unobtrusive. This is one of those times. Your coffee's ready. I should leave you and your friend in peace . . .' She was interrupted by Khalil's emergence and by Simeon raising a hand.

'No need for that. We're all adults. In any case, Khalil has something interesting for you. Well, you might find it interesting.' He gestured to the Arab, who leaned himself against a wall, unspeakably elegant and still naked, his near perfect physique worthy of sculpture.

'Simeon will not have mentioned that I am a policeman of a kind. There are many kinds of policeman, as you know, and there are more kinds of policemen in Israeli cities than in most others. It is possible that every person in Israel is a kind of policeman.' He shrugged. Chastity held his gaze, carefully expressionless.

'Simeon has told me that he saved you from the desert near the scene of an event.' He paused.

'An accident of some kind,' offered Chastity. Khalil smiled, shrugged gently, shook his head lazily.

'No. A murder. An assassination. They are not uncommon in the region, as you will be aware. Chas.' He smiled, sipped his strong hot coffee, waved a hand down at himself. 'My nudity bothers you?'

'I'm happy to look if you're happy to be looked at. Although I fear that I have no effect on you.' She smiled, as did Khalil.

'Maybe a little later. Once the coffee has worked its magic and the tale has done its telling. It was an assassination. A rocket attack. Two vehicles, six dead. Destroyed.'

Chastity dropped into the seat which obscured her belongings. Looked appropriately impressed. 'Wow. You don't see much of that kind of thing in England. Anyone important? Not friends of yours?'

'Not at all. Why were you in the area? It's not a place of beauty, not at all.'

'I was touring the desert with a friend, who was showing . . .'

'I know what you've told Simeon. Simeon is a trusting man, as are all half-Americans . . .'

She interrupted him. 'And you're an Arab. What's this about?'

'I am an Israeli, Chas. It is possible to be both an Arab and an Israeli at the same time. The men who were killed – they were all men – were Arabs, but they were not Israelis. Why were you there?'

'I told you already.'

'It's not easy for a policeman to believe that you and your friend were simply touring an area of desert famous only for an assassination which had not happened yet.'

'Try harder.'

'I've no need to try at all. I simply want to understand what happened. How were you travelling?'

'Land Rover. A British SUV.'

'Really? I would never have known. A white one.' A statement.

'Yes. Long wheelbase.' Déjà vu was becoming all too familiar to be comfortable.

'We may have found it.'

'Really? Where? Was Liam with it? Is he OK?' She exuded interest in this, suddenly.

'It was abandoned. Flat tyres. Someone had removed the valve cores.' He looked at Simeon; 'Cores, yes? Valve cores?'

'No idea. Whatever you say.' Simeon's entire attention was on Chastity.

'No one was with the vehicle.' Khalil was a man of some determination, focus. 'Your friend is called Liam? Liam what? What happened? Why were you alone? You could have died if Simeon had not rescued you.'

'Maybe. We'd just . . . argued. Had a fight. The last of many. We fought a lot. He took the Land Rover. He would have come back for me. Come looking for me.' She sounded appropriately doubtful.

'Why were you there? Your visas will just tell me that you were a pair of tourists, yeah, yeah, but why there? There is nothing there except sand and snakes. Not a place for lovers. Even goats refuse to live there. Even Palestinians.'

'We just wanted to get out into the real desert. Where there was nobody else. To be alone together. We had . . . issues.' She was sounding angry. Anger is a good disguise. It disguised her concern that although her own visa was authentic, an authentic tourist visa, Liam had no visa, authentic or otherwise. Improvised imaginary associates don't need visas. There was no Liam.

Khalil smiled, snapped upright from the wall he'd been supporting. He glanced at Simeon, who shrugged.

'Coffee's working.' Chastity nodded towards Khalil's dick, which had been growing in silence and in stealth as if to emphasise their conversation and was now beyond the point of being overlooked. The Arab smiled at her, spoke to his male friend.

'Time to get dressed. We need to be moving, Simeon. Chas – what sort of name is that? – Chas, would you do Simeon and myself the honour of joining with us for dinner this evening? At eight, say. Here.'

'I'm not going anywhere, am I?' Chastity stood to face him. 'And you don't believe me, either, do you?'

'Hardly a word. But no matter. The dead men were not friends to any Israeli and certainly not the state. They are no loss. I'd like you to do some thinking before we eat. Think about . . . you cannot leave my country if I want to stop you, and if you fail to appear for dinner I will stop you. I believe that you or your companion were involved in the assassination in the desert, and I would like to learn who and what were behind it. Think about that. I also believe – something else for you to think about – that Liam is dead, that is why he didn't return to pick you up after the attack. Or he ran and left you out there, for reasons of his own.

'Or you are as completely innocent as you want to appear, despite the sudden change in appearance, which may of course be a women's fashion thing. I wouldn't know. Shall you be joining us for dinner, Simeon and I, Miss Chastity?'

She bowed, gracefully. 'I shall. I shall go and buy a dress before the shops shut.'

Khalil bowed in return, steepled his fingers in a gesture of respect. 'I shall explain to my wife that this evening is reserved for dinner *à trois*, for my friend Simeon and his friend Chas, who I hope will become my friend also. I think she will understand.' He returned to the bedroom and returned dressed before Chastity and Simeon had exchanged more than some awkward and bewildered pleasantries, and swept out. 'Five minutes, Simeon. Hurry up!'

Chastity turned on Simeon. 'What the fuck?'

He was dressing, at a more conventional pace, and ignored her question.

'Simeon. What is going on?'

Guest stood up from tying his shoes. He looked at the floor for a long moment, then raised his eyes to meet hers. 'There's maybe $5,000 in the nightstand. Taking it would be no proof of innocence.' He left, pulling the suite door shut behind him.

6

JUST LIKE JOHN

Traffic heaved and hauled and occasionally hurried. Mostly it stood, boiling and blaring, cursing and constrained, while heroic invulnerable pedestrians swarmed like large ants through it, around it. The only cure could be coffee.

Stoner sat and sipped, watched and waited. In the distance his horizon was a vast, towering and beautiful garden provided for some reason by the Bahá'í, one more interpretation of man's endless quest for a fantasy immortality. One more among many, many others, here in one more land which claimed outright to be populated by some god's very own chosen people. Stoner had no gods. Occasionally, when he'd watched the life lift from the fading eyes of some hapless casualty, he had considered whether his life would be improved by a mystical belief system, by some omnipotent imaginary friend. He could not see it, could find little, maybe nothing, to believe in but himself and those few close to him. Exactly why some immortal, omnipotent, all-seeing deity should have any interest at all in the humanity which teemed across the surface of just one planet out of an untold multitude of planets . . . he had no idea. And if that deity did not in fact care about each human, such as himself, why should each human care for the deity? It was a selfishly simple philosophy, but he didn't worry about that.

Coffee, though. Coffee cured many things, including the bleakness of soul produced by sitting in a city populated by some god's apparently chosen people, surrounded by those people, people who, though they dressed in many and occasionally strange ways, appeared to be no more saintly, saved nor sympathetic than any other randomised city population. They pushed, they shoved, they fought, they swore, they bled and they died. Just like everyone. Just like everyone had done since the day humanity coughed its first cough and started its first fight. Even though his current neighbours claimed to be the chosen people of some cantankerous, possibly bearded and certainly male and demanding deity, and that they had a god-given right to live in this god-forsaken place . . . they behaved pretty much like any other urbanised, westernised, selfish, rude and violent population. They were by their actions godless. He would never understand it.

The meeting had been set for noon. It was past noon. Well past. Noon had been marked by a clangour of bells as one god's chosen people were summoned to churches, mosques and synagogues to be appropriately devout, and by a wailing of almost exclusively male voices singing the song of another god – maybe the same god, depending on who you listened to – being called to their holy places to be appropriately devout. And although the followers of all gods, who may or may not be the same god, preached forgiveness and love, they killed each other with at least as much vigour and enthusiasm as the followers of no gods at all. It was all a source of wonder to Stoner. He understood coffee. And this coffee claimed to be Starbucks coffee, famous the world over for its high standard. This particular cup was burned and over-strong. Possibly a victim of too much religious fervour, although it was as hard to understand that as to understand the godly themselves.

'The beard suits you.' A female soldier was standing to his left, her hands in plain view, as was the sidearm at her belt and the semi-automatic slung at her side. He looked up.

99

Looked down again, drained his coffee and waved for a waitress, acknowledging that second coming with an order for two coffees, cream, as little coffee in the mix as the machine and the barista could manage.

'I'll be awake for a week after this,' he complained gently, waving vaguely towards all of the three unoccupied chairs around his table. 'Am I supposed to know you?' He looked up at the military woman, the ultra-short, dark hair, the athletic build, the weaponry and the dark sun-dried skin.

'You're waiting for me, Mr Stoner.' He knew the voice. Smiled as the coffee landed on his table, and the waitress cleared the debris of his previous caffeine overload, the dried stained cups replaced as table furniture by what looked to his expert eye to be an Uzi.

'If you say so.' He sat back and took a closer look. 'Tell me who I'm waiting for, should you feel so inclined. Could be I'm waiting for anyone who happens along searching for company and truly intense coffee. Soldiers welcome, of course. How could it be otherwise, here in the peace-loving Holy Land?'

'I'd never expected you to be fooled by appearances, Mr Stoner.' The soldier had removed her cap, swiped a dark hand through the much darker stubble of her scalp. 'Do you really not recognise me?'

'Let's see. Plain identifiers. Height? Check. Eye colour? No. Hair colour? No. Complexion . . . How'm I doing with this? I was waiting for a little blonde lady lost in the violent city of . . . which city was it to be?'

'Ashdod. But you stood me up. Typical of you, Mr Stoner. Why? All original excuses are welcome.' She smiled at him. Sincerity was an unavailable option, it seemed.

'Palestinians threatening to rain rockets onto my ship, so I'm told, though I get told so many strange and surprising things that it's not easy to tell the fact from the bull. I was also told, for example, that you were stuck, which I found hard to believe, and that you need extracting, which I also found hard to believe. Now I discover that you're a sergeant – quite a senior one, looks like – in some unremarkable branch of the Israeli infantry and that you've been decorated a few times and carry several guns. I thought you preferred blades to bullets. That's the Charity I know.'

'Chastity, Mr Stoner. It's more than simply a virtue. You have a ship? Of your very own?'

'As you say. Charity sends appropriate affection. I made that up. She did send something, though, apart from me. Everything we thought you'd need to get you onto my ship – surely every well-dressed man about town has a ship? – is in the bag tangled around the legs of this unstable table. But . . .' he paused, staring as he sipped the coffee. She stared directly back, meeting his gaze. Waiting.

'Did you really plant a bomb in my club, back in England?'

'I did. Two, maybe three in fact. But I also disarmed them. Tell me about this ship? You're reputed to be resourceful, and you've been around long enough to be fairly affluent, but a ship? Some millionaire's drifting gin palace you happened to borrow? Or is it something left to you by your previous employer? Your recently-deceased previous employer. I could believe he had enough clout to own a ship. At least a big boat. You'd better be clever; they search boats, big and small, coming and going. And they hate stowaways and they lock them up and . . . that does not bear consideration, Mr Stoner. I hope your plan is better than that.'

'Have you finished yet? I don't remember you being so garrulous, Chastity. A woman of action rather than words, no? How much of your Israeli super-tan is genuine? You'll need to do magic with the make-up to look like your sister. She's still strikingly pale.'

'We're blondes, of course she's pale.'

'She's not a blonde, not currently. More . . . bottle black. With blue streaks.'

'How fine for her. And this matters how, exactly?'

'Her hair is in the bag, the bag below.' He shuffled the bag with a foot. 'And her ship ID is in my pocket, along with a passport which works well enough for Brit and Israeli officialdom. In the bag there is also one of her more striking going-ashore outfits, but she is very pale-skinned and the outfit shows a lot of skin, which could be a problem. You need to do a little tourist shopping. Buy some clothes. Get pale. You can turn your brown eyes blue again?'

'Yes. And I can do shopping. I'm a woman. All women can do shopping. I even know where the shops are here in Haifa.'

'Impressive.'

'Of course. How long do I have? Tell me about your boat? Ship?'

Stoner stood. Pointed. 'Over there. Big. White. Shiny. Ship-shape.'

'Impressed, Mr Stoner. That's . . . yours?'

'A wonderful sense of humour, as ever. It belongs to a great big American company, comically called Carnival, although it pretends to be British and pretends to be owned by a fine bunch of British chaps called P&O. Whatever, it's a very fine vessel, packed with a couple of thousand of the most innocently tedious people you're ever likely to meet. And it's your transport away from this toasted place. Everyone on that fine vessel has been checked and deemed to be kosher by the Israelis. They only check entries, not exits. Got the plan yet?'

'Uh-huh. And Charity is aboard and has gone through security? Won't anyone notice that there are suddenly two of her?'

'Only if you're standing side by side and sharing the same man in a public sex contest, at a guess. There are over two thousand other proles on there. It's not hard to get lost among them.'

'Can we do shopping together? I doubt you want to sit here for another hour waiting for me.'

'Thank you for that kindness and consideration, ma'am.

You need to ditch your military mien soon. You can't get on my ship looking like that. Sadly. I think you look great, though. Great style. Suits you. The Uzi matches your eyes. Show me the shopping.' He folded a few notes under a saucer, stood, and they left together.

'Have you been on one of these before?' Stoner asked. Chastity shook her head. 'Should be easy. There's a shuttle bus service from the town to the ship. Security check it at the dock entry, but it's only a light thing, a gesture. They may want to see your passport and your ship ID card, the cruise card, and maybe the immigration entry permit which is folded inside your passport. But they probably won't. You can't get on the ship without the cruise card, and you need to walk through a metal detector set on low and probably another scanner too, but that's looking for narcotics. You're not carrying?'

Chastity shook her head. Her Bible-black hair with its vivid blue streaks attracted stares from all around. The soldier was gone; uniform and weapons into a busy hotel's trash and already heading for a city dump, military ID dismembered and lost down several drainage gratings. Her eyes were blue behind the huge sunglasses. She appeared far more of a tourist than did Stoner, who towered at her side, doing his best not to observe their surroundings, to stare ahead. Stoner looked like a bodyguard, somehow. He often did.

'D'you feel watched?' He sounded cautious, appeared unconcerned as they walked together towards the shuttle bus pick-up point.

'No more than usual, to be honest. I feel lost without the armoury, though. It's surprising how rapidly you get used to it. Will passengers expect me to talk to them?'

'Just take my hand and act like a groupie. That should cause outrage. If you were tagged somehow or followed, they'll pick us up either as we get on the bus or as we board the ship.'

'I wasn't followed. Even now they're looking for me in

Ashdod. If they followed me somehow to the railway, I bought a ticket for Tel Aviv, not Haifa, and I told anyone who'd listen that I was from Tel Aviv. But that's just caution. I wasn't followed at all. They're not missing their sergeant yet; she had forty-eight hours leeway.'

'Cool.' Stoner looked around some more, disguising his scanning behind much wiping of sweat from baking brow. 'How is the sergeant? Who is she?'

'MIA, I'm sad to say. She was OK.'

'Gotcha. Here cometh the bus.'

They boarded, as did maybe forty other tourists, mostly fully paid-up members of the jabbering classes, recently retired, a few of whom nodded to Stoner and stared with open interest at his companion.

He leaned close to Chastity, whispered, 'I forgot. Stupid of me. Remember this. You're Charley, like it says on your ID. I'm John. Plain John. John Hand.' He pulled his cruise card from a shirt pocket and showed it to her. 'Follow my lead as we board.' The bus roared and blew an environmentally catastrophic cloud of diesel smog across the dock, attempting to drown his whispered words. 'You pass the card to the security stooge; he scans it, your image pops up before him, he waves you through. You ignore him like the last relic of a once-great empire that you are. Then it's just scanners.'

'The ship's system won't pick up that I never got off earlier? That I only got on?'

'I confused it earlier. Accidentally scanned myself off and on and off again. Silly me. Swiped your card once during the kerfuffle. Easy. Before you know it we'll be subsiding in some bar. I'll be chatting up Charity and you'll be taking a long bath. You need to do that.'

'You saying I smell?'

Stoner nuzzled her neck a little, passengers looked away. 'Blondes bloom, I believe. Here we go. Prepare to get shoved around by little old ladies. Watch out for spiked walking sticks. This lot are more frightening than Mossad. And watch out for Mossad, too, of course.' He climbed down from the bus, Chastity close behind, clutching her cruise card, and they walked together towards the ship's boarding gangway. Two very bored Israeli soldiers of some impossibly junior rank stopped passengers at random and asked for passports. They stopped Stoner. Both soldiers wore weapons, well-worn semi-automatics. Chastity scanned for threat. Habit. Stoner handed over his cruise card; the soldier, a small dark woman, waved his hand away.

'Passport. Please.'

'I'm sorry.' Stoner dug into his pockets and retrieved his dark red passport, handed it to the soldier, who flicked it open at the photograph, looked at him once with heavy disinterest, handed it back, waved both Stoner and Chastity through.

Stoner watched the dock for unusual activity. None was apparent. He gestured Chastity forward and up the long aluminium stepway towards the big white ship's entry. Two vast and varicose English women pushed themselves past him, separating him from Chastity. One turned back to face him and with a horrendous impersonation of a teenage flirt told him 'We really like your music, Mr Hand. Are you playing tonight after dinner? My friend thinks you're a rock star incognito!' Her friend blushed beneath her already fiery sunburn and sun hat and looked away, embarrassed.

Chastity reached the ship before them, turned with a wide white smile; 'John! Come on. Save your fans for later!' Turned back and handed her card to the security staffer with the scanner, who grinned at her, returned the card and waved her towards the metal detector arch, through which she passed without any electronic comment. Stoner joined her, waving to the ladies, who lurched, wobbled and wandered off towards the bank of lifts.

'Welcome aboard. Your cabin awaits.' He gestured towards the empty stairwell.

'Stairs? We do stairs?'

'We do. It keeps us fit and it keeps the throngs at bay. Remember, John Hand now. Always. That is who I am.'

'Do I get a drink before a shower?' She sounded almost friendly. Relief showing through, perhaps.

'Don't care. Do what you want. I'll deliver you to your sister and what you do then is up to you. It doesn't concern me at all.' His friendliness had packed its bags and left. Chastity nodded and followed him.

'It isn't as exciting as most people think.' Stoner was sitting high up in the ship, in the bar again, a quiet corner behind a door, almost invisible from the main body of the lounge itself. The first officer, uniformed, cap stationed on the table between them like a white dove of peace, should an observer be feeling lyrical, sat nursing a soft drink and a non-committal expression. He had more to say. 'Mostly it involves watching, learning, gathering facts and probabilities, possibilities some-times, and then passing those on or acting on them. Depends on the gig. Who's paying. What they want. It's all contracting.'

'You found your missing person? Solved the problem? Is life getting back to normal now?' Her voice was carefully neutral.

'Missing person is found, missing person appears safe and sound. No longer a concern for me.'

'Can you do that? Detach yourself from your . . . colleagues? Your friend Bili doesn't seem keen to detach, although to be fair Charley is inconspicuous enough. Saw her having lunch. She seemed OK from a distance. Head down in a book. How's Bili? You two are very close. Should I be worried?'

'I can't stop you worrying. Worry away if you want to. You have a husband. Bili is nowhere near as connected to me as that.' Stoner smiled, reached for her hand, then nodded an apology, remembering the uniform. 'She and I could be closer than a married couple, of course. Only joking. She protects me against evil women. No, I'm serious, she does that. It's . . .

endearing. Also sometimes inappropriate. You two would get on fine. You're both into control in all its forms, I reckon. With any luck at all, she'll turn up here sometime. She's great company when she's sober, and better than most even when wrecking herself again. If you're really lucky I'll persuade her to play a little, sing a little, although the music here is way too . . . tame for her.'

'Why does she do that? Drink so much?'

'Ask her. She'll either tell you why or tell you to fuck off. The latter's more likely.'

'You know why, I suppose?'

'We're friends. Knowing each other's answers is part of that. As is not talking about someone else's secrets, I think.'

'Are my secrets safe with you, then?'

'Yes. If I knew any, they'd be safe. Why? Is it that strange? Are sailors a gabby, untrustworthy bunch?' Stoner detuned his comments with a smile.

'You and your . . . friends in need have secrets from me. I know that. Are you going to share them with me? Or are their secrets safe too? Can you really balance friendships like that?'

'So long as there's no conflict of interest, yes, I can. You do the same, I'm sure. Everyone does. It's a matter of judgement. And . . . I wouldn't ask you to give away any secrets, betray any confidences. Why would you, anyway?'

'I might believe in truth and trust, things like that. Are they alien concepts in your world?'

'Now you're just picking a fight. I don't do fights, Jenny. I'm just a guy on holiday, an expensive holiday. You can't lecture me on trust and truth when you're a married woman having a fling with some guy on holiday. Really.'

'Hey guys, having a fight? Can I join in? Is it a free for all?' Bili was standing close by, hands jammed into jeans pockets. 'Take no shit from . . . John, lady. He tells the truth, mostly, but it's truth with holes in it. Like those Italian cheeses.'

'Dutch,' the first officer corrected her. 'They're Dutch cheeses.'

'What. Ever. You can get pedantic about cheese? Fuck's sake. Don't you have a job to do, lady in uniform? Or are you beating up JJ . . . John . . . just for the crack? Good sport, I'm not knocking it. I can join in if you like. On both sides, even.'

The first officer stood, collected her hat, smiled at Stoner. 'She is priceless, this one. Look after her, John. I'm off watch at midnight. Will drift up here after that. If you want me to, of course?'

He grinned. 'Of course. I'll sit here for a couple hours, get beaten to bits by Bili. Then throw her over the side. Keelhaul her or something nautical.'

'Something naughty sounds better. I'll snag a drink. See you later, Jenny, unless I get lucky. Which will not be easy, given the average age up here.' Bili waved an inclusive arm around. 'But a girl needs to try!'

The first officer refitted her hat, sketched a mock salute and left, replaced almost instantly by a waiter, a quiet Indian with a wide smile he reserved entirely for Bili, balancing a tray bearing two large glasses, both of them filled with thick, pale liquids topped off with fruit, paper parasols and a drinking straw. The waiter unloaded them and passed a bar check to Bili, who signed it with a flourish, beamed radiantly at the waiter and turned back to Stoner.

'What are those?' Stoner understood cocktails, from a safe distance, but couldn't recall actually drinking one.

Bili tapped the paler of the two concoctions. 'Kahlua colada. It's just the same as a piña Colada only made with kahlua instead of . . . piña? Whatever. Tastes of chocolate and comes with a slice of pineapple. I'd thought the pineapple made it qualify as a piña, but who gives a fuck?' She tapped the second, darker glass. 'And this is a BBC. Isn't that a crack? Baileys, banana and chocolate. I think. Tastes like chocolate and has banana in it. Sticks in the straw. You need to drink them through a straw or they get up your nose. I had no idea that cruise ships were so . . . big.'

'Having a good time, though, Bili? Do I get a drink?' Stoner mimed distress.

'Get your own. Is it true I can spend as much as I want on this card?' She flicked the cruise card across the table towards him.

'Pretty much. You need to square up before they'll let you off the ship back in England, though.'

Bili stopped drinking. 'Oh.'

'I wouldn't worry about that too much. It's not your name on the card, is it? I expect that Charley has done some sort of deal. Enjoy yourself. Buy a hat.'

Bili drained the first of the glasses, slid it to the side of the table, contemplated the second. 'I was witless shitless about you, JJ.' She spoke quietly, seriously. Eyes down. 'Really worried. You just vanished. And your whore, her too. I called you, called everyone I thought might know where you were, what was happening. It was shit. Absolute fucking shit. Stretch told me not to worry, told me to stop drinking and to play more music. He said you'd turn up, like a bad rash or something, that I mustn't worry. But I did worry. Made a real sad-ass show of myself. Every night I'd go down to the club, every night I'd fire up that crap old amp of yours, pull that crap old Fender out and tune it and put it on its stand, and every night I'd play the fucking blues for you. I never knew about the blues, JJ. Never really knew. Played "Sitting On Top Of the World", "Rollin' and Tumblin'", even "I'm So Glad", but just kept on crying. Pathetic. Fucking pathetic. Just like some fucking girl.' She wiped her nose with the back of her hand, reached for the remaining glass. Stoner shrugged, turned both hands palm-up.

'I'm sorry . . .'

'Do not fucking apologise. Just do not fucking fuck off again without a fucking word, JJ. I don't care if you fucking go away, why the fuck would I? You're not my fucking father, fuck's sake. Just . . . just tell me. OK?'

'Can't. Couldn't.'

'I'm not a fucking child, JJ. You can tell me when you're going away.' Her eyes were developing fierce red rims. She sucked so hard on her straw that she really did resemble a little girl.

Stoner rang the hard fingernails of his right hand hard on the tabletop. 'Stop it. Stop now. How many people asked you where I was?'

'Dunno.'

'Try. Guess.'

'Apart from the club regulars?'

'Apart from them.'

'Maybe . . . three. Four. Apart from the audience. Loads of those asked after you. But maybe a half dozen police types. Why?'

'What did you tell them?'

'What do you think I fucking told them? Don't go all soft, JJ. I told them that you'd fucked right off without a fucking word and if they were friends of yours then I wanted them to come back and tell me when they found you because I wanted to fucking slap you for just . . . for just . . . for . . . I was so worried, JJ. Jesus Christ, I thought some murky fucker from your private life had finally offed you.'

'You didn't think I might have met a tough husband?' Stoner waved for a waiter.

'I didn't for one single minute think you'd gone on a fucking cruise, JJ. It was all so tense. You were tense, you were attracting these tense women – Charley before her hair went blue, she was a blonde before, no? – and that cop. Then you were just not there. No one knew where you were. They really didn't know. I even went around to the place you let your whore live and spoke with some Chinaman. He didn't know where you were either. No sign of the whore, either, so I thought you'd gone away together. Then she turned up in the club one night with another guy, one of your military mates, and he asked where you were. I threw a bottle at him.'

Stoner beamed at her. 'You did what?'

'Threw a bottle at him, useless twat. Missed. Expect I was pissed a little. But it got better after that. I didn't see your whore again, but the guy came back, him with the tattoos and the stupid nickname like all your mates, and he brought Charley and two really weirdy guys, all in black, like goths from the stone age, then it all picked up speed and here I am. Why didn't you just fucking tell me you were heading out, JJ? Aren't we friends?'

'If I'd told you where I was then one of the men asking for me would have hurt you until you told them where I was. I didn't want that. Neither did you.'

'You think I'd have ratted you out? Come on!'

'You can't not tell guys like that what they want to know. No one can. Not me, not you. You never want to find it out for yourself. They aren't funny.'

She looked at him seriously. 'You mean like they're killers?'

'Worse than that. Far worse than that.'

'Why do you know them? Men like that?'

'I'll tell you one day. Not this day, another day, but I will tell you. Promise.'

'So how come you're on a cruise ship, hey? And playing with, what, the house band? The fucking house band. Soft jazz and daydreams for the night-time. That is *so* you. I should have thought of that. Nah . . . no, I'd never have thought of that.' One subject closed, another subject open. Stoner believed in that moment that he was actually in love with Bili. The one woman who was never bored and was never boring. Insane, emotionally disastrous, but never boring.

'I've been here a while,' he began.

'And what's with the John Hand shit?' Interruptions may indeed be good for the soul.

'It's an alias, a work name.'

'Like Bono?'

'Yeah, makes me into an Irish millionaire superhero so I can whine continually and lecture away on any subject I please while wearing a silly hat.'

'You don't like Bono?' She appeared genuinely surprised.

'Love him. Like a brother. Especially when he tells guys poorer than him to give away their money to his chosen causes or some such. I so admire major hypocrisy in all its forms.' She thumped him, hard, on the nearest bicep.

Their waiter coughed and attempted conspicuity. They ordered more drinks, Bili more adventurous cocktails ('You choose it, man; I'll drink it!'), Stoner a litre of sparkling water. He felt that he deserved dilution, absolution, that his blood needed cleansing a little.

'What's the scene, then? The music scene here on the *grand bateau*? Why are you playing with a house band? You after a job?'

'Why? It's no mystery. There're some very good players on board. Really. Several bands and guys who play in more than one. I just sit in from time to time. I've been on here a while now. They're cool, friendly. Late nights, after they've all done their sets, sometimes we play a little jazz.'

'Jazz, JJ? Fuck off. MOR, more like. Never took you for a "Girl From Ipanema" kinda guy.' She was plainly feeling better. 'You actually play "Girl From Ipanema"?' Suspicion clouded her voice.

He nodded soberly and drained a half-pint of water. 'And so should you. It's soul nourishing. Inspirational.'

'You are so full of shit, JJ.'

'Takes a . . .'

'Yeah. Takes a tosser to spot a tosser!' She smiled. Started to hum "Nowhere Man" . . .

*

'It's sweet, don't you think?' Two women talking across the same lounge, one darker-skinned than the other and possibly a little older; one conventionally attractive apart from the unconventional bright-blue glossy streaks in her otherwise matt black hair, the other boasting a short dark scalp stubble, a military or maybe a statemental stubble of some kind. If the intended statement was that the short-haired woman pre-ferred the services and company of her own gender, then the couple may have been identified as lovers. As it was, they were sisters. Neither of them was naturally brunette; an ironic state of affairs for some.

'What happened, then?'

'A lot. Be more specific.' Their soft drinks drifted towards the room's ambient temperature, ice melted, largely ignored.

'You took the shot?'

'I did. Complete success and accuracy. The plan was a per-fect plan, everything worked as per that plan. Up to that point. Beyond that point it was simply chaos. Someone took out both vehicles with a rocket of some kind.'

'Both vehicles? Some rocket.'

'As you say.'

'Any idea what sort?'

'As if. A blue one. Pink spots. How would I know?'

'Ground or air launch?'

'Good question. Very good question. I'd not considered that. Air launch opens another whole new nest of nastiness.'

'You didn't hear an aircraft?'

'No. But I wasn't listening for one. And in any case, don't some drones operate almost silently? I was mostly surprised. And understood straight-up that I was the patsy, the fall girl with the gun and nowhere to run.'

'Good to have you back, Chas. Really good.' The blue-streaked woman squeezed her sister's forearm and reached for her own glass, stared into its transparent ice. 'Talk me through it.'

'In a minute. Stoner. Why's he here, and how is he here? He's the latest in an increasing line of surprises, and I am truly tired of surprises, big sis. I am also suspicious and more than a little scared.'

'Scared? Of what? We should be safe enough on a ship, Christ's sake.'

'Of the coincidences. Tell me the how and the why of Stoner and I'll share with you my romantic flight across hostile territory. Lawrence of Arabia and so on. You will be gripped.' Chastity rolled her eyes.

Charity laughed quietly. 'I bet. Stoner vanished after Hartmann's . . . disappearance. Vanished completely.'

'You spoke with him after that event, though? At his club? The music club?'

'Yes. He seemed completely calm and in control. Unemotional. He sang me a song, even.'

'Fuck. A lullaby?'

'Something by The Beatles.'

'Not a blues, then?'

'No. Not that it can matter at all, little sister.'

'Maybe it shows the balance of his mind was disturbed. I thought he only played endless, tedious, self-abusing blues guitar solos from mother's time.'

'No. "Norwegian Wood".'

'Oh yes. Cool song. Lennon. Then he vanished? I heard no more, but I wouldn't have; I was working up this fiasco. Stoner was smart to disappear. Must have been a lot of unhappy troopers after the Hartmann thing.'

'Yeah, yeah. No one could find him. Did all the usual searches, trawls, known haunts, rousted all his contacts, but nothing. Not worth the effort of a deep dig. Couple of governmental departments were well knicker-twisted about Hartmann, but they're not the efficient torturing kind and gave up too easily, as usual. Leave him be, was the general agreement in our sphere. He'd either come back or he wouldn't. Cool either way. Then your operation went tits-up.'

'And what? He popped up like the white knight and offered to come find me? I think we only met the once. Sensible conversation, as I recall.'

Charity sipped and sniggered. 'Not exactly. Charm, in her role as great white mother, dug her claws into the whole business of pulling you out of that hideous shithole, and contracted the techno prisoners to come up with ways out, pronto. Your cover wouldn't hold deep scrutiny.'

'Yeah. Good just for the quick in-out. Thought so. Didn't use it. Used feminine wiles instead. Techno prisoners, though? How is the good lady Menace? Or is Menace the guy? I forget. Crazy couple, those. Creepy in black.'

'They're good, I think. They took about three seconds to tell Mother Charm that your best hope for a painless extraction was to use Stoner.'

'Of course they knew where to find him?' She laughed. 'You gotta love them; bats as a bag of bats, but they are always a surprise. Brilliant.'

'They knew where he was. They found him very rapidly. They just didn't want to share it with anyone. Considerate of them, and worth remembering for the future. I don't think they lied, exactly, I don't think they'd looked for him before your need arose.'

'OK, enough of the mystery, sister. Where was he?'

'Here. On a big ship, seducing hapless passengers and at least one of the officers, and playing guitar with some of the bar bands. His identity was neat; one of Hartmann's ancient covers from his own ops days. Technos traced long-dormant bank accounts, found the one Stoner's using, reasoned quick as a quick thing that MIA men rarely use checking accounts and even more rarely go on long cruise holidays, and bingo. Here we are.'

'The girly-girl? Bili? And the blue hair? Which suits you, of course, sweet sister.'

'Of course it does. Like you look so good as a soldier-boy. Bili came because we all thought that Stoner would do something rash and irrational if I just turned up and asked him for help. Threats would have done nothing, and it was fairly plain he didn't want to be found, so he was unlikely to be welcoming. Bili being here encouraged him to cooperate. She's useful leverage. She distracts him. The blue hair was so you could look just like me and fool the ship's security into thinking you were me. Just for a little while.'

'Where do I get off, and how?'

'Same method. Go ashore with Stoner at Barcelona, collect your revised papers, give my ship ID back to Stoner and I'll see you in England. Assuming I survive the Bay Of Biscay.'

'Stormy? Rough?'

'Stormy. If there's a way I can get off with you I will.'

'You don't like the naval life? Not about to sign up? Sign on? Whatever?'

'I've had a week of it and I'm bored senseless. Why do people do this? For what kind of fun? Anyway, I can catch up on my reading and they have a good gym as well as a couple of short pools. Maybe I'll throw some of the Johns overboard or something. The nights are too long. That's more or less it. Tell me your tale, dear sister.'

Chastity smiled, flagged down another soft drink, kicked off her shoes and did exactly that.

The rhythm of feet on teak. A double tapping. Early morning at sea; cool sun, brightening skies and the running rhythm of feet on teak. The white ship slipped through the Mediterranean waters with ease and considerable grace. Stoner ran the promenade deck, deck seven, the teak-surfaced deck intended for ladies and gentlemen to promenade upon but in modern times too often clogged by oiled-up sun-worshippers who considered little but their own introverted, self-obsessed lives. At this hour of the morning they were invisible, either sleeping off yesterday or preparing to break their short fasting with another sixteen waking hours of sloth and gluttony. Stoner ran alone, as was the case more often than not, although maybe another forty individuals, a possible two percentage points of the fine ship's paying population, ran or walked as he did, or swam in the pools or paced themselves in the gym.

After a half hour, maybe five easy miles, a second set of footsteps approached from behind. He pulled from the centre of the deck as a courtesy to let the runner past. They did not pass. Instead they pulled alongside and matched pace to his. They ran on in step.

'Chastity.' Stoner's gaze was straight ahead, plotting an efficient course between the deck furniture while always allowing space for his companion.

'I owe you a thank-you.' Neither of them was breathing hard, not yet, not at this pace. 'And, I think, an apology.'

'For what?' Stoner had been running for almost a half-hour longer than Chastity; there is efficiency in brevity when the running rhythm is matched to the breathing rhythm.

'Thanks for the extraction. It was excellent and effective. Apologies for ruining your vacation, your holiday. My understanding is that you had wished to disappear. So . . . an apology. You can no doubt disappear again should you wish. I doubt this is your only legend, and I doubt that the techno prisoners would give up another without some serious weight.'

'You're correct.' Stoner ran on, Chastity beside him.

'Any thoughts on why they chose to give up your location? It's been puzzling me.' Chastity's pace matched his exactly, their feet counted cadence together.

'Thoughts? No, not really. Theories, though. Can theories wait until breakfast? Half an hour or so?'

'Of course.' They ran on in a comfortably shared silence for another half-hour, until another half-dozen of the ship's less terminal passengers had joined them, while the ship's fit and efficient deck crew started to arrange loungers for the sun-soakers to pass another day of spiritual development and cultural fulfilment, disguising themselves modestly as idle, pointless products of an idle, pointless, endlessly consuming society.

On the four wide flights of stairs, heading heavenwards for breakfast, Stoner paused on a landing to stretch a little. 'Why did Mallis give me up? It'll be a bigger picture thing. Bound to be.' They completed the stairway to breakfast together, shambled around the carousels, hunters gathering trophies; bread, fruit, pastries. 'Was it Mallis? I'm just curious.'

'Don't know.' Chastity chewed on her second peach. 'I wasn't there.'

'OK. Thought you might know.'

'I can't tell them apart, anyway. Creepy guys. Hardly deal with them. Is it OK for a health god like yourself to fetch a lazy lady like me a coffee? Strong, black. This is a ploy to tempt you with some pastries. I can't be seen to eat pastries alone. People will notice. My reputation will suffer.'

'You have a reputation? How . . . impressive.'

'I might have. I'm a good shot. Does that help?'

'Tell me zip about the job you were on. Really, Chas, I just do not want to know. I don't want to get into it. I don't really want to do any more work like this.'

'I was set up.'

'Good for you.' Stoner stood, headed off for coffee and croissants. Returned. 'I already have too many ghosts. Just like you do. Too many offended, wounded, damaged souls who might like to talk with me about it. Talking as in . . . in terms of extreme prejudice.'

Chastity chewed pastry, in an interrogatory manner. 'That bothers you? Actually really bothers you?'

'Of course it does. Only a complete ass wouldn't be bothered. Do you have big ears and a tail? Do you eat carrots and make hee-haw noises?'

'I don't think you're likely to make me feel a fool, Stoner.'

'I'm not. I don't care what you feel like. Not at all. I think that Mallis and Menace will have had a long reason for involving me. It will be a long reason in a long game. I want as little a part in it as possible.'

'Then don't play.'

'It's not that easy with those two. Have you ever fallen out with them? Pissed them off badly?'

'No.'

'Don't. If you had, you'd be dead now.'

'No need to exaggerate.'

'I'm not. If Mallis – I get on better with him . . . possibly her, it's not easy to tell and I do not wish to investigate – if he'd told me to terminate . . . to kill you, you would be dead now, not rescued. That could also be why you have Bili along with you.'

'To keep you on a leash? Would it?'

'No. More as a gesture of good faith, is my interpretation. Madness follows all attempts at understanding those two. I just accept that they're very clever and brilliant and subtle as two drops of oil on the surface of an ocean. We owe each other a lot of favours. No idea who's in the lead.'

'I don't think I owe them anything.'

'Bully for you. May all your camels have rabid fleas, *inshallah.*'

'Oh thank you. So kind. No, smartarse, what I'm saying is that I don't understand why they gave you up and helped me. I don't think they owe us anything.' Chastity picked up both cups, plainly ready for a further caffeine infusion.

'Could be payment in advance, on account. Could be that someone to whom they do owe a debt asked them to either help you or find me; could be that there's another, longer game in play. Could be anything. You don't need to know, I don't need to know, and even thinking about it gives me a headache, makes me want to harm myself and to drink coffee so strong that it'll dissolve the enamel from my teeth. That was a hint. Subtle or what? Coffee eases my suicidal feelings.'

'That true?' Chastity paused in transit to the coffee pump.

'No.'

Coffee replenished, seat straddled once more, Chastity pressed him again about the motives, mysterious though they may be, for the techno prisoners' apparent generosity.

'Truly, Chas, I have no idea.'

'It doesn't bother you?'

'Nope. I can't affect it, so I try not to even think about it. Like many many things. Fretting does nothing. Gives you a gut ache. Maybe a coronary. Get over it. If there's a reckoning, a price, then at some point they'll present an invoice, send a bill, deliver the black spot, whatever. Remember . . .' his expression became serious, bantering momentarily banished. 'Remember that it's true what they say – they take no prisoners, none at all. Forget the techno joke; they really do not take prisoners. There'll be a calling to account, an account to be settled. Or there isn't and there won't be. Worry about them when they tell you to worry.' He smiled gently once again. 'Until then . . . oh I don't know, party, get laid, sing a song. Whatever you do for kicks. Kill someone.'

'There are two more. Two more hits on the contract.' Chastity aimed a long stare out of the ship's window, leaned her head and added intensity, focus, to the random wandering of her gaze. 'Are they dolphins?'

'Could be. That is the sea, and dolphins live in the sea. More likely to be dolphins than camels. Don't tell me any more about contracts. Talk about something else. I'm an old man. Show respect for my age and discuss the weather. Make like an Englishman. Woman.'

'You did sex with Charity.' A statement, not a question.

'Did she say so? If she say so, she must be tellin' de truth, lordie-lord.' Stoner rolled his eyes in a dismal impersonation of a bluesman.

'Two more. Talk sense.'

'Not in Israel, I hope? That would be a dark place for you to visit, sweet Chastity. Unhealthy.'

'No. Middle Europe, then in the UK. Charity is like a sister to me.'

'She is your sister.'

'You know what I mean, old man.'

'Nope. I wish it was night and not morning.'

'How so?'

'I could play dismal pop songs, seduce faded ladies and become dissolved inside.'

'You . . . do you enjoy that?'

'No.'

'Then why. . .'

'It eases the hate. Stops the killer thing. Sex instead of violence. You should try it. It may not be too late to redeem your immortal soul.'

'What are you going to do with your officer? Does she know who you are? What you do?'

'Do you never stop asking questions?'

'Should I be worried?'

'About what? About the state of your immortal soul? Of course you should. If I had the energy I would invite you to lie wrecked and naked with me in a quiet place. Save your soul in sex.' Stoner added a pointless creamer to his curdling, cooling coffee.

'Does it make you happy?' Chastity's cup was empty, as far from running over as it's possible to be.

'Don't be foolish. Of course it doesn't make me happy. I'm clinging onto the shreds of passion, pretending it's important. If having a decent fuck isn't important any more, then what is? Worrying about your immortal soul?' Stoner looked around at the gaily-clad breakfasting holidaymakers. 'Ever get the impression that everyone's listening to your every word?' He beamed at a nearby clump of fat, frilly, forty-somethings; one of them waved a wobbly hello, heaved a hideous smile.

Chastity was unrelenting, undistracted by talk of sex. 'I was set up.'

'You said.' Stoner stared with pointed purpose at the spot on his left wrist where there would have been a wristwatch, had he been wearing one, which he wasn't. 'Oh fuck it. Who by and why?'

'No idea. I'd hoped you might help here.'

'How? I've been cavorting on a ship, not carting heavy weaponry around deserts.' He paused. 'You're going to do them, aren't you? The hits. Despite the set-up, the maybe betrayal?'

'Reckon so. Why not?'

'That's the kicker, isn't it? Why not? The story of life, the answer to everything, the meaning of no meaning at all. Just words defending an action which has no justification. Killing someone. Someone you know; someone you don't know. Scars the soul, dulls all senses. I am out of it. Right out of it. Do you need the money?'

'Don't think so.'

'Do you even know how much you get paid for a hit any more?'

'Not really. Charm handles that. Takes the contracts, does the deals.'

'So a life is worthless to you now? It has no value at all? Monetary value, not that immortal soul crap.'

'Always has been. You arguing?'

Stoner paused. 'Do I sound like I'm arguing?'

'How far away am I?'

'Not very.' Stoner caught her gaze, held it. A bleakness shared. 'From taking the last life?'

'Yes.' Chastity was still as stone, more still even than Stoner. 'The last life.' Her voice was sibilant as sand on sand, a dry breeze in a desert, the shuffling of a desiccated tree.

'That's your own life.'

'Yes.'

'You can accept that?'

'You mean, welcome it? Yes.'

Stoner stood, fluid and silent. All around their tiny bubble of grief, merriment, clattered cutlery, shouted greetings, spilled food and laughter in equal measure. He rested his left hand on her shoulder. She glared at nothing, shook her head, breaking their rhythm, the mood.

'Did you really do the dirty with Charity? With my sister?'

'Hard to recall. Hard to say. I am a gentleman.'

'You would remember.'

'Remind me. Does she have hair?'

'Not for some time.'

'When do you move?'

'On the target?'

'I am uninterested in your bowels, frankly.'

'Off the ship in Spain, same way as you brought me on, if that's OK with you. Then a long, dull drive east. Mountains and lakes.'

'Austria?'

'Nearly. But . . . that's enough of that. Gym, I think. Then hit some salads. You'll be seeing to your harem, Mr Stoner?'

'The gym does sound appealing. Any objections to my sharing a little sweat and bad music played too quietly?'

'Tiring of your lady in uniform, Mr Stoner?' Chastity looked amused, faintly chilly.

'I think it's an age thing. Getting off in Barcelona, then?'

'Care to walk me ashore? Day after tomorrow?'

7

DUCKS ON A POND

Preparation is king. Also queen. Preparation is the only way to take a life while preserving another; someone else's and your own, in that order. No leeway for improvisation here. Chastity had prepared. Researched. Established the patterns of her target. Easy to achieve; he was a creature of habit, like most men. Routine and ritual, the stuff of ordinary lives, of comfortable people. The target was on holiday. A spa hotel. Slovenia. Beautiful Slovenia, a tiny country with its own alpine range, deep, dark lakes and dark, deep woods. Cold War era party resorts had transformed into hidden quality hideaways, unknown to most. A perfect location for anonymous unwinding.

The target's guards were muscular, hard as flint and of similar imagination. Less intelligence. Chastity had approached one of them for directions and a little help with the translation of a menu. The guard was bored, and helped her, his broken English making no more sense to her than the Slovenian original. They had shared a laugh, broken his boredom a little. Sloppy.

The contract specified no particular preference in the departure style for the target. After the desert disaster, Chastity favoured silence and no communication at all. So she applied both conditions without consultation. Silence is the best secrecy, the most effective secrecy of all. She learned the target's routines, and took complete advantage of the sloppiness of his guards. Three of them. The target rose in the mornings before his guards did, and although one of them was plainly supposed to stand guard in the corridor of the hotel, even having a seat for that purpose with the evident cooperation of the hotel management – and why not? – in fact every other evening he repaired to the bar with his fellow fools.

Chastity waited, Chastity watched. Chastity took a keen interest in her own security, but could detect no signs of untoward activity. Holidaymakers. Swimmers, hikers, boaters and climbers, every Euro-language. Chastity hiked, she swam, she climbed, she rediscovered the delights of canyoning and white-water rafting, and she worked out every morning, every afternoon, every evening, in the hotel's gym. She shone with health, and she fitted right in with the majority of the hotel's guest population; with the brightly-clad shining fitness brigade. Nodded and smiled to everyone, avoided all conversation with a laugh and a rueful smile, the skilful disconnections.

And at 23:23 on a day chosen at random, it being simply a day when all three escorting guards were answering Nature's lustful calls in the bar and when a tasteful rock band was playing tasteful rock music on a makeshift stage in a nearby drain, she dropped from the balcony above onto the target's own wide one, a move she'd rehearsed three times and could perform not only in the dark but also blindfolded if need be, swung her right arm through the open window, caught the security latch on the balcony door, lifted it, withdrew her arm and opened the door. The door was silent. She was unsurprised by this, mainly because she had oiled its lock and hinge mechanisms the previous three times she had practised her balcony-swinging Tarzana impression. The door opened cleanly and silently, and she slipped inside and stood in silence for a moment before closing it.

The target would be alone. She had no idea why he was alone, why he was isolated, despite the boisterous charm of the resort and the gregarious nature of his fellow guests. But he appeared to be happy enough, and she was unconcerned for his long-term welfare, unsurprisingly.

The target was alone. He was lying in the dark, breathing steadily. If not actually asleep, then heading to that fine place. Chastity didn't care. The tasteful rock music was a good mask for any noise they might make, there in his rooms, acting out their own one-way ritual of infinity in its own unique two-step. She slid the long black Teflon blade from its sheath, checked its balance in her hand, and floated like a dark dancer to the side of the bed, one more shadow in a crowd of shadows in the room.

'You're here, then.' His English was excellent. Not a native speaker, but excellent all the same. She stopped dead, senses reaching out for the untoward, detecting nothing. 'It's been a long wait.' He made no move to rise, showed no sign of panic, no emotion at all. 'Be quick.' He folded the duvet down to his chest, arms resting at his sides, both hands in view, eyes closed. Chastity leaned over him and slid the razor edge through the vital network at his throat, applying the full weight of her body and the full strength of the muscles of her arms as she sliced the long, black blade swiftly and smoothly, parting everything in its path. Blood flew, sprayed, pumped, poured, pooled, hot and blacker than the black blade, stinking in its volume and heat.

'Goodnight,' she whispered, and ran silently to her waiting door, her gentle valediction interrupted by the scream of lightweight, high-velocity ammunition shredding the living room's main door, lifting it while destroying it, and as the door danced its own desperate dance of death, she dived to the floor at the feet of the two men with the busy automatic guns, the fastest moving shadow in a sudden hotel of shadows, sliced ankle tendons, relaxed and rolled and sliced a second set of ankle tendons, relaxed and rolled and ran like a black rabbit through the warren of the hotel's suddenly unlit corridors, cool and calm, elated and driving on adrenalin and rage until she kicked through the fire escape into the night, then doubled back and ran around to her point of entry, her point of intended exit and stared, standing within a terrified gathering crowd while the characteristic high-speed scream of a fully automatic small-calibre high-velocity short gun discharged inside the bedroom, her body's bedroom.

A sudden flash, a flat detonation, shocking against the enveloping dark, and a fire was born. Two men, the one supporting the other, appeared at her point of entry, her exit, and a gun spat leaden fury over head height into the night; the crowd vanished like snow on warm water and a van, a lightless, dark van drove in to collect. She was in the full power of her rage. Again, she had been used. Set up. Again. Disappointing, puzzling and somehow unexpected. Invincible, she sprinted to the edge of the woods, to the concrete crazy golf course which had provided perfect cover for her own heavy handgun, which she emptied into the driver's compartment of the dark van and into the bodies of the stumbling black-clad gunmen, firing until the firing pin snapped on empty.

Then she ran to the lake, backlit and shadowed by the light of the fire, ignored by the terrified and confused and excited crowd. Kicked off her shoes, walked down into the dark water and swam, strong, steady, silent strokes, shedding all weapons, swimming powerfully in a wide arc until she was able to see her rental cabin.

Which was lit up like party night, two cars outside, four dark figures watching the track approach to the cabin, making no secret of their presence, their intent. She changed tack, and swam straight and true to the opposite bank, towards the church, the church with the roof somehow designed to resemble a camel's back, the roof which would provide a little sanctuary, a little rest.

The band had stopped playing, sirens providing an alternative night music. The hotel was lit once more and a wide crowd was staring, necks rubbery with interest. The dark van sagged on its wheels, bodies lay here and there, as motionless as the crowd in shock. Chastity sought salvation at an altar in the night.

Altars are often hollow tables, with brick sides supporting a stone block. A relic from the days of live sacrifice, perhaps. Chastity had no wish to be that sacrifice. She was her own Angel of Death, and death-dealing angels did not die. Not yet, not in their prime. And she was indeed in her prime. No blushing virgin, she.

From behind the altar, she removed a package, a nondescript nothing of a package; a wrapping in sackcloth. Ashes optional. The dirty, nondescript wrapping parted beneath her killer's fingers, producing a small bundle of pipes, slender pipes and stubby pipes, one finely rifled pipe, pipes with threads and pipes with fittings. She fitted them and threaded them together. Attached them to a wooden stock and a metal mechanism which had been taped together beneath the second bench behind the carved misericords and their lost messages to a lost god. From a pouch hanging around her neck inside her wetsuit she produced the final component: the firing pin.

At the bleeding feet of the crucified Christ stood more tubes: a bipod, wearily acting the part of part of a candleholder, holding a single tear of flame in a red glass jar. She collected the bipod, tottering the candle in its jar, and moving at a speed not far short of a run, she negotiated the stairs, entered the belfry and set up the bipod and the DIY rifle, snapping the most complex tube into place last of all. The night-sight lit up green. She stared across the wide lake, her enhanced vision locating her rental cabin easily enough. It was still lit up in welcome. For whom, she was uncertain. She felt no welcome at all for the four figures she'd seen earlier, and she looked for them again, finding one, two, three.

Deep, steady breaths, followed by shallow, steady, rhythmic cadence. Adrenaline and delight coursed through her, powered her. Two shots. The first was high, the second on target. Man down. Aim. Two shots. The second intruder was staggered by the first, demolished by the second. Man down. The fourth man was in the vehicle, its lights were lighting, while the third man ran for it. Two shots. The first missed, the second caught the running man. Man down. Two shots. The first exploded the glass of the driver's window, the second followed through. The car rolled forward, accelerating steadily until the driveway turned through a curve and the car drove straight on, stalling into stationary silence at a hedge. Lights lit, no vapour from the exhaust now. Not an automatic, this.

Her ears chimed and rang like a cascade of jubilant church bells; the belfry reeked of gunfire. The residents of the resort could maybe mistake their incendiary evening for Halloween, or they could instead consider the dark and none-too-distant days when the former Yugoslavia fell apart in a rage of gunfire. It was their choice. Chastity had no views either way. But she did have an agenda. Time to go hunting.

8

WASHED UP

The Blue Cube. A club, a bar, a refuge and a responsibility. Noisy at night, somnolent during the daytime. Stoner was at a point where he preferred the dark daylight hours to the bright of the night. Preferred to play the blues alone for his own ears rather than for an audience of strangers, or worse, an audience of admirers. He leaned against a wall. It was sticky. He'd been away for a couple of months and already the walls were sticky.

The carpets were sticky, the tables were sticky. The air itself seemed tacky, tired and laden with waste; wasted effort, wasted talent, wasted music and wasted dreams. Stoner wanted to break something, to fight someone, to hurt them. He shrugged off his jacket, kicked open the door into the kitchen behind the bar, pulled out buckets, bleaches and cleaning cloths. Set to, starting with the higher surfaces and working down to the lower ones. Poured away environmentally disastrous quantities of diluted filth and cleaners, and refilled and refilled his buckets again.

Two hours. Every horizontal surface above floor height had been cleaned. Next, the vertical surfaces. He stopped. What to use? How do you wash a wall? How do you wash the sticky shit from a wall without turning the carpets into quagmires?

He pulled a bottle of expensive sparkling water from a

refrigerator, cracked the seal, poured a glass and asked the empty air the question.

'Damp cloths. Tiny amount of detergent. Too much detergent and you'll flood the place getting it off.' The voice was calm, impressively so. 'And keep some dry towels to catch the spills. Hello, JJ. Welcome back.'

'Shard.' Stoner poured another glass of expensive water. 'I'm beginning to feel like the queen of England. It's impossible to take a leak in private without announcements and an audience.' He drank the water. 'Do you never knock? Do you in fact not know how to knock?'

Shard walked into the hard light. He was towering tall, tired, hard-faced. Harder hands hung loose at his sides. 'Thought maybe you were gone for good.' He didn't sound unhappy at the idea. 'Why did you come back?'

'Babysitting. Bili. Wanted to see her home safely.'

'Well, you left one fuck of a mess behind you. It's not cleared up yet. Your old master, Cheerful Charlie, the Hard Man, call him what you want; Hartmann, ex-Member of Her Britannic Majesty's Parliament . . . offing him and then disappearing into the blue like you did was a tough thing.'

'You never liked him. Why the grumbling?' Stoner spoke softly, neither of them seeking nor accepting eye contact with the other. The out-of-hours club was cool, quiet. Had they been dogs in the desert, they would have been circling now, sniffing, vultures would have been gathering overhead, ready to become an audience or to dine on the outcome, whatever.

'But you did.' A flat statement. 'I'd almost thought the two of you were friends.' No relaxation from Shard.

'You did? OK. How would you react to the cheering discovery that your . . . friend . . . had been doing the dirty with your own true love? Would the milk of human kindness have flowed through your veins? Friendly forgiveness all around?'

'She's a tart. Excuse my honesty. A hooker. She fucks anything with a wallet. I never understood the attraction, JJ.

Never. Didn't think it bothered you, strange man that you are. In any case, slicing the guy's throat seems a little extreme. A harsh word or two would have been more . . .' he shrugged. 'Recoverable.'

'You reckon?' Stoner relaxed, suddenly, as though a control had been reset, which might have been the case. He turned his back on the other man, deliberately, and walked to the huge chrome-laden coffee generator, poured water into receptacles.

'Catch.' Shard threw a half-kilo of fresh-ground coffee. Stoner caught it without comment, returned to his self-appointed task. Water spat, coffee soaked and dripped.

'Not going to kill me, then?' Shard appeared unworried by his own question, more curious than concerned.

'Not today. What would be the point? I want out of it all, my friend. Been like that for . . . a while. You know that. It was always plain, in everything I told you. I'd hoped that we could have done a deal, with you taking over the jobs I did for the . . . for Hartmann. That would have suited me. I'd have felt safe enough with you handling all the lost and found.'

'But he bought sex off your tart – sorry Stoner, don't want to piss you off. He did bad things with your woman so you offed him? That was it? All of it?'

'You know it wasn't.' Stoner did the serving thing. The fragrance of companionable coffee brightened the stale-beer atmosphere. 'And you know it was self-preservation. And you know that he'd ordered a hit against me. You did know that?' A mild enquiry, one murderer to another.

'You're sure about that? Really sure? I heard several versions, all of them certainly true, all of them contradicting each other.'

'That's the way it is.' Stoner refilled them both, calm, collected. 'Whatever. It's history now. And anyway, we've been through all this before. Straight after the event. Don't you remember? Did the petrol wash out OK?' He watched his companion carefully.

Shard ignored the barb. Answered thoughtfully. 'Never hurts to ask the same questions again. See if you get the same answers.'

'Yeah. And so now you're here to . . . to what? Arrest me? Bury me in a deep pit somewhere quiet? Arrange a traffic accident?' He sounded unconcerned, though there really was no other way to sound, given the circumstances.

'No. Not me. You're good with me. Any case, I think it's all had the whitewash treatment. Tragic accident. Ex-military man, ex-MP. National hero of the unsung kind. That kind of thing. Under the carpet. Remarkably quiet. Suppressed, probably.'

'They wouldn't trust you to do it to me, anyway. They'd expect you to tell me what was what, and to be mysteriously unable to locate me until I was far away. That's what I'd think, were I them. Assuming you're working for the good guys? Who are now the bad guys from my point of view, I expect. Who is going to come after me? Do you know?'

'No one, so far as I'm aware. Mind you, those bizarre sisters could be hiding in your cupboard and I'd not be surprised. The blonde ones with the stupid names. They were working for your deceased fat friend, no? That's the story I have.'

'And killed him, in fact.' Stoner set his coffee mug down, raised his eyes and stared deep into those of his companion, like improbable lovers discovering an impossible secret. Shard was utterly still, utterly silent. Then he shook his head, once, twice. Held Stoner's gaze. Intense.

'Is that so?'

'It is.'

'How?'

'Long black knife. Cutting knife.'

'Fuck.'

'As you say.'

Stoner turned slowly away from the other man. Deliberately. Reached up to the top shelf of the mirrored bottle display, high among the spirits, slid aside a small mirrored glass panel, revealing a keypad. Tapped a set of keys. Tapped a second set of numbers. The keypad proved to be the front of a small door, which he opened. Removed two cell phones. Then two more. Then two more. Closed up, locked up, slid shut. Replaced and adjusted the bottles. Laid the phones on the counter. Shard watched. Looked up. Smiled.

'His master's voice.'

'As you say. These have been switched off since I left. Unless you know different?' He switched on the phones, one after the other, checking their displays.

'Nope. I looked around here a couple of times. Missed your secret stash. You always were a phone fetishist, JJ.'

'JJ? We friends again?' Stoner worked his way steadily through the phones' memories, reading and deleting as he went. 'You're not going to kill me now you know where I hide my phones when I'm out of the country? That's a comfort.' He lined up the devices on the counter top. 'Messages from a dead man. That is seriously strange.' He ran his fingers through his hair, stretched. 'I need a gym. I need to run. Toxins in the muscles.'

'None after his death, then?' Shard was plainly thinking of the dead man.

'Beg pardon?' Stoner was already elsewhere in his mind, it seemed.

'No messages from your formerly fat friend post-mortem? He really is dead? You saw the body?'

'Dead men rarely make phone calls. You been on the strong stuff again? It'll do you no good. You can trust me. Scout's honour, so forth.' Almost a smile.

'Did you see the stiff? Behold the man with your very own eyes?'

'No. No, in fact I did not. No need. He was bleeding out. Carotid. Clean entry. I left him with a phone, but I do believe he called the wrong number. From his perspective.' Stoner stretched again. 'Where is everyone? I go away for a little while and no one does any work. What a way to run a bar. Coffee again or a drink – a real drink?'

'Where is everyone? This is a nightclub. There's a clue in the name. You are one cold fuck, JJ. You know that? My body is a temple to fitness and immortality. I'll have a whisky. Your best, as it's on the house. You knew Hartmann for years, worked for him for years. You didn't care for him at all? Not at all? That is cold.'

'He . . . this sounds melodramatic. He betrayed me. On every level. He would have done it again. Once the trust is gone, it never returns. You need to work it into a little ball of hate, bad experience, then throw it away. Move on. That's the theory, any rate.'

'And that's all because of your tart? Your black woman? Jeez.'

'No. Yes. No, not really. He'd ordered a hit on me. That discourages feelings of loyalty and respect, also admiration and fondness I think. I was pretty disgusted by the whole thing. Played me for a fool. So much for trust.'

Shard sipped incrementally at his whisky. 'You didn't see the corpse?'

'I told you that already. He was breathing – badly – last time I left him.'

'So you topped your long-time employer, who you'd worked with for, what, ten years? You topped him because he betrayed your trust. Then you trust some other tart, an insane blonde tart you've just met and don't know at all . . . you trust her when she sells you the old ding-dong the king is dead thing? You're cracking, JJ. Lost it.'

'There was a funeral. I watched it on the BBC. They never lie.' Stoner sounded increasingly unconvinced. 'You're being persistent. You know something I don't? Is he still alive? Did he survive? Where's Lissa?'

'Your black and blonde tart? Don't know. She was here in

the club a lot after it all went bad and you did your disappearing act, but I've not seen her since. Our circles don't overlap. Hartmann? No sign. No signals. Nothing at all.'

'So why all the paranoid shit?'

'That feeling. You know? Gut feeling? Back in the outfit, you always told me to believe and react to gut feelings. Always have. So've you. We're both still standing. Many others are not. My gut keeps telling me that this thing with Hartmann isn't over. You?'

'My guts? They have no views either way.' Stoner poked his stomach. 'Nope. No reply. Would you look at that?'

All of the six cell phones lit up. Simultaneous incoming. A digital barrage targeted on Stoner. Shard ignored him, reaching for a leg pocket and the cell phone it contained. All six phones registered receipt of a text message, and all fell silent in unison. Shard flipped open his phone, Stoner picked up the nearest of his own. Both read.

'Stay where you are. Is that what yours says, Shard?' Stoner dropped the first phone, picked up the next, read that, picked up and repeated the exercise. 'They all say the same. Spooky.'

'Yes. The same. ID withheld. Time to get out fast then.' He dropped from the bar stool and headed for the fire escape.

'Don't think so.' Stoner strolled around the bar and walked towards the main door, unlocked it. 'You locked the door behind you? Good man. Silent tradecraft. Awareness. Going to need some of that.'

'You know who the callers are? Is?'

'So do you. I'll break out the best bottles of water for our imminent guests.'

The door opened, quietly, allowing one man to enter. Just one. He closed the door silently behind him, left it unbolted, unlocked.

'Stoner. Harding.'

'Mallis.' Stoner spoke with careful neutrality. 'Bottle of

water? Cold? Sparkling or tap? Just you this morning? You're without Menace?'

'Shining wit as usual, Stoner. Consider me convulsed at it. Can we have a conversation? I was glad to find the two of you together. Convenient.'

'You want both of us?' Shard displayed rather more caution than did Stoner. Seemed nervous, suddenly nervous.

'That's really up to Stoner. He and I have a matter, a subject, a topic, to discuss. He might feel more comfortable with you here. I don't know. Stoner?' Mallis looked at neither of them. Made no eye contact at all. The lack of inflection in his voice made him sound as though he was talking entirely to himself. The skin of his face was as startlingly powder white as ever, eyes dark, small and slitted, shifting, restless, nervous. Hair was far too black to be natural, matching the black lipstick, fingernails, clothes and eye make-up. The sexless oddity of his dress somehow emphasised the flat, toneless delivery.

'I may prefer to leave.' Shard's level of alertness showed no sign of diminishing.

'Why?' The odd androgyne asked the question. Stoner's attention was locked on him. He lifted his gaze from the third man, looked at Shard and raised a quizzical eyebrow.

'I feel like a target.' Shard's conspicuous alarm was increasing. Stoner couldn't understand it.

'Fuck's the matter with you?' Stoner, not unfriendly. 'You want to leave? Fine by me. Hello goodbye, all that. Mallis is just here to welcome me home. That's it, no?' He looked at the man in black.

'No.'

Shard was standing by the door. He hesitated. 'I can leave? Is this that hail of bullets as I walk through the door moment?'

Mallis addressed no one directly, stared with studied disinterest away from the door. 'There's an observation team outside. They won't bother you. They know who you are. I'll pass your current contact details to Stoner. In case he needs them. Wants them.' He looked up, addressed Stoner directly. 'Want, not need. I doubt that Stoner needs you at all. He never has before.' He looked down again, poured a half glass of still water, a study in indifference once more, sneer delivered with perfect accuracy.

Shard took the words at face value. Departed. The door closed with impressive oiled silence. Stoner returned to his original station behind the bar.

'Well?'

'Are you open for business, Stoner?' Mallis could have been wondering about the bar's hours.

'The bar? It's always open. We barkeeps never sleep. Famous for it. You give me your money and I'll mix you some drinks. I can do great cocktails. Have you tried a kahlua colada? Really is some . . .'

'It's happened again.' Mallis could manage mysterious. Years of practice.

'Oh good. What?'

'A contract undertaken by the woman you know as Chastity has been compromised. Desperately so.'

'Nothing to do with me.'

'I know that. We . . . my sister and I . . . we have an obligation to her. To Chastity.'

'Menace is your sister? She's a woman?' Stoner laughed aloud. And sobered swiftly enough. 'So? I have no such obligation. To them or to you.'

Mallis sat in silence, sipping the water with all possible focus; maybe it was an elixir of the gods. He was paying as much attention to his drink as if it were the wine on an improbable altar. Time passed. Stoner sat opposite, in an identical silence, slowly working his way through the whisky he'd poured for the recently departed Shard.

'You said "the woman you know as Chastity". What's her real name?'

'Chastity.' Plainly smalltalk was on another agenda for

another day, maybe another life, another reality.

'You want me to help pull her out of some other faraway hot hole?' Stoner's surrender to his own curiosity almost made him smile.

'I have no idea where she is.'

'That's a start. No idea at all. I suppose I'm now supposed to start asking questions, to get interested, to get involved, to . . . all those things which I have no wish to do, but will end up doing because you'll offer some manipulative morsel I can't resist. You can be a right pain in the ass, frankly.'

'I'm in a curious position, Stoner.'

'You're sitting at a bar in a nightclub during the hours of daylight. That's unusual, but it's not curious. And you're here by your own free will, no coercion. Even the drink is free. Especially the water. Maybe I should start charging for the water.'

'One day, your sense of humour will prove fatal, Stoner.'

'Was that a joke? Did Mallis, the superficially sane half of the fabulous techno prisoners, crack a joke? My life is com- plete. Your prediction is self-fulfilling. I shall perform *seppuku* as soon as you leave.'

'There's one obvious reason for your inability to find friends, Stoner.'

'I have no problem finding, them, Mallis my friend, but they do keep dying. Occupational hazard, perhaps. Maybe I should advertise. Friends wanted. Must be immortal. The replies would be interesting, at least.'

Mallis closed his eyes, the lids diminishing as they closed, slitting to a single item and disappearing in the deep black- ness of the make-up. He sighed, a weariness staged with perfection.

'The contract was placed through us. I have a concern that we are being manipulated. That's unacceptable. You can see that. Stop with the jokes, Stoner, I'm in no mood.'

'I don't want a job, Mallis. I . . .' he paused to apply as much emphasis as possible. 'I do *not* want involvement any more. I want out. I want to be someone else. I want to go live the quiet life. I was getting there. I have everything I need, at least in a material sense. I'm back here earlier than I would have preferred, but I was glad to help out the sisters. The two of them, Chastity and Charity. I felt a small debt to Charity, none to Chastity.'

'Killing scars your soul. The more killing, the more scars. Every life you take, takes a little life from you. It can't not. Not when you kill in close-up, as I prefer. Preferred. It's why cowards and Americans kill their victims from a distance. They just pretend that they're pushing a button, not ripping a blade through the throats of a dozen people, a hundred people. Let them get on with that. It is the future. One of several. One day the sons and daughters, brothers and sisters of all those faceless victims will arise and they will exact their own vengeance. It will be foul. And justified. An impersonal killing is the very worst kind.'

'You can do vengeance, then? Vengeance doesn't scar your soul? You believe you have a soul, Stoner? I'm surprised by that. Thank you for the surprise. They're rare enough, valuable, even.' Mallis rose, leaned across the bar and poured more water. Sat down once again.

'You're pretending the surprise, Mallis. Nothing surprises you. You'll have predicted and calculated and assessed and judged every response I make here. I think that if I stripped naked and danced a conga on top of this bar you would be unsurprised. You probably have a probability calculated for that.' He smiled. 'Always a pleasure talking with you. We should do it more often. Could do it more often if every fucking conversation didn't end up with me needing to murder someone, bloodily and personally. Chastity, the slightly less psycho sister of the pair I've met, she's killed too many, too often and too personally. Her head's fucked. She's a fruitcake. She's . . . you want an opinion from me?' He paused, caught a glance from his companion, who nodded, to the surprise of them both.

'She's going to get herself killed. She'll be aware of how she's diving into insanity, how horrible the inside of her head is, how she's starting to dream of it, how she can't shake off the grimness of it, how all the protections she's built no longer protect her, how all the distancing, distracting and recovery mechanisms no longer do their jobs, and probably she'll just do her own Butch and Sundance moment, dive from the shade into the sun and catch the hail of bullets. Not because there's no mission alternative, but because there's no personal alternative. She'll want to die and she won't want to leave her sisters with her blood on their hands. So she'll make it look like a mission failure. There'll be tears and wailing and tearing of hair, but she'll be gone, the other sisters will shut up shop – they must be loaded by now – and she will die in delight, knowing that she's in no more pain and that she's provided an exit for the others.

'Are there really three sisters, Mallis? Have you met the other one?'

'Charm? Yes. Why?'

'Because I think they're all a fantasy. Something you and your own sister have cooked up. No idea why you'd do that, but it's a thought.'

Mallis was simply static for a moment.

'How close to that condition, the one you've described for Chastity, are you yourself, Stoner?'

'Balanced, Mallis. I'm balanced. Why?'

'If I thought that completing my request would drive you over that line, I would be reluctant to ask you to do it.' Flat tone. Glass-smooth, ice cold. No bias. Mallis the old-school goth playing the part of a twenty-first century zombie. Terrifyingly convincing.

'Really? I'm supposed to believe that? Can't you do a threat instead? You drive me to drink. You know that?' Stoner picked up the whisky bottle by its neck, walked between the tables empty of audience and stepped up to the stage. Unlocked the guitar case which lay by the switched-off Marshall amplifier, pulled his old Fender guitar from its rest and sat down on his stool, his old guitar resting easily in his hands, his weight taken by the old familiar stool while a sense of balance restored came over him. He fingered an unplayed, unamplified chord, fretted a silent solo into the silence of the absent audience. While his left hand played in silence, his right held the bottle, undrunk. He gazed up at the greasy ceiling.

'When the music leaves you, Stoner. When the internal scream is louder than the music you play. Then you'll end your own journey.' Mallis sat in near darkness, unmoving. 'You're a long way from that.'

'So you say. I don't think I can handle all this philosophical crap. She will kill herself. Chastity. One way or another. Conscious or not. The decision will be hers. The mind or the whole organism. She will decide to die. I don't think she'll go quietly into her own long night, either, and I have utterly no wish to be anywhere nearby when she does it. She'll make her very own big bang. Let's all hope she decides to take out only the bad guys when she blows. It would be tedious in the extreme if she decided that her sisters and you guys, even me, were guilty tormentors and all deserved to share her dramatic exit. Had you considered that?'

'Yes.'

'Can't you do the carrot and stick routine for me? So I can pretend that it's all your fault that I'm taking on a gig I don't want? So I can pretend you coerced me?' Stoner smiled at himself, to himself. Flicked the Marshall's power switch and watched as the tell-tale lights lit.

Mallis spoke softly, his voice somehow carving through the rising ambient noise from the guitar and amplifier, cutting above the electric announcement that music was imminent. 'I will answer any of your questions truthfully and directly and fully at the point at which you ask them.' Not a hint of a sug-gestion of an inflection. The words could have been spoken by a machine.

'That's the carrot. A convincing carrot. The stick?' Stoner continued his examination of the ceiling. The guitar and its amplifier muttered together, scheming machines.

'I can remove all of your resources, money, property and identities. I can certainly have you killed, along with anyone I consider might be important to you.'

'Including yourself? We could almost be friends, Mallis, you and I. Professional friends.' Stoner placed the open bottle on top of the amplifier and looked over at his companion.

'That's not a mistake many have made, Stoner. It's your sense of the humorous again. It's potentially fatal, as I said.'

'The carrot is a lot larger than the stick. I'd assumed some-thing more serious.' Stoner hit and held one note, a mid-register A. The guitar's volume was turned way down low; its power held in check. 'Was that another of my jokes? Mallis?'

'No. Are we going to talk again? If so, it needs to be soon.'

'If not?'

'If not, then we will activate another asset, promote someone else into the role we need filling. Someone, frankly, less likely to achieve the result we would prefer.'

Stoner nodded, held the A note, shaking the single string gently and winding the volume control up and down with the little finger of his right hand, waves of sound and silence. The guitar shook with the resonance, the bar glassware shud-dered in sympathy. The bottle drifted like a live thing on top of the amplifier.

'Not here, Mallis. I dislike polluting this place. You're the prediction wizard; tell me where we'll meet.'

There was no reply. Stoner lowered his gaze from the greasy ceiling. Mallis had left. In silence. The same way he'd arrived.

9

EVENING SHADOWS FALL

Stoner tapped gently on the blacked-out window of the matt-black SUV with the vivid fluorescent green anarchist graphics. The window wound slowly down. An incongruous powder-white mask of a face floated into view, surreal in the night.

'Nice night for an exorcism, father.' Stoner's humour fell on stony ground. He tried again to compete with the drifting silence. 'You decided against breaking in?'

The white face spoke, gently enough. 'We could see no point in breaking in. Even if it were possible to do it without damaging the place severely. And what would be the point of that? Breaking things is more your style than ours.'

'Am I graced by a visit from the pair of you?' Stoner tried his hardest to sound welcoming, friendly even. The only way he could see further into the cab would have involved breaking eye contact with Mallis. An improbably dangerous action, he felt. 'Or was that the royal "we"?'

'Just me. I'm the sociability freak. Nothing royal about either of us.' Mallis powered up the window, opened the door and stepped out into the quiet night. He and Stoner stood side by side for a moment. Two tall men, both in black, one bulky and broad, the other not; both relaxed, self-confident. The matt-black SUV uttered an electronic synthesised whisper as

Mallis released the door, which eased itself silently tight shut. A second whisper spoke of a security system arming itself. The two men walked in a shrouding silence to the main entrance of Stoner's industrial unit, its Transportation Station sign unlit apart from a small green light in the centre of the first 'o'. Stoner walked to the door. Looked once again at the small green light above, gestured to his companion.

'The door seems to be unlocked. Let yourself in. Oh, I guess you already did that. And you make cracks about my simple unsophisticated sense of humour?'

Mallis made no move to approach the door. 'Your sense of humour?'

'Yeah. Good joke about not breaking in. Ho ho, so forth.'

'I didn't break in, Stoner. But I did introduce myself to your security system. It's very good. If you like, we can improve it a little for you, but there's no need. Very few individuals and no agencies could disarm it.'

'But you can, plainly. That is, frankly, irritating. It's been happening a lot lately.'

'Indeed. Harding broke in using keys provided by your late employer, didn't he?'

'You knew about that?'

'We hear about most things we're interested in. It's a matter of survival. We read his debrief.'

'That . . . who was that report to? Presumably you know all that as well?'

'Are you intending to make us stand chatting like old friends on the threshold all night, or is there a better illuminated welcome within?' Mallis still showed no sign whatsoever of opening the door himself.

'You afraid of the dark, Mallis? Neat change of subject, too. Admirable.'

'No. I merely wondered why you'd chosen someone else – who? – to upgrade the security here at Parkside. And why you've not done the same at your other properties. I'm now curious that we didn't know about the upgrade until I actually appeared here and found it.'

'Curiosity does bad things to cats. Do you worry about curiosity?'

'I treasure it. I live for it. You know that. Why do you ask?'

'Because I didn't upgrade the security here. I wasn't aware that it had been upgraded. How did you unlock the door?'

'Using your old key and date codes, the key sequence and a clone of the original card.'

'So what's changed?'

'A system arms – becomes live – as the card swipes.'

'It does?'

'It does.'

'How do you know that? The light in the sign is correct.'

'A professional question with a technical answer. The gear is in the vehicle.'

'You weren't joking about giving me real answers to questions, then?'

'No point in joking about that, Stoner. Less point in lying about it.'

'Do you know what the new system does?'

'No. We may find out when we cross the threshold. How many possibilities are there? If you had altered your system, what would you have included in the addition?'

'Either a very big bang or a signal to a third party that access had been granted to the premises.'

'That all?'

'Surveillance too, I'd guess. But that would be the installer bugging the place, not me bugging myself. I already have a system inside for that. You installed it.'

'Indeed, and it's active now.'

'The vehicle tells you this? Smart car.'

Mallis pulled his impossibly black hair away from his artificially white face, revealing an earpiece and the smallest throat contact microphone Stoner had seen. He let the hair fall back.

'Wired for sound then?'

'Nice joke, Stoner. Wired for much more than sound.' Mallis lifted a hand from a pocket. 'This is a device.'

'I can see that. You are full of surprise devices tonight.'

'Much as we relish curiosities, Stoner, we prefer not to be surprised. Surprises kill more cats than curiosity ever did. There is a wi-fi connection here which we did not install, and it is active. I doubt I can deactivate it from outside.'

'It's two-way? Someone else can activate a – a device inside remotely?'

'All wi-fi is two-way, Stoner. There would be no point to it otherwise.'

'Will you be able to shut it down once you're inside?'

Mallis was distracted for a moment. 'Yes. Although it would be more intelligent to understand its purpose, who installed it and why. Assuming you're being truthful and did not install it yourself, or cause it to be installed.'

'Now you sound like a lawyer. I prefer your usual mysterious gothic nutter persona, frankly. You know where you stand with those. Lawyers are too slippery for my taste. Shall we go in? Should I go first? I am presumably dispensable from your perspective.'

'You are a man of action, Stoner. Perceptive.'

'And you are more intelligent than that, I suppose?'

'Exactly so. Are you planning on having us stand outside until it starts to rain?'

'Is rain forecast?'

'No, no it's not. Not for this evening. Later in the week. I was being figurative.'

'Is the wi-fi device transmitting at the moment?'

'It is.'

'Is it receiving as well as sending?'

'I imagine so. That is how devices work, Stoner. They communicate both ways – all ways – at the same time.'

'They don't just do a handshake then. They handhold too?'

'Exactly so. We are still standing here. Outside.'

Stoner walked to the door, hesitated. 'Would it be more prudent to enter another way? Through another entrance?'

'Would you, if you'd added the new systems, have added them only to the front door, knowing who uses this place and for what?'

'Of course not. You're right. As always. No one loves a smartarse.'

'Love is a many misunderstood thing, Stoner.'

'Well then. Today is as good a day to die as any other. I suppose.'

Stoner slipped a card into a reader at the side of the door. Nothing happened. The light in the sign above them remained a cheery green. He opened the door and walked inside. Stepped away from the door and flicked a switch on the wall. Lights lit. All looked normal.

'It all looks normal. You can come in if you want. I'm still standing.' He walked inside. Four VW Transporter vans stood impassive in a row. A Harley-Davidson motorcycle perched on a hydraulic workbench, flanked by tool racks and a pair of armchairs. Stoner walked past the motorcycle, opened a refrigerator, removed a vacuum-sealed container of coffee. Mallis stood in the centre of the wide room, consulting the device in his hand.

'Anything recording or broadcasting is disabled. Our conversation is as secure as I can make it from here.'

Stoner measured out filter coffee; filled a jug with water from the tap.

'Coffee? Tea? Something else? The electronic intruders haven't left any fresh milk, I'm afraid.'

'Eight dead.' The offer of a carefully brewed beverage was plainly lost on Mallis. Stoner carried on, prepping a serving for one, though he would pour two, believing in courtesies to absent friends.

'None of them Chastity, I imagine. A sweet girl. Looked so good with blue hair.'

'I can imagine. Anyone would. The first to die was her target, her contract. She killed him quickly and efficiently . . .'

Stoner interrupted. 'Killed him how?'

'Long knife, clean slice through all the soft tissues of the neck. The victim was in bed, presumably asleep. No struggle. Why?'

'When we last talked, y'know, as guys and girls do, about murder, mayhem, more stuff like that, she was grumbling about needing to use a long gun on the Israeli hit. She seems to think there's artistry in knife work. Hard to argue.'

'You prefer guns?' Mallis managed to sound almost interested.

'They have their place. Did the Hard Man survive? Is he still alive?'

'She wounded two of the men who attacked her as she took the knife to her victim. Achilles tendons. Beautiful piece of work, I understand. Surgical. Wish I'd been able to watch. After escaping the building, she procured a decent weapon, an assault rifle of some sort, and shot her attackers as they left the building, as well as the collection driver.'

'Good girl. Has a talent for this, wouldn't you say?' Stoner busied himself with his seemingly endless coffee ritual. Soft gurgles and sibilant hisses appeared to delight him in some way.

'Then, using a different calibre of weapon altogether, she shot and disabled the second team, the team who had been sent to her rental chalet, her base. Long shots. Difficult. Excellent work.'

'Proper little dynamo, that one, wouldn't you say? Outstanding performer, that kind of thing. You absolutely certain that my coffee's not good enough for you? How do you keep all this mass murder nonsense out of the foreign press? Easy for you guys to do that here, but over . . . where? Mainland Europe somewhere? Not your usual sphere, is it?'

Mallis managed to produce a complex sigh, mingling infinite weariness with hints of condescension and a touch of irritation. 'You never watch the television news?'

Stoner sat back in one of the armchairs, studied some particular feature of the Harley-Davidson's muscular power train. 'No. Not unless I'm being paid to do so. It's all lies, and it's bad for the mental health. Should be banned. Like newspapers, the internet and the like.'

Mallis paced over to where Stoner reclined, soaking in caffeine and apparently absorbed by the intricacies of American motorcycle engineering, and placed an electronic slab between Stoner and the motorcycle. 'This . . .' he began.

'Is a device. I know that. I'm not entirely ignorant. It's a pad, a tablet or something marvellous like that. Infinite possibilities. Like cancer.'

'At the moment, let's pretend it's a television. Let's pretend that you're going to watch the headlines on last night's news channels.' The two men watched the garish, shrieking recording in silence. Stoner spoke first.

'The Angel of Death. Is that really what they're calling her? No marks for originality, but it's a decent description. Bodies all over Bosnia, and they're all her fault.'

'Slovenia. Slovenia, not Bosnia.'

'How did the media guys get the idea that there was only one survivor, and that she's a woman? Who told them?'

Mallis said nothing. Stoner continued, 'And now they're all running in circles playing *cherchez la pissed-off femme*, huh? Why are you here, Mallis, and what does it have to do with me?'

'Are you sitting comfortably?' This was plainly a Mallis attempt at humour, or something similar. Stoner looked up at him, his expression as screamingly blank as the large goth's.

'I'm sitting. It's probably impossible to be comfortable given the present company. Why are you here?'

'Why are you not back on the ship, Stoner? Why did you stay ashore?' Mallis stared past Stoner, seemingly transfixed by the Harley-Davidson before them.

'Oh, please.' Stoner poured weariness into his voice. 'No little boys' school games. I asked first. You're in my place, you almost broke in, you agreed to answer my questions. Not with another question. I'm tired. Just tell me.'

'I did. You're being disappointingly dull, Stoner. I'm here for the same reason you are. Concern.'

'Yeah, yeah, yeah. Concern for weeping humanity. I can see that. Can't believe it though. Concern for who? Me? Chastity? The wider world? For yourself, I assume, though I can't see any direct threats to you in whatever's happening with Chastity. I would have expected you and Menace to be invulnerable by now.'

'So many things there. Quite a speech, Stoner, though you probably didn't realise it.'

'Insult away. Care I do not.' Stoner suddenly bounced to his feet and mounted a raid on his coffee pot, coming away with a further dose and leaving the refilled machine spitting aggressively to itself. He returned to his chair. 'Well?'

'It's a question of priorities. Everything is linked to everything else. All our interests are the same. What level of analysis do you want? You're a man of action, Stoner, I'm a man of analysis. I think a lot. Mostly all I do is think.'

'And I should maybe try it too, before it's too late? Is that your subtle underlying suggestion?' Stoner sipped and smiled.

'Not at all. We all have strengths. Also weaknesses. Chastity is very unstable. She . . .'. He paused. 'I'll have a glass of water.'

'Help yourself.'

'We've worked with Chastity and her sisters for a while. With any working relationships, it's inevitable that loyalties develop. That may be an unwelcome consequence, but it is a consequence. There are several courses of action . . .'

Stoner interrupted. 'It's OK, you can spare me the deep

thought thing. I know how relationships work. Even I, brainless thug though I might be, even I can understand loyalties. Also that they make you blind. Make it impossible to see when you're being set up, stitched up, carved up.'

'And there are conflicts of interest.' Mallis spoke over and through Stoner's outburst. 'The most difficult task Menace and I face is reconciling those conflicts.'

Stoner interrupted once again. 'At this point you should also mention trust. Loyalty, too. A speech like this one should be long on trust and loyalty.'

'Thank you.'

'That's fine. I just wanted to demonstrate that I was keeping up. That I was in tune with your theme.'

'I'd already mentioned loyalty.'

'True. But only in relation to that strange clump of murderous bitches. You and I have been dealing with each other for a long time. I forget how long, exactly, but it surely must be longer than you've been dealing with Charity, Chastity and the invisible Charm.'

'Charm is hardly invisible, Stoner.'

'OK. More like entirely absent, then.'

Mallis sat, swaddled in an almost tangible cloud of theatrical weariness. 'Charm is the controller in all this. You know that.'

'Do not. So far as I'm concerned, she doesn't exist. People talk about her, but they also talk about the Virgin Mary, and I don't think she exists, either.'

'You are being obtuse, Stoner. You know Charm. You have . . .' he paused. 'Made her acquaintance. More than once.'

'Really? I have? That was plainly so memorable that it's slipped my mind completely. I assume there's a certain blurring of the truth involved? Like false names, that kind of thing.'

'Certainly. Legends. Worknames, you call them. Such as John Hand.'

152

'Is Mallis your real name?' Stoner smiled.

Mallis smiled back with equal sincerity. 'Yes.'

'Menace? No one's called Menace. It's more of a description than a proper name. Like, say, Charm. Perhaps?'

'You've got me there. Menace was not always called Menace.'

'What was she called previously? Petal? Flower? Beautiful angel of the early dawn?'

'She was called something flattering in another language. I'm not interested in talking about us, Menace and I.'

'OK. I understand your shyness. Charm?'

'Chastity.'

'Why not Charm? We'll need to get around to her eventually.'

'Chastity. It's her time. This is her tale. Her story. I want your help. That's why I'm being so . . . communicative. It's not something I enjoy.'

'It doesn't come naturally to you?'

'Exactly. Well put.'

'No master of small talk, you? That sort of thing.' Stoner smiled. 'Coffee?'

'Talking with you would tempt a saint into narcotics abuse.'

'I'm mainly gauging your interest in this. How sincere is your appeal for help. If you can put up with lightweight idiocy from me then . . . well, you're being serious.'

'It would be a lot easier and a lot quicker if you merely asked me whether I was being serious, Stoner. I am entirely serious. Being interrogated, however gently, is not a pleasant experience, and time is always short. Chastity is our concern. Not Charm, and not Charity.' Mallis paused, waiting for an idiotic interjection from Stoner. None came. Stoner remained silent, staring and almost motionless. Staring at nothing obvious.

'Chastity is becoming unhinged. She will unravel.' Mallis paused again. 'You have no comment on that? No views nor opinions?'

'None. No argument. She was unravelling the first time we met, her and I. Everybody told me this. Endlessly. But so far as I can see, she's always been like that. Unravelling. She shot my car's lights out while I was standing between her and them. The lights. She may be unravelling but she is an excellent shot. No argument. There is a question, though, and it is . . . why are we having this conversation? Why should I help Chastity any more than I already have? You – that's you, Mallis – ruined my new private life. You involved Bili, which is a subject we will return to at a time when I'm less irritated about it than I am at present . . .'

'So your judgement will be less clouded?'

'Exactly. We'll get back to that. In the meantime, I feel no obligation. None. I see no benefit to me. I see no reason why I should help any further.' Stoner attempted to mask his increasing irritation by pacing around the open spaces of his building.

'You're getting really irritated, Stoner. Why not sit down and relax? Save the irritation until later. Build it up and change it into violent action. Kill someone.' Both men suddenly burst into shared laughter.

'Why am I here, though?' Stoner sounded genuinely puzzled. 'I was happy on the ship.'

'Not true. You were hiding on the ship. I gave you an excuse to end the hiding.'

'Crap.'

'If you say so. You took no persuasion at all. Why are you here, instead of on the ship? Because you want to be.' Mallis paused again, expression faded from his powder-white features. 'I'll make you an offer. It's a serious offer. Genuine. If you help Chastity, we will disappear you if that's actually what you want. If we do that, you will never be found unless you actively want to be found.'

'You can do that?'

'Yes.'

'Even in this electronic age?'

'Yes.'

'Even your fellow travellers on the Silk Road would be unable to find me?'

'Those too.'

'Impressive. You've done it before?'

'Yes. No one you would want to know. Not that I could tell you if I wanted to. Which I do not.'

'What's going down with Chastity, Bosnia's new Angel of Death?'

'Slovenia.'

'Whatever.'

'The sisters have accepted a contract. A genuine contract. Multiple targets, all of them prominent in their own worlds and well protected. Chastity has removed two of the targets. At both locations, locations she selected herself based on intel provided. She was set up, set up to be vulnerable after the event. You helped pull her out of Israel.'

'Your involvement in this? Oh I see. You brokered the contract, researched its veracity? OK. Go on. Sorry.'

'Yes. The contract is sound, a series of clean hits. Nothing complicated, no weirdness. Complex logistically, but that's not our concern. The sisters can do logistics as well as anyone and their security is excellent. After the first hit, there was a second executive in play. Chastity fired a long rifle to remove the target . . .'

'Who was?'

'Doesn't matter. Chastity took out two vehicles and their occupants, then a second – unknown – executive used what we think was an RPG to explode the lead vehicle, killing everyone inside once again, and sending up a smoke signal. At the same time, Chastity's own vehicle was immobilised. The rest you know. At the second event, the ongoing mess . . . Yes?'

Stoner had been waving an attention-seeking arm. 'Chas did not get from the scene to Haifa on foot. How and who?'

'She hitched a ride.'

'With the three bears? Come along now. Who and how?'

'We'll need to do more work on that to be accurate. You want that?'

'Yes.'

'All right. We have background chatter, suppositions, innuendo on her route north. It'll take a while, but we'll need her back first to do some verification. At the second event, at almost the exact moment of completion, an attempt was made on her, either to take her out or to detain her.'

'And you verified the contract? You know who the principals involved are? You can vouch for them?' Stoner's query was as predictable as its answer.

'Yes and yes. Payments have been made, and we know the . . . ah . . . principals, so far as that's possible. You mentioned the Silk Road, so you are aware of it?'

Stoner nodded. 'What version is running now? The Feebs still closing it?' He smiled.

And received an unexpected smile in return. 'Version 2.8, so the story goes. The dark web in all its gory detail. Untraceable, designed by US government agencies to be invisible to everyone but themselves, hijacked by renegades but still used by those same agencies . . . and by people like us. It is impossibly easy to hide true identities on the Silk Road, by its very nature. But regular travellers are trackable, and references are available.'

'Essential, I would expect. References.'

'Yes. It's as easy to peddle misinformation as it is to supply facts. People do this.'

'No! Surely not. Dishonour among thieves? Who would have thought it? I am shocked.' Stoner's wide smile suggested the opposite. Mallis maintained his preferred non-committal countenance. And continued.

'Chastity will extract herself from Slovenia, I would expect. She is exceptionally capable . . .'

'Even though she's unravelling?' No smile from Stoner to

accompany his interruption. 'If she really is unravelling, she could be excused for being at least a little bit crap. Does she need help?'

Mallis paused, a typical and predictable absence of expression on his pale features. 'I would doubt that she does.'

'But you can't say for sure? You're not certain? You're – well, well – you're out of touch. Glory be. You've lost contact. Excuse me for saying this, but I am surprised. Really surprised.'

'I'd imagine she's simply exercising a little tradecraft and is keeping entirely silent.' Mallis shrugged. 'But yes. Nothing from her directly for forty-eight hours. We're tracking her through security services traffic.'

'Her sisters? She's avoiding them also?'

'Appears so.'

'And you would know if she was in touch with her sisters. I suppose?'

'Almost certainly.'

'You installed their comms and security systems? Like those here? Clever. It hadn't really dawned on me before. You install the systems, you monitor them. Neat.' Stoner's face was as impassive as his companion's, if rather less pallid.

'Yes. The only way to be sure that the systems we install . . . for our friends . . . the only way to check that they are working as intended is to monitor their performance. Stop glowering, Stoner, we're all on the same side.'

'You sure of that?'

'Let us hope so.'

'So who modified the system here?' Stoner wandered from the subject again, as was his way when he wanted to think. 'And why? And if whoever it was is good enough to break into one of your unbreakable, beyond compromise, so forth, mega-systems, how could they also be not good enough to make their tampering invisible?'

'Had you spotted it?' There was possibly a hint of irritation hidden within Mallis's question.

'No. So far as I'd know without you to tell me different, the system is working perfectly. No alarms. Which raises several questions, no?'

'Yes. And we will answer them all as soon as we can.'

Stoner was on a roll, plainly. 'And you have no idea who's receiving the transmissions?'

Mallis held up a hand and paused, listening. 'No. No, we have no confirmation of who modified the system, or who caused it to be modified. And the listeners – assuming that it's not just a robot monitor – are currently hearing something entirely different to our actual conversation.' He smiled, eyes lighting up with a very rare display of humour.

Stoner's suspicion was instant and justifiable. 'OK, I give in. What are you broadcasting?'

'A sexual encounter between you and a friend. It's very diverting, and loud. Distracting.'

'You bug me when I'm making love?' Stoner produced a decent impersonation of outrage.

'No. Only when you're fucking. You once assured me that there was a big difference. And in any case, the event took place quite some time ago.'

'Anyone I know?'

'It's possible.' Mallis could also do dry.

'And you have a collection? You are sick, Mallis. I knew you were sick, but not how sick.' He paused. 'You also have video?'

'For amusement in the long evening of your retirement, Stoner? For an approaching time when you amuse yourself only by abusing yourself? No. We don't have a collection, and we weren't bugging you at all. We were bugging your partner – your sexual partner; your emotional partner was . . . someone else. You were just the cream on the cake. It was a surprise at the time. Can we talk about Chastity, or must everything revolve around you?'

'Fine. That's fine. You say that Chas can extract herself . . . can perform her own extraction, a rare talent among dentists,

I expect, and if that's the case, where do I come in?'

'We want you to accompany her to the next target.' A flat statement from Mallis.

'She won't like that at all. She'll refuse that.'

'She won't know unless you tell her or unless you are spectacularly clumsy. We would expect neither of those failures from you. You were once the best, Stoner. No longer, but you are still very good. We want you to watch her back until whoever is tracking her and interfering with her business is plain to you.'

'Not the best? Huh? What kind of flattery is that?'

'The honest kind. You want lies, speak to a whore and pay for them. Speaking of which . . .' Mallis drifted to silence, watching Stoner for a cue. Which did not appear. Instead, Stoner returned to the major topic.

'How will I know when Chastity has performed her very own extraction?'

'We'll tell you.'

'So you'll know? For certain?'

'Yes. We shall also provide the details of the next commission. In advance, probably, depending on whether Chastity requires a break.'

'Or surgery. Medical attention. Splints, traction and the extraction of unwanted ballistic lead, for example. What happens if she's physically incapable of performing . . . of completing the next commission?'

'Charity is likely to handle it. Maybe Charm.'

'Charm? The invisible lady? She does hits? Really? If I sound surprised it's because I'm surprised. I thought she was the brains of the trio.'

'It may do you credit that you speculate, though I doubt it. We prefer facts; it's easier to base any form of plan on facts. Speculation is pointless. Until we know otherwise, we work with Chastity. Via Charm.' Mallis was beginning to sound bored.

Stoner was currently unavailable to Mr Boredom. 'Where and when? The next contract, commission, call it what you like; the next killing? And who?'

Mallis considered, then answered carefully. 'Germany. By the Rhine. Königswinter. Does that help?'

'I was stationed in Germany for a while.' Stoner paused. 'Königswinter. It's on a railway as well as on the river, I think?'

'It is. Correct. You should be a guest on a quiz show. How does the railway help you?'

'I like trains.' Stoner smiled. 'And the more options for entering and leaving a location, the better I like it. When?'

'Four days. Maybe five.'

'You don't have an available operator, Mallis. That does sound a little optimistic.'

Mallis stood, as though he was planning to leave. 'You need to have more faith, Stoner. You also need to speculate less and base your planning on previous results. Chastity may well be there already. It's not far from Bohinj to Königswinter. It's all EU now, so travel won't be a problem.'

'You have that level of faith in Chastity? I'm impressed.'

'As you should be. She is as competent as you were, and she is in her prime.'

'Yeah, yeah. Yet still you're sufficiently worried about her that you want me to go in and perform the protection shuffle?'

Mallis was very still. He looked at a far wall, and sighed before he answered.

'Not protection, Stoner. Not really. There's an operational distinction between support and protection, as you once understood. Are you going to Germany? If so, do you need any logistical arrangements? Will you need us to provide armaments, accommodation?'

'No to both. But thanks. The less you know, the less I'll worry about the Angel of Death taking exception to my presence, and topping me while I carefully explain to her the operational distinction between support and protection.

Heaven's sake, Mallis, you do spout some jargonised bollocks.'

'Thank you. While you are merely imprecise. You said "no to both" – does this imply that you are not going to Germany?'

'No. It implies that no, I am going to Germany, but also that I'll make all my own arrangements. Who's the hit, and what's his – his? – itinerary?'

'It's all on your email and as an SMS on your usual operational numbers. Usual contact regimes with us, if you don't mind.'

'My phones are silent, Mallis. No incoming since we got here.'

'They'll all work again as soon as I leave.' Mallis walked atypically stiffly towards the main door.

'You turned off my phones?' Stoner appeared more surprised than irritated.

'Of course. We provide decent security, Stoner.' Mallis was at the door. Stoner interrupted his exit.

'Are you going to remove the bug, the whatever it is, from my security system? You can't just broadcast an endless soundtrack of sex, it would get tedious after a while.'

'Also physically improbable for a man your age, Stoner, despite your fantasies to the contrary. We'll check it out properly while you're away. In the meantime, assume that you're being observed. Do we need to discuss a fee at this point?'

Stoner smiled again. 'Not at this point. There'll be a reckoning later. There always is, no?'

'Always. There is also always a final parting shot from whoever is actually doing the parting. Which would be me. Employ one hundred percent tradecraft, Stoner. We don't want harm landing on either Chastity or yourself. We would also prefer that she remain unaware of your activity. There is a high probability that if she is aware of you, and if her activities are indeed compromised again, she would connect you to that compromise and take effective action against you.'

'You think I wouldn't survive an action from Chastity? You

really are not playing the flattery card today, Mallis.'

'It's most likely that you would damage each other in such an encounter. There would be absolutely no point to that. I am simply being practical. We always are. Practical. Simply observe, identify and report back. Save your parties for later.'

And he was gone. Four of Stoner's cell phones awoke with their characteristic flashings and vibrations within three minutes of his departure. Stoner collected them and read their contents.

10

TIME TO PRAY

Chastity was in church. Kneeling before the altar. She prayed, very quietly, almost inaudibly, but she prayed. 'Forgive me, father, I know not what I do.' She stopped, considered. 'Forgive me, mother, they know not what they do.' She stopped once more, silence drew itself around her as she considered. 'Forgive me, sisters, for what I am about to do.' She stood, smoothly, slowly and silently. Damp in black, viewed from the back.

'Chastity, I presume?' A man's voice. She retained her penitent air before the bleeding plaster Christ on his wooden cross. Crucified saviour and mortal executioner gazed into each other's eyes. Neither pair saw much. Plaster eyes are always blind; Chastity was listening, all senses bar hearing detuned into the background. She said nothing.

'Simeon told me to mention his name to you. He felt it might save on misunderstandings. He says hello and I am offering assistance on his behalf. You've had quite a night.'

Chastity turned to face her uninvited guest. Who was confronted by a tall, well-muscled woman wearing flat-black combat kit, her short tar-black hair frizzing around her skull as it dried, the black camo pancake on the tanned skin of her face streaked where it had been washed and wiped, her eyes bright and white and staring with complete focus and intent at him. Her left hand held a black knife with a wickedly long Teflon-black blade; her right a black pistol, which she elevated slowly and steadily until it was aimed with almost no shake at all directly between his eyes.

'You're armed.' Her statement was as flat as the unremitting black of her attitude. Her guest raised both arms until they were clear of his sides, both hands empty of weapons, his pose empty of threat.

'I'm armed.'

'With what?' The gun did not waver, nor did her voice.

'Two Glocks. Thirty-something rounds.'

'Blades?'

'One'

'Strip. All the way. Throw your clothes and shoes away, like you'll never need them again.'

'That's a threat?'

'It is what it is. It is an instruction. You carry it out or you die. Your call.' Voice and handgun were steady.

'Simeon said you were one hell of a lady.' Her guest was still fully dressed.

'You're still dressed.' Chastity's tone of voice was unchanged. 'It's too melodramatic to do all that "if you're not stripped by a count of five" nonsense, and I'm all out of patience in any case. Strip now or it's bang-bang time.'

He stripped in silence, threw away the clothing and the two handguns and the knife.

'And the pants, and the socks. Let's see what's left. Let's see whether god made you the only black man without a howitzer in his shorts.' No smile, no humour. He obeyed in silence and stood naked before her, a large darkness in the plaster white of the church.

'Satisfied?' He held her gaze, and she held his.

'Only rarely, to be honest. Take a seat. Relax. Tell me stories about who you are, who you think I am and who Simeon claims to be – whoever Simeon is.' Chastity sat on the back of the front row of benches, feet propped on the seat; she waved the knife towards an opposite bench where the black man would be visible, vulnerable and too far away from her to pose a threat. He sat as instructed. The gun remained aimed, her expression neutral. He said nothing.

'Go ahead. Entertain me. Time is limited. Much to do. Places to go, people to see. You know how it goes, I imagine.' She sounded bored.

'You have a friend.' The black man spoke slowly, American English, clearly enunciated and without overemphasis. A soldier delivering a report. 'Your friend is called Simeon Guest.' He stopped, his expression a question. An ignored question. So he continued.

'Your friend suggested that I should offer to help you if it appeared that you were in need of help.'

'Is that how I appear to you?' The edge in Chastity's voice wavered towards amusement. 'In need of help?' The gun's aim drifted downward, re-centred its one-eyed gaze at the dead centre of the black man's chest. 'A curious interpretation of our current situation. Unless of course you've brought the entire US Marine Corps along with you, they are currently encamped around the lake, all their guns trained on this sweet little old church, locked and loaded and ready to end my short life unless I come out waving a white flag and disarmed by your charm and imposing black toolkit. How am I doing with this?'

'I'm alone.'

'And therefore unwise. If your friend – not mine – Simeon suggested that interrupting this lady at her morning devotions was an activity devoid of risk and that you would not require at least a little support . . .' the knife flicked towards his groin in a macabre suggestion of humour '. . . then he may in fact be no friend to you at all. Why are you here, who are you, and what do you want? No jokes, please. I am in no mood for jokes.'

'What? Ever?'

'As I said. We are a little short of time, in case you were working on some prolonged nonsense while your cavalry gallop up. Speak now, or . . . dream up your own alternative.'

'You'd shoot an unarmed man?'

'Very soon. It's easy.'

'I was instructed to watch and wait here in Bohinj until the action – unspecified in my instructions – took place. I was then to identify the hunter, the operative, and if that operative was a woman, and if necessary I was instructed to introduce myself and offer assistance. If required. That's it.'

'That's not it. How was I described to you?'

'White woman, active, five foot eight, ten, blonde. Fast, efficient. Name of Chastity. Nothing more; simply Chastity. That sounds like you, despite the wrong hair.'

'What help do you offer? What do you think I need? And why do I need it?'

'The place is awash with police. Everyone's out to get you. I have a vehicle, resources, facilities. They'll be looking for a white woman. I'm a black man. No one's looking for me.'

'What's this guy Simeon's interest?'

'You do know him, then. You are who he says?'

'I've no idea what he says. What's he said to you? What's he like, anyway? Another imposing black guy?'

'Never met him. Spoken twice. Can I get dressed? I am not exactly overheating here.'

Chastity shot him, twice in his left knee. Then again, twice in his right knee. He roared to his feet, howling with pain, and collapsed, crumpled back into his seat, hands reaching reflexively for his destroyed joints.

'Maybe the Christian desert god doesn't feel the cold. Who knows?' She walked steadily, unhurried, through the screams of his agony to the small pile of his possessions. Sifted through them, collected weaponry, wallet, keys, sliced through all the seams of his clothing, searching for transmitting devices, found none apart from a cell phone.

'You're not going to survive this.' Chastity spoke pleasantly, calmly. 'This situation is not survivable from your perspective. The best I can offer is to reduce the suffering. Its duration, at any rate. That depends on whether I believe what you're going to tell me, really. You need to understand that I default to distrust. Everyone lies, everyone dies. Got that?'

The black man summoned impossible energies, thrust himself upright, arms providing the acceleration, shattered knees tottering as those long, hard arms reached for her. His eyes were wild, tears and sweat forming twin rivers on his cheeks. She shot him, twice, almost exactly halfway between his navel and his groin, and light left his eyes. He fell back, both knees collapsing into impossible geometries, hunching over his own ruin, weeping now in silence, shaking.

'It gets no better. Tell me who you were and what your plans were, and we'll finish this nonsense now. Mess around, and you'll take about two hours to bleed out.

'Who I was? I am still . . .' His voice strangled into sobbing incoherence.

'This is not a good time for existential debate. It is a time for answers. I have very limited patience. Your time remaining is defined by that limit.' She spoke almost gently. He remained hunched over himself, no sense in the sounds he made, only pain, defeat and desperation.

'Please,' he said.

Chastity put down her weapons, way outside his reach, though his streaming eyes followed them. She stripped off her clothes, smoothly, efficiently, completely, folding them neatly and placing them carefully beside her small arsenal. Picked up her long black-bladed knife and positioned herself in front of him. He stared, confusion diluting the bursting pain of his situation. Almost silence. Chastity approached him, almost softly, placed the black blade of the long knife against his sweating, corded throat and pushed his head back. His shoulders followed, his eyes widening to an improbable extent, the dead white skin of her arm an impossible contrast against the gleaming, sweating, straining black of his body. She reached down between his legs and took hold of him. Shook her head sadly, while holding hard eye contact.

'You men. You're about to end your days. You're dying. You are completely broken and beyond hope. Your blood is leaking all over the floor of a church and still your stupid stupid stupid man brain wants to have a fuck. Your stupid man brain sends what's left of your blood to your cock. You do not deserve to live.' She dropped him, picked up the handgun and shot him, twice in the heart or thereabouts. He shuddered and sighed and the light of life left him.

Chastity stood stock-still for several minutes, her skin chilled by the cold, her eyes and attention elsewhere. Then she walked behind the black man and she drew the black blade across his throat. Despite the absence of pressure from the stilled heart, blood spurted, but briefly, as arteries parted. A last sigh escaped his lungs. She cut again, this time down to the bones of his neck, the muscles parting as the blade slid through them, razor-edged and under pressure. His dead black head with its open white eyes lay between her impossibly white breasts as though seeking a last comfort.

She pulled the body, still warm and willing, to the floor of the nave, carefully slid the long blade between two of the exposed neck vertebrae and sliced. The bones parted. One more slice and the head fell free. Black skin and wide white eyes staring at the religious painting on the ceiling. Chastity glanced up.

'Can you still see? That's some bad old white man's god on his big white cloud, welcoming the sinners to their hereafter. But there is no hereafter, is there, buddy? None. Just one big fat silent nothing. Hope you enjoy it.'

She stood. Stretched. Placed the handgun beside her

clothes and walked, naked apart from the long knife, to the church door. Opened it. Stepped outside, crossed the small car park, the small road, and ran lightly down the clean beach to the calm waters of the big lake. Waded in. Squatted down and relieved herself luxuriously while scrubbing the black blade clean with sand from the lake bed, walked back to the beach and laid the long knife to dry in the sunshine. And she swam, ignoring the remote sounds of traffic on the road, the distant movement of small boats on the water, and waved once at another passing swimmer.

Back in the church, she dressed swiftly, still damp, but humming some tune. Took the dead black man's keys, went outside and plipped open his car. Removed a laptop computer, and returned to the church. Fired up the laptop, checked that it was decently modern, opened a connection to a familiar web address, a familiar site, and set the machine's camera so that its one-eyed focus was on the dead head of the dead black man still leaking onto the altar. Her own bloody sacrifice. To someone. Somebody. Somewhere. She stepped into invisibility behind the unblinking gaze of the computer's eye, looked up at the crucified representation of eternal optimism, bowed solemnly from the waist and spoke, gently but loud enough for the computer's ear to collect and transmit. 'For you. For the three. For the trinity.'

Then she left.

11

AN ELEPHANT MEMORY

Suicide may indeed be painless, but surveillance is not. Select your preference. Watchers have two core briefs; they must see everything and everyone but be seen by no one. This is not an easy combination. The best way to accomplish both ideals of surveillance is by operating a skilled team of nondescript experts, girls and boys of several ages and physical types, all of them convincingly occupied carrying out entirely unremarkable everyday activities, activities which are usually dictated by the location of the surveillance. It is a rare talent, for example, to appear nondescript and invisible while wearing a formal business suit in high summer on a busy surf beach. Likewise, the wearing of a Hawaiian shirt, shorts and a blue pork-pie hat is unlikely to go unremarked anywhere outside a bad bar or a home for the sartorially insane. The team thing, though, is the only true path to surveillance. Snag is, teams are costly, cumbersome and complex. Best left to government agencies which can luxuriate in spending funds not their own and being rewarded handsomely whether they succeed or do the other thing.

Shard was on his own. His favourite position. Sometimes. He had been trained over several years by the military machine, finally specialising in marksmanship. Given a decent weapon, decent visibility and decent light and luck, he could drop a bullet-sized object into a man-sized object at a decent distance with a decent degree of consistency. But he was never entirely top class . . . except on military firing ranges, where his scores were as high as scores ever get. This is almost always a great thing, and Shard could – and did – shoot for his unit in marksmanship matches, almost guaranteed to come away with trophies, kudos and the like. But the first time he was called upon by his country to pop a small morsel of military metal into a representative of an opposing military group, he missed.

His shot was close enough to send the target heading – successfully – for cover, and his superiors put the miss down to bad luck, bad light or bad something else, and everyone lived to fight another day. Most members of most armies are not in hot combat for most of the time, and Shard's own unit passed several tours in overheated suburban warzones, where sniper skills were rarely in demand, and when they were, that demand was often filled by other, more specialised, units. The second time Shard was called upon to utilise his award-winning and actually fairly famous shooter abilities, to behave as a sniper, was over a year after the first miss. He missed again. Same closeness; same result. A theory gained ground higher up the chain of command that maybe soldier Shard had a problem with killing people. Which can be less than the most desirable attribute in a front-line combat soldier, although other callings are of course available.

The military mind being what it is, some faceless someone, somewhere in a remote and safe location, comfortably removed from actual reality and real risk, posted Shard's unit to a truly hot spot, a spot where the climate could boil a Caucasian brain in its box and where the natives were restlessly intent upon killing the foreign invader . . . which is always simply understandable unless they are good at it and persistent, at which point it becomes understandable but undesirable. Shard revealed that far from having some liberal pinko scummy moralistic problem with killing people, in fact he had no problems with it at all. Provide him with a weapon: gun, knife, RPG, howitzer, claymore, whatever, and a target – 'the guy over there in the hat' – and he would, could and did execute, terminate or just kill the target with no personal problem at all.

He did this manly stuff for some time, one thing led to another, and at a point close to the end of his tour he found himself once again on a lonely urban rooftop, lying alongside a long gun, waiting for the arrival of the person deemed by his military masters to merit ultimate discontinuity. The two main differences between this sniper event and the sniper events which had preceded it were that the operation was successful, and that Shard did not squeeze the trigger. His companion did. His companion on that day was a civilian. An ex-soldier but now a contracting civilian expert; one of the 'specialists' preferred by the powers at some times to genuine military men, mainly because they were disposable, deniable and deliverable in ways that most military units are not.

Shard spotted for the shooter. JJ Stoner squeezed the trigger. They worked excellently together. The military might was delighted with the result, being as always keen on team work, cooperation and things like that, and teamed them together again; similar situation, location and resolution. And they did it again. And again.

Shard explained to Stoner that although he was an excellent shot – his range scores were decently higher than those of his shooting partner from the latter's time in the military – he seemed somehow incapable of translating his superlative hand-eye coordination into actual individual fatalities. Stoner sympathised, in a mostly disinterested way, and said no more about it.

Until their next job together. Shard arrived at the scene equipped with the paraphernalia of the business, and Stoner arrived, not empty-handed, as had been the case previously, but with a totally impressive set of binoculars, the kind of bins capable of observing the weather on Jupiter. Shard shared his sense of awe and wonder at the resources available to the private sector, and followed that with surprise when Stoner laid himself prone in the position usually adopted by the spotter, not the shooter. Ignoring all attempts at conversation and discussion, Stoner started reading the range, passing the figures to his companion, who set up the long gun. The target arrived. Shard took the shot.

The target passed on to a higher plane, or whatever dead men do at the point of their death experience, and Stoner rose to his feet, grumbled about the effects of gravel on his delicate knees, and left.

The two men worked well together, sharing the shooter's role in a seemingly random way. Sometimes Stoner showed up with his NASA-standard binoculars, other times he did not. If Stoner brought the bins, Shard took the shot. Their record was 100 percent. As everyone with an interest remarked, they did indeed work excellently well together. That was all they did. Work together. Shard would return to his unit, to the end-lessly macho camaraderie of serving soldiers, and Stoner would not. Stoner went wherever it was he went. They did not discuss this, nor indeed anything unrelated to their shared objectives. It was a non-issue; neither of them was exactly aware of it; both were quiet men, self-contained and effective. On their final joint assignment, Shard remarked to Stoner, as they both watched, waited, waited and watched, that this was his last detail before his discharge. Stoner continued to scan the tenement housing their target. Shard spotted, as spotters do, passed the details to Stoner, who sighted, shot, sighed and sat back from the long gun. 'Target's down. Look me up once you're out. If you want.'

Years passed, as they do, and Shard was once again surveil-ling a dreary suburban location. On his own, which was not ideal. Looking for Stoner, such are the ironies of the civilian freelance life. Another of those ironies was that he was rather less than inconspicuous, a bulky, muscled and well illustrated man in a cyclist's outfit, bicycle by his side, reclining on a park bench in a small park directly facing a large house belonging to Stoner, long since converted into at least two apartments, one of them inhabited for a long time by a working girl as close to Stoner as it is possible to be, and by a moveable, variable Asian population. Parked outside the house was Stoner's usual vehicle – a black VW Transporter, sufficiently nondescript to be laden to its lid with surveillance kit and personnel, although Shard doubted that that was the case.

His controlled watcher's reverie was shut down by the opening of a side door to the house and the emergence of a compact Asian man who jogged across the road towards Shard, vaulted the park's decorative fence and approached the bench, hands held open.

'You must be bored!' The Asian man sounded faintly excited. 'And cold. Come inside and share some tea. You can tell me who you're expecting so diligently, and maybe I can expect them alongside you.'

Shard slowly raised his gaze to meet the smaller man's. 'I'm not bored. I'm thinking. And I'm not cold. Thank you.'

The Asian man smiled broadly and held up his hands in an unmistakeable gesture of non-threatening behaviour. 'I am Mr Tran. You are looking for Mr Stoner. He's not here.' He operated his body posture to express his probable regret at his statement. 'You are welcome to wait inside. There is no sense in sitting out here. You may catch a chill. And in any case, Mr Stoner will observe you observing his house. He is smart like that. Very smart, that one.'

Shard sighed and stood. 'That's the point. The point is that he observes me. That way we can have a conversation.'

Mr Tran considered. 'I would recommend taking tea rather than sitting out here. It will get only darker. Darkness brings many problems, not only those associated with conspicuity.

Darkness is however always the correct time for teas to be shared. Please.'

Quite suddenly and for no reason he would ever be able to explain, Shard understood that the polite smiling Asian man was threatening him. More than that, in fact he felt under threat. That the threat was real and substantial. He leaned towards Mr Tran, as if seeking a whispered confidence. Mr Tran moved closer, into his personal space.

'Tea is best taken hot, and without milk,' said the Asian man, in a confidential, conspiratorial way.

Mr Tran was plainly not alone in the big house. Waiting for them on a low table in a high-ceilinged room stood a loaded teapot, three cups and their saucers, a larger vessel filled with steaming water and a plate bearing a number of wrapped sweet treats.

'Fortune cookies?' Shard was uncomfortably aware that he probably sounded as mystified as he felt.

Mr Tran smiled again, a man whose features appeared to arrange themselves into a celebration of good humour at every opportunity.

'Missy is fond with them,' he announced. 'She may join us later. If not, then sooner. We have met before.' When Shard failed to reply to a sentence he had failed to recognise as a question, Mr Tran repeated it, this time with a gently comic exaggeration of an interrogative inflection. 'We have met before?'

'No. I don't think so. Do you live here?'

'Yes. Yes we have.' Mr Tran's smile was relentless, all-conquering. He moved to pour tea, swilling two cups one after the other with the steaming water before resting them in their saucers and filling them from the teapot. No strainer. Loose, large leaves. Gentle, dark scent. Relaxing, deliberately so. Mr Tran leaned over his own cup and inhaled theatrically, closed his eyes. 'Americans prefer coffee,' he revealed. 'Their empires will last only dozens of years. Not hundreds of years. They are inscrutable.'

'The blonde is joining us?' Shard lifted his own cup to his lips, discovered that the tea was still too hot, and lowered it back to the saucer. 'Stoner . . . Stoner was asking after her.'

Mr Tran maintained his smile. It became augmented with the faint but perceptible air of an elder adult dealing with a dim child.

'Mr Stoner is not likely to join us,' he shared, gently. 'Hence the three cups. If Mr Stoner were to be joining us then there would be four cups.' He closed a chapter and moved on.

'I have lived in this house for a lot of time. Mr Stoner inherited me and my . . . tenancy when he inherited the house. It is very warm and very comfortable. Missy – she is on her way, by the way, on her way – has been here for a lot less of a long time. Very little time.'

Shard sipped at his tea, which was predictably delicious. 'Stoner inherited the house?'

Mr Tran nodded. 'He was at the death of the previous landlord. Mr Stoner is an excellent landlord.'

Shard stared hard at his companion, who sipped gently at his tea with every appearance of relish and delight.

'Stoner killed the guy who had this house? Why? For the house?'

'Here she comes now!' Mr Tran settled his drained cup in the perfect centre of its saucer and rose to his feet with the fluid perfection of a gymnast, the simple power of his ascent dragging Shard with it, so he too rose to stand in greeting. 'Welcome!'

A plainly unnaturally blonde woman appeared, silently, in the doorway, and bowed deeply to Mr Tran, who took both of her hands in his own, then gestured her to the spare chair and snapped the fingers of his left hand, suddenly, loudly, before returning to his seat. Shard remained standing, an ancient inbuilt politeness asserting itself, and the silent blonde smiled gently at both men and seated herself. As one, the men sat. Neither said anything, while Shard simply stared.

Into the suspended conversation stepped a second Asian man, of similar build and demeanour to those of Mr Tran. He carried a tray, from which he removed two teacups, their saucers and a second teapot, switching them with their earlier incarnations on the table. There was no soundtrack to this silent movie, and when the substitutions were complete, the latest player departed.

'You're not . . .' said Shard, somewhat unsettled that the newcomer wasn't who he'd expected.

'Missy,' said Mr Tran, 'is our most recent arrival. She prefers lemon with her tea, but I am persuasive as well as educational.' He laughed, softly and with delicacy. The artificial blonde smiled, extended her hand to Shard while Mr Tran warmed their cups, set them once more on their saucers and filled them with fresh tea.

'Blesses,' she said.

'Thank you,' said Shard, feeling a little confusion while privately wondering who'd sneezed. Mr Tran leaned almost imperceptibly towards him, gestured to the quiet blonde.

'Blesses, this is Mr Harding. He is a friend . . . a colleague of Mr Stoner, who usually calls him Shard. Can we also call you Shard?'

'If it helps.' Shard studied the blonde woman, whose pale eyes were lowered below the close-cropped golden stubble on her scalp. 'You're white,' he said, stating an obvious truth as though it were a divine revelation, which it may have been, at least to him.

Mr Tran's smile had cooled a degree or two. 'And I am Hmong. Is it important? We are all who we are. It is the best way. Among friends. The tea is still hot.'

'Sorry.' Shard accepted the mild chiding. 'I was expecting someone else. When you spoke of Missy, I understood that you meant Lissa, Stoner's . . . ah . . . companion. Recently.

Previous companion.' He coughed, maybe disguising the increasing stumble of his speech, his own confusion. 'Missy . . . Blesses. Have you. . . have you lived here long, miss? Blesses?'

'On and off,' she replied. 'You?' She sipped at her tea. 'Excellent as always, Mr Tran. Hmong may brew the very best of teas.'

Mr Tran clapped his hands gently and beamed broadly. 'Better than those Han Chinese!' They celebrated something which excluded their companion. He turned back to Shard. 'Blesses and I first met in mainland China. It was exciting.' Both laughed once more.

Shard sat back. 'Sorry. Again. I'm lost. Confused. Apologies. The woman I was expecting to meet is not this woman, and I was hoping to catch Stoner, not a Chinaman, hospitable though you both are. For which thanks.' He rose to his feet, and Mr Tran raised both of his hands in a calming, pausing gesture.

'Please sit with us for a little while. You need be in no rush. It is important for you that you do that. Enjoy the tea. Share a fortune cookie with Missy . . . with our Blesses. They're too sweet for my tastes. I worry for hyperglycaemia. Two things for your attention. Firstly, I am not a Chinaman; that is a description as offensive to me as referring to you as a dumb Mick would be to you.'

Shard sat down, interrupted. I'm not Irish . . .'

'You are acting like a cartoon comedy Irishman, Harding. Hence the careful insult. I am Hmong, as I said. Vietnamese, not Chinese. Blesses here is Irish, but not a Mick. Secondly, you can wait outside in the rain for a long time. Stoner will no doubt return at some point, if only to repair his Volkswagen, but it will not be any point soon. He is on his way to another country.'

'Another county?'

'Another country. There is no need to act like that comedy

Irishman. You're among friends. Your secret intelligence is safe with us. Relax. Stoner is probably meeting the person who shot out the headlights of his Volkswagen. Maybe he will ask her to pay for its repair. All things are possible. More tea? Another cookie? We should probably talk about the elephant.'

Shard was speechless. Almost speechless. 'The elephant?' He shook his head, gently. 'Which? Which elephant?'

'A figurative elephant. A pachyderm of parable. Not a parabolic pachyderm, which would be ridiculous, of course. A geometric nonsense, if nothing else.' Mr Tran smiled again. He smiled a lot. Plainly he was a happy Hmong. He had more to say to a silent Shard.

'Why do you wish to locate Mr Stoner? This may sound to your complicated intelligence operative's ears to be a simple question, obvious even, but it is a question which I – playing my part as the wily oriental – need to ask. I will explain a little of my wily reasoning. My reasoning goes like this: Mr Stoner and you have worked together several times, and with some success. Mr Stoner has plainly not kept you appraised of his movements for some time. Two things, then. Firstly, if Mr Stoner wished you to be aware of his whereabouts, he would have told you himself. Secondly, when Mr Stoner took himself off, away and out of the frying pan, he also failed to advise you of his departure and of his destination, fluid though that may have been. I see no pressing obligation, you see, to discuss Mr Stoner's current activities or locations with you. Or anyone else. Please do not feel offended by this. I am a quiet man, and am well known among Hmong for being quiet. And secure. So, again I ask, why do you wish to locate Mr Stoner? You can contact him in several secure electronic ways, I am certain.'

'He doesn't reply. Not to email, phone or through third parties.' Shard was calm, more comfortable now.

'Then it is probable that he does not want you to locate him. Others know where he is, some of them know what he is doing, and many individuals have a serious interest in the outcome.'

'I simply want to help. He's a friend, a good friend, and I want to help.' He stopped, plainly considering. Reached a decision. 'The last time we met I . . . left early. I may have . . . panicked a little.' Confession time was over, and his resolve and confidence returned together. 'OK. OK then, will you tell me how to locate him? How to get in touch?'

'No.'

'Why not? No offence, but we have fought together and we trust each other.'

'Of course. As have Stoner and I, more than once. He is a full-grown man, he is capable of deciding who will benefit from sharing in his several lives. Several people are aware of his current situation, some of them have an interest, as I have said before.'

'If you could be kind enough to suggest someone who would trust me enough to share that information, I would thank you and ask them.'

'There is no reason at all why I should do that, Shard. And none of them would tell you anything which could endanger our mutual friend in any case. I will tell you this. Stoner will soon be travelling, possibly quite far. The only act of a friend would be to provide support if he needs it, which he may. And to remain contactable and available. He knows how to find you if he needs you.'

Shard sipped at his cooling tea, waved away an offered cookie. Mr Tran had more to say.

'There is always a complexity to Stoner's work. There are times when no one is reliable.' Mr Tran sounded serious. 'There are times when the only way to operate in security is to operate alone. When the only way a friend can help is . . . well . . . by keeping out of the way.'

Blesses interrupted, softly. 'Mr Tran is telling you that there's nothing you can do to help, and that you could – by accident of course – actually hinder. Or get hurt.' She gazed earnestly into Shard's eyes. He gazed back, in some irritation at the idiotic ritual of afternoon suburban tea as well in his increasing view that he was being mocked.

Blesses did not blink. Shard was suddenly aware of this. He was a little puzzled by why it should be important. He didn't blink, either. The long fingers of her two hands traced patterns in the fabric of the tablecloth, somewhere at the remote edge of his vision; peripheral patterns. Her eyes were pale, ice-blue. Maybe green. Her voice was addictive, although he had somehow lost track of what she was actually saying.

Morning. Sunshine. Deeply rested, sighing with comfort, Shard awoke and swung his feet over the side of his bed. The smell of freshly brewed coffee was almost arousing, sexual in its associated memories. He padded barefoot through his morning routines and toiletries, decided that he would drink a first strong, dark cup before shaving and sorting the day. And stopped. Dead in his tracks. Memory kicked in. Or rather an absence of memory. He was at home. He had no recollection at all of his journey from Stoner's place – one of Stoner's places – and tea with . . . Mr Tran. And someone else? Or not? He found a mental cavity where there should have been the memories of an entire evening.

His home was as secure as need be for a man of his profession. A rapid check showed that no infiltration was apparent. His clothes were hung correctly, folded neatly, as was his routine, while his shoes, wallet, watch and lucky charms were where his military training always placed them. Undisturbed. No phone with them, however.

The phone sat by the full coffee-maker in the wide open, bright and white kitchen. He poured a first cup – why not? – and contemplated his phone, his window to the world. Flicked it to life. To reveal a single SMS message. From Stoner.

'Hope you enjoyed tea for two. Mr T's tea is the very best. Called away. Try NOT to be involved. Back soon. Catch up then. JJ.'

12

TWELVE BLUE BARS

Bili astonished everyone – including herself – by jumping backwards onto Stretch's baby grand piano. She sat swinging her legs like a child while pounding her red Rickenbacker bass guitar in approximate harmony to the rousing rock 'n' roll chorus battering from the piano beneath her. Stretch roared with almost audible laughter and yelled an imaginary inaudible verse at a switched off microphone. The audience enjoyed the show; more general entertainment than merely music, the piano and the bass thundering along a rocking road together. Good humour was everywhere.

Bili dropped to her feet once more, and she and the pianist brought their improvised and unconventional duet to a surprisingly coherent close. Stoner walked through the audience, hands high over his head, applauding and encouraging players and audience alike. He picked his weary-looking Stratocaster up from its accustomed resting place, flicked the amplifier from standby to full on, then wound the tone control pots on the guitar up and down in a vaguely successful quest to defeat the dreaded Fender crackles and hum. Gave up and grinned.

'One day,' Bili grinned at the audience over her own, live microphone. 'One day, this mean man will buy a new guitar and save us all this noise! Yeah!' The audience yelled back.

Stoner moved to her side, leaned down almost a foot so his mouth was close to hers and to the microphone.

'Yeah,' he breathed. 'Yeah. Come that day.' Then, swinging his gaze around the crowded bar, he said, 'We'd like to try out a new number for you. Not a cover, not our take on some tired old standard. This is new. So new that only Stretch knows the words, only Bili knows the tune. All I know is Stretch and Bili have spent more than one whole minute rehearsing, and that it was so dreadful to hear that they swore they'd never do it again. This song – this new song – is so appalling, so completely frightening that they'll have to play it as fast as they can to get it out of the way. They asked me to play a kazoo solo for it, to keep in the spirit of the thing, but the kazoo is too difficult for me and I left my swannee whistle at home tonight, so we'll have to see how it works with this old guitar.'

He grinned and stepped back. Quiet fell, a clinking, drinking good natured quiet. Stretch and Bili swung into a dirty country groove, and the huge pianist sang his song.

> She was talkin' with Jesus
> Talkin' with him behind my back
> She been talkin' to Jesus
> Talkin' with him behind my back
> Talkin' with that white man
> Down by the old goat track

Bili and Stoner chugged a vigorous twelve-bar beat behind Stretch's stripped out piano chords, quieting on cue to allow the black man his second verse.

> Now Jesus was a white man
> In the wide lands of the black
> Yes Jesus was that white man
> Walkin' the wide lands of the black

Talkin' love and revolution
Down by that old goat track

Stoner's guitar eased solo sustained notes into the mix, playing with a fluidly melodious tone which was unfamiliar to most of the regulars in the audience, while Bili and Stretch worked hard to build their own version of a power trio, piano and bass providing the tension behind the lyrics. Stretch loomed towards the microphone, plainly poised to deliver another half-formed verse of racial theft and betrayal, but before he made a sound the strident brazen bellow of a tenor sax powered by a decent set of lungs split into the mix, not from the stage but from the audience. Amanda, eyes squeezed tight as though to focus her pressures entirely through the reed, rocked on her feet as her impromptu solo pulled all the attention of all the audience away from the stage. She powered through a full twelve-bar verse, then another, walking through the audience to the edge of the stage, walking with confidence though her eyes were tight shut, fetching up with her ass resting on the edge of the stage as her solo and the verse ended together.

Eyes locked on Amanda, only hearing each other, Bili and Stretch pulled the song to a close. Bili raised her hands and brought them together in applause for Amanda's solo; Stretch bounded from behind his baby grand, dropped to the edge of the stage next to the sax soloist and threw his arms around her. The audience whooped and whistled. Amanda was flushed, either from exertion or from excitement or both. Stretch released his huge hold, swung her to arm's length and shook his head in delight. Then hugged her again. She grinned. The audience quieted to an appreciative murmur. Bili spoke through the microphone; 'Hell, Stretch doesn't have any more verses anyway! Let's hear it again for Amanda, Blue Cube's own sax goddess!' The audience obliged.

'To the bar!' sang Bili, and stopped in mid-movement.

'Where's JJ?' she asked the noisy air. No one heard her. She asked again with the same result. Stretch and Amanda had gone, absorbed by the cry of the crowd and by the call of the bar. Bili walked slowly and in private to Stoner's Stratocaster, resting in its stand, the amplifier switched to standby, as though it had been silent all evening, waiting for a player who'd failed to arrive. Bili switched off the amp; an almost inaudible contribution to the background hum was silenced. She was alone in hearing its absence, and stood still, motionless and filled with questions in the half-light at the side of the stage, until finally she shook her head, a cascade of blonde tangle framing her face, and turned to the steps, walked down them and stopped dead to avoid contact with a tattooed man, standing with his back to her, facing away into the audience.

The man spoke. 'He's gone again, hasn't he?'

Bili slipped silently to his side. 'Yeah. Reckon so. You up for a glass of something?'

'I'm Shard,' the tattooed man said quietly, his attention elsewhere, eyes roaming the club.

'So you are. Like you were last time we met. I remember,' said Bili. 'I wasn't that wrecked last time. Did he tell you to meet him here?'

'No. Seems he's avoiding me.' He turned to face Bili, who stood her ground, entirely familiar with the physical proximity of powerful men and unmoved by the experience. Her eyes dropped from Shard's face to his chest, to the exposed skin, to the inked illustrations.

'What's that?' she asked. Then opened two more buttons of his shirt, revealing more of the artwork. 'Your life story? You're the illustrated man? An open book? Still life in pictures? Dreams and realities captured in ink.'

'You're a poet.' A flat statement. 'An artist. You make art for others. Other guys make art on me and I carry it for them. And I talk shit. They're tattoos, little lady. That's it. They meant something on the day they were made.' He looked at her. 'You delaying me? Holding me up? So Stoner can get away?'

Bili shook her curls slowly. 'Fuckwit. No. He's gone. He can do the big disappear better than anyone, that man. Welcome to his very own waiting society.'

Shard buttoned his shirt. 'You wait. I'll find him.'

Bili smiled a vacant smile. 'You can try. It's a big world, so they say.'

13

HANDY CANDY MAN

'Nice day for a long walk.' Stoner pulled back a chair next to the dark-haired lady who had watched him approach with no sign of interest nor recognition. He sat, kicking back the front legs of the chair. 'OK if I join you?'

She smiled, in a notably grim way. 'You already did, I think. It's late for breakfast, Englishman.' Chastity leaned forward, across the table, forming a vague symmetry with Stoner's backward tilt. 'Why are you here? Come for the cure? Hiking is good for the immortal soul, so they say. The more strenuous the better. As in all things.' She waved an arm for a waiter. 'What do you want with me, Stoner? Conversational ecstasy? A guided tour of Königswinter with a special emphasis on the history of the Drachensfels and the importance of the Rhine in the rural economy of Germany through the ages?' The waiter arrived, oozing an Italian smile and brandishing an order pad. Chastity ordered two double espressos and two ice-cream pizzas. She ordered in Italian. The waiter's appreciative ooze was replaced with a delighted gush.

'You speak Italian?' Stoner pantomimed his wonder.

'So do you.' Chastity mimed nothing at all. 'My accent's better.'

'Only in Germany. I'm not supposed to be talking to you. What's an ice-cream pizza?'

'It's a confectionery orgasm. Sort of like the old "see wherever and die" idea; eat an ice-cream pizza and then die. Your
arteries will clog and a slow painful death will result. Are you
man enough for a pizza ice cream?'

'Are you?'

'My second of the day. All today's calories have come from
ice-cream pizza.'

'The espresso balances the diet?'

'You are that man after my own heart, Stoner. Marry me
now. There's a church over there.' She gestured at the adjacent religious structure. 'Make an honest woman of me.'

'There's not enough time for that, even if we both live forever. And in any case, the church is defrocked.'

'It is? How can you tell? I suppose we could burn in hell
together forever. Sounds romantic.'

'Only to you. Hell is rammed with people I have no wish to
see again. I plan on paying all the gods' representatives on
earth enough to at least get a passport to purgatory. Do the
men in frocks still sell indulgences? Plenary indulgences?'

'I hope so. Purgatory sounds good. Heaven sounds dull; hell
– like you say – too many tediously familiar residents. But I
like the idea of a church wedding. I like churches. Only a day
or two back I killed a guy in one.'

'Was there any particular reason? Was he a bad guy? Is this
why I'm sitting here with you now? Directed here by a higher
power to hear your confession and provide absolution for
your sins?'

Chastity sat in silence while the oozing waiter delivered
improbable edibles and restorative potables.

'I'm not sure whether he was a bad guy.' She seemed
thoughtful for a moment. 'It's rarely easy to tell.'

'So you kill first then find out afterwards whether the vics
are good guys or bad guys? Seems harsh.'

'Just like bombing. Impersonal, that's me. Blowing shit up
along with anyone nearby who you've never met is OK, but

removing a tedious intrusion is not. It's all a question of values. I needed a car. He had a car.' She dug into the ice cream. 'Your turn to talk. Eating, me. In any case, if he was a good guy, then he's a martyr and I've sent him straight to heaven, where he'll be fucked forever by virgins. What's not to like?'

'Confusing your theologies, Chastity?'

'I'm entirely unconfused. You talk, I eat, then maybe we try to take each other out.'

'That what you want?' Stoner threw back the coffee, gestured for a refill, and assaulted the ice cream. 'This is . . . awesome.'

'To die for, as they say.'

Stoner grimaced. 'Questionable taste, that.'

'You just said it was awesome. Make your mind up.'

'Such searing wit. Cutting. I was asked to come and watch over you. Don't ask, because I can't tell you who did the asking.'

'Not a problem. An amoeba could work it out.'

'Amoebas are very small.'

'It's amoebae, surely?'

'Someone is burning you.' Stoner dropped that, left it to drift between them while he devoured improbably glorious ice cream. 'Two hits on the trot, you get wild men chasing after you, screwing up your carefully-laid, so forth.'

She nodded. 'All good so far. Did you read that in the newspapers?'

'Do they serve anything drinkable apart from espresso?' Stoner flapped an irritated hand, trying to catch the attention of the oily waiter, who was nowhere to be seen. Chastity smiled remotely, raised an eyebrow a fraction and the oily waiter appeared from nowhere. A bottle appeared, plates were cleared, glasses raised in an uncertain toast.

After a decent, relaxing, digestive pause, Chastity remarked, as though discussing the wine, 'It's worse than that.'

189

'How do you mean?'

'The man in the church . . . the dead man in the church, he claimed to know me through my saviour in the desert.'

'You killed him for that? Fuck.'

'I killed him because an inexplicable, irresistible, mysterious, murderous rage overtook me.' She smiled. 'I wanted him out of the way, I wanted a car and he had one, like I said, and I was tired of everyone knowing more of what I was doing than I did.' Her expression became serious, quiet almost. 'I shouldn't say this, but I'm almost pleased to see you.'

'Hence the proposal of marriage.'

'No, no. That was a joke, pure and simple.'

'I weep. OK, wild sex will do as well as marriage. Better and cheaper. Do you do wild sex? I've not booked a hotel yet. You'll be in the Maritim, I expect. Great views. Good swimming pool. You like wild sex in swimming pools.'

'Was that a guess? It's a good one. Yes. And yes I am in the Maritim. Let's skip the wild sex. You'd hate it.'

Stoner poured and smiled. 'I doubt that, somehow.'

'Did you fuck Charity?'

'You always ask that. No.'

'OK.'

'Do I need a room of my own? I'll stay in the same hotel, if only in hope of that wild sex, and also to watch . . . which is what I'm here to do, as I said.'

Chastity waved down a second bottle. 'And then?'

'And then we do wild sex . . .'

'Just stop that. It's un-fucking-funny.'

'Wow.' Stoner poured and attempted an uncertain smile. 'Mad psycho bitch killer woman hates sex shock.'

'That's not in fact true. I would enjoy it, assuming you have a certain skill and a certain vigour to match. Can't we just avoid this? You're no James Bond, I'm no Mata Hari and this is a genuine matter of life and death. Complicated enough already. There are enough night cruisers in the hotel lounge;

you'll get a bedtime rumble if you want one. You've still got the beard. Romanian whores love guys with beards. Especially rich English guys with beards.'

'Or without beards?'

'There is that.'

'OK, I can take a hint. What's your plan?' Stoner unconvincingly acted the jilted lover and waved for another bottle.

'I've killed every man who's fucked me.'

'The little death? *Petit mort*, as our French friends call it? There must be worse ways to go. I've died on stage loads of times. It's a musician's nightmare.'

'I've killed every man who's fucked me.' Chastity was not smiling. Not smiling at all. She was defiance, cold irritation and menace. Stoner lowered the glass he had just raised.

'Why tell me? Even if . . . even if it's true.'

'It is true. Completely.'

The darkening evening was drawing frigid wings around them. There was a mist on the Rhine. Cheerful drinkers' clamour spilled from the restaurant. Time passed in silence for a while. Chastity and Stoner emptied the bottle. He broke the tension, voiced the only acceptable decision.

'I'll book a room.'

'Good move. No rush.'

'You're not worried about being observed by your target?'

'He's not here yet. Arrives tomorrow. His minders are here. They'll ignore a happy couple.'

'All of them?' Stoner's tone was carefully neutral. He wasn't talking about the target.

'All of them.' Nor was she.

'Fuck.'

'As you say.'

'Why? Habit? Inadequate performances? Awful puns? Halitosis?'

'Joke if you want. I can do laughing – though I can't really see the humour.'

191

'You've . . . you've had a lot of lovers?'

'Who keeps count? Thirty. Maybe more.'

'That's a lot of dead soldiers. For a woman.'

'I've discovered that. I discovered that a long time ago. But most of them performed only once. Very few encores.'

'I can see that most men would feel threatened by this.'

'They don't. Generally speaking, men are blind and stupid. I've told several of them that they're about to die. Not one has taken me seriously.'

'You are being serious? Seriously?'

'Yes.'

'OK. Thanks for trusting me with that.'

'Thank you for spotting that trust.' Chastity was 100 percent serious. Absurdly calm. 'I told you because you helped me in Israel. Because Charity told me I could trust you, and because this business of uninvited guests appearing when I'm working is a bitch. I'm not worried about it – pissed off if anything – but it's making things tricky.'

'Do you fuck every man you kill? Sorry. Had to ask that.'

'No. But it's an easy way to get inside a man's guard, and most of our contracts are against men.'

'Mine too. What does it all mean?' Stoner attempted some form of levity, though the subject had no light in it. None.

'Only men are worth killing.'

'You reckon? And women make the best killers?'

'Women are great for making babies.'

Stoner tried for lightness once again. 'You told me no wild sex.'

'Wild sex is nothing to do with babies. Wild sex is only for entertainment. Recreation, not procreation.'

'You hate it, though. You told me.'

'I love it. You'd hate the result, experience suggests.'

'You really think you could kill me? Me? Really?'

'Yes. Everybody dies, Stoner. Everybody. If I wanted you dead . . . you would be dead. Several times over. The first time

192

we met it would've been easy. Killing people is easy. Especially men. Fuck their brains out, blow their brains out. Always works.'

'You think I should try this?'

'You enjoy sex with men?'

'Does it pay well?'

'You're being flippant.'

'I am.'

'I'm being serious.' Chastity's expression confirmed the statement.

'OK.' Stoner mimed the very model of contrition. 'You're the famous international Angel of Death. I'm just some kind of . . .'

'The Angel of Death? Excuse me?'

'That's what the Slovenian press are calling you. The Angel of Death.'

'Marvellous.'

'I knew you'd be pleased. Flattered, maybe. You don't look very angelic. In fact . . . not angelic at all. What's with all the head cutting off nonsense, while we're being thoroughly distasteful?'

Chastity sat back in her chair, lifted her attention from Stoner and stared away into the distance. 'Didn't we discuss you getting a room? It's increasing cold out here and a mysterious event just took place.'

Stoner was already on his feet, moving very rapidly behind her, drawing back her chair for her, acting the gentleman he was not. 'What happened?' To the point.

'The mark's here. He's early. That's a question, no?'

'OK. Who is it?'

'He's inside now. I'll point him out.'

'Who is he?'

'Does it make a difference, Stoner? I have a contract, we've been paid, I'll complete.' She named a name. Stoner shook his head.

'Means nothing to me.'

'Is that permission?' Chastity's smile was colder than the frigid evening.

'You need none.'

'Be aware of that. At all times.'

'I am.'

They moved inside, heading for reception, an island of order in a Germanic sea of orderliness, no rushing stewards, no squalling babies. Chastity took Stoner's arm, leaned to his ear. 'He's at the counter. Good looking guy, mid-forties, balding, fit, thousand-dollar suit, thousand-dollar shoes, thousand-dollar . . .'

'I get the point.' Stoner squeezed her to his side, smiled into her eyes. 'What did you call him? Guertler? Is that what he's calling himself? I wonder why.'

'That's not his name? You do know him? Do we have a problem?'

'His name is Boekkerink. He's Dutch, not German at all.'

'OK, so what? So he'll be a dying Dutchman rather than a good German.' Chastity was performing a fine impression of either a besotted new lover or a professional bedfellow. Onlookers might have asked themselves which she was, if they asked anything, which they probably would not. Most onlookers looked away at overt and intense displays of affection. 'Are we . . .' she slipped her tongue between her teeth, suggestively, '. . . going to have a problem? Is he a friend of yours?'

'No.' Stoner, with a convincing display of attempting to hide the gesture, rubbed the back of his left hand along the side of her breast. 'I don't have friends.'

'I can believe that. Can you save the foreplay for the bedroom?' Her eyes tracked her target as he moved towards the lift.

'I don't want to die.' Stoner beamed at the receptionist, who regarded him with a buffed and meaninglessly professional smile.

'Shame. You'd do it so well.' Chastity turned to include the receptionist in their private conversational circle. Stoner spoke before she had the chance to begin. 'Can you get me a decent room? Third floor? The front? Looking over the river?' Chastity glittered her teeth at the receptionist. Or maybe at Stoner. It's hard to tell with teeth.

Stoner extracted himself from Chastity's embrace and extracted his wallet from its hiding place, every inch the tourist. '*Guten tag.*'

'Good evening, sir. How may I help?' The German receptionist replied in perfect almost accent-free American, icing it with the special tang of condescension reserved for idiot Anglophones who believe they've mastered a proper language. 'A room? A suite, maybe? For you and your . . . lady friend?' The interrogatory pause was a thin sliver away from overt mockery.

Stoner smiled, an innocent abroad. 'A suite, yes. At the front. Good view. Anything to please the little lady.' His accent drifted from mid-west to mid-winter and his smile froze. 'And add a little courtesy. *Bitte.*' A flat tone, a flat gaze with ice. The receptionist was flustered, but only briefly. Maybe she remembered the postwar occupation, although given her age it seemed unlikely. She processed the room, handed over a key, then a second key, wondered whether Mr LaForge and . . . ah . . . Mrs LaForge required assistance with their luggage? Stoner revealed that his luggage would arrive later, in its own time and possibly before he checked out, airports being airports, that his lady companion was not his wife, that he was staying alone in the suite, that his guest would be leaving later. He smiled, relaxed. The receptionist refreshed the static, plastic, bland, blank face of her trade, along with an optional extra superior sneer. Stoner ignored her, disappeared the keys and swept the pair of them to the lounge, where women bearing drinks appeared, unobtrusively.

'Why's he here early?' Chastity clinked her glass against a bottle, companionably.

'Why didn't Ms Efficiency recognise you?' Stoner countered. 'You have a room here, yes?'

'Different receptionist. There's more than one, you know. Are you unfamiliar with hotels? Do you usually camp out in a park? Sleep under the stars, under hedges? With loose women? Sheep?'

Stoner walked to a corner table, excellent views of the room, of both doors. Pulled back a chair for his companion.

'All of those and many more. Just like you.' They sat companionably side by side, like a tourist couple in a tourist hotel. Held hands, clinked glasses. Spoke in their private bubble of quiet. Polite drinkers ignored them and watchers dismissed them.

Chastity gazed earnestly into Stoner's eyes. 'He's on the third floor.'

'I know. That's why I wanted a room on the third floor.'

'I know that. Why?'

'Which floor are you on?'

'First.'

'Ah. Windows.' Stoner sipped and nodded, knowingly.

'The rooms are air conditioned. The windows don't open.'

'Did you know that when you booked in?'

'The aircon, yes. The sealed windows, no.'

'Tricky.' Stoner radiated thirst and big tips; a waitress replenished glasses, brought a bottle for them to contemplate, should their enthusiasms run to dinner. 'Can you see his minders?'

'That's the thing. They're not minding him. They're watching elevators, stairs, doors. I can point out the four I've identified.'

Stoner shook his head. 'No need. They're looking for you, not me. Blonde woman travelling alone, not some blue-streaked brunette with a dribbling bloke in tow.'

'Blonde? Why blonde?'

'I don't think they're up to speed. Don't think their photos are current. Are you often brunette?'

'No. I'm a true blonde.'

'I bet. Let's save that for the Discovery Channel. Along with my boy scout curiosity over the blue streaks. Watch the guys.' He rose, lightly kissed the top of her head, and walked to the wide staircase. He mounted a half-dozen steps, stopped, paused, turned, walked back down the ground level and headed for the elevators. Stopped again, ran his hands through his pockets and walked rapidly to the washrooms, vanishing inside. Shortly he emerged, returned to his table and to Chastity, kissed her scalp once again, shook his head sadly, and sat. She raised a quizzical eyebrow.

'What was I going for? Have you got both room keys?'

She reached into her bag, discovered that she did indeed possess both keys, both cards, and laid them on the table between them. He took one. She smiled and patted his hand.

'Neat trick, Stoner. The world's first reverse pickpocket.'

'Not the first. Not by a long chalk. Good, huh?' He smiled a lust-filled smile.

'No one was interested in your star turn. A shame. That was an Oscar of a performance. You could be the next Matt Damon, *The Bourne Complacency*.'

'*Bourne Calamity*, more like. No one interested? OK, that's cool.' He got up again, apologised, waggled his retrieved key at her with a wink and left her sipping solo, attracting attention. She called the waitress, received a current newspaper and started a hunt for stories about the Angel of Death.

Stoner walked briskly up the stairs, a man with an evident purpose and no problems in the world. Found his room, entered and walked immediately to the balcony, stepped outside into the cool of the early evening air. The Rhine sped by, maybe a hundred metres away and across the road. Couples took the air, bicyclists bicycled, no one paid him any attention. He leaned backwards over the rail of the balcony, checked that the rooms on either side of his own were lit. They were. Both balcony doors were opened to the evening airs, also.

He turned, took the air with deep sighs and an appreciative expression, then returned inside, closing the door behind him and turning out the lights. He left the room, wedging the door as he did, and walked to the door of the adjacent suite to the right of his own, the room nearer to the lift. Knocked. Knocked again. It opened. The not-German, Herr Guertler, stood there. Behind him, a meal on a table, an empty tray by its side. A meal for one. Mostly eaten. A single bottle of wine, mostly drunk.

'Herr Guertler?' Stoner's accent was plainly regional. Guertler nodded with no trace of suspicion. 'You ordered another bottle of wine?' The German showed a little surprise, shook his head. He'd not ordered anything after his meal and Stoner was plainly not a wine waiter.

Stoner punched him hard and fast with all his strength and a complete follow-through; a puking blow to the gut, low down, dirty and irresistibly painful. The German doubled over, collecting a hard left cross to his temple for his trouble, and Stoner slammed him back into his room, tripped him, and kicked his falling head the moment before it reached the carpet. Guertler fell and lay still. Groaned. Moved his limbs, with no rhythm to their movement. No intelligence to the groans.

The room was a mirror image of Stoner's own. No one else there; a pair of unpacked cases, airline, carry-on size. A laptop was lit on the dressing table and toiletries were in the bathroom. All the comforts of home.

Stoner kicked his companion hard in the temple. Twice, then again. Bent down over him and unbuttoned his shirt, lifted him by the shoulders and stripped his upper body. Old scars, a decent level of musculature, nothing too remarkable.

He dropped the body again; the carpet removed all sound from the fall. Trousers next; the unconscious, dying man hadn't soiled himself in his final moments. Stoner offered a silent and insincere prayer of gratitude for this small mercy, lifted the failing body by its shoulders and dragged it to the bed, lifted it onto the sheets, laid it on its side in a decent approximation of a relaxed, sleeping posture, and pulled up the duvet.

Next, he hung the trousers and shirt, neatly next to the jacket, the coat, and above the shoes. Germanic neatness. No fingerprints nor recoverable trace. No blood, no shit, no noise nor smells. He checked the corpse for a pulse, for breath. Nothing. Checked out.

Stoner closed the balcony windows, switched off the lights, placed the remains of the meal back on its tray, parked the tray outside the door, hung the Do Not Disturb sign from the handle and checked his watch. Returned to his own room, washed, checked himself in the mirror, splashed a little of the hotel's aftershave onto his beard, locked up and returned to the bar.

Chastity smiled her least sincere smile at him. 'It wasn't the aliens, then?'

'The what?' Stoner glanced around. All was pretty much as he'd left it. 'Aliens?'

'You were gone so long that I was worried about you.' She leaned across the table and took his hand, gazed profoundly into his eyes. Anyone of a squeamish disposition would have looked away at that point; public nausea is poor form in a German restaurant. 'I was worried that the aliens had beamed you up. Happens all the time on the TV. So. You're back. What's the haps, my lover?'

Stoner maintained their shared fictional intimacy. 'All quiet. Comfy rooms, the quality rooms boast not only French windows that open but decent balconies. Ideal for young lovers to gaze with romantic intent upon the fast-moving waters of the mighty Rhine. Inspirational stuff.'

'Perfect for unexpected midnight visitations, then?'

'Exactly. What have you been doing, my pretty? Shining those razor-sharp fingernails, loading your secret brassiere rocket launchers?'

'No bra, small man. These precious babies support themselves.' She thrust her chest skywards and Stoner suffered a small lack of focus, as would any man at that point. Charity was watching every man but him. She disarmed her bosom.

'We're not being watched. You can stop staring now. And I sent my plan to mother. She acknowledged it.'

'Your mother? Your mother is involved in your killer games? Does Mallis know this?'

'My mother's dead. We chatter on Facebook, mostly. Everyone's dead there. It's Charm. You remember her?'

'You lot are too weird for words. No, I've not encountered Charm. Yet. You still use Facebook?'

'Uh-huh. So much traffic that no one could monitor it in real time, and we have a private code anyway. Even if you could read it – if you knew our Facebook IDs – you wouldn't have a clue what we're talking about. There y'go; I've told you a secret for free. Now we may as well do that wild sex as I'm gonna have to kill ya anyways.' She'd lapsed into a Deep South patois so insincere that any southern gentleman would have winced with pain on hearing it.

'My seas are dried up. Terror does this.' Stoner smiled and drank half of her remaining drink. 'What's the plan? Do I need a Facebook account to read it?'

'You've got one. Several, according to trusted sources.'

'Is nothing sacred? Hey, can we be Facebook friends?'

'Of course. I'll send you a request right now,' and she reached for her phone. Stoner stopped her.

'You do actually know a Facebook ID for me?'

'Bluesman One. Right?'

'Right. Who sold you that one?'

'It's too long a tale for right now. Later though, if we both survive the next couple of days.'

'OK. I live a life of constant anticipation. What's the plan? If Facebook knows about it, it's only fair that you share with me, no?'

'Yes. Tomorrow. I'll introduce myself to the mark at dinner – he's already booked a table for one – and invite myself to his room. He's a straight alpha male, so he'll simply drip at the chance. I'll dress up especially nice.'

'And his watchers?'

'They can follow if they're still with us. French windows and balconies work both ways. Your room is nearby?'

'Next door. I'm a light sleeper, so please be quiet about it. Do you actually need to bang him first? Is that a ritual I need to be aware of? If so, please be quiet, I'm also the jealous type.'

'Depends. Maybe, maybe not. It's the exciting potential that makes it so thrilling, don't you think?'

'No.'

'Are you drunk yet? You swill drink like a squaddie.'

'Takes years of selfless, dedicated practice. But no, I'm not drunk. Why?'

'I need a walk.'

'You need to eat something. You're trying to live on booze and ice cream. Noble in a teenager, tragic at our . . . at your age, perpetual youth though you are, of course.'

Chastity grinned at him. 'Walk first. Then food. Then you can carry on drinking and I can gaze at you with my famous death angel air of feminine superiority until you keel over.'

'You want to do something electronic away from the hotel.' A statement, not a question.

'Maybe I just want to hold your hand, stare into your deep eyes and appreciate the sweet aroma of the mighty Rhine. But yes; a little electronic confirmation.'

'Your mother? Didn't you just speak to her?'

'My life insurance agent. Book us a table for an hour's time. I need to walk alone; go have a scout around or whatever it is boy scouts do.'

Stoner did exactly that.

And almost exactly an hour later, they met again. The same restaurant, a better table, a table in a corner, ninety degrees to each other and covering the entire room as well as affording a decent view of the river. Having an alternative somewhere to aim the stare is often useful. Chastity was stunning to look at.

'I'm stunned, your beauty to behold,' said Stoner. 'You look hardly at all like a murderous assassin bitch from hell.'

'Really? How sweet of you. What do I look like?'

'Someone sinful. Every bishop's wet dream.'

'You have a fine turn of phrase sometimes, Mr Stoner. Thank you.'

'Grammar school education. A lot to be said for it. Taught me how to speak proper and shoot straight.'

'They taught marksmanship at your school? That is really progressive. I got domestic science and fingernailology. But maths too. You got guns at your school?'

'Army cadets. Play soldiers. Inspired me to become a real soldier.'

'You liked that?'

'I did.'

A waiter appeared. They placed orders in a confusion of languages. The waiter left.

Stoner poured for them both. Water. The wine breathed, rested in peace.

He passed Chastity's glass to her.

'You? Military?'

'Quakers.'

'Ah. The Society of Friends. Far more murderous.'

'You jest. But it is. SAS training is more friendly and more sympathetic than a Quaker college. The SAS doesn't have God and righteousness to beat you with. And the endless polite moderation and restraint are worse than gods and bullets at their worst.'

'My parents did have their god. I was an altar boy.'

'Beautiful!' Chastity clapped her hands.

'Yeah, yeah. It sort-of never went away. In the mil I got known as Father Jean.'

'That's cool. Why?'

'Jean The Confessor. Before we boldly went into really grim stuff the lads would come talk with me. Unload a little.'

'Did it help?'

'No idea. They died anyway, or they didn't. Lost a lot in some places. What got the troops down was the lack of recognition. Their families never knew how they died, or that they were heroes. No medals. No big parades on gun carriages. No political party time or TV twonks singing their songs or wringing their hands. That got to them more than the missions. They chose the work because they wanted to do it, but when they caught it in Beirut or Bulawayo doing something really worthwhile then their families and friends got told that they died in Iraq or Afghanland because we were never active in Beirut or Bulawayo. No one got told the truth of it. And regulars still get the praise for doing their jobs while the specials go unrewarded.'

'Except in heaven, Jean The Confessor?' Chastity watched her companion steadily.

'There is no heaven. You know that as well as I do.'

'Let's drink to that.' Chastity poured the good wine for them both. 'Why does this feel like the evening before a battle, real knights in armour stuff? Tomorrow we may die, all that jazz?'

'It does, doesn't it? It's not. It's just me. They also called me Jean Dark at one point.'

'Joan of Arc? That's a little literary for grunts, surely?'

'John Dark, not Jeanne d'Arc. It was the British Army not the Foreign Legion. It wasn't really a time for jokes. Towards the end. We did nothing but deniable jobs by that point, and that has to be *the* most thankless occupation. Then the unit got badly caught out, I did a very bad thing, and a very hard man in a very bad suit wearing wraparound shades and cool foot-wear came to see me in my own private hole in hell, and I went from being a spec to being a merc. A subtle shift. Pays better, though. No need to pretend you're doing it for queen and country any more. Makes it a lot easier.' Stoner's glass was empty. He refilled them both and sipped in silence. Sighed, looked up at his companion.

'Sorry, Chastity. It really is enough to make a guy love the blues and hate society.'

She smiled at him, gently, almost.

'Call me Chas. It's less formal, somehow.'

'Yeah. Tell me about the whole Chas Chas Chas scene? Do you all really look alike? Are you the interchangeable sisters?'

'Not really. If you saw us all together you'd see that we look pretty unalike side by side. Chas . . . Charm in particular. She's mother.'

'Your real mother?'

'Long gone. Likewise father. They were both good guys, made us what we are.'

'Bloody hell! Having three crazed killer daughters makes you a good guy?'

'Don't let your alpha male lack of understanding ruin your judgement, JJ. Dads are proud of their soldier sons, mothers too. Ours were proud of their girls; we girls are proud of each other. All for one and one for all is not a male preserve. Come on, you're more together, more grown up than that. You never fight with women soldiers?'

'No. Against them, sometimes.'

'Bet that was a bundle of fun for good wholesome Brit boys.' Chastity's expression was as grim as their shared mood.

'You learn fast. You hesitate the first time it's a woman in your sights, then she takes the shot, spins the knife, and you remember what happens to he who hesitates. You don't do it twice, even if you do get a second chance.

'Talk about yourself, Chas. I'm too familiar with me to be happy alone with myself, unless I've got a gun or a guitar in my hands. You say you guys are all different. First time I met you I thought you were Charity. Last time I met Charity I thought she was you. Gives a guy a headache.'

She stared steadily across the table at him.

'You know Charity's dying?'

Stoner swirled the wine in his glass. Raised it to eye level.

'Absent friends, then. I did wonder.'

'You've seen her naked?' Chastity looked down, as though willing the food to arrive, to provide a break in the conversation. The food duly arrived. Both parties were relieved, grateful even. They ate, drank, together in silence. Stoner broke it, finally.

'She is bloody fit. Body like a greyhound. Beautiful. Bald head and missing tits gives the game away a little. Respect for her. Lay down your weapons, Chas, let's toast her again. I'd take a bullet – have taken bullets – but when the reaper spreads tumours he's not playing the game.' His face shifted to a bleak landscape of its own. 'Doubt I could handle that. Fuck. To your sister!' He raised his glass again.

'Are those tears in your eyes, Jean-Jacques?'

'Yeah. Anger. Maybe rage. Soldiers go down fighting, not being eaten alive from within. Fuck!' He raised his glass again, drained and poured. 'How bad, and how long does she have?'

'Full remission. Could live a decade, two, or fail tomorrow. She cut out everything cut-outable. Now she thinks she's repellent to all men.'

'Not true.' Stoner met her eyes across the table, dry-eyed again, the two of them. 'Not true at all.'

'The chemo was bad for her. She wanted to die. But she wanted to beat it, too. Both at the same time. Made her very angry. Us too. Rage.'

'Good to have close family at a time like that.'

'Crucial. The work helped. Maybe.'

'The work? You make it sound like mission from God. You mean your killing people work?'

'From God? Told you you'd met Charm. She sometimes believes she is on exactly that mission. It . . .' she hesitated, sank her wine. Gazed out towards the German river as it flowed by in the dark. Stoner poured for them both, clinked the glasses, said nothing.

Chastity caught up with her thoughts once more.

'It changed everything. Not just Charity. Charm got more godly, more into music and spiritual shit. I shouldn't call it that. She has beliefs. We don't, Chas and me. We believe in our survival. Chas became so tired, exhausted really, that she couldn't handle the contracts – the wetwork. And after her surgery she couldn't face a man. Not like that.'

She stopped again.

'So I took over the wetwork. It's . . . wrecking. Wrecks your soul if you care. So I need to work hard to not care. You know all about that, Jean-Jacques.'

He nodded. 'Yeah. Makes us what we are. So you don't enjoy it, then? You pretend well.'

She shook her head. 'Maybe I do. Sometimes.' She paused again, as if reflecting. 'It helps. When Chas was struggling, I compensated by being brutal. When we had no gigs I'd go act the whore and pick up fat, old, dirty married men and beat the living shit out of them when they aimed their dicks at me. It works. They never report it. Violence is addictive.'

'But it escalates.'

'It does. And then you need to stop. Can't kill marks for free. Bad for business. And not one of the cheap sad bastards I beat up went to the cops. Guilt is good. You'd know that, being a Papist deviant. Why am I telling you all this? If I say much more I'll have to kill you.'

'If you're going to kill me anyway – and why not? – can we

do the wild sex thing first?' Stoner worked to break her mood. Chastity wasn't easily distracted.

'You've seen Chas with her kit off. You really OK with it?' Chastity watched him. 'You're the first guy . . . as far as I know . . . the only guy she's got naked with since the surgery who wasn't actually a surgeon. It's that decision of hers, her judgement, which lets me relax a little with you. She stopped me killing you.' Chastity appeared transfixed by her wine glass.

'She did?'

'She did. I'd laid charges at your club, remote detonators. The full thing.'

'She stopped you? How? Told you I was a cool and groovy guy with great taste in women?'

'She visited you there. Stayed with you there.'

Stoner met her gaze across the table. 'You were there? Watching? In the club?'

'Calm down, big boy. No. She has a trace on her phone. I was outside. She buzzed me before she left you. Not seen her so easy with herself or with a guy for ages. Were you just playing with her?'

'Not in the sense you mean, lady. She's one unique woman. She is who she is.' His tone softened. 'Like you. Do we need to fight now? Are you never tired of fighting? Do you never stop, never rest?'

Chastity stood, surveyed the tired, cold table, flagged a waiter. The service in German hotel restaurants is excellent and prompt. She asked the waiter to put the bill onto Stoner's room, spelling out his alias and adding the room number, then reached into a mysterious hidden place within her dress, produced a bright euro note with a large number on it, dropped it to the table and reached for Stoner's hand. Pulled him to his feet. The waiter drew back her chair, then Stoner's chair, and appeared ready to serenade their departure, such was the power of the number on the euro note before him.

*

207

'Keycard.' They stood outside Stoner's room. The room service tray from the adjacent suite had vanished, German hotel service being predictably fine. Stoner passed the card to Chastity, saying nothing at all. The least said, the least to regret later. She spoke again. 'Is the room clean?'

'No reason for it to be otherwise.' Stoner's tone – neutral. Chastity unlocked the door, he entered before her, casually. No surprises. He strode to the French window, stepped out into the night. Returned to the room, turned to close the window and its heavy curtains, turned again to find his dinner companion standing with her back to him, her clothes entirely removed and neatly hung, her shoes parallel parked by the door. She was very still.

'I should frisk you. Check you for hidden weaponry.' He removed his boots and walked quietly to the door, positioning his own footwear next to her own. Turned back. She was still naked, still holding her back to him. He hung his jacket, approached her. Hesitated. Backed away.

'You have a great arse. Swimmer's arse. Great back, shoulders. One hundred percent in the rearview beauty contest. Care to turn round, beauty queen?'

'Care to turn me around yourself, Mr Stoner?'

'Not without a Kevlar vest and bulletproof pants, if that's all the same to you. Curiosity does bad things to cats, remember, and they have nine lives to learn from. I don't.'

She turned. He smiled. Her hands were empty. She held them up, palms open. 'Do I pass the test? Can you undress yourself?'

'If I must.' He proved it, quickly and neatly, and stood before her, out of reach.

'You don't trust me?' She smiled. 'You can. No need to run away. Stay and fight another day.' She closed the distance between them until her breasts were resting against his body.

'You say that to them all? All the marks?'

'Oh fuck off.' She spun on the balls of her feet and bounded to the bed, dived precisely onto the centre of it. Turned, sat, facing him. 'Your mind elsewhere?' She waved a hand at his obvious lack of arousal. 'Thinking of someone else? Your black whore? Your shipshape officer? Charity? A motorcycle?'

'If I thought of them I'd have a hard-on.' Stoner lifted his cock, let it fall back. 'I'm thinking only of tomorrow. I'd like to be alive this time tomorrow. And the next day, given the choice. I'm attached to my life, so forth.'

Chastity pouted theatrically, crossed her legs. 'I thought you military types craved danger. Especially when the first flush of youth has passed you by.'

Stoner walked slowly to the bed. Very slowly. She uncrossed her legs, at exactly the same pace as he walked. He stopped. Held her gaze. Or she held his, it was tough to tell. A steady, slow, inexorable arousal occurred between them. She spread her legs, and he took a single further step. The last step. The hairless lips of her sex parted with a soft but entirely audible sigh, labia majora and minora swelling slightly in anticipation; she was plainly ready to receive him. His eyes dropped from her face to his cock's resting place between her parted pink lips, which were mingling their own fluids and his own with immortal enthusiasm for the imminent penetration. Their shared statuary tableau was broken as she reached for him.

And he gently pushed her hand away. No violence, no real force. With affection, if anything. Chastity laid back and closed her eyes. 'A man of steel.' There was plain regret in her voice. 'Just a survival instinct, I suppose. Was it something I said?'

'Shut up.' Stoner was beyond courtesy, and sank to his knees between her thighs, spreading them as far as they would go, which was impressively wide, the wide legs of a seasoned swimmer. He wrapped one of his arms around each of her legs, hoisting her into the perfect position for his mouth, and sank into her. No gentle probing; tongue into her as far as it could, his top lip and the base of his nose pushing her clit from side to side as he worked with his tongue, lips and teeth. She groaned, hauled him to her with all the power of her swimmer's legs and shook beneath him.

He surfaced, came up for air, looked up her shuddering body. Chastity had grasped her breasts with her hands, was squeezing them together. Her eyes were tight shut, her mouth open as wide as her cunt, and breathing as hard as if she were swimming in a race. He dived to her again, surfaced again, dived again, and she started to climax, noisily, bouncing against him and up from the bed in her pleasure. She grabbed his head, first pulling it into her as she came, then pushing it away. He resisted, holding his face hard between her legs. She rolled to her side; he rolled with her, clamped. She rolled the other way, growling and panting at the same time in her series of spasms, and he pulled his face away at last, and sank first one, then both of his thumbs into her arse. She shrieked then, and banged the mattress with both arms and shoved him away with her legs. Stoner lost his balance and fell to the floor in a tangle of duvet. Sat up.

Chastity rolled to her side, pulled her legs up and squinted at him. Stoner remained where he was, face as blank of expression as he could make it.

'Potato,' she said, distinctly.

'OK.' Stoner maintained his air of monkish self-control. It was, very visibly, a struggle.

'When I was younger I called them potatoes.'

'OK. Called what potatoes?'

'Orgasms. I only had orgasms with myself, sometimes with Chas . . . with Charm. And I called them potatoes. We could discuss them over supper.'

'Who? You and Charm or you and me? You want more to eat? I'll need a decent wash. That's the thing with beards. They stink of pussy for days unless you wash a lot.'

Chastity smiled at him, a gentle and honest smile. Probably

the first she'd shown him. 'I expect there's something I should do for you first?'

Stoner shook his head. 'No need. A teenager I'm not. That was pretty . . . draining, to be honest. And . . . great for me. Hope it was as good as it looked. Sounded.' He smiled back at her. 'Felt. Tasted. I'll make some . . . tea? Would you like tea, coffee, something with . . . ah . . . more bite?'

She laughed out loud, rolled from the bed and walked like the athlete she was to inspect the hotel's refreshment facilities. 'Tea. They have a whole range of teas. How very English. For Germans.'

Stoner rose to his feet and walked towards the bathroom. Chastity stopped him, a hand on his chest. 'No need to wash. I'll share your memories for tonight. We'll clean up in the morning, make like animals 'til then. OK?'

He stood behind her, reached around her and squeezed her breasts gently. She leaned back into him. Then stood up straight. 'Tea. English.'

'Talk to me.' Stoner lay beside her, tea steaming to itself either side of their shared bed. 'Do you need to kill me now?' He smiled and brushed her hair from her face.

'Don't joke, JJ.' She reached between them, found his cock and squeezed it. He wheezed a little. Held her hand still.

'Steady now.'

'Do we need to do the analysis thing? Do we? Do I need to explain what a fuck-up I am and how my childhood was a disaster, with interfering relatives and catastrophic relationships, broken shit marriages, abortions and that shit?'

'Only if you want. We can just lie here and sing songs at each other in the dark if you like. Songs by The Beatles are best, everybody knows them all. My favourite is . . .' She interrupted, resting a finger against his lips.

'"Norwegian Wood", I bet?'

'"Paperback Writer".'

211

She laughed softly. 'Yeah, I bet.'

'You can't bet twice. You already lost the first bet.' He kissed her forehead.

'A kiss! How romantic!' She was playing with him, they were both aware of it. 'Our first kiss.'

'And the last?' Stoner's fingers had walked down her body and were playing with her clit and the wet folds of her lips again. She squeezed her thighs around his hand and held it still.

'No. I hope not. But there is no trust in this world, so we don't know. No truth.'

'Oh come along. Wasn't that good for you? Don't you want to do it again?'

'I'm very fucked up, JJ. More than you know.'

'No shit, Sherlock. You mean that the crazy killer psycho bitch routine isn't an act? Not a persona? That it's really the real you? Really?' He extracted his hand and rolled onto his back. The tea had cooled. He drank it off as though it were water, which it mostly was.

'Did you notice my lips? Pussy lips?'

'A fine array. Healthy. In the pink.'

'Thank you. They're uneven.'

'So? Everybody's are. I don't think there's a beauty contest for cunt lips. They come in all shapes and sizes.'

'You speak from experience. Of course you do. The average man screws less than four women.'

'Really?' Stoner wondered where the conversation was heading. 'That's a quiet evening in a music club, after hours. If you want it. They must have peculiar lives, these average men. What do they do with their time?' He stopped. 'I'm sorry, Chastity. Don't mean to be flippant. What about your lady lips? It's not as if you stare at them every time you look in a mirror.'

'Done with a brush.'

'What was? You've had them painted? Most girls make do with photographs.'

'He raped me with a brush.'

'OK.'

'A hair brush.'

'OK.'

'The sort with the metal bristles.'

'Ouch. Ouch seems a little inadequate. Who did this?'

'Two of his friends watched.'

'This gets better and better.' He shook his head slowly. 'Who?'

'The first man who fucked me.'

'Good choice. You have a knack, plainly. You killed him?'

'With the brush. Straight into an eye.' She was breathing hard. 'Then the other eye.'

'Jesus.'

'No divine intervention. Then I pushed it into his mouth – he was screaming a lot – and smacked it into his spine, where it's easy, behind the throat.'

'That would do it. Jesus wept, Chas. How old were you? What did his friends do?' Stoner had rolled over, propped himself on an elbow and was staring at his companion.

'Fifteenth birthday. One of his friends puked, the other ran and called the cops.'

'I think I need a lie down.'

'You are lying down.' She regarded him as though he was a cretin. Her breathing had slowed to normal. 'You're a lousy audience.'

'Lack of practice. What happened next? The cops?'

'It's a bit hazy. It was a while ago. It was very frantic.' She paused, thoughts plainly swirling together with memories. 'His friend – the puke – tried to pull me off little Romeo. I shoved him away and stood there with blood running down my legs and all over my hands and face. Yelling. Either he fell down or I knocked him down, because when the plods arrived I was sitting on his chest yelling; "Do you want it, do you want some of this?" over and over. When they pulled me off him, off the puke, about a pint of blood dropped out of me all over him and the cops, and they were all puking then. Must have given their forensics a bit of grief.'

'The courts? Self-defence, stuff like that, I suppose.'

'Juvie stuff. I was a minor and my snatch was shredded. I passed out from the bleeding. Needed transfusing. But yeah, justifiable homicide. I was in care for a time. But by the time the psych hearings and social work and religious nonsense were under way I was calm again, pussy was whole again and I was missing my sisters, so they convinced themselves that I was no risk to society and I got away home.'

'Your parents? What did they. . . I can't picture that scene at all.'

'I don't talk about them. They're dead. They always were. For me. They were . . .' she stopped for a moment, closed her eyes and released a huge breath. 'They were Charm's parents. I won't talk about them, so don't push. OK?' The steel in her stare pushed him away.

'Yeah. Fine. Talk about what you want to talk about, Chas.'

'Water?'

'For two.'

Chastity bounced back onto the mattress and handed over another glass of water. 'Cool stuff, huh? Do we start singing Beatles ballads yet?'

Stoner admired her musculature. 'If that's what you want.'

'Whatever. I'm horny.' She bounced around some more.

'Talking about getting raped with a hairbrush makes you horny? That's freaky.'

'Talking about killing that stupid fuck makes me horny.' She bounced onto her back, spread her legs and planted Stoner's hand between them. 'Do a girl a favour, mister.'

He leaned over to kiss her, but she rolled her face away from his. The kiss landed on her cheek. She placed her own hand over his, squeezed it and guided his fingers onto her and into her. And as her skin deepened into red and her breathing caught in her throat, she pulled her two hands around his head, arched her back clear of the mattress and held his face between her breasts. She groaned as she shook, groaned again and fell back against the bed, eyes screwed shut. Pushed him away. He said nothing, watched her face as her colour fell to normal and her breathing eased. Once again, as her eyes opened, she reached for his cock, and once again he caught her hand.

'It's OK. I'm fine.'

She looked steadily into his eyes, disbelief on show.

Stoner shook his head lightly, and raised a smile. 'Your pleasure is my pleasure. Really. And doesn't that sound stupid?'

She nodded. 'It does.'

'It's true, though. Wouldn't it be cool if this could be a night of truths?'

'It can.'

'It can't. We're both liars. We couldn't be here if we weren't.'

Chastity planted a dry kiss on his forehead. 'You need something. I'd like that.'

'And yeah, yeah, we can make shared jokes about how I'm already too old to die young, and then you'd stab me in the eye with your hairbrush while I'm revelling in the fuck of a lifetime.'

'I don't have a hairbrush with me.'

'Borrow mine. Or you'd just wait until we're somewhere else, which would be worse.'

'You're joking, right?' She stared into his eyes.

'Not really. And . . .' He stopped again. 'This is going to sound like shit, but . . . I get quite enough. And it gets tiring sometimes. A night of truths? OK. I'm completely happy to spend the whole of it having you come as often as you want in whatever way you want. That means more to me than . . . oh . . . another fuck. Why d'you tell me you've killed all your lovers? Jesus. It's hard to be lighthearted about that.'

'I didn't say that, Stoner. I said I killed every man who's fucked me.'

'Same thing, babe. Same thing.'

'Not so.'

'Yeah?'

'Yeah. Feel better now? Feel like getting into something good?'

'No.'

14

BRAND NEW DAY

A voice breathed into his ear. 'Morning, glory.' A gentle laugh accompanied it. Stoner snapped awake, fully awake. His eyes remained closed, his breathing steady. He knew where he was. Sleep – a remarkably deep sleep, of the sort he'd not experienced in a long while, not since Lissa – had departed, had run away giggling, leaving him hard aroused and unable to focus upon much apart from the steady rhythm of the hand working him between his legs.

He lifted his upper body from the bed, opened his eyes and took stock of the proceedings below. It looked good and it felt good, the hand was expert. Chastity was sitting on the floor on his side of the bed, and she was smiling. Her hand maintained its steady rhythm, he was as hard as he could ever remember being, as hard as a teenager. He began to roll towards her, but she shook her head.

'Lie back, soldier. Think of England.'

'I can think of nothing else.'

'You lie.'

'I lie.' He sighed, reached behind him and bunched pillows beneath his head, the better to observe.

'Feel OK?' Chastity's grip on her rhythm faltered not at all. 'How long do you hold out?'

'For England? For ever. I am everlasting, me.'

'Hmm. Doesn't look that way. The clouds and the rain appear imminent.'

'Trust me.' He sighed. His rigidity, his sexual tension eased. 'He's a trooper, always bows to royalty.' He sighed again.

'He needs to be strong. He needs to be sure. Has he been tested? Is he loyal and true?'

Stoner beamed at her. 'Tested in more ways than you can imagine.'

'I doubt that. But he is looking chipper again.'

'At your service, ma'am. However, and speaking on his behalf because he is an organ who prefers to be seen and not heard, I must share with you that he is perfectly content with his current situation. No advancement is required at this time. No insertions nor elevations. He thanks you for your interest – as do I, your humble servant.'

'You do talk some shit, Jean-Jacques. This thing looks like a dick to me, not a ventriloquist's dummy.'

'Ma'am. Humble Dick and I are at your command. What time is it?'

'You seriously want to know what the time is?'

'Just making conversation. You should also be getting something from this interaction. Looks like rain.'

She laughed, slapped his cock hard. He rolled his eyes theatrically and groaned, equally theatrically. 'More please. Can we have breakfast soon?'

She laughed again, slapped him again. His eyes were closed. No words now. She slapped him again, and again, and again. His head fell from the pillow and his arms spreadeagled at his sides. He was silent, focus targeted on a single area of his body. A whole world in a few inches. She pulled his foreskin back as far as it would pull, and then a little more and raked her fingernails – short, sharp fingernails – down him. He was done. Pumped hard, and again. And then again. Relaxed, quite suddenly. Lay there.

He smiled. 'Well. Hey.'

Chastity rose to her feet with the easy grace of the supremely fit, leaned over him and dragged her fingernails across the pool on his stomach.

'You done?' She smiled, but her smile, like his passion, had passed its peak.

'I'm done. Lots to do.' Stoner caught her hand, held it. She did not pull it away, though her eyes drifted from his.

'Yes. You are an odd one, Jean-Jacques.'

'Not to me. I'm the only one I've got. Let's not have an oddness contest, huh?'

'What happened to your impressive seduction technique? Your endless need for that wild sex?'

'I want to live longer. Simple.'

'You really believe I'd kill you?'

'Yes.'

'That's it? Yes? That's all?'

'If you want to, you will. I'd prefer that you didn't. Nothing complex in that. The world is packed with pussy. If one's unavailable, there are a thousand more. OK. Maybe a hundred. A few dozen. Here and there. You kill the guys who fuck you? That's fine with me. I'll fuck with someone else.'

'You still believe I'd kill you? After spending the night here?'

'Yes. Absolutely yes. There are a few things worth risking my life for; a fuck is not one of them. Half the world wants fucking; never any need to stick it where it's not wanted.'

'And if I wanted you to?' She smiled, but her tone was harder than her words.

'I'd need to believe that and I'd need to believe in the consequences. I'm forty-two, I'd like to see next year. What time is it? Really?'

'Guess.'

'Oh, eight-seventeen.'

'Oh, eight-ten. I thought you strong silent military men had dead accurate internal clocks.' She smiled again, walked to the bathroom.

'You read too many books.' Stoner sat up, mopped himself with the sheet, fumbled it into a bundle and tossed it to the floor. Walked to the windows, opened them and stood on the balcony, nude, watching the scene outside. After a few minutes, Chastity joined him.

'You're an exhibitionist too . . .' her voice trailed away. The road outside was closed by a silent ambulance and two police cars.

Stoner led the way back into the room.

'Do you think I can get a full English?' he wondered.

They stood together, holding hands like lovers do, waiting until the receptionist came to them. She was the same receptionist who had booked Stoner into the hotel on the previous day, but appeared distracted.

'I want to extend my stay. Two more nights.' Stoner spoke polite and faintly formal German. 'And my . . . friend would like to check out. No need for you to return her passport; she'll be staying with me. In my room.' His tone suggested mild embarrassment, no more than that. The receptionist made no comment, assaulted the hotel's computer system with a hatred born of long familiarity, and produced an invoice for Chastity to sign. Chastity signed it.

'What's going on?' A lift door slid open, two policemen and a medical man in whites emerged, the latter pushing a wheeled stretcher. The receptionist followed the party with her eyes.

'There's been an accident. One of the guests . . . one of the guests has been taken ill.'

Stoner shrugged. 'Happens to us all. Risky places, hotels. Can you have my friend's luggage shifted to my room?' Once again holding hands, Chastity and Stoner walked through to breakfast, following the medical melee as the ambulance loaded, lit lights but sounded no sirens in silent chorus with the police cars and left.

'Not in a hurry,' Chastity remarked as Stoner pondered his next meal. 'Either nothing serious or too late for treatment. Judging by the plods, it's the latter.'

Stoner ordered for them both.

'You feeding the five thousand, or something? No two humans could eat all that.'

'Condemned man. Hearty breakfast. Coffee?' He poured for them both.

'Meaning what?' She leaned back in her chair, gestured with the coffee. 'OK. Tell me.'

'Watch everyone.' Stoner was already following his own instructions.

'I am. Talk.'

'That was Guertler.'

'Talk some more. You know this how, exactly?'

'I want to see whether you've been recognised, and if so by whom. Oh good, here comes the food.' A waiter danced attention around them, mountains of food and rivers of drinks descended. Chastity's silence impressed them both. She cut into her eggs Benedict with the ease of decent practice, wasting none of the yolk.

'Any signs, good or the other thing?' She looked around as she ate, exactly as innocent diners behave.

'Nope. No sign of the enemy.' Stoner chewed, steadily.

'How did you kill him? Why? Do we have a problem, you and me?'

'My foot slipped. More than once. So far removed from your own famous MO that you should be above suspicion from any nearby professionals. And you told them that you were taking the hit this evening, I think. Hence the lack of interest.' He chewed, reflectively. 'The sausage is outstanding. You just cannot beat the Germans when it comes to sausage.' He poured more coffee for them both.

'I told who, exactly?'

'Only you know that. Who did you tell?'

'My mother. And she's dead. Not easy to trace.'

'On Facebook?'

'Yes. Why . . . Are you trying to pull some stunt, Stoner? Are you contracted?' She pushed two forks together and twisted their tines out of shape. 'When . . . last evening when you went to . . . what was it? . . . to check your room? You do work fast. And you're very cold. Cold about killing.' She looked at him with a lover's rapt attention. Or the attention of a botanist examining an orchid. 'The sex was just a distraction? An alibi?'

'Just so. I hated every minute of it. Would rather shag myself with a pineapple.' They both creased into laughter, muffled, like lovers do. Reached across the table and held hands again, like lovers do. A waiter refilled the coffee, evidently entertained by their overflowing delight.

'Jean-Jacques?' She was suddenly serious. 'Are we on the same side, in the same team, playing the same game? Or are you doing something else? Is this just another game for you?'

'Have we reached the sudden fatal honesty moment? Do we declare a truce now? Tell only the truth?'

'I didn't know we were at war.'

'Everyone's at war.' Stoner looked suddenly ancient. 'Everybody lies. Everybody dies. And sometimes they even lie about that. You know what I mean, Chas. You more than anyone. You get your rocks off by killing people.'

'You're confusing me with my sister. With Charity. It's probably the blue streaks.'

'Not so. I am one hundred percent unconfused. So should you be. I came here to be helpful. I am being helpful. Do you need me to explain?'

'Do you really feel nothing when you kill someone?'

'Someone like Guertler? No. Nothing.'

'He'd done nothing to you. You really aren't under contract to kill him?'

'No. I told you, I don't contract. Not any more. It wrecks

your head. You know that. You're insane. Pretty much.'

'Gosh and golly thank you. Nicest thing you've said all morning.'

'Just honest. I can do respect as well if you like.' Stoner spread conserves onto fresh toast. 'Finished with the breakfast?'

Chastity said nothing.

'We've a long walk ahead, lots of exercise, so if you need to stoke up with the carbs, now is the time.'

'Man of mystery, Mr Stoner. Long walks? Healthy exercise? How so?'

'We're the hot news in the hotel today. Hardly any of the staff know of Herr Guertler's untimely demise, so they're busy gossiping about our blossoming romance, teenage passion in the over-forties. That kind of thing. We must not disappoint. I'm going to the desk to ask about train times for the Drachensfels castle, *schloss*, whatever the damn thing is.'

'What thing?'

'The castley thing on the hill. Keep up. You're supposed to be smart.'

'I'm way under forty, too, so don't go pedantic on me, lover boy. Why did you kill him? Why didn't you tell me?'

'You really can't work it out? Sweet thing . . .' Stoner reached across the wreckage of breakfast and took both her hands in one of his. He smiled, a secret lover's secret smile.

Chastity smiled back, professionally, musing. 'You wanted to look for watchers? You think I'm being watched? You wanted me to look all wide-eyed and innocent in case of expert spotters spotting me and identifying me, despite the groovy new hair and wide-eyed innocence?'

'Good so far. And I wanted to see who was following who. Guertler had protection. It vanished after you contacted your mother – I wonder why and where to. His team is gone. I've not seen them in the lobby or through the windows. So they got the message – even though they showed no sign of recognising you. The watchers' plan was the same as in Israel and in Slovenia. They'd be waiting for you when you made the hit.'

'You're forgiven. What now?'

'If we pack our bags and leave immediately then the police as well as your own fan club will be after us. We're going to do the young – in your case at any rate – lovers bit, and when the police question us – as they will – we can act all baffled, helpful but no help at all. Looks like innocence to a policeman, that sort of thing.'

'Why will they question us? You think they'll grill every guest? Doesn't seem very German.'

'It's entirely German. In any case, Guertler's room is next door to mine – to ours, my lady.'

'Fuck.'

'Not until you sign a peace accord. Until that moment, your virginity . . . your honour, is safe. Let's go do tourist things. Maybe ice cream afterwards if you're very good.'

'How come you know all about the tourist stuff? You've been here before?'

'It's called research.' Stoner grinned and stood up.

'You had it all planned before you got here? Impressed, I am.'

'Nope. All busked. Not my preferred method of operation but needs must and all that. I'd not understood before that whoever is shadowing you is privy to your comms. As you so rightly said, Facebook is utterly secure in realtime; even the NSA can't watch every comment all the time. Messages between you and your . . . mum have no keywords to trigger ECHELON, you being a pro, so forth, so someone, some actual person, must be telling the black hats what you're up to.'

'Elementary. Clear thinking, JJ. Who's telling who?'

'JJ? We're friends again?'

'Always and forever.' She propelled him towards the door. 'Your thinking – and the puzzles – make a lot of sense. And not

just because we should stay a while to demonstrate our innocence and endless, boundless passion.'

'No?'

'No. There's a second target, and he's due to arrive soon.
I've no intention of leaving. Not yet. You've made yourself
multiply useful just by being here. A girl could hardly ask for
better camouflage than your notably upstanding self.' She
grinned with sudden, genuine delight. 'So let's make like tourists and go grab hats and coats and crampons . . .'

'It's summer. We'll travel as we are. They . . . *someone*, will
be along to search the room very soon, if they've not done it
already. Wouldn't do to interrupt them.'

'Mr LaForge.' The German detective radiated charm and efficiency. 'And Fraulein Weise. Can you help me with my
enquiries?' His English was excellent.

Stoner glanced at the proffered identification.

'Of course. Can we freshen up first? It's hot out there! Ten
minutes, then back here . . .' he gestured vaguely around him
at the hotel's reception. 'Or in the bar?'

The German smiled. 'The bar. In a quarter hour. There's no
rush, just some questions I need to ask you.'

'Do you want our passports? They're with the desk.' Stoner
was ploddingly helpful.

'Of course. In one quarter hour. The bar.' The German was
polite, but plainly had no expectation of intelligence from the
Englishman. He spoke in German to Chastity, who replied in
English, suggesting that as her companion was English it
would be polite to discuss him in his own language. She was
as glacial as she was fluent. The detective bowed, amused.

'An accident. The guest in the suite next to your own, Mr
LaForge, suffered an accident last evening. Can you tell me
where you were last evening?'

'Here.' Stoner gestured around them. 'Here. We ate in the

restaurant, drank in the bar. Retired quite late, I think. You can get the bar tab, I expect. What's the problem?' He was confident, assured, vaguely irritated. 'I don't think I heard anything last night. Good quiet rooms, no music or TV. You disturbed at all?' He included Chastity in their conversation. 'Ms Weise spent the evening and the entire night with me. The hotel moved her luggage into . . .'

'Yes. So I understand.' The detective was plainly losing interest.

'What sort of accident?' Chastity appeared to be as interested as the detective, and looked around, catching the eye of a bar waiter. 'Is he OK? She?'

'Dead, I'm afraid,' the detective was watching her now. 'Suffered some kind of attack.'

'Oh, a heart attack. Poor fellow. Did he call out for assistance, or something? I didn't hear a thing. But then I wasn't listening. And I'm not a nurse.' She ordered two coffees, large, two pastries, larger. 'I can't help you. Is that all? Can we enjoy our stay now? Our holiday?'

Stoner sat back and enjoyed the performance. The detective turned back to him and asked how long he planned to stay, was apparently satisfied with the answer, rose, bowed courteously, and left them.

Chastity busied herself with the pastry. 'Two of dead boy's minders are on the terrace. They look a little stressed.'

Stoner nodded, dipped a biscuit into his coffee. 'They'll be wondering how to get paid, I bet. Wonder why they're still here and in the open. They can't expect you to appear in all your best blonde finery and do a little Here I Am dance, surely? And they'll know that Guertler wasn't killed by a woman. Not on her own at any rate.'

'How so? How did you kill him?'

'Kicked him in the head a few times. Their concern will be that I also lifted him onto the bed. He was a big guy; a woman would have struggled on her own. I made it plain that he was lifted, not dragged. Real he-man stuff; he was not a light-weight. You couldn't have done it. Not without leaving signs of the effort. Maybe a crane.'

'You said he was Dutch, not Deutsch?'

'Yep. He was Dutch last time I was aware of him.'

'Did he recognise you?'

'Don't think so. In any case it hardly matters. He's dead.'

'I'd wondered whether he'd clocked you in the lobby, reported that.'

'Your paranoia is impressive, Chas, even to this paranoiac. Dead men hold no fears for the living. Reported to whom, in any case? I have no idea what he was doing here – do you? Do you care when you're contracted? Do you care what the tar-get's actually doing and who they are?'

'It's all just detail, isn't it? Where the devil is, so forth.'

And then she stopped short. Her eyes widened and she shifted her focus to the ruins of the sweet pastry. 'Order another coffee or a spirit or something.'

Stoner raised a hand, caught a waitress, ordered. Chastity smiled at him, a secret lover's smile. Reached for his hand and held it.

'Marriage?' Stoner caught her mood. 'You've decided that if we marry I can fuck you and survive?' He gazed into her eyes, establishing a small lovers' circle of privacy – hard to ignore; the other diners looked away, left them to it.

'In the lobby, behind you.' Chastity looked down at their hands, caressed the back of his. Stoner said nothing, did not lift his attention from her.

'There's a man I know from the Palestinian up-fuck. Israeli Arab, Israeli security.' She paused to sip coffee, chew sweet pastry.

'He recognised you? Does he know you with your cunning disguise as a human female? Or a brunette?'

'Don't know. He's seen me . . . once I think . . . as a brunette, but less the tasteful blue streaks. And the hair was a lot shorter then than now. Called Kahlil. Identified me as a suspect in the desert hit.'

'And let you go? That's . . . unprofessional, and seriously unlike any Israeli I've known. Seriously.'

'He was the lover of the guy who gave me a lift out of the desert. Guest. Simeon Guest.'

'An alias so obvious it's probably his real name. Lovers? OK. Your lover? On your deathwish list?'

'No. I ran before our date. You rescued me, knight in armour most shiny.'

'You had a date? Impressive.'

'What's he doing here? I couldn't get a handle on what they were up to in Israel, and now he pops up again. Stop arsing about, Stoner, this guy's heavy.'

Stoner displayed the amusement he felt. 'Heavy compared to who, exactly? To you? To the Angel of Death herself? I doubt that. Compared to me? I doubt he can bend the strings of a Stratocaster as well as I can, and that's all that really matters.'

'You're a fucking idiot.'

'True. My only concern is that you sound worried. There's never a need for that. Almost never.'

'Go take a walk. Take a leak. Go have a look at the guy. He's the only Arab in the lobby. Oh. Fuck. No he's not. There's a stack of them. What the fuck is going on here?'

Stoner stood, brushed crumbs from his legs, glanced around. 'What's he wearing? Blonde wig? Funny hat? Joke bow tie? Give me a clue.'

She did. He left, walked into the lobby, and was immediately intercepted by the German detective who had questioned them earlier.

'Are you leaving, Mr LaForge?' The question, delivered in English, seemed innocent enough. Stoner smiled and shook his head.

'The bathroom. Why?'

'We have some distinguished guests. Arriving here from Israel. They have their own security, and may wish to ask you questions.'

'Because I have the room next door to the dead guy? The heart attack?'

'Exactly so.'

'Don't think I ever saw him. Was he with them? He was an Arab? An Israeli?' Stoner gestured at the small crowd, their luggage and their confusion.

'Known to them, certainly.'

Stoner raised his eyebrows. 'Curious.'

'Exactly so.'

'Am I under some suspicion?' Stoner's genuine amusement was plain, and plainly genuine. 'Is it OK if my friend and I take a swim in the pool? You can observe if you like. I bet she looks wonderful in a swimsuit.'

'Of course!' The detective dismissed all and any concerns, expansively. 'I think our Israeli friends are just being cautious.'

'Jews in Germany being cautious? Surely not. Heart attacks are the scourge of our age. Too much soft living and hard eating. Not enough exercise.' Stoner excused himself and headed for a restroom, returning to his shared table after a suitable interval.

'We're going for a swim.'

'We are?'

'We are. The nice policeman and his Israeli friends may want to question me. How sweet is that?'

'How sweet . . . How sound is your passport? Your papers?'

'Perfect. Genuine. Total cover. Unless they're looking for a George LaForge, in which case I'm shafted with a broom handle.'

'George? Darling!' She beamed at the detective, who was suddenly at their side.

'Fraulein Weise, Mr LaForge.' He was on the verge of an

announcement. 'There is no further need for you to be concerned.'

Stoner beamed in parallel with Chastity.

'I wasn't concerned, detective. Should I be?'

Chastity rattled off a fast stream of German. It sounded like anti-aircraft fire. The detective bowed.

'My English fails me a little. Our Israeli colleagues will not need to take up your time with questions.' He smiled again.

'Just as well. Let's hope heart attacks aren't contagious. Tell them to avoid the fatty meat. Especially the sausage. Hardens the arteries.' Stoner savoured the moment, squeezed Chastity's arm. 'Swim? Bracing sex in the pool?'

She thumped him on his arm. The German detective merely appeared bewildered. They laughed softly, privately, together and headed for the elevators, hugging like lovers. Doors closed behind them.

'You saw him?' Chastity was all calm.

'Yes. Cool guy.'

'You know him?'

'No. And before you ask, I worked a lot in the Middle East. Know lots of the spooks to nod to. But there are a lot of spooks in the Middle East. Lots. Nasty lots. Efficient lots. You say this guy made you for a suspect? And let you go? That's one cool guy. He'll recognise you. Probably. What's your passport photo look like?'

'Like someone else of the same name.'

'Weise? How solid is the workname? Used it before?'

'Only as a smokescreen. Not carried by me, but Ms Weise has been to several Euro lands, never on a kill job. Done courier work.'

'No end to her talent.'

'You think he'll make me here?'

'Bank on it. If not, you've got a bonus extra life.'

They entered Stoner's room, closed the door, chatted for the benefit of any newly installed uninvited audience about the heart attack, about their new-found passion, love and swimming, while Chastity produced a costume from her luggage. Two hard knocks announced a visitor to their door. Stoner walked to it, opened it.

The man known to Chastity as Khalil was leaning against the opposite wall, across the corridor, arms held out either side, jacket open, legs spread. There was no one else in sight.

'Can I help?' Stoner, asking in English.

'The lady.' Khalil made no move from the wall and maintained his search-me, no-threat pose. 'May I speak with the lady?'

'Why? And why are you standing there like a scarecrow?' Stoner was calm. Chastity appeared next to him, silent.

'We've met before.'

'OK.' Stoner cleared a passage into the suite. 'Come in. Is it too private for me to be present?' He smiled, chill, clearly dishonest friendliness.

Khalil remained by his wall, adopted a less submissive, more comfortable posture. 'Maybe the bar, a restaurant, would be better.' He made no move towards their door, spoke quietly. 'The lady can decide whether she and I are to talk in front of you.'

A tableau. Nobody moved. Chastity spoke, quietly.

'Who is he?'

'He says he knows you.' Stoner's focus was entirely on Khalil.

'I doubt that. We may have met before. Lots of people meet lots of people. There are a lot of people. Does he say where we may have met?'

'Ask him yourself. There he is, dark guy, over by the wall, ask away.'

She did.

'Where did we meet? And why? What do you want to talk about?'

Khalil looked at Stoner, who looked right back at him.

'You . . . we met in Israel. Following a murder, an assassination. It's up to you to decide whether your friend needs to know more about you than you may have told him. We have a mutual friend – Simeon. Are your bells ringing yet? Am I so easy to forget?' He spread his hands before them, his eyes still holding Stoner's own. 'Mr LaForge. My name is Khalil, and I am a policeman of sorts. There has been a crime . . . a murder. The last time your friend and I met there had also been a crime, another murder. A policeman is trained to observe connections, maybe where there are none, but I dislike coincidences.'

Stoner held his gaze.

'A murder? How so? Do you think Ms Weise here is a murderer?'

'What I think about Ms Weise isn't important, not at this time. What is important is that she understands that if indeed my memory for faces and voices is as efficient as it usually is then she can be placed at the scene of two violent events. I am not her concern. But . . . what should be her concern is that as soon as records are examined her presence will stand out.'

Stoner nodded. 'OK. Who's been murdered? A guy in the next suite had a heart attack, but . . .'

Khalil interrupted. 'He didn't have a heart attack. He was murdered. Beaten to death. The heart attack story is simply a story, to avoid scaring the guests.'

'And you think I did that?' Chastity pushed her way in front of Stoner. 'Me? Beat someone to death? Don't be an idiot.'

'Can I speak plainly in front of Mr LaForge?'

Chastity nodded. 'Go ahead.' She held onto Stoner's arm. 'I didn't beat anyone to death. But this gentleman and I might have met before, as he says. It's a long story.'

Stoner nodded. 'And we should talk somewhere away from my rooms? Why? Bugs? The police in Germany bug hotel rooms?' He shook his head. 'Why don't we all head to the pool? It can't be easy – or sane – to bug a pool.'

Khalil nodded his agreement.

'I'll wait for you there.' And he left them, called the elevator and waited for its arrival, pointedly watching the electric numbers changing as the lift headed towards him. Stoner nodded to Chastity and joined Khalil by the elevator. Chastity collected a bag, pulled the suite door closed and walked to the stairwell, disappeared from view while the two men waited for the elevator.

'And what line of business are you in, Mr LaForge?' Khalil watched the slow progress of the elevator.

'I drive a van.'

'You must be very good at driving a van to stay in a hotel like this one, Mr LaForge.'

'I own the company which owns the vans, Mr . . .' his inflection asked the question.

'Khalil is enough.'

'So you're what kind of policeman, exactly? The kind with no surname? A spook, then.' A statement, not a question. The elevator arrived. Doors opened and closed behind them.

'Have you known Ms Weise for very long?' The Israeli plainly preferred to ask questions rather than answer them.

Stoner shrugged. 'A short while. You know how it is.' He smiled amiably at Khalil. 'But I can't see what business it is of yours. Are you married?'

'No. Are you?' Both men smiled. Khalil spread his arms wide. 'I am concerned that Ms Weise may be involved in some way. Many more individuals are involved in crimes of this kind than is obvious. Not killers of course . . . but involved all the same.'

Stoner met his eyes as the elevator arrived at its destination, the lowest floor of the hotel, the gym and the pool. He pressed a finger against the 'door closed' button.

'Do you have a time for the murder? I've seen the movies. Time of death, you guys call it.'

'Yes.' Khalil provided a time, a reasonably accurate time.

Stoner was impressed with German efficiency and communication skills. He sketched a slightly theatrical sigh and released the door.

'That's OK. She was with me in the restaurant and the bar then. For a decent amount of time each side of your estimate. How exact is your time?'

Khalil nodded as they walked together out of the elevator and down flights of marbled steps to the pool. 'Accurate enough. This is Germany.'

Stoner stopped walking. Chastity ran towards them from the changing room, waving gaily and heading past them for the pool. He turned to face Khalil.

'Then we both know that she didn't murder the guy.' Chastity had hit the water running and was stroking her course for the far side. Stoner gazed at her, a long stare. 'Handsome, isn't she?'

'Of course. Do you . . . Are you involved with her? Forgive me for saying this, but you do not seem the type.'

'For what? For a holiday fling? For some heavy relief away from the non-existent wife and family? I seem like a hard-faced cynic to you? On such a brief encounter, too. I'm shocked.' His laughter was hollow, forced. He watched Chastity as she turned and swam another length. 'Are you warning me? You think – really think – that she's dangerous? To me? Is that what you're saying?' Stoner shook his head.

'It may just be a coincidence, Mr La Forge, but no policeman believes in coincidence.'

'Yeah. Policemen call it circumstantial evidence. The Americans would call in a drone strike for less.'

'You were a soldier?' Khalil's interest was obvious as it was sudden.

'I was. Pensioned off a long time ago.'

'Ah. The peace dividend?'

'The what? Oh I see. No. Only Americans get peace dividends, British soldiers get retired. Same result, just no fancy names and less money. The British way. The Army taught me how to drive, great training for a career as a van driver.' Both men smiled.

Khalil leaned closer to him as Chastity began another lap.

'Then before I leave you to your vacation, I will trust you with this. A message from one soldier to another. Should the subject arise, please tell Ms Weise that I am not a concern for her. Not an enemy. I have no regrets at all for the death in this hotel. And none for the gentleman who died in the desert the last time our paths crossed, although one of my colleagues was killed in the same action. Both men were . . . if not enemies then certainly not friends. Let us call them enemies. That way it is easy to recall the old saying that the enemy of my enemy is my friend.' He handed a business card to Stoner, who took it, his face expressionless. 'This is where I can be found. If Ms Weise and I are fighting on the same side, she can ask for assistance should she need it.'

'And if you're not? Not fighting the same good fight?'

'Then our encounters were indeed coincidences, and we shall not repeat them.' Khalil bowed in a peculiarly gracious way, and returned to the elevator. Chastity waved to Stoner from the pool.

15

JOYLESS ROGER

A blizzard of thinking rattled the shutters of Shard's consciousness. He was answering a summons. A text message from a withheld number, suggesting that he meet the anonymous sender at a certain place at a certain time. He'd marvelled a little at the unprofessionalism of it. Then he'd laughed aloud, for his own benefit as he was alone, and dismissed the suggestion as being simply silly.

A little while later, after reading the message for maybe the tenth time, he changed his mind, deciding instead that someone demonstrating such arrogant unconcern at his willingness or lack of it was someone who felt themselves to be in total control, of themselves and their situation. No need for code, subtle and sinister systems of oblique communication. Confident. Secure. He decided that simply because the sender was behaving in an unconventional manner did not mean that they were not to be taken seriously. On the contrary, double negatives notwithstanding, they knew who he was and, indeed, they had his number. It couldn't hurt to find out more about this person, these people. Taking appropriate precautions. He approached the designated park bench, walking alongside his freewheeling bicycle, just another physical fitness freak taking a breathless breather before assaulting the pedals once again.

The bench was occupied. A strangely unremarkable woman, unfashionably substantial in build if not height, was sitting, relaxed, reading the screen of some hand-held device. Shard parked maybe two hundred yards away from her and watched, waiting for unnatural patterns to emerge in the steady ebb and flow of the park. He saw nothing to concern him, so approached her from behind, swung himself onto the bench and leaned his bicycle against the armrest. He shook his head and leaned his elbows onto his thighs, the perfect picture of a weary pedaller.

'Thank you for coming.' Blesses, then, looking remarkably more bulky than a short time earlier. 'I won my bet.'

'With Mr Tran?' Shard pulled off his cyclist's helmet, ruffled his hard fingers through his short, sharp hair and wheeled his bicycle around in front of him, taking a studied interest in the adjustment of its gear-changing mechanisms.

'Have you been contacted by anyone else?' Answering a question with another question is a technique as age-old as the question itself. Blesses leaned forward and pointed a trim finger at a beautifully crafted and curved piece of finely formed and extremely light metal.

'Many times and about many things. Stupid question. Stupid answer, then.'

'All right. Try this. Are you currently employed? Are you currently under contract?' She showed no sign of irritation, and anyone watching from out of earshot would have assumed a shared interest in the mysteries of derailleur gears.

'Of course I am. You can probably check.'

'I have.' Blesses pointed to another part of the bicycle. 'It's a triple clanger. Why do cyclists call chainwheels clangers?'

'Have you lost a lot of sleep worrying about this?' Shard tested the tension of the bicycle's chain with an immediately oily finger, wiped the digit on the wood of the bench. 'It's plain you're a friend of Stoner. Only he knows women with a passion for machinery.'

Blesses stood, stretched and sighed theatrically and sat herself down again.

'I'm no friend of Stoner. I don't know him. Not really. We've met.' She shook her head, turned to face Shard directly. 'We're not friends. Not enemies either, before you go rushing off with some strange fantasy notion. I simply don't know him. Except by reputation. Mostly.'

Shard leaned back into the right angle formed by the bench's cast metal arm and slatted wooden back and looked at her. Her eyes were blue, an extremely pale blue, and large, wide and compelling. She gazed into his eyes, smiling gently, calm. Confident. Shard relaxed, comfortable, held her gaze. Their combined attention held them both rapt, somehow, as another pair of hands lifted the bicycle from Shard's grasp. His own hands, released from their task, fell to his knees and rested, fingers retaining the shadow of the shape of their relinquished grip. His world was all calm, tranquil, unnatural unconcern.

Blesses stood, gently, smoothly. Looked away, along the path and into the park itself. 'Walk with me,' she suggested. Shard stood, silently, moved to her side. His progress paralleled her own, along the path and deeper into the park itself. He said nothing; felt no need to interrupt a perfect moment. She simply began to walk, and he walked with her. His steps matched her stride, his pace was exactly her own. He said nothing. They walked for the entire length of the path, turned right onto the perimeter path and performed one complete lap. She stopped. He stopped. She turned, and walked another complete lap in the opposite direction, turned left and returned to the bench, Shard matching her step for step, direction change for change. She spoke again, gently, not unkindly.

'Seat yourself. Take the weight off.' And silently, with a calm lost smile, he did so, leaned back into the right angle formed by the bench's cast metal arm and slatted wooden back.

'Impressive.' Another voice, a man, his hushed tone attempting to sound gentle, easy, relaxed – all lies, overlaying a profound hoarseness and a harsh rasp of forced breath. He spoke as though fighting to form every word. As though every word caused pain for its speaker. 'Very fast. Good. How deep is your control?'

Shard reacted with curiosity, with half-recognition, to the new voice. He half-turned, his normal knife-sharp reactions stifled into slow-motion. Blesses once again caught Shard's attention, caught his eyes before he found focus on the third party. Drew his focus away from the older man and back to herself. His interest restored, she smiled softly at him, took his hand and spoke.

'Don't worry about him, my treasure. You don't know him. He's no one to you, no one to worry about. Only think about me. I'm all you need here. Now, what's your current contract? What's its duration?'

Shard blinked, frowned. 'Steady state. Open ended. Availability and readiness.' He fell silent, frowned again.

The sound of Blesses' voice matched the smile on her lips. 'It's good. All good. Just relax now, sweet boy.'

Shard's frown faded, replaced by an inattentive neutral expression. The older man spoke from somewhere immediately close by but at the same time impossibly far away, calmly and with little inflection. The underlying rough grate of his voice vied with its calm tone. Despite its pained hoarseness, it remained familiar, somehow.

'Could you take him deeper? He's protecting himself, he's not giving much up to you. But you are excellent at this.'

'I could move him further, make him more responsive and less in control of himself, but not here, not without background and more time. This is surface, very lightweight. We'll need another session in private. A little more chemical encouragement. But he is a natural, has no resistance to me.' She smiled sadly. 'He could probably believe in miracles, maybe even religion. Really believe, I mean, not just paying Sunday lip service.'

'A weakness?'

'Oh yes, always.' Blesses lifted her eyes once more to Shard's.

'Take a little while before you leave, lovely boy. No one turned up here. You met no one. You enjoyed a brilliant ride on clear paths. You're falling in love with me, and it feels so fine, so very fine. It's what you've always wanted. Rest now, relax and dream, dream about me, about Blesses, my soft hands and my beautiful Irish voice. Dream about my head next to yours on your pillow. You'll feel so fine when you've rested enough. You're falling in love with me, and it feels really good. Nothing better.' She reached over, took his hand, lifted it to her lips, kissed it and let it fall. She stood, and walked away, alone down the path, leaving the park. Two pairs of male eyes tracked her every step, following her with intensity, one pair with love in its stare.

'Lovely day for it.' A man's voice, quiet and impossibly close. Shard's eyes snapped open, wary, alert. Then he yawned and stretched as habitual tradecraft asserted itself, and looked around him, the very picture of an afternoon athlete feeling a little guilty about a secret doze. A conventionally dressed man of uncertain years, tall and well built, but baggy somehow, as if he'd recently mislaid a substantial proportion of his body mass, was sitting at the other end of the bench, smiling conversationally, if oddly, the smile attempting to break free from skin too big for its face. He looked weirdly familiar, too, but probably no more than would any other middle-aged man in a suit sitting on a park bench.

'As you say.' Shard smiled back, leaving a pause for the stranger to say something to confirm that this was the meeting to which he'd been summoned. Instead, the stranger checked a watch and shook his head.

'Time flies. Must get on.' He stood and flicked a pair of

glances down the path, one each way. 'Enjoy the rest of your ride.' And he walked away, in the direction of the town itself, towards the crowds. There were hardly any other walkers, cyclists, strollers or runners to be seen, so Shard stood, lifted his bicycle, swung aboard and propelled it lazily in the opposite direction.

The cell phone in his pocket summoned his attention almost immediately. A message, a withheld number, an apology for failing to meet as promised. No excuse, simply an acknowledgement that Shard had wasted his time. He dropped the phone back into its place, resumed his pedalling and his circuit of the park. The anonymous individual with whom he had shared a park bench was standing outside a bank, talking into his own phone. It appeared to be a fractious exchange. Shard smiled to himself, to his own audience of one. The suited man, who appeared less familiar the more Shard observed him, ended the call, Made another immediately. From his facial expressions it appeared to be as fractious as the conversation which had preceded it. The angered man's gaze drifted as his conversation continued, rested for almost no time at all on the cyclist and moved on. No hint of recognition. The feeling that Shard should have known who he was . . . faded.

Shard's observer instinct was almost silent, only a peculiar residual curiosity kept his eyes on the suited stranger, the angered man. His phone buzzed once again, and he lifted it from his pocket once more, still watching the man, who was still enjoying his fractious conversation. Another message, text only, number withheld: 'Same time, same place, tomorrow.' The phone sending him messages was obviously not the phone operated by the other man. Reassured, and confident that his memory would at its own convenience remind him who the angered man had been, Shard headed into the traffic.

*

Two women. A cafe. Expensive, elegant, extremely busy. One woman tall, both blonde short-hairs, one black-skinned, one not. Both friendly, animated. Regal as queens in their familiar world.

'He turned up, then.' A statement of a shared fact, not a question. The black queen had spoken, while her companion sipped at a glass of something frilly.

'He did. This is very good. Refreshing. You should try some.'

The black queen shook her head, her close-cropped and improbably blonde hair glittering in the lazy sunshine.

'Does he know where JJ is? Stoner?'

'I have no idea. Not yet. It doesn't work like that.' The white queen sipped some more. 'I've asked him to meet me again tomorrow. If he appears I'll ask him then. He's a pro, Lissa, he's not some john with a permanent hard-on for bad women. He won't give up much. Not easily.'

'But you can do the stuff with him OK? Your mind control thing?'

The white queen smiled. 'You make me sound like a Venusian she-monster. But yes, he drifted off like a good boy. Some of the . . . ah . . . herbs I added to Mr Tran's beautiful tea would help a lot, though. If you didn't want me to do all this slo-mo skull and daggery nonsense we could both just meet him and be up front with him.' She paused, sipped. 'Shard knows you're looking for Stoner, so why not just ask him outright? I would know if he was lying to you.'

'You think?'

'I know. He drifts under really easily, but like I said, he's a pro and he's not far under. Not yet. He'll fall deeper every time, but it takes time. I asked him for details of his current employment status and he was noticeably struggling with himself.'

'But he answered?'

'Yes. Grudgingly. And with nothing of value. I'm a bit concerned that he might simply surface when I ask him something he thinks is important and is uncomfortable talking about – really uncomfortable, I mean.' The white queen picked nervously at a pastry. 'I want to eat this so badly . . .'

'Do it then. Just do it. Go on. I will if you will.'

The white queen shook her head, scraped a little sugar from the pastry with her fingernail, licked it. 'So badly . . .'

'That's disgusting. Didn't your mother tell you not to play with your food?'

'It's not my food, dear, it's yours. At least, it will be when you pay for it.' Both women laughed. 'Why can't you just ask him outright where Stoner is? It would save a lot of messing around, stumbling around in the dark.'

The black queen looked away, picked up the mauled pastry and broke it into approximate halves. Said nothing.

'Are you scared of him?' The white queen picked up her share of the pastry and inspected it for nail damage.

'Of who? Scared of who?' The black queen picked at her pastry, examining it for bugs, maybe. 'I'm not worried about Shard. He's a lot less hard than he thinks he is, and I'm sure I could . . . ah . . . charm him in an appropriate way.' She smiled. 'JJ is something else. He's a lot harder . . . a lot more . . . he's a killer, a stone killer.'

'A Stoner killer!' The white queen had amused herself. She sobered quickly enough. 'You are afraid of him. Of your lover. Stoner?'

The black queen nodded. 'Yes. And Shard would tell him that we'd spoken.'

'So?'

'If JJ is as pissed as he . . . as he might be, then he might tell Shard to . . . Oh I don't know, anything up to and including killing me. He really might. He really might decide that he cares so little that he would just throw me away permanently. And if he told Shard to top me then he would. No question. None of your Venusian mind control would help. I don't know whether to laugh or cry.'

'Eat cake. It always works for you humans.' The white queen reached across the table, took her newfound friend's hand. 'Do you really think Stoner cares enough? To get Shard to kill you? Really?'

'Really? I don't know. JJ killed Hartmann. He killed him for . . . for offering me a home. For a betrayal of our . . . trust. Which it wasn't. He misunderstood. I want to explain. That's why I need to find him.' She looked up at the sky, three tattooed tears on her cheek were washed with real tears as she stared upward. 'I love him. It's just rubbish. Sorry, B. I keep dissolving like this. Don't know what I'd've done if you hadn't come along to pick up the pieces. I'm a mess. I don't know how, either. I've not felt this useless and fucked-over since I got out of Africa. And there's nothing here as wild as the wild things in Africa, believe me.'

The white queen watched this performance with a smile. 'Save the tears for your johns, Lissa. And the declarations of love. No need to act the wounded angel with me. You're a hooker, God's sake, not Mother Theresa. Stoner knows that. He knows you get paid to get laid. He can't care who you choose as customers, lovely girl. That's irrational, and you've always said he's completely rational. Cold, even. And how do you know he killed your top john? This . . . Hartmann?'

The black queen's eyes dried, only the tattooed tears remained, stained blue on her cheeks. 'Hartmann, yes. He was an MP once. A Member of Parliament. I thought he was a bishop or something. Always a bit tense. I always knew he was loaded. Several houses. Big ones, not scuzzy pads like JJ has scattered about. Do you know, Blesses, I really do miss him? JJ. I would give anything I've got to just sit with him and act the arse, try to get him to talk about the jobs he's doing. He could be really funny. Really funny. Then sometimes he'd go all serious, suddenly, and I could see through him, see the detective he really is.'

'Detective, even? Is that what he told you he was? Is.'

The black queen licked at a piece of unhappy pastry. 'He didn't tell me he was anything. He just talked about his work, which was always about finding people for other people. People who didn't always want to be found. He looked for killers. Sometimes he would talk about the crime scenes he'd been to. A real buzz. I was scared of it all at first, reminded me too much of home – home in Africa, not home here – but somehow when JJ talked about it I felt safe with him. It was, like, an exorcism. The ghosts sort of went away and took the bodies and the dreams of bodies and the smell – I hated the smell of it – away from me. Yes, a detective. A specialist, I think.'

'And such a good detective that he didn't know you were screwing Hartmann, his . . . his what? Employer? His friend?'

'I don't think JJ even thought about it, B. Never even considered the possibility. He was all wrapped up in everything. The music, the jobs, the people he played with. And when he was working he was really working, know what I mean? His phones would be buzzing all the time – he had more phones than anyone I've ever heard of – and sometimes he would just go out, drop everything, me included. Like . . . like he was always thinking. Sometimes there wouldn't even be a phone call. He'd just stop whatever we were doing, and go. Scary and weird. Even when we were in bed he'd just suddenly stop. Like a switch. Get dressed and go.'

'You accepted that?' The white queen appeared regally unamused on her friend's behalf.

'All functional relationships are dependent on compromises. Of course I accepted it.'

'You sound like a marriage guidance counsellor.' The white queen was plainly unamused. Again. 'Making excuses for his behaviour. Sounds to me like he just treated you like a whore.'

'I am a whore.'

'That's no excuse. Didn't he tell you that he loved you?'

'No.'

'Never? Never at all? Not even once?'

'You mean, like, in a moment of weakness? No.'

'I didn't mean in a moment of weakness. More like a moment of truth. Understanding. That kind of thing.' The white queen radiated certainty. Dug deeper. 'So he didn't love you, you reckon?'

'I don't know. Most men are just meals on wheels, wallets walking. They do what they do, pay for it and move on. JJ is very different. Was different.'

'He did love you. And you let him go. Let him get away. Love is blind, so they say, so maybe you love him too.'

'Of course I do. I really miss him. Why do you say he loved me, anyway? He just . . . just left.'

'He killed a man for screwing you. Maybe for violating you or something.'

'No. He killed Hartmann because his own pride was hurt.'

The white queen studied her companion with unkind humour. 'You don't understand men at all, do you?'

'And you think you do? How fine, how very fucking fine for you. You going to share these giant balls of understanding, my new best friend forever?'

'Stoner offered to let you live in his place for free, right?'

'Right.'

'And you refused, right? You insisted on paying rent. And fucking him for free?'

'Yes.'

'So?'

'So what?'

'You did that whole pointless independence thing, right? You turned down what Stoner thought was the best thing he had to offer you. The chance to get off the game, get a place to live. He was offering you a chance to be free.'

'What? I don't mind being on the game, being a hooker. I like it. Sometimes. It's only temporary, anyway. When the looks go, the worthwhile johns always follow them. I just want to be independent. Africa – home – made me like that. Hooking pays and there's no tangles. Once I've got enough, once I've made my own pile, then I'll stop. Buy a place, rent a big place, whatever.'

'Unless the looks and the trade fade first.'

'Yeah. Not going to happen.'

'You reckon? You move in dodgy circles, that's how you get the big bucks. Bad men do bad things to women. Stoner offered you a way out of that. And you turned him down. And then you accepted exactly that – what he offered – from someone else. Not just anyone else, either, babe – you went off to set up house with his employer. His boss, for the love of God. And you thought Stoner wouldn't find out? Thought he might not notice? He's a detective, you say? How did he find out, anyway?'

'I invited him over to the house where I was playing house-wife . . .'

'You did what? Are you really stupid?'

'No. The house was one of Hartmann's spare houses. He didn't live there. He lived with his Number One Wife some-where else.'

'And you don't see how refusing Stoner's offer to get you out of the game but setting up to play housey-housey with his employer – a seriously heavy spook and a politician – you can't see how Stoner might get just a tiny little bit unhappy with that?'

'I always told JJ that I couldn't stand Hartmann. That I wouldn't let him into my place . . . my apartment in JJ's house, next to Mr Tran . . . willingly. Which was true. I didn't like him. Hartmann. He was vile. Violent. Got off on knocking women around. I told JJ that. Told him that Hartmann was a twat. That very word. A twat.'

'Hartmann knocked you around? You let him do that? You are sounding sick to me, babe.'

'Why not? I've been beaten all my life. Men beat up on

women. I'm used to it. I don't care. Never takes them long. They're limp, soft, they beat up on a woman, they get hard, then it's all over. Then they pay and they go away. The guilt always makes them pay and leave. Always.'

'And you were OK with that? Really OK?'

'You just switch off, don't you?'

'No. No I don't. I do not permit it. You're not right in the head.'

'Says you.'

'Says I. That said, Stoner wouldn't have killed Hartmann for that. He would just have left.'

'He did leave.'

'You know what I mean.'

'Not really. Do you think he'll come back? From wherever he is? Do you really, secretly know where he is? You're thick with Mr Tran, he seems to know everything.'

'Ask him, then. Work your hooker charm.'

'Tried that. No joy. He pretends not to understand, but he does really. He just does the "Me Mister Tran the Chinaman" bit just so he can pretend politely and say nothing.'

'But he makes great tea.'

'The best.'

'And Stoner's been back.' A tactical bombshell dropped almost casually by the white queen. Her black companion was mute, staring. Eyes filling again.

'Say what? Where is he? Do you know where he is? Can I see him? Is he all right?'

'He's gone again. He's overseas somewhere. Not sure where.'

'Where overseas?'

'I told you, I don't know. Keep up.'

'JJ always told me to keep up.' The black woman sniffed, a touch theatrically. 'He would call me his dirty blonde, and he'd ruffle my hair.'

'I still don't know where he is. And I don't know whether

he'd still want to ruffle your hair and call you petnames, either.'

'Spare me the sarcasm, sweetie, just tell me how he is and where he is. You know. I bet you know. You do know, don't you?'

'No. Don't ask again. Repeating myself gets old very quickly. Really does.'

'All right. Is he well, though? Did he seem OK to you?'

'I didn't see him. I just heard that he'd been back and that he'd gone again.'

'Who told you? Mr Tran?'

'Uh-huh. Mr Tran's a wily oriental, he knows everything. Softlee softlee catchee monkee . . . that kind of thing. They learn it in the jungle.' She smiled. 'Sorry, no offence.'

'None taken. I . . . If . . . *When* JJ comes back again . . . If you hear he's coming back, will you tell me?'

'Sure. No problem. Soon as I hear – which I will. Hey, you tell me something. How well do you know Harding, Stoner's friend Shard?'

'Shard? The guy you've been doing the mind-control shit on? They were soldier buddies.'

'So you know him?'

'I know who he is, and he knows who I am, but I don't know much about him. Why?'

'Does Stoner rate him? Trust him?'

'You're asking me? I don't know. How would I know?'

'He must have mentioned Shard. They worked together a lot. Stoner talked about his cases with you. You being his very own dirty blonde. I do like that. He has a decent sense of humour for a policeman.'

'I don't think he's a policeman, exactly.'

'Clever girl! He's not. I asked Shard where I could find Stoner, like I said, but he doesn't seem to know, and he does seem to be pissed about it. We'll see if Shard turns up tomorrow. A longer conversation might just do the trick.'

'What do you want JJ for, exactly, B?'

'Easy with the suspicion. I know someone who wants someone found. That's what Stoner does, right? And I'm helping you, too, because you want your boyfriend back, and you're my friend, my new best friend, the dirty blonde. That is so you, so extremely you.'

'Fuck you, Blesses.'

'Many have tried, babe. Many have tried.' They both laughed, tension and unhappiness draining away like the last dregs of a summer wine.

16

MOVING ON

'Who's next?' Stoner shared another new day, another break-fast after another night. A second night. Their fellow travellers at the efficient German hotel had forgotten about the untimely demise of one of its guests, or had never even been aware of it, which was more likely. Or had simply ignored it, which might have been the easiest way.

'How's that?' Chastity was sitting in the morning sun, her pale blonde complexion contrasting strangely with the artificial black of her hair. 'Who's next for what? Tennis?'

'On your very own private hit list. Who's next to perform the great "time to die" speech?'

'*Blade Runner*, right? The robot.'

'Replicant. Roy Batty. Rutger Hauer. Very good indeed. Excellent.'

'For years I wanted to be Pris. More than anything.'

'Wows. My dream girl. Me too.'

'You too what? You wanted to be Pris? You're too fat to be convincing. And your beard would give the game away.'

Stoner pouted, badly.

'Why do you want to know? Silly question. OK. What are you going to do? I don't have details, just know where, approximately. You coming with me? Bodyguard? Spare assassin?

Emergency repair kit in case of disasters? The dark voice of conscience?'

Stoner poured glasses of expensively aerated Germanic water for them both. 'I was asked to look out for you. That's what I'm doing. I'm going to carry on doing that. Either out here in the open, which lowers the hotel bills but raises my frustration factor, or by shadowing you in another dimension, secret-like. Spooky noir stuff. So I was just asking, friendly.'

'The frustration is self-inflicted. Your neck's safe with me. Honest injun.'

'Yeah. For now.'

'I'm serious. You can have a special entry permit. Guaranteed non-fatal.'

'Oh lady . . .' Stoner's sigh could have swallowed entire worlds of doubt, clouds of cynical sadness. 'Then there will come another day, another place, and you'll decide that I really am the enemy because of those hot nights, that you need to remove me, whatever the real reason, and I'll be a legit target, and you'll do a non-refundable transaction, and I'll be history. Being history is junk, as I think Henry Kissinger might have said.'

'Fraud. Henry Fraud. You still think . . . You do think that.' She paused, contemplated. 'I see it. Your thinking is that I'm all warm and happy and content now, here, with you and safety and all that. I'm stable. You also think I'm mad enough to lose it all when you go back to that black tart you were screwing, who lives in your house – one of your houses – and I'll go batshit and jealous and do the furious scorned woman thing. It may be that you flatter yourself, JJ. Your charms are resistible, even though you're good to have around. How'm I doing?'

'You're good. Close enough. I'd rather not be a threat to you. You put a bomb in my club . . .'

She interrupted. 'More than one, but I also removed them. We've been down this road before. It's an old road.'

'It only gets older. Your sanity will slip at some point – your own point of no return. You'll come after me and take a punt. You'll either hit me, which would not be an optimal outcome, frankly, or you'll miss me, which means that I'd need to work out it was you, then come after you, then we'd have a big fight, and one of us would be dead. All that so we can share some meaningless fucking – memorable I'm sure, but also meaning-less – and you can see me as some kind of threat. No. Not me, babe. I'd rather we were friends.'

'Jacking each other off in the meantime? That's enough for you? It's a little bit teenage angst, no? What if I have a summit meeting with myself and redefine fucking as either party having an orgasm in the company of the other? Huh? What then, smart guy?'

'Oh please. Don't go all terrorist on me. I'm only some guy.'

Chastity was relentless, though her voice was calm and quiet. 'It's important to me, JJ.'

'Christ. Just don't fall in love with me, right?'

'You flatter yourself.'

'Just telling you what you sound like. You sound scary.' He reached for, caught, her hand and smiled. 'We need to stay iced while the deals go down.'

'You reckon I sound scary when I talk about normal things? I don't sound scary when I talk about hacking guys up, flushing their dicks down the toilet and filming their bleeding heads for the benefit of sad fucks on the MurderMayhemand-More website? You are one curious individual, JJ Stoner.'

'So they say. So, who is next?'

'I'll get hold of mother . . . Charm on Facebook, and find out.'

'Can I come and play too?'

'Yes.' She looked steadily across their shared table, and the music left her voice, the warmth her eyes. 'I shall say this only once.' Stoner nodded with an equally flat expression. He looked suddenly old, tired.

'I've never worked with anyone apart from my sisters.' He

nodded once, no wish to interrupt. 'I trust only my sisters. Tell me I can trust you.'

Stoner said nothing.

'Tell me, then? I can trust you?'

'I won't lie to you. That's the best I can manage. Don't trust anyone. I don't trust anyone. Neither should you.'

Chastity's pale face paled further. Anger, perhaps. 'You don't trust me?'

'Of course I do, but not in the way you might expect. I trust that you'll do what you do. You kill people. I trust that. It defines everything about you. I can't see any reason for that to change. I'm being honest. Trust me on that.' He rolled out a small smile. None returned.

'You're . . . difficult.' Chastity's voice was quiet, almost gentle.

'Am I coming with you?'

'You want?'

'I want.'

'OK. I'll get hold of mother.'

Stoner raised both of his hands, palms outward. 'But.'

'Here comes the but, then. Which but is this but?'

'Do you always contact mother in the same way? On Facebook?'

Her irritation replaced itself with interest. 'Yes, mostly.'

'Do you have a supersecret known only to you three musketeers last resort ohmigod panic coms channel?'

'Yes.'

'How's it work?'

'I should tell you?'

'You're the one who talks about trust and bright shiny things like that. You choose.' No joking going down here.

'Key words. You need to know what they are?'

'No. Not yet. Then?'

'The two words after the key words, reversed, with numbers replacing the letters L and O; mother sets up a new

Gmail account using those words as the account name and I mail her there from a Hotmail account of the same name. Quicker to do than to tell.' She smiled, briefly.

'Passwords?'

'We choose our own; no need to know the other's.'

'Will mother . . . Charm, will she also tell Charity? Anyone else?'

'Sisters only. Just Chas and Charm.'

'Not Mallis, Menace?'

'No. Is that secure enough for you?'

'It should be. Do it.'

'Explain?'

Stoner shrugged. 'Your contact is compromised. Has to be. You need hundred percent paranoid setting. And we both need to believe in it.'

'You're starting to sound seriously paranoid yourself.'

'That's an accurate assessment. You should join the NSA and become a profiler, skills like that.'

'You're thinking about the FBI, not the NSA.'

'Is either of them in charge of the purity of drinking water?'

'No.'

'Then either will do. Where would you like to go to resurrect your mother?'

'What's wrong with here? No one knows we're here . . . at least, no one knows who we are.'

'They do.'

'Who does?'

'Your pal Khalil for a start. The Deutsch detective will know as soon as he talks to his own spooks, and . . .'

She interrupted again. 'You really think it's that easy to work out who we are?'

'Yep. How much deep cover work have you done?'

'None. Not as such. I'm normally in and out in no time. If you see what I mean.'

'I'm forty-two. I've worked in Ireland, in Iraq and in Iran.

I'm still standing. There's one simple reason for that.'

'Point taken. How do you want to play it?'

'I don't want to play at anything.' Stoner's eyes were following every moving body, then every stationary body, then every moving body again. 'We're going on a train ride.'

'We are?'

'You don't need to act incredulous every time I say something which isn't in the *Girl Guides' Big Book of Murder And Stuff*. Yes, we're going to a railway station and we're going to catch a train. If I was a real bluesman I'd be catching me a freight train, but bastards can't be choosers. So they say.'

'They say that?'

'Not to my knowledge, but bullshit drips from the tongue.'

'It sounds better to say that venom drips, rather than bullshit. The shit is not an attractive image, to be honest. And it's beggars who can't be choosers.'

'I'll remember that, come the revolution.'

'It needs to be a train to nowhere.' Chastity waved for a bill, signed it with an illegible but aggressive slash of the proffered pen.

'Of course it does. Do you know many blues songs? That's a good one, "Train to Nowhere"; "Hellbound train goes to God knows where; I don't know and God don't care. . ."' he half-sang, half-tonelessly.

'Spare the romantic singing shit for your sweet baby bass player. I'll go grab a bag.'

'Leave your cell phone in the room. Switched on.'

'OK.'

They paced the platform while an endless freight train rumbled by, slowly, reliably conveying the produce of the German industrial depths into the slavering markets of the rest of the world. Implacable and unrelenting. A most modern invasion.

Stoner took a phone from a pocket, wrapped it in a stolen glove, dropped it into a stolen plastic bag and swung it onto one of the passing bogies.

'Stealing a ride,' he said, watching the train run relentlessly away from them.

Chastity held her hands in her pockets. Watched and wondered aloud.

'So any crazed obsessives are now convinced that I am lazing around in the hotel, *toute seule*, as we say in Europe, while my baby done gone left me on that ole freight train lordy-lord. That about the size of it? You really think we're being watched that closely?'

Stoner shrugged. 'Don't know. It's possible that being prepared is better than being dead. Better this way than suffering an unwanted invasion of the body-snatchers. The plan is – if there is a plan within a plan, which is always possible, were I really to be one of those smart guys who makes plans – that a band of body-snatchers may well invade your room. If you're under suspicion by folk not unconnected to your pal Khalil. It's impossible to perform even the most frustrated body-snatching exercises without leaving a trace. And if they leave a trace we can make all manner of entertaining and hopelessly paranoid deductions about who they are.'

'You're just weird.' Chastity shook her head sadly. 'Paranoid beyond dreams.'

Stoner shrugged back. 'I'm still standing, OK?'

'As seen here, Mr Stoner. Point duly taken. Which train? And to where?'

'It doesn't matter. The first to this platform will be fine, wherever it's going. We won't be going there – not all the way anyway.'

Chastity raised a smile. 'And we buy our tickets with cash on the train itself, making it just about impossible to follow us?'

'Yes indeed. It doesn't matter much, in some ways, but the fewer clear indicators we leave, the more doubts and options, the less we appear to be what we actually are to any low-level investigator. The best tradecraft is invisible tradecraft, unrecognisable. So we look at first, second and maybe even third glance to be a couple in the throes of a fresh new fuckfest, filling in the time between athletic bouts of passion with fairly aimless wandering around, tourist style.'

'That sounds fine.' A train arrived, slowed, stopped. 'But will it hold up to close scrutiny?' They boarded, talking, like lovers do.

'No. But if the scrutiny is close and carried out by a pro as weary and cynical and experienced as me, then we really are in trouble. All we want to do is obscure our trail and hide our intentions. At some point we need to go back to the hotel to collect passports and luggage; dumping our kit and disappearing is only a practical option if we've decided to run for it. And I'd rather not be doing that at the moment. Even leaving lies behind tells the bad guys something about you. Also prints and bodily identifiers on passports, clothes. You know all this, surely? It's all pretty basic.'

'I'm not a spook, JJ. I never was a soldier.' Chastity smiled at him in a brittle saccharine manner. 'I'm just a simple little girl with a difficult family background trying her best to make her way in this cruel man's world.'

'Is that so? In a world of cruel men, or in a world belonging to a cruel man? These things are important.' A uniformed official appeared before them.

'We will never know.' Chastity switched effortlessly to German, asked for a couple of tickets to Frankfurt. Stoner produced a wallet and a banded bunch of notes to pay for them, accepted the change and a receipt, all delivered with Euro-courtesy and meaningless Euro-politeness.

'We're married now, huh?' Stoner's smile was relaxed.

'Feels like it. We don't fuck and we argue all the time. Perfect harmony in all things. He won't remember us.'

'True. How come you don't do tradecraft? How did you get

into a life of murdering the innocent? It's not too obvious a career choice.'

'Am I after a job?'

'What?'

'This can't be an interrogation, so it must be an interview, judging by the questions.'

'The more I know about you, the more I believe in you. The more I buy into you, the more I'm likely to be useful or helpful.'

'Sex isn't enough to bind you to me, then? Whatever happened to the knights of old and chivalry, things like that?'

'Died out when wimples went out of fashion, I think. You kill your lovers. That is – as we've agreed – unattractive to me. How did you get into the life? It's almost exclusively home to ex-soldiers and the like.'

'Like you.'

'Like me. How are you being leaked? If all you sisters are as careful as you say – and I don't doubt it as you've survived this long – then how are you being set up?'

'Who asked you to watch over me? Did he really tell you not to make contact with me?'

'Mallis. And yes, he did. His view was that you would surely hate interference of any kind.'

'Correct. If no one knows where I am and what I'm doing then they can't get in the way and they can't betray me. You dig?'

'I dig. That's very Seventies. You're not old enough to remember the Seventies.'

'Neither are you. What should I do when we find an internet cafe?'

'I don't want you to do anything. You're in charge.'

'I would appreciate your advice. In my normal world, I go in using a route prepped by Charm, do the deal and leave, also using a route prepped the same way. It's always worked. Until recently.'

'How does Charm prep your routes?'

'How would I know?'

'You're her sister. You work together. The family that works together . . .'

'Fuck off. But you're correct. You did sex with Charity. You going to try it on with Charm?'

'I didn't do sex with Charity. She did sex with herself. It's a family thing with you ladies. Oh . . . I see.'

'Oh good. Rough ape regains consciousness at last.'

'Spare me. You and Charm have had a falling out.'

'Not really. We just don't talk much. Hardly at all. There's no need. She tells me were to go and what to do when I get there. I do it, she transfers pots of gold to my hoard.'

'And you live in a big cave under a mountain, get pestered by dwarves and breathe fire in an entertaining way. Sounds perfect to me. What did you argue about?'

'We didn't. She thinks I'm going mad. Charity thinks the same.'

'Are you? Going mad? Don't take that as a criticism, it's quite common among soldiers. Battle fatigue and the like. Being near death experience, or something.'

'Don't patronise. At some point I started to enjoy killing men. They think that's insane. But as you know, Charity did the wetwork before me, mostly, and I think the conflicts, the stress, gave her cancer. Turned her from a bubbly outgoing girl of the world into a sexless, hairless freak with tumours, no tits and no friends. I think killing men and enjoying it is a lot more healthy than that. But – if I may be philosophical for a moment – realities become divergent. What is reality for TV-watching housewives of the world is not my reality. The more realities diverge, the more unbelievable they become to the occupants of alternates. And the more they hide away watching daytime garbage television without understanding that they are just turds in a vast meaningless valueless pool of steaming shit, the less they know about true realities; the realities which exist in a world where living life is real and watching third-hand while others live it in an acted fantasy through the goggling-glass is simply insane. They are worth-less.'

'And the men you kill are also worthless? No one important enough to attract a killer contract is going to be a stay-at-home daytime TV addict.'

'How would I know? They're worth more to me dead than alive, which is sufficient. What's your point?'

'Aren't empty trains a great place for an argument?'

'We're not arguing. What's your point?'

'By your standards, you're killing the wrong people. You should kill the useless turds. I simply doubt anyone would contract a hit on someone who was a worthless, purposeless pleb.'

'Why would I . . .? Oh, I see. You're justifying your sol-dier-boy antics. Killing large numbers of anonymous and probably innocent people who just happen not to wear the same silly clothes as you is somehow more justifiable than taking out some fool who's fallen out with some other fool who's quicker on the draw than he is? That's nonsense. And you know it's nonsense, Mr Stoner, sir.'

'You know something? You sound distinctly uninsane to me.'

'Then we're all fucking doomed, soldier boy. Is this where we get off? I need a swim. And the internet so I can tell my mother all about you. Blind dates are such fun.'

17

IN PIECES

Rain. Hard rain on a roof. Shard quite suddenly felt himself snap awake, felt as though he'd been asleep for hours, very deeply, and had been dreaming, one of those dreams which are completely real and only recognisable to the dreamer as being dreams because they are impossibly perfect. Or impossibly dreadful. The rain was real – he was becoming really wet, not that he was in any way concerned by that. Summer rain is supposed to be warm. He was cold, and he was leaning against a wall in a dark street he recognised, with no real idea about how he had come to be there. Apart from the dream.

Footsteps. Footsteps in the rain. Hard to disguise or to hide, the softest sneaker soles still splash, just like cheap, hard plastics. Shard remained where he was. Stationary and silent. His level of wet had reached the point at which the same amount of water was running from his clothes as the heavens were pouring onto him. Saturation. Cyclists have no fear of saturation, and Shard was a healthy urban cyclist. He knew no fear. Concerns about the cold and the wet were for lesser souls than his own.

This thought amused him so much that he wondered whether he was still dreaming. Then he wondered whether he'd ever been dreaming in the first place. Distraction can be fatal for a watcher. Was he here to watch? He should know that, at least.

Two voices, approaching. Their cadences and tones were familiar, but the words spoken were indistinct. Shard was more interested in there being only one set of footsteps. They were walking in step, like soldiers. They approached. Two women, well wrapped against the rain and talking closely, their words muffled by their collars and by the rhythms of the rain and the patterns of their feet. A companionable mumbling, good-natured by its tone, lively in its cadences. They approached, then passed him, neither even glancing in his direction. Their surreal behaviour surprised him a little, given his dreamy state. Was he invisible? If so, he certainly was still dreaming.

In fact, he was far into shadow. The rain's insistent hiss and constant movement blinded both ears and eyes, his rain-slicked, rain-blacked bomber jacket and denim jeans offered no interruption to the background visuals the women were passing through. And in any case, they weren't looking in his direction. Shard wondered whether he was supposed to be watching the women. Was he looking for them? For someone else? Although he was feeling more awake with every drip, every muted splash, he was still unclear about why he was where he was, leaning against an eroded brickwork wall in the dark and in the rain.

He hauled himself upright, balanced on the balls of his feet, and prepared to follow the women. He knew where he was and he knew where he was going, whether – he decided – the women were heading there or not. The Blue Cube, JJ Stoner's very own jazz club; the least bright-blue fluorescent sign in the whole world tried to pretend that there was life inside, but in only a weary, dull, waterlogged way. It was just around the corner. There would be warmth and a welcome of sorts. He was suddenly aware that although he'd been there several times, he had almost always had business with Stoner himself, none worth remembering with anyone else. He wondered whether anyone would recognise him, and whether it would be a good or a bad thing if they did. Or if they did not. He stepped from shadow and into the relative light of the footpath.

Two men walked silently into him, colliding out of the streaming evening. All three men stumbled and fumbled, one of the younger men dropped something. The unmistakeable clatter revealed it to be a knife. Shard fell to his knees: plenty of practice and extreme fitness made him as fluid as he was fast, and he was extremely fast. One of his hands closed over the knife's handle, lifted it away and into the protection of his own body. It was a clasp knife, not a good one, unbalanced, and its blade was folded out. It was being hand-carried, then, intended use imminent.

Shard relaxed and rolled, away from the startled men and up again onto his toes, turning to face them and dropping into a casual fighting stance. Almost on autopilot, no cognition required. A man of action, in action. Against men with knives. Two men. Where there was one knife, there would be another, at least one, maybe several, depending on who these guys were and what their purpose was. He lifted the knife between them, held it steady. Right hand on the grip, the point of the blade resting gently on the extended forefinger of his left hand. His feet were steady, his legs splayed, he eased back towards the wall, shuffling, both feet in constant contact with the ground. Where there were two men, there could be more men. He'd not hear a quiet man behind him, the rain would muffle another man as well as it had blinded all three of the present tableau into a simple mistake, an unremarkable accident. He reached the wall, knife, hands and eyes holding steady. The cold, the wet, the weird dream were all forgotten. He felt good. He said nothing. Smiled, slowly, steadily widening his lips, then pulling them apart to show his white teeth. A wide white grin, and a hard knife.

Two younger men faced him. One black man, one white man. Racial balance. Both were wearing raincoats, ski caps. Stubbly men, weirdly nervous, unsure of their position. Amateurs. Shard flicked the knife from his right hand to his left, then back to his right. Made a display of testing its sharpness against the pad of his thumb, shook his head, the grin never faltering. Then he made a theatrical display of testing the point of the knife against the palm of his left hand, shook his head again. He spoke.

'Ooooo . . .' he said. 'Scary big knife. Too scary for little girls like you two.' His eyes flicked past them for a rapid glance; the two women were long gone, innocent of the tiny sodden drama unfolding in their wake.

The men facing him separated, moved apart from each other. Not entirely without awareness, then.

'Rape? Mugging? Bit of a laugh?' Shard's tone was easy, relaxed, confident.

The black man shook his head. More nervous than Shard, but not too nervous, and less so as the seconds flipped by.

'Just dropped it. Easy mistake. No harm intended. Just pass it back, OK?'

'You always carry an open blade? Dangerous. Cut your nuts off if you take a fall.' Shard moved a little closer to them. 'Can you run?'

'You what?' The white man spoke. 'What you on about? You're the one's got the problem, not us. You want to run, you run.' He produced a knife of his own. Another clasp knife. He opened it. Tried to match Shard's white wide grin.

'Catch.' Shard tossed the knife from his hand, both men followed it with their eyes. It flew into the air, over his head and landed behind Shard, clattered to the roadway. Two sets of eyes, two puzzled looks focused again on Shard, who was now holding a pair of very different blades, both night-black, both set into black handles, one in each hand.

'Oops,' he said. 'Dropped it. You running yet? I don't hear

any running. I don't even hear any walking away very quickly but with dignity.' He flipped the knife in his left hand over, caught it by the blade. 'This is very sharp. Do you want to try it?'

Shard stepped forward one pace. The two men remained where they are. 'I kill people for money,' he said. 'It pays very well. I could do you for free though, just to stay in practice. To keep my hand in. Most professionals don't practice enough. Never understood it myself. Got to stay sharp. Stay sharp, gettit, gonzos?' He waved the blade in his left hand in an encouraging way. 'I'll do you a deal, OK? How's this; one of you – you with the stupid blunt knife – attacks me. I'll perform the old slice 'n' dice, nicely does it, and then I'll explain what I did to the man left standing. And, wait for it . . . you can have a go at me to check out that you understood and got the message. How's that? Care in the community and such.'

'You're off your fucking head, mate.'

'It has been said, and by better men than you. No offence.'

The black man attempted fierce. 'Give me back my knife.'

'It's behind me somewhere. It's yours. Go get it.'

The dark door to the Blue Cube opened, emptying a bathful of dirty light into the street. Shard's eyes remained fixed on the two bemused men. The dirty light reflected the dirty street, and faded, slowly, its own enthusiasm waning. There was a silent and almost sudden darker dark behind the two men, and quiet American drawled from it.

'I would leave now. Gentlemen.'

They ran.

Shard disappeared both black knives from each of his hands. Stood his ground.

'Thank you.'

'Never were thanks less required, but politeness is underrated as a virtue. I feared that if I left you to it all on your own you would be forced to cut them, which in itself would not be a bad thing, not exactly, but unnecessary. Were you heading for the club? I've seen you there before. A friend of Stoner's, am I right?'

'I hope so. Hope I'm a friend. You never know exactly with him.'

'He calls you Shard, right?'

'He does. Hi.'

'Hi yourself. I'm Stretch. I play . . .'

'Yeah, I've seen and heard. You play piano. Hello, Stretch. A pleasure.'

'All mine I'm sure. You coming inside before the rain starts again?'

'You reckon it will?'

'Surely. This is England, right? In summer, right?'

'Right both times.'

Stretch, a hugely inconspicuous black man wearing black in the evening's sodden darkness, walked with confidence to the doorway beneath and to the side of the dimly flickering blue light. Shard spoke to his broad back.

'You'd think that the club's owners would replace the sign. Get more trade if it was a little brighter.'

'Owner, Stoner,' said Stretch, a deep southern American humour lacing his tone. 'Reckon as he likes it like that. Reckon as if he want to change it he change it. He don't, so he don't.' And he laughed, the laugh a rumble like a mountain coughing.

'Stoner does actually own the Blue Cube, then?' It was impossible to tell whether Shard was surprised or was merely acting surprised. The games some men play with each other. Another rumbling half-laugh was the only answer. Stretch reached the door and pulled it open, beckoning that Shard follow him in.

'Assuming you were heading this way?' The black pianist was making a polite enquiry. Shard shook his head but walked towards the door anyway.

'I don't think I had any idea where I was going. Sounds crazy, yeah? But it's true. Can't think of any reason I'd come down here right now, and I can't remember getting here either. Odd.'

'As you say. Excuse me for not sounding surprised. This is one long life of surprises.' Stretch headed to the bar. Shard followed him, walking more slowly, looking around as his eyes accustomed themselves to the dim interior. 'Know where you are now? Recognise this? This is a bar.' A wide white grin split Stretch's shining black face. His eyes glittered as he rolled them. 'Bars are bad places, where bad men buy bad drinks for bad ladies. Or for each other.' He gestured to the barkeep, a thinning, wiry white man whose face carried a professional lack of expression. 'What's your personal poison?'

'Do you make coffee? Anything weaker than that could be fatal.' Shard smiled a weak splinter of a smile. 'This is a very strange day.' He observed that the two women who'd passed him in the street outside were now sitting at a table, deep in an animated and plainly passionate exchange of views with a smaller woman, a woman with a mass of wild curls and of singularly indeterminate age, who repeatedly rose to her feet to emphasise some lost point, then sat down again once she'd made it. She appeared to be in disagreement with one of the women from the street, a woman more rounded than herself, dark-haired and relatively undemonstrative.

Stretch nodded towards them, waved a hand and shook his smiling shining head at the tangle-topped fury, who glared in recognition, then grinned at him. And sat down, raising a mostly empty glass in his direction. Shard in his turn stared openly.

'She's called Bili and she plays bass. Yes?' Shard said, as if not entirely certain of those facts, as much to himself as to Stretch.

'She does. You know her?'

'A little. Not much. We met. I know who she is. I was supposed to go on a trip with her once. Can't remember why. Don't think I know the others, though. Are they players, too?'

'Amanda blows the sax. Also JJ whenever she can get her lips around him.' Stretch sipped, smiled, possibly at his own wit. 'But Stoner is Bili's in truth. Bili don't know it, and Amanda would lie about it, but it is true. Together forever, those two, though it takes a sayer of sooth to know it. I got dem ol' voodoo vibes,' He rolled his eyes in a bad impersonation of the black man he actually was. 'And that other lady with them was blonde the last time I saw her. That's the kicker with chicks. They vary with their moods. I got only one me, me.' Bili stood once again, patted Amanda on her shoulder, and walked towards them. 'Oh my my, here comes little Miss Lightnin' . . . How you doing, sweetie?'

'Hey, Stretch. Don't tell me how it's hanging because I do not want to know.' They both laughed.

'This here's JJ's friend Shard.' He expanded his circle of careful bonhomie to include them all. 'You fighting with Manda?'

'Daft bitch says she's not here to play. She's here to chat with Charity. I told her she can chat to Chas over a nice cup of Darjeeling in a nice cafe; if she's in the Blue Cube and it's night-time and she's drinking free drink, then she's playing.'

'She drinking free drink?' Stretch mimed shock and scandal. 'Hey, baby girl, that's a hanging offence.' He banged his empty glass on the counter, called in a deep bass for the barkeep. 'Hey hey hey, Chimp man. How come those ladies get their drinks for free while us working men need to pay for ours or sing for our supper? That ain't right. Fill us up.'

Bili punched him on the biceps. 'Fucking A, Stretch. We going to play today? Place is filling up and I don't see a house band.'

'You and Amanda could do a nice duet. Harmonise till dawn. Something sweet and cool, together like sisters.'

'Stretch stopped a knife fight outside,' said Shard, half to himself. The others fell silent and stared at him.

'Do what?' said Bili.

269

'I was preserving two young men from imminent destruction.' Stretch smiled as widely as ever. 'This guy was about to demonstrate the old slice 'n' dice, and they were just too darned stupid to see it for themselves. So I explained the many errors of their ways and they departed, joyous, unto the arms of the night.'

'Do what?' Bili repeated herself, incredulous.

'I didn't know where I was.' It was plainly an evening of continuing surprises for Shard, who did indeed appear to be only partially present.

'You would have taken them, man.' Stretch watched his companion. Bili watched them both. Stretch was serious now. 'You would have killed them. The look was in your eyes. The killing look. You were a soldier once.'

'I was.' Shard spoke slowly, slurring words.

'Me too,' said Stretch.

'I didn't know that.' Bili looked from one to the other, then watched her glass refill at the hands of the barkeep, who poured coffee for Shard, a long whiskey for Stretch, then left, silently as he'd arrived.

'Didn't know what?' The woman known as Amanda rested her two hands upon Bili's two shoulders. Bili nodded at Stretch.

'Stretch was a soldier.'

'Yes,' said Amanda. 'Sea, Air, Land, am I right? One foot in the water, things like that? Boy things. And he plays off his rage on the piano almost every night. Am I right?' She lit the light of her too-bright eyes on Stretch's gleaming black skin. 'You're right, Bili. We should play. You're always right.'

Stretch smiled a wide, wide smile. 'Chief Petty Officer Stretch, re-tired and at your service.' He stretched long southern vowels.

'Ruins.' Shard quite suddenly stood upright. 'In the ruins.' The silent assembly stared at him. 'I'm in the ruins. Me.' As suddenly as he'd stood up, he sat down again. Shook his head, then shook it again. Stretch reached a long, heavy, muscled arm around him.

'Man. You are wasted.' As Shard tried to rise once more, Stretch held him in his seat, two big men, holding things together. Shard sat, sighed and closed his eyes.

'This man needs sleep.' Stretch looked around. 'Who got the keys to the apartment upstairs?' Bili pulled a chain from around her neck and passed it over. Stretch raised Shard to his feet, knocking two chairs off balance as he did so. Bili caught one, Amanda the other, synchronised saves.

'We need to make some noise.' Stretch looked back over to them, sharing his thoughts. 'I'll be back soon as I can lift our friend here onto a mattress.'

Amanda nodded, and surprised Bili by walking to the stage, through the building crowd and around any empty tables, finally climbing up and taking a seat behind the piano. The piano more usually manipulated into music by Stretch himself. Bili followed her, stood quiet at the side of the stage, watching, her expression unreadable. She turned to face the audience, the filling crowd, but their collective attention was more on themselves, on each other, than on the stage. Music drifted from the stage. Bili turned back to watch in silence as Amanda keyed a familiar set of chords, leaned towards the microphone more usually used by Stretch to announce the performers and the songs they sang, and eased her voice around 'Cry Me a River', a quiet, confident performance which by its conclusion had silenced every speaking voice and turned every head in the house towards her.

'Thank you.' Amanda adjusted the height of the seat, swept her glance across the islands of expectant faces, waved Bili up onto the stage and revealed to the audience that although amateur piano and virtuoso electric bass were hardly a commonplace duet, she and Bili would now like to perform a small set of quiet, traditional, romantic folk songs while Stretch was upstairs in the bedroom . . . with a man. She rolled her eyes, and the audience applauded and wolf-whistled in a long-shared joke. As soon as Bili stepped up, plugged in and stood to, Amanda stamped the piano's loud pedal and belted full-tilt into the unmistakeable intro to The Beatles' 'Lady Madonna'. Bili pounded her big bright red Rickenbacker along for the ride, anchored her lead voice to Amanda's accurate harmonies, and the evening swung into action.

'Didn't know you played the piano, Amanda.' Bili was offering warmth and congratulation in an unusual direction. 'That was seriously smooth.' Amanda sipped at a long, tall glass and nodded her appreciation.

'Cool music, little lady.' Stretch subsided into a spare chair at their table. It groaned. 'I can see I'll be out of a job. Old man piano plainly likes his ivories tickled by a fine young woman rather than some gnarly old fool like this one.'

Amanda smiled her appreciation, looked more concerned than flattered.

'How's your guy? Shard?' she asked. 'What's up with him? He OK?'

The habitual smile which decorated Stretch's face slipped a little.

'You know him? Know him well, I mean? He a user? Shard, man, does he, like, relax with a needle? Play the spoon?'

Bili and Amanda shook their heads. Bili spoke first.

'He's friends with Stoner. Work friends. You see JJ working with a smackhead? Nah. Me neither, black man.'

'Never seen no crackhead ride a bicycle, neither, nor have a body like his.' Stretch's smile was restored to its former glory. 'Then he been doped. Easily done, either deliberately or by accident.'

'Doped by accident?' Bili stared. 'How the fuck do you dope someone – like – by accident? You, y'know, sort of accidentally drop a half pint of, oh I dunno, arsenic into his Pepsi and he goes la-la? Don't see it. Doped with what, anyway?'

'He don't know where he is. He don't know what he's doing. Anything from a tequila slammer to one of the Chimp's coladas can do that, get enough inside you. But Shard don't smell drunk. And he was sharp an' fast enough to take down a couple of bangers outside – I wasn't foolin' 'bout that; I saved their dumb asses from him. Reckon he'd have hurt them bad. Both of them. But he went straight down the pan from there.'

'He OK now? Where is he?' Amanda stood up, looked around. 'Anyone seen Charity?'

'Not since I was a child, little lady.' Stretch grinned more broadly than before. 'Charity was a white Christian high school illness, permanently cured by vigorous exercise, cold showers and limitless self-control. Never give anything to anyone for free. No. I've not seen the lady who styles herself in that fashion since you went on stage. Shard? He seems OK. He's upstairs in the flat.'

'Locked in?'

'Strange question, Manda. Why should he be locked in? This ain't no prison and he ain't no prisoner. Why'd I lock him in?' Stretch's voice trailed away into the background roar and he joined Amanda in a visual search of the club. 'You want I should go see him? See he's all right?' He didn't wait for an answer, just launched through the milling drinkers, the party people parting before him as he headed for the back of the bar.

Amanda turned to Bili.

'It's surprisingly easy to dope – to poison – someone by accident. It usually happens that the poison was intended for someone else.'

'And you know this, how, exactly?' Bili squinted through her curls, peering into the depths of her drink.

'Maybe read it in *Practical Poisoning for Petite Piano Players*. Some old book in the library.'

'You are so full of shit, girlie.' Bili grinned and waved an empty glass over her head. 'But I forgive you.' The glass was replaced by a fresh, filled one. Bili smiled an invisible smile of thanks to no one in particular. To her invisible benefactor. 'Can you see your friend? Lady Charity? You reckon she's a demon poisoner?'

Amanda sat down. Lifted the filled glass from Bili's hand, sank maybe a half of it, pulled a bad face, and passed the glass back.

'Doubt it. But I reckon she'd know a poison working when she saw it.' She nodded to herself. Bili finished the drink, stamped the glass down hard on the table between them and nodded. Belched. 'Pardon. Me. Reckon you're right. JJ treats the pair of them like they're compadres, so who knows.' She leaned back in her chair. 'We going to play some more?'

Amanda shook her head. 'Let the house band take the applause, now they've finally rolled in. What pair of them? Pair of what?'

Bili's eyes were closed. 'I'm just going to sit for a while. Listen to Mellow Yellow Jello or whatever the band call themselves this week.'

Amanda leaned across the table. 'Pair of what?'

'Sisters.' Bili's voice was a small thing, fading fast. 'They're sisters, aren't they. Chas and Chas. Welcome to each other, too. Thieves. Thick as. Ah, fuck off, Amanda. I'm pooped. Need to sit for a while.' She rolled a single eye into view. 'And no, girlie, I'm not poisoned. Pooped. Pissed. Pissed and pooped. My favourite condition. Just need a rest. OK with you?'

But Amanda was gone.

Charity was sitting, relaxed in an easy chair, in the dark and the surprising cool and quiet. Surprising given that the apartment was above a night club, and that night clubs tend to be hot and loud, if they're any use as a night club. Cool music, and a heated atmosphere to appreciate it.

These and similar thoughts were a million miles away from Charity. She leaned across the easy chair, resting her right shoulder against its back, with her legs hooked over the arm. She was watching Stretch, who was stretched out along a chaise long, reclining gracelessly and watching Charity. Being persons of talent and ability, capable of multitasking in the modern manner, they were also both watching Shard. This required little effort or concentration, because he gave every appearance of being asleep. No snores, but a sure lack of movement and easy, regular breathing.

Amanda entered without knocking.

'He asleep?' she asked no one in particular.

'Ask him.' Charity's divided attention maintained its twin interests.

'Hey, dude. You asleep?' Amanda asked. No reply. She shrugged. 'What's up with him?'

Stretch unrolled into a more conventional seated position.

'He's drugged, somehow.'

'Poisoned?' Amanda walked in silence over to the wide bed, entirely occupied by Shard, who maintained his senseless silence.

'Same thing, miss.' There was no humour in Stretch's voice, though his mouth smiled the words as it set them free. 'He's been out for a couple hours. Pulse steady, breathing clean, temperature stable. Check yourself if it makes you happy.'

Amanda walked to the horizontal Shard, leaned over him, breathing his breath. 'Yeah,' she said. 'And he smells OK, too. No puke.'

Charity and Stretch each raised an eyebrow to the other.

'You expect him to puke?' Charity asked.

'Not really. He's no ace guitarist so far's I know, but even non-musicians can inhale their own vomit, so I believe.' Amanda stood upright, stretched her back and yawned widely. 'I reckon we should wake him.'

'Why?' Stretch, short and to the point. 'If he's just sleeping – which is an idea of appeal to me, to be honest – why don't we just leave him be? Check on him in the morning.' No reply

275

came, and he looked over to Amanda, who stared at Shard, who stared right back at her, eyes wide open. Charity joined in with the new game of everyone stares at Shard. The focus of their interest stared at Amanda. Looked around, counting heads.

'Fuck,' he said. 'That was weird.'

'Hey, Shard.' Amanda breathed like she was recovering from a passion. 'Tell me how it was. For you,' she added.

Shard's gaze was held by hers. The others may have been invisible so far as he was concerned. Maybe they were invisible to him.

'Weird,' he said. 'Well fucking weird.'

'Yeah?' Amanda breathed some more. The others craned in to hear her better. 'How so, big man? How . . . weird? Huh?'

'Like . . . like . . . I'm still in the club, yeah?'

Amanda nodded. They all nodded. Shard nodded. Conformity is a wonderful thing.

'She wants to know where Stoner is.'

'Who does? Who's she?' Amanda's hands silenced anything the others might have been about to say.

Shard said nothing.

'Who? Who's after Stoner? And why?'

'I don't know.' Shard grew pale. 'I'm shattered. I don't know who. She . . .' his voice trailed. 'I can't see her face. At all. Not at all. Weird. I can hear her voice. Lovely voice.'

'Can you try to put a face to it? Come on, it's important.'

'No it's not. She's . . . she's OK. Really. She's OK. Really like her.' He sank back onto an elbow. 'OK if I crash here? Really tired.'

Stretch moved across the room, silent, fast, implacable. Amanda stepped back to allow him access. Stretch caught Shard by the shoulders, raised him up to a more or less seated posture, though he was very slumped, folded on himself.

'Remember me?' Stretch was nose to nose with Shard, who opened his eyes and looked steadily at his questioner.

'Yeah. Black brother. Player piano. Got to sleep, brother. Nothing left. Let me down gentle . . .' And he was gone, asleep in Stretch's grasp. With the careful consideration often characteristic of men his size, Stretch lowered the sleeping subject of the evening's entertainment back to rest. Turned him, adjusted him.

'Recovery position,' he said to Amanda. 'In case he chokes.'

'Drugged,' she replied. 'Him, not you.' She smiled. 'Who's good with the pharmacy? Anyone recognise this? Delayed action downers? How does that work? He was lively enough when he landed in the Cube, huh?'

'He was about to slice a couple of guys when I caught him.' Stretch was thoughtful. 'Psychotropics. If anything.'

'You know about those?' Amanda lifted her attention from the sleeping Shard to the looming black man.

'Yeah. Enough. Not convinced, though. Looks like voodoo to me.'

Amanda smiled at him. 'Go on, roll your eyes, do the whole lawdy-lawdy thing. I can see you acting out a decent Uncle Tom, and all that.'

'Yes ma-am,' he drawled out his long southern vowels. Sobered quickly. 'I wasn't kidding. Reckon he's doped. Doesn't look like anything psychoactive. Not really. Not now I think about it. Most like some kind of serious gris-gris. Voodoo.'

Amanda walked to stand next to him, took his arm, walked them away from the silent Shard. 'You're serious?'

'Uh-huh. Operated out of Florida some time for some time. Long time. You see lots of weird shit. When you're a musician.' He suddenly laughed aloud. 'When you're a spooky musician. Where's Charity?'

She was gone.

18

GETHSEMANE AGAIN

'Long gun.' Stoner's voice echoed softly in the church. They were alone. No one else there to frown at their defilement of some dead god's sanctuary. Except maybe that god himself, if he cared. Which he so plainly did not. Even though his I Am Here candle was burning in a red jar suspended above the altar, any supernatural presence was way beyond intangible.

'I'd have to use a long gun for that.'

'You said.' Chastity's reply was even more muted in its enthusiasm than the reverence of their situation called for.

'Better ideas? As in, have you got some?' Stoner was lying on his back, stretched out over a series of heavily embroidered cushions, whose heavy religious depictions were endlessly failing in their purpose of inducing tidings of goodwill to all men. They were, however, more comfortable and less unyielding than the wooden benches themselves.

Chastity hefted herself from the stone pillar which had been providing unwitting support and walked, silent in her bare feet, down the nave. She stopped when she approached the altar screen, and, unexpectedly, fell gently to her knees and crossed herself. Stoner's eyes tracked her. His face showed no expression at all. Neutrality rules within churches as without them. Chastity's head bowed, her face fell to consider the ancient stone slabs and the patterned tiling of the floor.

'Murder from the cathedral,' she intoned, the reverence of her tone matching her supplicant posture.

While she rested unfocused eyes on the ground, Stoner raised his to the heavens, contemplating the barrier of a finely-wrought and perfectly maintained ceiling.

'It's all fake.' His voice continued its echoing path to heaven. 'Us bastard Brits bombed the fuck out of the place in the war. We did that a lot. Discourages a chap's belief in angels, quiet or otherwise, if they couldn't be bothered to protect their favourite god's own roof. Some of the churches keep bits of bombed-out bells to . . . to what? Remind them of something? Provide a mortality lesson? Discourage their leaders from attacking Brits again? No more daft than the rest of the holy relics, though. You asleep?' His gaze remained heavenward.

'Where do we get it?'

'Divine intervention or a long gun?' Stoner's voice smiled for him. 'Where would you usually get it? Carrefour? Lidl on special killers' discount day?'

She was sitting by his head, quite suddenly, any flaw in her silence disguised by the godly echo of the huge building's suppressive ambience. She leaned over him, closed his eyelids with the tips of her finger and kissed him. At length and with skill and deliberation but little intensity. When lips and fingers lifted away, his eyes remained closed.

'The killer's kiss? The Judas kiss? You about to betray me? Should I be getting prepped for my very own Stations of the Cross as I totter towards my very own Calvary?'

She leaned over him again, murmured, 'Do you ever, ever stop talking? Just a little bit? This is a house of prayer.'

Her lips moved once again to his, which managed, 'Yeah, when we need a den of thieves . . .' before the contact and comfort of a second kiss silenced them. He reached for her head, she caught his hands and held them away from her, returned them to his sides. He lay, relaxed, returned her kisses, companionship rather than passion their possibly shared motive.

She sat back at last, breathing easily and relaxed in his company, in the comfort of the huge religiously-intentioned building.

'Gun,' she said. 'A long one. OK. Where would you get one? Charm usually arranges my ordnance. I say what I want and she provides. Usually. You super-secret soldier boys have your very own super-secret sources, I expect.'

'Theft.' Stoner's eyes remained closed. He appeared as though he could set to stone and stay there forever. 'I'd steal one. Crap handguns are less of a pain than a decent rifle, though.'

'Who from? Who'd you steal guns from?'

Stoner sighed. 'Crims. Crims have guns. Shops. Gunshops have guns. If there's time, answer an ad. It's supposed to be impossible to buy a gun illegally, but it's not. Especially if you have a decent amount of cash.'

'Which you do?'

'Cash is easier to acquire than guns.'

'Who do you steal cash from, then? I'm assuming you do steal it?'

'Correct. Hookers and dopers, mainly. Sorry, pimps and dealers; they're the ones who carry the cash. Knock over enough of them and buy a gun. Sometimes you get lucky and a dealer or a pimp has a pistol as well as a roll of notes in his pants. And it's an unusual pimp who reports a robbery to the police.'

'Easy as that?'

'Mostly. In a decently big city, at any rate.'

'I thought you'd head out into the underworld, seedy night-clubs and the like.'

'You can do that, but you run a bigger risk of taking a serious beating. Which is one way of discovering the joys of the local public health service but has little else to recommend it. It's hard to operate effectively if you've been smacked around too much. Or, of course, you ask someone you know. Depends on whether you know someone and whether you've got the time and the currency.'

'You know someone?' Chastity was sitting upright now, resting her hands on her thighs, watching the church's main entrance as if anticipating a divine visitation. 'You know someone from your old spooks' network?'

'Oh yes.' Stoner was as static as a statue. 'Fancy a little more lip service? I enjoyed that. Domestic. Blissful. Makes a chap consider retirement.' She leaned down to him again, rubbed the tip of her nose against the tip of his.

'You don't fancy some of that wild sex of yours in a church? You ever made out in a church?'

Stoner grunted in reply and sat up.

'Yes and yes and yes and . . . We'll have company soon.'

'We will?'

'We will. A particularly nice religiously inclined lady who will satisfy our every need. Ordained and into ordnance. Who could ask for more?' He stood up, reached for the sky with his hands, then bent down, touched the toes of his Caterpillar boots and repeated the exercise a half-dozen times. Chastity stared at him. Tilted her head and bulged her eyes in the silent question.

'Huh?'

'While you were doing all your loving family routine, asking after your mother's health, the state of the family finances, acquiring the target, so forth, I just sort of asked around, like you do.'

'Like *you* do.' Said flatly, emphasis on the second word. She punched him, not gently, on his left bicep. 'Like you do. And like nobody else does.'

'Not true. Lots of us. Several hundred across Europe, most likely. You really don't know much about it, do you? It's a miracle you survived. Any of you.' He raised a shout to the godly rafters, 'It's a miracle!'

'No need to shout, Jean-Jacques. God will always hear you if you want Him to.' An impossibly wide woman, dressed from head to toe in religious black, addressed them from the pulpit. Chastity spun around, dived behind the nearest of a long array of benches. Stoner bowed from the waist.

'Sister.'

'Mother.'

'Really? How did that happen? Another immaculate conception? They sound like no fun at all. Best left to the funless Jews. Mother.'

The figure in the pulpit rearranged the numerals in the list of hymns to be sung by the faithful, whenever they next appeared. '"Jesu, Joy of Man's Desiring", one of my favourites. Great melody. Sounds superlative when sung by a choir in a church. You'd be after guns rather than redemption, Jean-Jacques.'

'You know the truth, Mother, as always.' Stoner bowed. 'I am still working on the redemption, though.'

'I believe you. No one else here does, but I do. I even pray for you.'

'Every night? That's almost a comfort. If a little spooky.'

'No. I pray for you whenever I hear your name. If I'm hearing it, so are too many others. One day when I hear your name, Jean-Jacques, it will be from the lips of a stranger asking me to bury you.'

'Which you will, Mother.'

'Which I will.'

'How is it with your god, Mother? He up to snuff lately? Challenging times for the Christians' lonely deity, I'd imagine. Confessions business should be good though. Do you still sell indulgences to the cautious faithless?'

'Guns are guns, Jean-Jacques. No need for hyperbole. If that's what you were trying for. Your German is – frankly –

rusting in pieces before me. Would you prefer English? Does your delicate and badly-named friend need translation, or does she speak the language of Kaisers and philosophers? "Angel of Death" sounds a lot better in German than in English. Better yet in Russian.'

Chastity bowed, replied in colloquial German. Meaningless fencing pleasantries were exchanged. Stoner walked to the pew before the pulpit, knelt on the hassock and rested his head in his hands. Supplicant.

'Forgive me, Mother, for I have sinned . . .'

They were soaking into the unique echoing silence of a large church. Chastity held her peace. Incredibly, the wide woman in the pulpit stretched out her hands over Stoner.

'I listen, Jean-Jacques. Only the truth please.' Silences grew around them. Not a cough nor a shuffle disturbed them. Chastity appeared to hold her breath. Tension displayed as a stiffened stillness.

'I have killed again, Mother.' Stoner's tone took Chastity by the throat and shook her like a dog. Its pain and the loss it contained destroyed the peace and the silence of the old church.

'Go on. There's more. There always is.'

'I will kill again. Soon. Sometimes badly.'

'Can your conscience comfort you? Can you believe in the rightness of your actions, Jean-Jacques?'

'No. Not always.'

The woman sighed. Her sibilance grew as it spread wings around them through the entirety of the church.

'You're asking for forgiveness?'

'No.'

'For what? You're in a church, confessing to a priest.'

'Not a priest, Mother. Never that. I share my pilgrim honesty with you; a crusader, with a warrior. This is no confession. There is no absolution, no forgiveness of sins, no life everlasting, no hereafter. Not for me. There is certainly power and there might be glory, but it has little to do with me.'

'You are your own penance, Jean-Jacques. You always were. Adding to it would be a sin. If you need me to help you, then in exchange you need to return what you borrow. You need to add to my knowledge and to undertake a task I'll set you once your debts are cleared.'

'Yes.' The single word. The day was dimming inside the church as the sun passed from one stained-glass window to another. While the small party stood in deepening darkness, the full stained light of the sun quite suddenly illuminated the high altar. The polished brass of the tabernacle lit up like the gold it pretended to be. Without appearing to move and with no sound at all, the female cleric was standing between Chastity and Stoner. She held out her hands to encompass them both.

'Come to the sacristy. We can talk death and weapons in peace in there.'

'How is your long black whore?' The hard, dark priestess was no less formidable in the relative sanity of the sacristy.

Stoner nodded an acknowledgement. Said nothing.

'Last I heard, she was looking for you.' The priestess shrugged from the black cloak and stared at Chastity. 'Women do that, don't they, Jean-Jacques? They look for you. Then they find you, and it ends in tears.'

'It always does, Mother.' Stoner walked to a small safe, opened it and removed a cardboard box. Flicked open the lid and extracted a small handful of communion wafers. Popped one onto his tongue, chewed and swallowed. Repeated the process. 'I always enjoyed eating these. They soak up the altar wine, too.'

Chastity stared at him, motionless, speechless. The priestess, suddenly considerably less bulky as she stood before them in a black outfit which appeared more suited to a midnight assignation in a gymnasium than for a celebration at a high altar, reached out a hand, patted Chastity on the cheek. She recoiled, shaking her head in strangely uncomfortable distaste at the contact.

'Don't get attached to this one.' The priestess shook loose the long, dark ponytail which had appeared from inside the bulky cassock. 'He's exactly what he seems to be, and there's no room in your life for honesty like that. "Angel of Death"? Great title. Are you? Or are you just another tawdry killer? Stoner would make a good Angel of Death, if your mythologies allow for male angels.'

Chastity turned to face Stoner. 'What is this woman on about? Why are we here? Is she really some kind of cleric? Or just another nut-job dressing up in a cape like some fat super-hero?'

Stoner smiled, for the first time in a little while. 'Bernadette is indeed a priest. Worse than that, she's Mother . . .' he glanced to Bernadette, who nodded and raised her left hand, palm uppermost, until it was level with her shoulder. 'Mother Superior of a convent or a retreat or something sexist which allows no men and no obvious pleasures of any kind, so far as I know. Bernie, say hello to Chastity; Chas, Bernadette.' He paused. 'We go back a long way.'

'I was part of a different organisation when we first met.' Bernadette's casual statement fell twitching to the floor between them. She had produced a melodic Irish accent from somewhere and had switched quite suddenly to English, rather than her fluent and precise German. 'That dates it. And him. And me.' She smiled.

'Are you just letting him eat all your holy bread?' Chastity waved a hand at Stoner, who had chewed his way through about half the box of wafers.

'Why not? It's only bread, and they're cheap enough. Do you need to eat something proper, Jean-Jacques? I can't vouch for the nutritional value of those.' Bernadette's neat German had returned to her.

'Don't you believe they're the body of God, or something?' Chastity was hanging on, her purpose unclear but her tenacity beyond doubt. 'He can't just chew his way through an entire box of gods, surely?'

'They're just wafers. Nothing more. Relax. Jean-Jacques? A meal?'

'But you're a nun, right? You believe.' Chastity made a sneer from a statement. 'You mumble mumbo-jumbo, wave your hands around and change a wafer into real genuine godstuff. You're smart. You can't believe nonsense like that.'

'Why not? I can believe what I want to believe. I believe what's real to me. You believe what's real to you. It's not a competition, there's no winner, no loser, only right and wrong, truth and lies, honesty and deception. Black and white and every shade of grey between them. It's not even a choice. You believe or you do not believe. People pretend, they pretend to believe and to not believe – but why do they do that?

'And you know exactly what I'm talking about, Chastity. You've looked hard into the eyes of the dying. You've seen their sudden understanding, realisation, fear and their need to make their own peace with what they see before them. They see the path and they know then that they need help along that path. You take that away from them. It will drive you more insane until you snap and you kill yourself. It happens to all women who walk the road you're walking, sister.'

'Only women?' Chastity sounded subdued, though her eyes signalled a different, turbulent tale.

'Mostly women. Most men lack the sensitivity. They're not very smart, most of them. Think mostly with their dicks, not their souls.'

'You OK with this, JJ?' Chastity flashed a challenge with her question.

'You girls carry right along. Make like I'm not here. I'll get on with guy stuff, OK? Don't worry your pretty little empty heads about the old gorilla over here. I'll just peel a banana and talk to myself about football.'

'I'm done. Fuck philosophy.' Chastity stalked to a chair nearby, wound herself down into it. 'Should I keep the door open? That way we can see any visitors.'

Bernadette answered, speaking into the air, not directly to either Chastity or Stoner. 'Keep it closed. You'd need to drill through it to eavesdrop. It was designed by generations of my forebrethren, so they could bugger their choirboys to ecstasy without disturbing the holy songs being sung outside by the mostly unholy.'

'Strangely cynical, Bernie.' Stoner stood close to her. 'You wobbling in your faith or just having another crack at us simple chaps?'

She smiled at him and replied in her Irish-accented English. 'Yeah. It's all about the crack, isn't it now? Isn't it always, Jean-Jacques? Fill me in. No more than I need to know. I need to be able to make peace with my God, as you know.'

'You really do believe in this crap? God in His heaven and water and wine and resurrection and the Pope in his palaces?' Chastity's voice was low, drifting across the ancient clay tiles of the sacristy.

Bernadette's reply was similarly subdued. 'If I did not, I would not be here, you would not be here, and I would be of no use to you at all. So . . . yes, I believe in all that crap. It's real to me. As true and as real as you sitting there sunning yourself in the dark. If the prayers I pray and in which I believe work well on behalf of an unbeliever, then I pray – I will pray this day – that you also come to believe before it kills you. Which it will. Which it will, my sister. Have no doubts at all. Without belief, you can hope only for a quick death, maybe a clean one. Pray yourself to all that is godless that your end comes from a man as competent as Jean-Jacques. Or just trust to luck. A firm belief in your own mortality is a harder belief than a quiet belief in angels, trust me.'

She spoke directly to Stoner. 'If you care to speak to me for a moment while Chastity considers her ways and others', you could drop a hint or two about what you're wanting.'

Stoner outlined their recent activity, carefully avoiding names and locations. Recited an obviously carefully considered wish-list. Bernadette listened. Even Chastity gave every appearance of listening. He wound to a stop and reached for a cup, walking to the hand basin and filling it from the single tap.

'It's the wafers, Jean-Jacques. They need to be blessed to soothe your thirst. Without that, they do dry the mouth.'

'No more than this tale of woe and incompetence.' He drank a second cup, filled a third, held it out to Bernadette. 'Bless this for me, Mother.'

'You remember her, then? Blesses? You do remember her? That's good. There may be hope for you, yet. Have you heard anything of her lately? It would be a comfort to learn that she's . . . secure.' She took the chipped cup into her left hand, made a sign of the cross over it with her right. Raised it to her lips and sipped, then spat softly into the water. Held the cup over her breast, then passed it back to Stoner. 'My heart to your heart. Peace between us, my son. My brother. My friend.'

'Mother.' Stoner took the cup and drank from it, draining it. Nodded to Bernadette and returned the cup to the table by the sink. He turned back. 'Always peace between us. Can you deliver the hardware?'

'Consider it done.'

'When?'

'Before you need any of it. But Blesses?'

'Not a word from her since Belfast. Ask Mallis. He'd find her for you. Can't be difficult. There's only so many prisons.'

'Ask him yourself. If you want. Maybe you should. Meantime . . .' an almost theatrical pause, an exaggerated thoughtfulness. 'There's a price for the ordnance.'

'Of course there is.' Stoner smiled. 'Let's all hope I can pay it.'

Bernadette turned her back on them, Stoner and Chastity both, a triangle of silence between them all. A respected silence. She turned back, waved Chastity to join them. 'All right. Untraceable, silent. Can you still do that, Jean-Jacques?'

'Hope so.' He nodded.

'In less than an hour, you'll be outside the church. A van will arrive and a group of women, girls really, will leave it. They need identities and saving. I can provide identities and the church has been a saviour for their kind since forever. But there's been the difficulty of the van driver, who would be reluctant to allow the girls their freedom, and is insensitive to kindly moral arguments concerning his immortal soul. It wasn't obvious how we'd deal with him.' She gestured at Stoner, at Chastity. 'God provides, as seen here.'

Stoner nodded. 'OK. No more driver, no van, salvation all round and we can return to our hotel?'

'That's it. Silent. Untraceable. Immediate. Immortal soul liberated from the confines of flesh.'

'An act of God.'

'An act of an Apostle, or of an apostate, more like.' Chastity had rejoined the conversation, her eyes never leaving Stoner.

Bernadette crossed to Stoner, took both his hands in both of hers. 'Be well, my brother.'

He nodded. 'You too, my sister, my little sister.'

She pulled aside a heavy curtain, revealing a door. 'You can leave this way. I think I should pray alone for a while.'

Stoner and Chastity walked through the early evening's spectral light, down the pathway through the graveyard and out into the busy street. Commuters, shoppers, office workers headed either to or from their homes, either to or from their employment. He led the way to a tall, wide tree, one of several with a steel ring of seating around its base. They sat.

'Christ, JJ. Don't tell me you believe all that religious

289

nonsense? You? A stone killer if there ever was one? You can believe that?'

'Makes no difference what I believe. What Bernie believes is important to her. I respect that. You should, too.' He crossed his left leg across his right knee and removed the Caterpillar boot.

'I can do respect. Though your friend is very strange.' Chastity watched with evident curiosity. 'What on earth are you doing? Changing your socks? Shouldn't you be watching for a van?'

Stoner pushed two fingers firmly into the cleated sole of the boot, at the same time pulling the heel backwards until it came away in his hand. The sole's steel reinforcement was revealed, and he slid a strong thumbnail under each side of it, prising it free then lifting it complete from the shoe. The heel replaced, the boot back on its foot, he repeated the process with the other Caterpillar boot, this time extracting not the reinforcing metalwork but a reel of cord and what appeared to be a small handful of pebbles from within the heel itself. He replaced the boot, as before.

Chastity sat in amused silence.

'There it is.' Stoner nodded to a van, drawing to the kerb across the street from their shared seat. 'I hope. Walk over to the driver, ask him for directions, if he's got a light for your cigarette, anything like that. Keep him talking for a minute and away from the girls.' Who were already climbing down from the van's side door, away from them. Chastity nodded, crossed the street and headed for the van driver, a brutally handsome man, tall, slim, dark and wearing fashionable pimp gear and facial stubble, standing beside the van now. She looked behind her, but Stoner had disappeared.

'Excuse me!' Chastity applied her most stunning smile, the driver turned and grinned back at her while his charges adjusted their short clothes and did things with their hair. She dug into the pockets of her jacket, producing a folded piece of paper and a pen. 'Can you help me?' His widening grin revealed that even if he could not, he would certainly try. His charges ignored them both, apart from an occasional sidelong sneer. 'I'm looking for . . .'

She stopped in mid-sentence, transfixed. The driver abruptly shuddered, his eyes wide, his hands rising from his sides and moving slowly – so slowly – to his head. Which suddenly snapped sideways, and he crumpled to the ground.

Chastity spun around, the working girls turned to face her, spotting their fallen master and starting to shriek, collectively. She knelt, reached for a pulse, found none, started to shout about there being an accident, maybe a heart attack, maybe someone could call the police. A crowd condensed around them, the shrieking girls, the fallen driver. Cell phones lit. She saw Stoner, once more sitting at the tall tree's circular bench, once again fiddling with his Caterpillar boots. She walked to him. He stood to greet her. They walked away, her arm through his.

'Catapult.' It was a statement. She was sharing understanding, not enquiring.

'Hmmm. Never leave home without one. Never know when you might see a scary squirrel or some other vermin.'

'Good shots. Both of them. Spot on.'

'OK, I suppose.' They stopped beneath a street sign, found the direction arrow to the railway station, and walked on. Sirens blazed. 'I had four stones. Two missed. I need to practice. Let's go catch a train.'

19

STARTING GATE

'Ah. Mr LaForge. Your luggage has arrived. Finally arrived.' Smart and efficient reception desk lady greeted Stoner and Chastity as they crossed the lobby. Stoner shifted from his original path like an oil tanker making a wide turn, and dropped anchor by the desk.

'Good. About time. Is it damaged? Intact?' His tone carried no undercurrent of concern; he was simply asking after his lost luggage. An everyday thing for a regular traveller.

'No. All the Customs seals look intact, even on the instrument cases. We had no idea we had a musician staying with us, Mr LaForge.' She simpered, a rare achievement for a German reception desk manager, and Stoner scowled a little in appropriate response.

'I trust that's not a problem?'

'No no.' The receptionist banished her moment of humanity, resumed glacial efficiency mode. 'We completely respect your privacy. Completely.' She passed two room keys across the desk. Stoner reinstated the idiot beam of the Englishman abroad, thanked her and rejoined Chastity, who was leaning against a wall by the bank of lifts, every inch the resigned companion to a star of unspecified luminescence. As he neared, she lifted from her slouch, summoned the lift and grinned at him.

'In character, JJ. However do you remember them all?'

His suite was cool, calm, well cleaned and only a little encumbered by a small stack of expensive suitcases and two guitar cases, both bearing prominent Fender logos and a skin of stickers proclaiming to anyone who cared to take notice that these cases, presumably accompanied by their instruments and their player, had travelled the world a lot, on expensive airlines and in the expensive seats. Chastity kicked off her inexpensive, comfortable shoes, bounced onto the bed.

'What. A. Day.' Stoner waved his hands at the walls, suggestively, cautioning unnecessarily. Then dropped his arms to his sides, walked to the bedside table and retrieved Chastity's cell phone from it.

'May I? I've no idea where my phone is. Must have dropped it or some thieving scum lowlife has lifted it.' He waved Chastity's phone at her.

'Go ahead. Knock yourself out. I'm sure I watched you throw it at a policeman. Or was it a nun? Whatever. I'll have a bath. I never want to see another church. My feet are raw with all that culture. Aching with it.' She headed to the bathroom, shedding clothing. Stoner fired up the phone and flicked through pages, sat in one of the easy chairs and studied the small screen. Nodded, studied some more, scrolled a little, nodded some more, and finally rested the phone on a table.

'We're good,' he announced as he walked into the bathroom. Chastity flicked soap suds at him. Accurately enough. 'Nothing's transmitting. Might be recording, but by the time they do the playback thing we should be on our way. Oh yeah, well caught. Memory kicked in just in time, huh?'

Chastity submerged, rinsed her hair, surfaced. 'You're not worried about hardwired bugs?'

'Nah. I'd take a chance on that. Hotel's hardly Soviet era so I doubt we're wired. Could be wrong. I can see whether there's an app for detecting telephone wires in the walls, but

I'd doubt it. A little bit steam age, no? Relics of the Stasi, things like that. Unlikely.'

'You have an app for spotting bugs?'

'Don't you? Doesn't everyone? That's what smartphones are for, isn't it? Apps for everything. I can see where my van is. In case it goes freelance, all on its own, before you ask.'

'You downloaded this app onto my phone? Show me how to use it. Or is it one-time, user-specific? Fingerprint recognition or some such magic?'

'No. Just plain old firmware, most likely Microsoft or Chrome – probably pirated from the NSA or some worthy body with too much money, too much time and not enough brains. You just tap the little icon and off it goes. You look nice enough to eat in that bath.' She grinned at him and raised a long leg above the water.

'Getting in, big bruiser? It's a big bath. Big enough for three, in case you have a special friend here too.'

'Nope. Going to check out the hardware.'

'Hardware?' She lowered her leg back beneath the surface.

'From Bernadette. You didn't think that the guitar cases contain, y'know, like, guitars? Why would I cart guitars around with me? Idiot.' He grinned and left the bathroom, closing the door behind him with some delicacy. No sooner had he reached the first of the cases than Chastity stood beside him, steaming, wrapped in fluffy towels. Stoner leaned towards her, breathed in her own private atmosphere.

'It gets harder. It does,' he remarked, squatting in front of the smaller of the two suitcases.

'So it should. Must be hours since you last got one off.' She put her hands around his neck. 'Keys to the cases? Or does the man from Milk Tray climb in through the window, give me a box of chocolates and you a bunch of keys?'

He shrugged off her hands, lifted the case to the rack, stared at the lock; an unassuming combination mechanism. Keyed in a set of eight numbers. The locks failed to release.

Chastity started to speak, but he shook his head, without looking up from the locks. 'Three strikes and we're fucked. And embarrassed. Possibly dead.' He entered what appeared to be the same set of numbers, this time from the right. The locks fell open with a silent oiled precision not usually found on flight cases. Chastity reached for the catches; Stoner stayed her hands. 'Steady. Bernadette is cautious. She needs to be with a god like hers. There'll be a Judas latch somewhere obvious.'

'A what?'

'You heard.' Stoner spun the case around, examined the hinges, tapped experimentally at their pivot pins. No activity from the case. He turned it around again, re-entered the same number sequence on the keypad, this time starting at the left. The lid lifted a fraction. Stoner sighed, and opened the case up.

'How did you know the numbers?' Chastity spread her hands. 'This is tradecraft trickery, right?'

'It really is a miracle that you guys have survived for so long. Look and learn. Pray hard to any gods you like that you never come up against someone like Bernadette if she's out to get you. Or against me. Or Shard, come to think of it. You'd need a decent set of gods to survive that. Or a long gun. For which . . .' he lifted two boxes from the case, 'we have ammunition. And keys.' He lifted out a metal foil envelope containing three plastic keycards.

'And yeah, tradecraft. Not seen one of these before?' He gestured at the open case. She shook her head.

'No. I could never guess the numbers, right?'

'Right. Three strikes. Failure ignites the case. See how thick the sides of the cases are?' She nodded. 'Magnesium something, depending on who the armourer is; maybe something explosive and nasty, too. Get the combo wrong and the box takes you out, also the room it's in and probably the other boxes too. They might be wireless linked, as well. Let's not find out.'

295

Chastity backed up, started to rub her hair dry. 'All seems a little *Man From Uncle* to me. A bit idiot melodrama. Why the overkill, the destruction? Why would it matter if the wrong person tried to open the box?'

'Because everything can be tracked back. Everything. Then you get the midnight callers, and you so seriously do not want those.'

'I am that midnight caller, JJ. You forget.'

'I forget nothing about you, Chastity. Someone knows what you're doing; someone who should not, someone whose motives are as unclear as their identities. We're going to find out who they are, and when we do, we're going to ask them the why of it. You normally go up against amateurs, maybe a policeman or two. You do OK against people like that. You come up against a pro, a pro spook and you can't even see where he is. I think you're great, really do, but I don't think any of the three of you can survive this.' He sat back and stretched, rocking his shoulders from side to side, flexing his fingers and breathing deeply.

'What the fuck? Survive this? What the fuck are you on about?'

'If Bernie wasn't seriously worried, she wouldn't have gone to all this trouble.'

'And expense.'

'She doesn't need to care about that. Alms for arms, sisters of mercy, all that. She's proper Irish.'

'What?'

'Never mind. There's only one reason I can think of for someone shadowing you and making sure of your kills. When we flush him out, we can ask him whether I'm right. He won't tell us, and we'll do bad things to him or give him over to someone else if we're feeling squeamish. You're used to working in a tight team of three, right?' Chastity nodded. 'Now you're in a big team.'

'A big team of two?' Her smile was scorn illustrated.

'No no. A really big team. This is what I mean. You don't know what you're up against, you and your sabre-toothed siblings. You're playing against a big team, not just taking a hit on behalf of some convenient customer. This is why Mallis wants me to help. Although, to be honest about it, I have no idea why he's bothered. Can't believe you've got meaningful dirt on Mallis or his sister. If you've got a lever on him, then two things. One, respect. Two, you're dead. But he's looking out for you. Why?'

'You asking me, clever soldier boy?'

'I'm asking. Think of me as stupid meathead soldier boy, and enlighten me.'

'Can't.'

'Or won't? Oh come along, this is no time for games, Chas.'

'Can't. Don't know why Mallis is involved or concerned. Truth. Chas . . . Charm may know, but she's not told me.'

'Is that unusual? Her not telling you what's going on? None too sisterly, no offence.'

'None taken. Time was, the three of us knew everything we did together. Then Charity got sick, Charm got, like, all executive and management, and they both got convinced that I was losing it.'

'You are.'

'That a question?'

'Not really. We all lose it. You either work through it or you get out of it or you get dead or too broken to be a threat to anyone with any clout. That's it.'

'I'm losing it? You really think I'm losing it?'

'Yep.'

'And you're happy to work with me? You, who thinks I'm a nutter? You, Mr Tradecraft? Mr guitar god and part time genius killer-man?'

'You kill everyone you fuck, Chastity. That is considerably insane. More than just a discouragement.' Stoner applied a key card to one of the guitar cases, which opened smoothly and silently, no clacking of latches, no scrape of hinge, to reveal a dismantled rifle and a pair of long, fat, telescopic sights. 'Thank you, Bernie,' he breathed, taking Chastity's bath towel from her and laying out the gun parts on it.

The second guitar case contained two handguns, two tube suppressors, oil and a comprehensive cleaning kit. 'H and Ks, very nice.' Stoner muttered, mostly to himself. He collected a second towel from the bathroom and spread the gun cleaning tackle out on it.

'Equal opportunity man, me. Do you want to clean down the long gun or the shorties?'

'Which is for me?' Chastity held his eyes with her own. Direct question.

'The long one. You happy with it?'

'Yes. Used one before.'

'Set up your own sights?'

'Yes.'

'Clean that, strip and build, strip and build. Do you need a stand for it?'

'What range?'

'Only you know that, Chas. You have the target and the location. Not me.'

She slid into a shirt, fetched a map from the hotel's supply. Lifted an iPad from her luggage, waited for it to wake, then called up a map and a location on that map. Passed it to Stoner, who nodded and passed it back, spreading out the hotel's paper map for them both to consider.

'Where would you take the shot?' Stoner looked at the map as he asked the question.

'Never mind where I'd take it from,' she replied. 'They'd work that out, wouldn't they, Mr Paranoid? Because they know how I do what I do. Then they'll be waiting for me? So you should choose the hide and fool them.'

Stoner looked up. 'Makes no difference. You can't use a suppressor at that range, not if you're going to be accurate. And you need to be accurate because the location is a railway halt and there'll be other people around. You need to take the shot, pack up the gun, leave the case with the gun and get out fast. They're bound to be waiting for you – whoever they are – and they'll be able to get a good idea of where you're firing from. Choose your spot, take the shot, get out hot. Simple. Will you need a stand?'

'Maybe. If there is one, I'll use it. What will you be doing, Mr Tradecraft?'

'I'll be part of the crowd.'

'Oh.' She sounded less than delighted. 'Checking that I've made the hit and doing the coup de grâce thing if not?'

'No. You'll do the job. No doubt about that. I'll be watching whoever's watching out for you. Who's your target?'

She retrieved the iPad, finger-flicked through pages and returned it to him with a series of images set up for his inspection. Stoner ran through them all several times. Considered.

'No one I know. You?'

'No. Always best. He'll be the only very fat Arab guy in his party of five, according to Charm.'

'And you know which train he'll be travelling on? And that he will definitely get out at this stop? Going up the hill or down the hill? It makes a difference in that you could do without the train between you and him when you take the shot, and you could do without the sun in your eyes.'

'Really? Well gosh and golly. I might never have thought that all for myself. I'm only a girl. One of three trains, a half hour between each. And yes, he'll be getting out at this stop on his way down. Or up. No idea why, before you ask.'

'Culture vulture. Crazy Arab tourist come to steal the flower of German womanhood and sausage . . . or something. What would a fat Arab want in the middle of tourist Germany? And who is he anyway?'

'Is that rhetoric? Do you care who he is?' Chastity sounded

vaguely surprised, dressing herself slowly while watching the weapons rather than Stoner.

'I never care. It's impossible to care. Do you?'

Chastity shuffled her damp shoulders, settling her dry shirt, then shrugged. 'I sometimes wonder who and why. Don't you? Is it something I'll grow out of? Did you want to know why you were taking a hit, back when you were new to it all?'

'That was a while ago.' Stoner was stripping a pistol steadily, fluidly, automatically, staring into space while he did so. 'I was a soldier. I believed in the honour, the purpose, the regiment, the queen and country, all of that. When I went solo it was an extension of the same thing, just better paid and with a lot more freedom and a lot less support. My first contract was in Ireland. I could have done it for free, for the crack as we said back then. The Hard Man – you can't have forgotten him – explained that was not an option. I must get paid. It must be a contract. It must be a job, not on a whim or for revenge or soldierly love or any unreliable fatuous crap like that. Not for the queen, not for the country, for the money. Anything else is insanity.'

'Who was he?'

'Who was who?'

'You first contract?'

'No one I knew. Could've been anyone. Any man. Any woman.'

'You'd be OK with killing a woman?'

'Sure. Why not? You're a woman, research reveals, do you worry about hitting men? Women?'

'All my targets have been men.' Chastity paused, rubbed her oily hands together. 'Not really thought about it before we started our intellectual debates.'

'You've never killed a woman?' Stoner's scepticism was clear.

'Yes. In Israel. Just before you performed your gallant rescue knight routine.'

'I thought your target was a man?' Stoner's interest was clear.

'It was. The woman was . . . she was . . . in the way. A necessary casualty. I told you then.'

'How d'you feel about that?'

'Nothing, why? She was OK, though. Attractive. She certainly liked me.'

'Is that important? Did that make it OK to kill her?' Stoner was watching her closely, a half-smile flickering around his eyes.

'Didn't think about it. It had to be done.'

'That's the only way, Chas. There's no high morality, no moral justification. There never is. The only high ground you want is so you can get a better angle for delivering the bullet.'

'How do you reconcile it, then?' Chastity laid the freshly reassembled rifle on the table before her, steepled her fingers above it and flexed them. The gun oil shone on her knuckles and fingernails, a killer's gloss.

'Reconcile what? Killing people? I don't. Correction. I try not to. But it's like fucking strangers; after a while you grow immune, cauterised. You can't care about everyone you fuck, it's just not possible, so the same applies. It's not logic or a justification, it's just an operating system. Anything that gets in the way, sooner or later kills you. Or hurts you so badly that you're out, then you depend on the same tradecraft to keep you safe in your retirement.'

'Most guys don't get to fuck as many women as you, Mr Guitarist. Most guys wouldn't know what to with that much pussy if it was offered to them in a parade. Most guys care about the tiny number of women they mate with, breed with, play housey-housey with. Or they say they do, pretend they do. Or they watch football. Same thing.'

'Most guys don't kill other guys, Chas. Show me a guy who kills other guys for money and I'll show you someone who most likely does the dirty deed with a lot of women. Even if he doesn't play the guitar.'

'Is that a rule?'

'No. Not really. I've known a couple of real warrior monks, guys who believe their bodies to be temples, purified killing machines above mere pleasures of the flesh, pseudo-religious shit like that. They always die. They're always motivated by self-absorption, and the self-confidence which always follows that takes them out.'

'How've you survived for so long, then? You some kind of guru, Mr Stoner, sir?' She sneered. Caught herself, replaced the sneer with a wry smile. Held up her hands in mock apology.

Stoner shrugged. 'You want the truth?'

She nodded.

'Friends. Capable reliable friends. People sometimes like me. Some people. You've met Shard. He's caught me twice before my mistake became fatal. Fatal to me, that is.' He shook his head.

'Bernadette? She been a mother to you? Alma mater? She should give me tips, helpful hints on how to inspire true devotion in my man.'

Stoner was motionless. Simply stopped. A hard moment was born and died between them. He leaned forward, parked his elbows on the edge of the table, folded his hands together and leaned his chin against his hands, stared with complete concentration into the eyes of his companion. Chastity ceased movement. Carefully raised her open palms between them.

'What?' she said. 'What?'

He said nothing. Stared at her, breathing with deliberation, long, slow lungfulls of conditioned air. Another moment passed. Both of them, woman and man across a table of stilled weapons, a silent, focused world of deadly intentions, were held by something in Stoner's silence, his posture, his vibration, a wound-up, pent-up energy quivering between them

– all of it his own. Not hers. No equals in this contest of . . . what?

'We should work out what we're doing tomorrow.' As suddenly as the clouded atmosphere had arrived it died, and Stoner was moving again, relaxed. He picked up the handgun, ejected the round from the breech into his hand, examined it, rolled it between his fingers, and replaced it in a spare magazine. Chastity released the breath she'd been unaware of holding, and simply nodded.

'You're going to kill an Arab. It's usually easy enough. They die as easily as anyone else.' He stood. Chastity pushed her chair back from the table, her hands invisible beneath it, her eyes on Stoner.

'I'm going for a run,' he said. 'See you when I get back. Let's do dinner, or something.'

20

JACK IN THE GREEN

'Where's the fun in killing by gun?' Chastity scoffed at her own situation, prone in a makeshift but competent hide between two luxuriantly foliaged bushes, sheltered from the sun, breathing sap-scented mountain air. The rifle was stable with no input from her. It rested relaxed and steady, sight and barrel aiming aimlessly above the scene across the valley. No distance for such a weapon, less than 500 metres. She felt that she could take the shot easily without the telescopic sight; could imagine the consequences of a miss, too. The sight was focused on the further platform of the railway halt before and slightly below her. A helicopter droned above. She wondered idly why some Arab worth enough to warrant a hit had decided to take a train to visit a castle – a *schloss* – rather than arrive by helo. She wondered briefly who he was, smiled again at her own expense and instead considered the still morning air: no desert haze to distract, an entirely welcome absence of crawling, biting things. European woods, altogether more civilised than a Middle Eastern desert.

She swung her eye to the sight and swung the rifle slowly, smoothly, to provide a panning view of the railway platform. Few loitering passengers, midweek, not a holiday. Stoner would be over there somewhere, doing whatever men like him did at times like these. He would be even more relaxed than she was, she reckoned, even though she was relaxed enough, calm as she always was when setting up a target. The geometry, the precision of it, all allowed her to focus completely on the shooting range mindset, where accuracy was all – placing the round into the centre of the target, twice for good measure, and to gaining approval from instructors and peers alike.

She wondered idly whether she was being watched. She'd left the hotel early, carrying the guitar case which contained the rifle, its support and ammunition. She'd loaded the case and herself into the first cab at the hotel's rank and asked for a ride to the station, bought a return ticket to the nearest city, observed no other cab pulling in behind her, no other car at all in fact, before the early commuter train arrived and collected its burden of office-dwellers set on another unremarkable day to add to the long list of unremarkable days which comprised their lives. She could see no appeal in that at all, and felt a familiar mild surprise that so many people felt so very differently about their own lives than she did about her own. She was the freak, the oddball, and she was relaxed about that.

First stop, she left the train. No one else stepped down from any carriage; all of the traffic was inward, city-bound. She crossed the track, caught the first train travelling in the opposite direction, returned to her original station, remained on the train until the next station, where she left it, caught the first train back to her original station, and left the train again, having gone exactly nowhere at some expense and taking quite some time to go there.

No pursuit. Why would there be? She felt faintly foolish following Stoner's instructions; anyone who expected her to take a hit on an Arab would hardly be discouraged by her catching a train, surely? They'd expect her to return, surely? Stoner's view was that as she thought that way, so would any pursuing team, and splitting the team would reveal its strength and weaken it, or reveal that in fact there was no team, that either she was clean and unfollowed or was followed by a single tracker who already knew her moves. The aims of the train-changing exercise were to learn and to confuse. Both were admirable goals, he felt. She could not argue, but left to her own devices wouldn't have bothered with all this alpha-male game-play.

While the deserted *Hausfraus* of Königswinter settled down to their morning chores and their husbands careered off to earn their euros – or the reverse – Chastity had hefted the guitar case and walked from the quiet station, taking the longer path up to the distant castle. So far as she could tell, no one was interested in her at all.

Her hide was simple to select and to construct. She wanted only a clear field of fire and not to be too easily overlooked. The whole situation appeared every bit as straightforward as had the desert exercise, an understanding which did make Chastity a mite more cautious. Here there was a lot more cover, it was far less hot, and somewhere out there Stoner was in support, though he'd been completely opaque regarding his intentions, and she couldn't see him on either platform at the halt.

A moment of sudden quiet, followed by the wing-beating flight of birds announcing the arrival of a train, this one heading up the slope. Or maybe more; birds were flying higher up the track simultaneously. Two trains? She smiled to herself. Hopefully there'd be just a single Arab.

The trains pulled into their parallel platforms and parallel parked with the perfection of a practised performance. Electric trains, quiet from her position, little hustle or buzz, platform activity, but not much, no milling crowds. The trains gathered their energies and departed, as quietly and with the same symmetry as they'd arrived. And there stood her Arab. No delay, no messing, no mistake. A single fat Arab, prominent in white. She had the range, there was insufficient wind to require compensation. The shot was easy and with the smooth ease of practice she took it. She rapidly chambered a second round, dropped the sight a little to allow for her target to fall and took the second shot. Both hits.

She stripped the sight, wiped the trigger, the stock, dropped the weapon into its case, removed the single glove she'd worn on her left supporting hand and dropped that into the case too. Closed the case, spun the combinations on the locks, and slid the case into the undergrowth, under the biggest of the concealing bushes. The case was black, its outline broken by the several stickers; not easy to see. She slid back from her hide, looked around her, stood, brushed ground debris from her hands and interrogated her immediate surroundings. Nothing. Commotion from the station. Not her concern. Time for a brisk walk back to the town, to the hotel. A late breakfast, maybe a light lunch, perhaps a little shopping on the way, or maybe a walk by the Rhine, majestic in its slow fall to the sea.

No concerns. None. A beautiful morning. Chastity breathed deep of the wooded atmosphere and began a winding, steady descent. In the distance, she could make out the scream of a siren. Two sirens, maybe more.

Stoner heard the hard crack of the first shot. Percussive or supersonic? He was never entirely certain. The second report was lost in the screaming panic of the impact. Slightly before the sound of the first shot came the blurring, the red, the look of . . . of nothing at all. The bulging disproportion of the head, the sudden stumble. Before collapse came the sound of the first shot and the impact of the second, followed smartly by the clean crack of the rifle; the round arriving with its intended energy release, violence and chaos. Stoner had been watching the Arab when his head blurred, misshapen and discoloured, and he'd looked away at once, the impact the signal for his attention to switch to all around him. Who else was not surprised, shocked and shaken by the unfolding melee?

Whoever failed to show appropriate shock and horror was likely to be complicit, unless they were both blind and deaf.

Two atypical reactions, discounting his own, which would in its turn be recognised as atypical by anyone watching him. The first was a woman, who dropped to the ground, looking around her and pulling down the man at her side. The second, reacting with the same speed as the woman, backed up against the shelter of the building and clamped a cell phone to his face, speaking while scanning the hillside opposite, the hillside which had spawned the destroying bullet.

The sound of the second shot made no impact on the man with the cellphone; the woman rolled to better cover, away from the target, beckoning her companion to follow. She looked around for a safe exit. Cellphone man was watching the hillside opposite and talking, smoothly and steadily. Stoner watched him, all the while appearing to stare at the fallen man and the pooling blood around his head, the disappearing white of his headdress. Like the professional he appeared to be, cellphone man switched his attention from the hillside to his companions. By this time, Stoner was as transfixed as everyone else by the spreading red drama of the killing, and the professional's gaze passed over him, aided no doubt by the hooded sweatshirt Stoner was wearing; face in shadow, hands jammed into pockets, shoulders hunched. Hardly the posture of a professional threat.

Railway officials clustered. Only three of them, this being a small railway for harmless tourists only. No weapons were in evidence as harmless tourists milled around, getting in each other's way and aiding the quiet departure of cellphone man, and of Stoner, who followed him, carefully and at a distance and in parallel rather than in pursuit. Cellphone man could feel his shadow, his rearward glances betrayed this, but Stoner had trod this path more than once and was alert to his own conspicuity. Finally, when his presence was no longer in question, though his motive still would be, he ran past the man with the phone, head down, eyes averted, running like the young man he no longer was and with his hands in his pockets and stride kept short; not at all the gait of a confident and regular runner, more that of a disturbed pickpocket or small time hood.

At the exact moment he reached the end of the station drive, was about to make the turn towards town with its sheltering bars and cafes, the morning's deadly still was shattered by a wild explosion from the hillside, from exactly where Chastity had taken the shot and then hidden her redundant ordnance, followed at once by the approaching twin howls of officialdom, arriving typically too late but from different directions. Stoner and his target both stopped, turned and stared at the remarkable fireball assaulting the lush greenery which had covered Chastity only a few minutes earlier. Cell-phone man was caught off guard, his confusion clearly visible. Stoner pulled a phone from his pocket and snapped as many images of his quarry – and everyone else nearby – as he could before turning away and for the benefit of any interested audience talking with considerable animation into the silent phone. He'd called no one; no one had called him. Much as it should be. Calls have ears. Phones have eyes.

Chastity swam, smooth and fluid as the dolphins she always admired, length after steady length, fluid turn at each encounter with the wall. Front crawl, four double lengths; back crawl, four double lengths; butterfly, four double lengths, followed by a fast length underwater, surfacing, pausing, stretching and beginning the sequence again. The hotel's pool was at the perfect temperature for prolonged swimming, for competition swimming, and Chastity swam like a competitor, even though she swam alone. She gave the impression that she was in the pool for the rest of her days, until she was interrupted by the arrival of two men, men in suits.

She surfaced and observed them from the far side of the

pool. She recognised them both: the German detective, whose name she'd either forgotten or had never known, and a face she would never forget – Simeon Guest, her Israeli saviour. She waved, and swam towards them.

'Miss Weise,' the German was the first to speak. Simeon stood at his side, watching her, his expression filled with interest and polite greeting.

'Inspector.' She floated in the water below them. Then turned, dived, immediately surfacing with sufficient vigour to lift herself from the water and place her backside on the poolside. She shook her head, water flew, the men backed off in a shared reflex. 'Towel? Please?' She stood, naked before them. 'Apologies for the full frontal. I wasn't expecting any company.'

Simeon Guest, part-time courteous Englishman, offered her a vast towel. 'Chastity,' he said, quietly, 'a charming surprise. I'd been told about the beauty in the pool, but hadn't thought it would be you.'

'You two know each other?' The German detective was obvious in his surprise and curiosity. Guest shrugged. Chastity towelled herself vigorously, restored her modesty and smiled, said nothing.

Guest turned back to his police companion. 'A brief encounter, some time ago, and in a place a long way from here. Social only, I'm afraid, and sadly brief.' He turned to the drying swimmer. 'How's the love life? A little more stable? A little less tense?' His face and his words smiled together.

'I'm a little embarrassed.' Chastity applied appropriate facial expressions and hand gestures. She turned to the German. 'I borrowed some money from this gentleman,' she stammered very slightly and returned her attention to Guest, 'but I can repay you today. My finances are sorted out again. Promise.' She grinned brightly and turned back to the policeman. 'He is a very kind man, helped me out when I had a spot of boyfriend trouble.' Then she repeated her statement in German; both men appeared surprised, and both assured her – in German – that she should speak whichever language she was most comfortable in.

'I must ask you about your whereabouts earlier today, Ms Weise.' The German lapsed back into policeman mode. Guest simply appeared vaguely amused and largely uninterested.

'Why?' Chastity shook her short dark hair, obscuring the fresh blonde roots. 'What am I supposed to have done?'

'Nothing. There's been a murder.' The German watched her closely, unsmiling, unlike Guest, whose vague amusement remained at standby level.

'What? Another one? And you think I've been murdering people?' She contrived to sound incredulous, amused and irritated at the same time. 'Not another heart attack? Bombs? Rockets? Guns? A tribe of mercenary pygmies toting blowpipes and poison arrows?'

'A gun. And a bomb.' No amusement penetrated the detective's expression. 'I would like to know what you were doing earlier today.'

'So you can eliminate me from your enquiries?'

'Exactly so. Now?'

'I hiked up the mountain to the Drachensfels, then I hiked back. And I've been swimming since. That's it.'

'You can prove this? There is someone who can vouch for you?'

'No.'

'Then I have to ask you what you were wearing for your hike.'

'There's also been an offence against high fashion?' Chastity's scorn was towering. 'You're going to toss me in the slammer for wearing hiking boots by Caterpillar rather than nice gold slingbacks by Jimmy Choo? Who said Germans have no sense of humour.' She paused. 'The clothes are in the changing room. Over there.' She gestured with a tilt of her head. 'Don't worry about me getting a chill. I'll just wear a towel to dinner and explain that the Stasi stole my clothes.'

'The Stasi were East German.' No humour from the detective, who walked over to the changing room, his footsteps echoing in an odd medley with his voice. 'You didn't change after your hike?'

'That's why I was swimming in the pink, officer. I was hot. I ran part of it. That's why the lack of Jimmy Choo footgear. Hard to run in lamé slippers. Unless you know different.'

'You run in boots?' The detective looked up, pausing from loading her clothes into a plastic bag.

'You don't?' Chastity's mockery was clear. 'German women walk home to change their shoes before running, even if it's a beautiful day, not a cloud in the sky, birds singing and not a single tedious cop to ruin the view? Or do German woman carry a few spare pairs in case they fancy a spot of running? Maybe flippers as well in case a swim appeals? For heaven's sake, officer. How long do you want my clothes? If you just want to give them to your girlfriend, just say and I'll buy some new ones.'

Simeon Guest spoke for the first time. 'Gunshot residue, Chastity. He'll want the lab to check for residues on your clothes.'

She turned to face him. 'Yeah, yeah, I watch *Crime Scene Investigations* too, and I know that GSR gets onto hands, gloves, sleeves, maybe a jacket. Will it be on my trousers, bra and pants? Or is this boxhead just so repressed that he thinks he can intimidate the blushing flower of British womanhood by stealing her underwear?' She laughed, not an amused sound. 'Tell you what.' She dropped the towel to the floor and folded her arms beneath her breasts. 'I'll just walk up through the lobby and tell everyone that this sad fuck stole my clothes. Oh. Maybe he tried to molest me too? Is that frowned upon in Germany? Hey hey! Maybe you both tried to rape me? Two big guys, one frail. That should make the news.'

The detective tossed her underwear to her. She let it fall, made no move except to face him. 'That's such a cool idea that

I think I'll do it anyway. Hang on while I summon a few tears.' She walked over her clothes towards the stairs. Simeon Guest strode over to block her way; arms spread wide, no attempt to touch her, just a shaken head and an expression of apology.

'He's just . . .'

'Doing his job. Yeah yeah. That's what they all say, isn't it?' Well fuck him. And fuck you too if you take his side, Simeon.'

'You're upset, Chastity . . .'

'No, really? This fucker's accusing me of murdering someone, is taking my clothes and . . . and what? You'd not be upset if he tried that with you? If you weren't here as a chaperone, I'd be screaming rape now. There's no residue on my clothes. Pollen, dust, maybe grass stains on the arse – I did sit down for a little while. Is that allowed? Oh, hang on, there might be some sunblock on them too. I put some on my neck and forehead before setting out. Never can be too careful with skin like mine.'

The German walked towards their tableau. Chastity turned to him, then walked back to her underwear, slipping into her pants and sliding her arms into the bra. 'How long do you need them for? It only takes about a minute with a magic spray in the movies.' Both her expression and her tone were more subdued. Politeness returned to his features.

'Maybe an hour. Maybe a little less. There is a magic spray, miss. I'll return your clothes at once. Please . . . apologies for the misunderstanding.'

Simeon Guest had walked away, and returned carrying a robe. He walked behind Chastity and hung it over her shoulders. 'With the compliments of the hotel management,' he said.

'Do they know they're giving away clothing?' She smiled at neither of the men in particular.

'Not yet. But they will when they see you gracing their dull robe while we have a seat in the bar. Coffee lounge? You'd prefer tea? While we wait for your clothing to come back.'

The German bowed and left them. Simeon and Chastity headed for the hotel cafe.

She was like a black island of silence in an ocean of riotously loud colour. The pavements outside the ice cream shop heaved with young life; children, teenagers and maybe some twenty-somethings were holding an impromptu noise competition, shouting, talking loud, courting and squealing – all of it an accompaniment to the massed consumption of imaginative ice creams. The single wide nun in a flat black habit sat alone, silent, surrounded by a quiet quarantine zone. She sipped at a black tea.

'You still know how to mingle, then.' Stoner dropped into one of the unoccupied chairs at her table. 'Still attracting every single man in the place, making every heart skip a beat. Hey, Bernadette, Bernie. And thanks.'

'You took your time, JJ, I could have been worried, if I was the worrying kind.'

'Don't you have prayer beads for that? Make your god a happy god by counting nuts on a string or something?'

'You make Him sound like a chimp, Jean-Jacques. Do not be irreverent.'

'You really do believe, Bernie? Truly? I'd heard the story, but never thought to ask. You know how it goes.'

'I do.'

'Respect.'

'Should I believe you?'

'Believe whatever you want to believe; my respect for you is straightforward. Your beliefs are yours, yours alone, and I respect them as I respect you. Unconditionally.'

'You always did talk like a dictionary.'

'Just like a dick, Bernie; all I ever was. Dictionaries are for clever people.'

'Blesses is out.'

'Oh.' Stoner stared at her, then his gaze drifted, attention shifted as he waved away an incoming waiter. 'Oh shit. Oh fuckety fuckety fuck. When? How?'

'Does swearing help you, Jean-Jacques?' Bernadette smiled gently at him.

'Yes. Who let that psycho loose? And why? If I didn't swear, Bernie, I'd need to break things. I thought she was away for good. If I'd thought anyone would ever let her out . . .' He ground to a stop.

'You'd have killed her, Jean-Jacques.'

'I would. I could have and I should have. How come she's out? It's been . . . what? How long? Has she changed? How come you know and I don't? Didn't? Oh fuck. Sorry, Mother. But fucking fucking fuck.'

'Any minute now you'll remind me that my God created her, so how can I be a believer? That right, Jean-Jacques?'

'No. Not one bit. No. That psychotic cunt was created by something malign. Your God is a god of love. No love in that one.'

'Now you're taking the mick.'

'It was a Mick who created Blesses, wasn't it? Or an entire damned wasted gods-lost nation of Micks. Blesses. Jesus God and all His saints in heaven. Her. Free? Walking around like a human? Cold blood this one, Bernie. Cold blood. Just a sanction. I'm not being taken in by that again. Where is she? Do you know? That's royally fucked up my day. I was feeling so . . . good. I thought we'd wrapped up this nonsense with Chastity and Mallis and his bizarre insistence that I look out for her – like she's some kind of limp vegetable, and . . . I lost one of your rifles, Bernie.'

'Think I heard it. Someone try to open the case?'

'Sounded like it. I've not been to look. Impressive bang though. Could it be survivable?'

'No. Hundred-foot blast radius.'

'OK. Thank you. You are the best, Bernadette. If you want to hold a debt, you have mine. If you ever need . . .'

'Shut up. I need nothing, Jean-Jacques. Not from you. Blesses is the one who needs . . . she needs what you're going to provide. She was talking with Harding.'

'Shard? Oh great. This just gets better. Does he know who she is? What she is?'

'How could he?'

'OK. That could be problematic.'

'Mr Tran introduced them.' Bernadette paused, interrupted by the expression of mounting round-eyed incredulity on Stoner's face. 'There will be a reason for that. He's very subtle, Tran the Man. Maybe he was trying to help you, who knows? Maybe he doesn't actually know her well enough?' She shook her head gently, a soft sad smile balancing Stoner's anger at himself. 'You were at fault only in refusing to believe how bad a woman can be, Jean-Jacques. And it was a long time ago. You wanted her to be put away, locked up somewhere she could do no more harm. If I was uncharitable, I might harbour the suspicion that you believed she would suffer more from incarceration than from a bullet through the head. Of course, your humanity took over.'

'Bollocks it did. I wimped out of killing her. A woman would never have given it a thought. Chastity here; she'd have snuffed her out without even a pause, no hesitation. Blesses set free. How in this flying fuck of a fucked up world did that happen? Presumably the nice public schools chaps of the Security Service or Six will find her and reel her in?'

'I think she's out clean and legit, Jean-Jacques. My understanding is simply that she's free. As in, time served, on licence, debts paid, getting a second chance to be a model citizen.'

'Time off for good behaviour? From a life sentence? She must have had a religious conversion. Led the prison choir in celestial song, that kind of thing. Sorry, Mother. It's enough to make me scream. What's she doing, Blesses? Do we know? What's Mr Tran's involvement with her?'

'No answers, Jean-Jacques. Precious few. She's been a free woman for some short time. No fanfare. I only heard she was out because her face flashed up at your place, talking with Mr Tran. And Harding.'

'That's more of a puzzle. Shard's a good guy. A trooper. What would she want with him? Thoughts? Suggestions? I'm done here, pretty much. I head home, hunt her down and take her out?'

'Why would you do that? Why would you want her dead today when you didn't all those years ago? What was it, ten? Must be a decade now.'

'About that, I think. Can you get out after twelve years for murder?'

'It seems that you can. Well, that she can.'

'I should simply have wasted her. There and then.'

'Does you credit that you didn't. Do you need to go back to England?'

Stoner paused, considering. 'No. That wasn't my plan.'

'Then don't change your plan, Jean-Jacques. There's no one gunning for you right now, is there? Chastity's in your debt. You neutralised Hartmann already, and who else is there with a good reason to do you any harm? So why change any plans at all?'

'I'd intended . . .'

Bernadette put her finger to his lips. 'Hush now. I don't want to know anything. Don't know, can't tell. She might come after me.'

'She'd need decent resources to find you, Bernie.'

'You found me. Mr Tran could persuade Mallis – even maybe Menace – to give him a big clue.'

'They'd do that?'

'Why wouldn't they? They meet you at Mr Tran's – which house is your house, and have no reason to doubt your being relaxed enough with him to let him live there – even though you inherited him when you inherited the house. That was way after the business with Blesses – way after your last time in Ireland. She's before their time with you. They might know who she is, what she's done, but I doubt they'd take sides, doubt they have any idea what she can do to a man. Doubt she'd be a threat to their cosy little world – in their eyes anyway.

'And in any case, Jean-Jacques, I want to stay away from it. It's been a long time. A lot can happen to a character in ten years – more than ten years. She might be OK now. You could practise a little charity.' She smiled. 'Sorry, man, bad joke.'

He returned the smile, the corners of his mouth sagging, adding a wry taste to it all.

'You believe people like her can change? Really? Is this the real Christian in you? And my weakness that I can't believe in leopards changing their stripes?'

'I want to believe, Jean-Jacques. And I can. That's the difference between us. But in this case – Blesses – I'd just stay well away and lock the doors at night. And I'd take to wearing sunglasses. Mirror shades.' She looked suddenly bleak.

'You've not forgotten Blesses' own private voodoo, then. The eyes?'

Bernadette shook her head slowly, sadly. 'No. There's a science to it, I'm sure, but it never felt like that when she'd magic-up the Paddies. Pure poison voodoo.'

'Spoken like a true Catholic, Bernie. Only the one God, remember?'

'Belief and trust in a single deity doesn't make me blind, Jean-Jacques. The opposite if anything. You should know better than anyone that the voodoo Mass is only one step removed from our own; they worship the spirits who we call saints. Our Lord told us to believe only in Him. He didn't talk much about other gods or their absence. People can believe what they choose. Our Lord gave us that choice.'

'So if Blesses believes in her voodoo mind games and practises them, that's OK with you and your God?' Stoner shook his head, signalled a passing beauty for a long coffee; two long coffees. Bernadette nodded her thanks.

'I can't affect what she does or doesn't think any more than I can expect you to take holy orders, Father Jean.' She smiled softly.

'And if she comes after you with a gun? You two were closer than kin for a time. I doubt she'll have forgotten that, and I seriously doubt that it's in her to forgive. You more than me, Mother. Would your God let you kill her? In self-defence?'

Their coffees arrived, the day was heading into evening. A black taxi appeared at the kerb, waiting to take her away. Bernadette stood, folding her black habit around her, holding the rosary at her waist in one hand while she poured down the hot brew with the other, a single swallow, no hesitation.

'We'll see,' she said, waving to the cabby. 'You're no man of God, Jean-Jacques. No need to ask you if you do revenge.'

The conversation between Chastity and Simeon Guest was not going well. In fact, it wasn't really going at all. He ordered afternoon teas for them both, ate his own. Chastity appeared to be at the limits of her patience. He told her, with a small flourish, that she could forget the money she'd 'borrowed' from him in Israel. She nodded non-committal thanks. She looked around the hotel's cafe, at the entrance door, mostly. He told her he was certain that the clothes inspection would be fine, that everything would be fine, that she would be fine and that the detective would be fine. She looked at him in pitiless silence, shook her head as though he were a slightly dim child, maybe the bastard progeny of a despised minor relative.

The detective appeared, finally. He bowed to Chastity, nodded briefly to Simeon, handed over a bag of clothes. 'With my thanks, Ms Weise. Your clothes are as you said they would be. No residues. Please accept our apologies for your inconvenience. If you wish to make a formal complaint, I can put you in touch . . .'

'No need. No need at all. It's just a worry, being under suspicion. Who was murdered? That's two deaths in as many days in this town. Is it always so exciting?' Her words were light, her expression devoid of friendship of any kind. She didn't wait for an answer. 'I'd like to run up to my room and change. If that's all the same to you guys?' Without waiting for an answer, she picked up the bag of clothes and headed for the door, ignoring both the German and Simeon Guest, who rose to his feet as though to catch her attention.

A guitar case and two smaller suitcases stood unattended by the reception desk. Chastity scanned the lobby for Stoner; nothing. She walked rapidly to the stairs and ran up them with the fluid ease of the athlete she was, ran down the corridor to their room and let herself in; the keycard still worked perfectly. Stoner's few impersonal possessions, mainly toiletries and new underwear, were in the places she remembered from earlier that day. But there was no sign of the man himself, nor of the hard luggage and the remaining guitar case. Her own belongings were – so far as she could see – exactly where she'd left them.

Chastity dressed rapidly, distributed her documents, wallets and money around her pockets, and turned to leave. A small padded envelope had been fixed somehow to the back of the door. Facing her was a large capital letter 'C', written in bright, clear ink. The envelope was plainly not empty, and caution suggested that she would be wise to leave it where it was. She pulled it from the door, opened it, breaking its seal to do so. Inside was a cell phone, its battery and a SIM card alongside it. She pocketed them, took the padded envelope with her, and returned to the lobby. The guitar case and the hard luggage had gone. Of course they had.

'The guitar case?' she called over to the receptionist. 'Has Mr LaForge taken it?'

The polished presence on the other side of the counter

smiled glacially. 'Herr LaForge settled his account this morning and left instruction that his packed luggage should be collected from his room – from your shared room.' The glacial cool of her expression fell by a few more degrees. 'He explained that he would be back for tonight but would be leaving early tomorrow morning, and that we should leave his small luggage for his use this evening. Which we have done. What time are you expecting him?' Her lips smiled politely, her eyebrows sneered. 'Would you like to reserve a table for this evening? For how many? You have several friends, it seems.' She nodded towards the restaurant, where the German detective and Simeon Guest were both staring at her.

Chastity shook her head. 'I think I'll take a walk by the river. Need some exercise. Fresh air. See you later.'

She strode from the lobby, out through the revolving doors and into the early evening street. Stepped back into a little shade and slotted both battery and SIM card into the cell phone. They booted with Germanic efficiency, and revealed that there was a message waiting, in the patient way that messages have. The message was simple enough; 'Recognise anyone? He's your man.' There was no sign-off, but there was a small selection of attached images, all of them figures in a familiar landscape, a familiar railway station, not a million miles away from her location, and indeed in the background of the best shot was the result of her own best shot, taken earlier that very day. One man in the photos was not looking in horror-struck fascination at the bloody cranial evacuation taking place before them. One man was looking away, squinting a little in the morning sun, as if estimating the direction and distance of the shots. A man she surely recognised. A man who had made a habit of turning up just when things stopped going to plan.

Chastity closed the cell phone, dropped it into a pocket, and returned to the revolving doors, just in time to observe the German detective leaving them and heading for the car park.

She watched him go, pushed her way through the doors, crossed the wasteland of the reception lobby and arrived with a smile at the cafe table now occupied only by Simeon Guest, who looked up, a smile of his own matching hers in welcome. He stood, walked around the table and drew back a chair for her.

'Changed your mind? Decided to fraternise with the enemy? Great to see you again, Chas. Really is. Regained your good humour after the German inquisition?' He tucked the chair behind her knees and returned to his own.

'Three's a crowd,' she revealed, grinning in what she correctly hoped was a predatory manner. 'Two's company. You here for the night?'

Guest contrived to appear surprised. 'Well. I can be. I have a room.'

'With only you in it? No surprise Arab boys this time? Does your inclination also swing towards dyed blonde British girls?' She beamed at his confusion, plainly enjoying herself.

'Khalil should join . . . He should be here now, but he's not. And anyway he does have his own room. Are you . . .' he was grinning now, eyebrows raised in his mounting amusement. 'Are you saying what it sounds like? I hope you are; unfinished business from Israel, I hope.'

'Even dyed blonde Brits can be direct. This has been a seriously strange day. Fancy helping out a lonely lady with what a less refined person might refer to as a decent fuck? No need to waste a meal. I'm not hungry. I just feel like that certain something. Like you say; unfinished business. Great way to unwind at the end of a busy few days, don't you think? And to say an honest thank-you for the loan.'

Simeon Guest stood. 'A gift, Chas. A gift and a pleasure. Your room or mine, then, beautiful lady. Beautiful British lady.' His words shared laughter with her; he truly was a most handsome man.

'Yours. Lay on, MacGuest. We who are about to die, and other mangled misquotations.' She slapped his arse, to the embarrassed delight of all around them.

21

I'M IN A PHONE BOOTH

She picked up. Third attempt at a call. Said nothing, though the line was open and crackling.

'Hello darlin', I'm on a train . . .'

'Not a space rocket, huh? Sounds like one. Signal would be better if you were in orbit, I expect.'

Stoner smiled, stretched out as far as was possible in the fast, powerful, plainly new Teutonic engineering excellence which was his train.

'You sound . . . almost cheerful. Did your day go well? Did you enjoy a brief night of passion with our distinguished Middle-Eastern gentleman with the Jewish name?'

She laughed, or maybe she blew her nose, the connection quality wasn't great.

'Yeah. Eased a girl's pent-up frustrations just a little. But not for long.'

'I did wonder . . . which is why the phone call. Did your international carnal relations have the result I'd expected? Have you maintained your profoundly worrying one hundred percent mortality rate?'

She laughed again. Or maybe she had the flu.

'Yeah. He checked out, then I checked out, everybody checked out, and now you're checking up on me, Father Jean. Do I need to confess over the phone, or can you see your way to administering last rites or penance or something in the none-too-distant? I'll make this plain for you: I would enjoy that. And I feel a debt.'

Stoner watched a uniformed railway official progressing slowly along the swaying carriage.

'Don't think a house call is imminent. I'm heading to a far-away land, where everyone is sweet innocence.'

'Sounds dull as old shit. But you are an old man. While you're here, how'd you work out we had a guest who wasn't what he seemed?'

'Tell me . . . Hang on.' Stoner passed his ticket to the official, who ran it through an efficient silent machine and handed it back in silence. 'Are you in a safe place?'

'I'm in a bar. Completely alone. I . . .' she paused. 'I have some doubts about my reception when I get home, so am in no particular hurry, and I've no particular place to go. But yeah, there's no one around. Certainly no service. I could die of thirst.'

'This is conjecture. Deductive reasoning. That's all. You shouldn't – granny and egg-sucking advice here – you shouldn't take any action based on what I think. OK?'

'OK. Oh, here comes a libation. Such joy.' Stoner could hear her issuing her drink order.

'No savoury snacks?'

'Diet. Tell me your thoughts, surprising sage.'

'It's not hard to work out. Your . . . the contract your sister accepted was from some Israeli faction or other. No idea which; there's lots to choose from. You were to diminish a bunch of guys disliked by the faction.'

'Cool choice of words.'

'We aim to please. I think the original idea – from the Israelis and presumably kept to themselves – was that you'd take the fall for the original desert song. I'd guess that your late guest was there to manage the situation, monitor it, or even to let rip with the fireworks, though he didn't strike me as the type for actual . . . y'know . . . effort. He'd have set up the bigger bang and the punctures.'

'OK so far as it goes. So why did he pick me up as I trudged along, weary warrior lady-like?'

'Can't be sure. Maybe you impressed him with your blonde hair, great ass – they like their donkeys, these guys – and accurate shooting. He may have decided that you'd be more use if he kept you running. There were other hits planned, as we all know now. They could have solidified after he'd seen you operate.'

'Solidified?'

'Yeah. Gone from partial plan to "Wow, let's do this!" after he'd seen your impressive attributes. Also target skills.'

'And then?' Chastity was sounding relaxed.

'That's it. Isn't it? You were always dual-purpose. You'd take the actual action, and fingers of blame would be pointed at some unseen, unknown assailant, or you, if you got caught.'

'The men in black? The stack of shooters in Slovenia? And the guy in the church there?'

'Dunno. Probably the shooters were mercs. Another layer of separation from the Israelis. They were pretty rubbish. Amateur. You should never have got out of that. Mossad would have been much more effective. If I get the chance I'll ask about them. Or you could ask Mallis. He'd have no trouble finding it out. He'd check for empty seats and insincere tributes and salutes in the pits mercs hang in.'

'You're a merc. So'm I.'

'Yeah. You say it; must be true. There's mercs and there's mercs, sweet and chaste one. They were unforgivably sloppy.'

'Fatally.'

'As you say. I think in Germany they intended to let you take Guertler, good and clean – they seemed to get on well with the local constabulary – then end your dazzling run of success after the fat Arab. Probably the other guy – Khalil? – was intended to take care of you, tying up several loose ends and getting backs patted throughout the land. There could've been medals. Who knows?'

'And we spoiled that?'

'Modesty forbids me to suggest that my interference in your masterly plan – y'know; you go in guns blazing in front of everyone and shoot anything that moves – actually helped, but it might have confused them a bit. I don't think anyone there had any idea I wasn't just a gormless tourist seduced by your most excellent company. And ass.'

'This isn't a very secure conversation, Mr Tradecraft.' She laughed. 'And hey, can I tell you a thing?'

'Go for it.'

'I wish you were here.'

'Thanks. Thank you. Really. Next time.'

'There'll be a next time?'

'Let's hope not. But . . . it's a small world.'

'Yeah. Got to give B credit, too. Her guitar case did for Khalil, right?'

'Yep. I doubt they'll find enough of him to identify, so they'll conclude – the police, that is – that the shooter took the hit and blew himself up somehow.' He paused, thought for a moment. 'But there's another thing to consider. You might not want to hear it, and you might not thank me for it.'

'Go ahead. What's said on a train stays on a train.'

'You're on a train?'

'No. You are, JJ. Don't be dim.'

'Habit of a lifetime. Perfected. Selfless dedication to dimness in all her forms. Chastity and Dimness, what a killer combo, huh?

'Sounds stupid. Stop dodging the issue. What's your bad news?'

'Did I say it was bad?'

'Bet it is.'

'Someone your end told the bad guys where you were and what you were doing. Every time. The cycle only broke when

I interfered with it. Remember also that my instruction was
not to be involved, not to speak with you, and only to look out
for you. That's a very soft set of instructions.'

'Thanks again, big man. I owe you a long comfortable one.'

'Not so, sweet ladykiller. No debts among friends.'

'We friends then?'

'Your call, Chas. Your call. But . . . if you decide to take it further, to find out more of what went down with your own
team, who passed on your logistics, locations, despite your
neat Facebook cutout, and you need back-up, then look me
up. I'm not difficult to find. Meanwhile – and I mean this – I
want out. No more cowboy crap. My offer is for you only. Not
for Charity and not for Charm.'

'No fee?'

'A consideration is always welcome. Money's useless when
you're dead. But you could do a thing for me. Something I
can't do.'

'Speak it, JJ, before I strip this phone and throw it down a
drain.'

'Find out what happened with your sister and Hartmann.
Can you do that?'

'Yes. If she lies I'll know. We're very close. Why though? He's
dead, right?'

'Remember that B mentioned a character called Blesses.'

'She did.'

'The new news is that Blesses is no longer resting at Her
Majesty's pleasure. B said so. The only person I can think of
right now who could spring Blesses is Hartmann. And Blesses
and me have some extremely bad history. The very worst
kind. And she is too dangerous to deal with.'

'Worse than – golly – me?'

'I'll ignore that. But if you could find out and let me know –
send a Facebook message, why not – that would be uber-cool.'

'Did you do fucks with Blesses? Like you wouldn't with
me?'

'Thank you for listening. Now have a great day, y'all.' Stoner pulled the SIM card and battery from the phone. Dropped them into separate pockets. Tried to relax. To sleep.

22

LIFE ON AN OCEAN

'I'm impressed.' Stoner looked up at the speaker from the newspaper he'd been reading and picked up his full mug of coffee. Thick, black and bitter. The coffee, not the newsprint. Although . . .

'This is truly an age of wonders.' Stoner was sipping carefully while splitting his attention between the speaker and the brimmed beverage; he appeared to view both with equal caution.

'I almost managed not to recognise you without the beard. But you told me you'd be here today, and here you are. Today. Bang on time. Now what?' The speaker placed her uniform hat on the table between herself and Stoner, outside likely spillage range of the powerful coffee, and sat down carefully, avoiding violent contact with table legs. Instability can be a hazard in an inappropriate environment.

'Now what?' Stoner spoke with a smile, looking firstly at the dangerous brew, then at the uniform hat, finally raising his eyes to his companion. 'I'm here. You're here. You said you would be here and I said I'd be here too. Nostradamus would have been proud; one hundred percent predictive accuracy. Impossible to improve on that. What happens next does in fact depend on you.' He returned his attention to the coffee, picked it up again and sipped with due care and attention. Leaned back in his chair and smiled at his companion.

'Jenny,' he said. 'You look truly fine. Fine indeed. It is so good to see you. Thanks for coming. I watched the ship sail in, wondered whether you'd come ashore, whether you'd remember. Whether you'd still want to after all this time. Two weeks is a long time in some situations, like being aboard a big ship surrounded by rich retired old men.' He grinned; no offence to his words.

She smiled back, with a caution often reserved for over-heated coffee in over-filled vessels. 'You went away. You didn't call. You didn't answer my calls. You didn't even text or answer my texts. I did wonder whether you'd just . . . thought better of it. Whether you were more involved with those . . . sisters or that musician lady than you'd said. Men do that; they lie. Or maybe you'd simply been off driving your vans – your Volkswagen vans – and it was just simply all too exciting for you to waste time with me.' Her expression suggested that although she was prepared for a fight, she did not in fact want one. And she was still smiling.

'My cabin's booked and paid for. And I need a holiday. Here I am. It's up to you now; do I go through embarkation and come aboard, or do I spend some time enjoying the art, culture and vice centres of St Petersburg? On my own.'

'Your cabin's been booked, paid for and completely empty for the last fortnight, Mr Hand. You'll need to excuse my slight doubt.'

'Excused. May I come aboard or should I cast off and clear off?'

'Do you have a preference?'

'Don't be silly. I'm here. I've endured several trains and too much Russian public transport to get here to have done it out of some mad desire to travel in Ladas which smell of cabbage and paraffin, drinking coffee distilled from asphalt. I'm here, like I said. Can we sail back to the UK together? It seems like months since I last saw Southampton. My heart dreams of Southampton. Rome, Istanbul, Bangkok . . . all are mere whimsies compared to the splendours of Southampton, cultural epicentre of the known universe. Home of the . . .'

She interrupted his flow by placing her hand over his and telling him to shut up. She smiled. 'I hoped you'd be here, John.' she said. 'It is John, isn't it?'

'John Hand, groovy guitar player and goodtime guy, at your service.'

'Not Jean, then? Not Stoner?'

'No. Left that other guy at the railway station. On a train to nowhere. Like I said, Jen, I need a holiday.'

'The captain told me I'd never hear from you again. He's met your sort before. Rich, idle men taking advantage of the flowers of English womanhood. Met your sort before, he did tell me that. More than the once.'

Stoner grinned. 'Let's give him the benefit of a doubt. He might have met my sort before. He's a sea captain after all. Maybe he drove a submarine in a previous life and dropped off spooks in dead of night on unfriendly shores so they could boldly go and get themselves killed. Who knows?'

She slapped his hand good-naturedly. 'He's sailed with the same company all his career. The same civilian company.'

'It could be a cover. For . . . international espionage. You'd never know. The entire ship could be used for massed infiltrations of geriatric Brit retired civil servants and teachers into previously civilised parts of the globe to incite unrest, revolution, that kind of thing. You might deny this, but how can I trust you? You could be one of them. Mata Hairnet, that sort of secret spy thing.' They both laughed, both stood, walked around the table till they made contact, hugged and finally kissed, at length. Followed by more of the same.

'You been doing the spooky spy stuff, John?' There was no

secret agenda behind her words, none that he could see anyway. He nodded. Shrugged. Shook his head.

'Did it go well?' She was watching him carefully.

He nodded once again. 'Mostly. One good result . . .'

'But? I could hear the but?'

'Yeah. Some unwelcome stuff too. It's the way of it, the name of the game. Rough goes with the smooth.'

'That's why you get the big bucks, though?'

He laughed. 'The big bucks come from theft, plain and simple.'

'You want to talk about it?'

He shook his head. 'No. I want to forget about it.'

'It'll wait until we're . . . until you're back in England?'

'I might not get off, Jenny. I feel like a long rest. I did before; didn't lie about that at all. I didn't think the job would find me – would even want to find me. Didn't think I'd get pulled back into it, even though I am – like they say – good at it somehow. I might not get off in England. Where's the tub going next? We're doing – what? – six days sail back to Southampton, timeless glittering jewel of the western world, then what?'

'Atlantic crossing. Canaries, then Florida, then New York, then Eastern Seaboard to Quebec via Boston, then New York, then Azores, then Southampton, then Istanbul via Malta . . .'

'Stop! Enough! You sound like the index to an atlas, a cruise ship catalogue. New York. I could do New York. I even know people there. Mostly sane, most of the time. Mostly. Reckon I could have the same cabin?'

'No idea. I can check. Where's your baggage?'

'I'm it.'

'No baggage at all?'

'Not in the sense you mean, Jen. Far too much in every other sense of the word. I left most of my stuff in the cabin anyway, I think.' He paused. 'Has there been a delivery for me in the last couple of days? Like . . . a guitar?'

She shook her head. 'Not that I know of. You expecting one?

One of your own? It would be cool to hear you playing your own instrument. Fender, yes?'

'Yep. And no, I wasn't expecting one, but a friend might have decided I needed it.'

'Uh-oh; a lady friend, John? Another lady friend?'

'Not what you're thinking. This one's a nun. An honest to goodness religious nun. And Irish with it. Although she lives in Germany. A truly superior mother. Simple to understand.'

'You know interesting people.' She waved him to accompany her to the terminal's check-in facilities.

'Just me? Am I the only passenger meeting the good ship here in Russia?'

'Yep.'

'Wow. I always prefer to blend in with the scenery. It's the mark of a decent spook. Being inconspicuous.'

They walked across an echoing concourse with a capacity of thousands, alone together, her heels providing the only accompaniment to their progress until they reached the single manned station.

'Did you enjoy your stay in Russia, Mr Hand? Your short stay in Russia.' A not unfriendly question said in a fairly unfriendly way by an unsmiling man with a sharply creased uniform and a savagely sharp haircut to match his almost comprehensible English.

'I always do. Thank you.' Stoner spoke in gruff Russian. Jenny the officer looked at him in surprise. The face opposite Stoner – the Russian face – erupted into a shining smile.

'Then we shall see you again,' the border soldier replied in his own tongue, stamping Stoner's passport with a vigour more suited to stamping out tanks from blocks of pig iron than impressing the double eagle onto the flimsy passport paper.

'God willing.' Stoner took back his passport, slapped the back of his left hand with the palm of his right, attracting an identical gesture in response from the border soldier, who nodded him towards the security scanners, metal detectors and other devices designed to oppress the innocent while providing little protection against the guilty.

'What was that about?' The first officer waved her card at the ship's security staff and walked past the scanners as Stoner walked through them and passed their various simple tests.

'Boy stuff. Soldier stuff. Meaningless stuff unless you know what it means, in which case it only means stuff to people who need stuff to be meaningful.'

'Military stuff?'

'Yes. If your captain was a military captain he'd know what it meant – unless he didn't. In which case he'd know it meant something but not what.'

'And it meant what, Mr Mysterious?' They were aboard, walking steadily to collect Stoner's ship identity card – his cruise card – confirming that he was John Hand and permitting him to live in luxury and spend freely while afloat. 'Can you tell me?'

'Safe entry into a dangerous area. I last used it in Kabul; expect he used it in the Crimea. What with the friendly Russian chat, he'll assume I'm on his side. Always handy. Whether it's true or not. It pays to make friends.'

'You're telling me something, aren't you, John?'

'Show more than tell. You need to know who you're dealing with, Jenny. If you're considering a mutual future, you need to know that this never goes away.' He collected his ship's identity, posed for a poor photograph. They headed into the white ship's quiet interior; the thousands of passengers and many of the crew were ashore, vulturing up Russian culture for reasons only they could understand.

'Never goes away? How d'you mean?' She led the way to his cabin, the same large comfortable suite he'd occupied previously.

'The border guard was active military. He's a vet. He'd not

be pulling a duty like that if someone in the port authority wasn't watching for something.'

'Watching for you?'

'No. If it had been me . . . I'd still be ashore, answering questions at least until after the ship sailed. No, they're not bothered about me. They've no reason to be. John Hand has been to Russia several times – according to the passport – and he's never been in trouble.'

'So why the hand gestures? Masonic rituals?' She grinned at him.

'Nope. In case he was at all bothered by the passport and identity. Now he'll think it's a dodgy Russian British passport rather than a dodgy British British passport.'

'Is it dodgy? You told me it was genuine.'

'It is genuine. My name is not John Hand. The passport is genuine, the man is the fake. I'm being honest with you so you can see that I'm dishonest. Is your head hurting yet?'

'You're like this all the time? What were you doing in Russia anyway? Can I even ask?' She stepped aside as he opened the door to the cabin, remained outside while he entered and continued to stand outside even after he'd beckoned her in.

He sighed, walked to the fridge, opened it and extracted a half-bottle of undistinguished alleged champagne. 'I've been in Russia for less than a day. I came here to meet the ship, to see you. That's all.'

'Came from where?'

'Germany.'

'You were looking for someone?'

'More like looking after someone, but looking for someone too, in a way.'

'Did you find them? Look after them?'

'Yes and yes. Is this going on all evening? I'm not going to give you the same third degree, you know, so . . .'

'That's because you know what I've been doing, you're not interested in it. I'm . . . intrigued. A real spook.'

Stoner stripped off, stood before her and smiled.

'I'm a grimy spook. I need a shower. Then a bath. There's no room for two in the shower, but there is room for two in the bath. Or questions. You choose.'

'I'll scrub your back. One last question then I'll shut up. Promise.'

'OK.' He dug out shampoo and shower gels, turned on the water, waited for it to run hot. She reached up and rubbed the muscles around his neck.

'The unwelcome thing you mentioned, John. Is it going to take you away again? Soon?'

He turned to her, took his hands in his, walked backwards into the steam of the shower, looked at her through its mists.

'My first thought . . . When I heard . . . OK. It's a person who got sent down – sent to prison – after a job I'd been on. I'd never really thought any further. Never really expected them to get out, but now they are out.'

'A bad man?'

'A bad woman. Very bad.' He shook his head. 'But here I am. I decided not to do what seemed like the only thing to do. So instead of sending you a message saying I couldn't meet you, and going back to the UK to look for her, or whatever, I'm here. I want out of it.'

'Will she be after you? Is she a danger to you?'

'No idea, Jenny, and there's nothing to be gained from conjecture, from worrying about it. At the moment I'm more inclined to book a trip to New York, to Quebec.' He stepped back into the shower.

'That's enough of the Spanish Inquisition for now. I just want to get clean, to climb onto the big bed and . . . to get some rest. It's a long way from Germany to Russia, and I don't sleep well on trains.' He laughed. She turned him around and started to soap his back, then turned him around again and started to soap the front of him.

*

'You're very kind,' Stoner was learning to answer to John once again. It was less easy than he'd expected, mainly because shifting identities on the fly is rarely comfortable and never seamless. The pianist in the ship's rather fluid jazz trio had invited him up to take a turn on a guitar. 'I'd rather listen to you guys. Play me something soothing, hey? It's been a long day, this one.'

The band obliged, and Stoner leaned over to the first officer, who was looking as stunning out of uniform as she did in it, while at the same time appearing to be almost another person entirely. 'It's good to be back. Good to see you again.' He caught her hand and squeezed it in his.

'Worth the train ride? Russian trains?'

'Surely.'

'Do you want to tell me what you've been doing? What you've really been doing?'

'No. Not really. I need a break. Need to think. Need to get a lot of things straight in my head. We've got lots of time before we need to make evaluations of each other, of what we're doing. Should I ask how your husband's doing?' His smile kept any unnecessary offence from his words.

'Point taken. Life on the ship has been quiet. Your departure while keeping the suite booked and paid for raised a few comments, but you got support from the captain – which was unexpected. He told the officers he'd met others like you while in the service of the mighty company and if duty called him or us other officers he'd expect us to ditch friends and family, shit like that, and just get on with it. Like you'd done. I think he was reliving the Falklands. He went there on a company ship filled with soldiers. I'd not known that before.'

'Wonder what he was on about? Duty? This isn't exactly the East India Company. It's American, for a start.'

'He did receive a long call from somewhere ashore in a very high building, and in Portsmouth not Southampton, I think. Well. I know, because I was there on the bridge when it came in. He told me it was about you because – old Boy Scout that he is – he'd observed that we're friends.'

'Clever guy. Admiral material, plainly. Salt of the earth. Sea. Whatever.'

'My husband's fine. We talk regularly and he tells me he's fine. I tell him that I'm fine too, so we're both fine.'

'Works well, then.'

'It does.'

'I like him more and more. He even knows what he's missing and I'm enjoying.'

'Was that a question? He does, anyway. Yes.'

'Then I like him even more than before and understand not a thing. Men are an endless mystery to me.'

'Women?'

'Them too.'

'Present company excepted, I suppose?'

'Nope. Why a woman as smart as this one – that's you – wastes her time fucking the very legs off a guy she mostly doesn't know and who lies to her all the time and never answers her questions and clears off when least expected . . . and then just turns up again and expects her to fuck his legs off again . . . Why would any even half-witted person do that? Everyone knows that everyone wants to meet the woman, man, whatever, of their dreams, fuck just the once, buy a house together in a new cardboard development and fuck just the once again to get a child, then once again to get another. Then they do debt and mortgage and football on the TV and self-hatred and mutual hatred and school fees so their kids can hate them and they can hate their kids and they can all go on a holiday to Benidorm for ten days off-peak where they can hate each other somewhere hot with peeling paint and cracking concrete walls and beer and pubs pretending they're in England . . .'

'You make it sound so good. My husband would like that. He wants to do those things. Some of them. The kids and school fees, but we already have a house – he lives in it – and now that you've revealed to me what I've been missing I think I'll hang up my epaulettes and hat and get pregnant. At once.' She flagged for drinks, which arrived with impressive speed and were exactly correct despite neither her nor Stoner expressing a preference or placing an order.

'Damn. I knew my eloquence would land me in trouble.' Stoner poured half the cold beer down his throat, shuddered and poured down the rest. Belched and apologised. 'Cool. I rarely drink beer. That was cold.' He shook his head to clear it.

The first officer laughed and sipped at her own drink. She shook her head in wonder at him; two heads, shaken in time but for different reasons.

'Tell me why you're a god to Joe.'

'Excuse me?' Stoner appeared taken aback by the suggestion. 'Who's Joe?'

'The band's leader.' She gestured at the small stage, where music was being played with considerable competence but little sparkle. 'He told me that you were some kind of guitar superhero whose socks he wasn't fit to wash or wear or something. I asked him why – it was a very quiet evening, most of the passengers were in Russia drinking industrial solvents they think is the real vodka and pretending to appreciate balalaika music played badly by disillusioned revolutionaries from Petrovsk or Peterborough or somewhere.' Stoner's beer replaced itself, a reflection upon a continuing age of miracles, perhaps.

'I can play a tune on a balalaika, too.' Stoner approached his refreshed drink with caution. 'Betcha didn't know that.'

'Which tune?'

'Don't know until I've played it. I compose my own; interpretive art, y'see.'

'Why does Joe think you're a guitar god, John?'

'Do you think I'm a guitar god? You're plainly in a better position to spot this, being a goddess – a sex goddess – yourself. Takes a god to spot a god, I do believe. Mere mortals gaze on in awe and wonder, so forth. More beer.'

'You play great stuff; you do. Different to the other guitarists we get on here – and we get through quite a few. Joe reckons you have a unique approach, says it's a talent; you either have it or you don't. He says you're a star – you've been a star in an earlier life or something. I can't see it. I can hear that you play differently – the last time you played "Girl From Ipanema" with the guys it was beautiful, but a guitar's got the same notes on it whoever plays it, so what's the difference, guitar god?'

'You really want a serious answer?'

'I really want a serious answer. To this, anyway.'

'I'll just switch off the false modesty button, OK?' He looked at her with a faintly serious expression. Just faintly serious.

'OK. Really.' Jenny tipped her glass at Stoner, took a sip and raised questioning eyebrows.

'It's like saying all guys got cocks and all girls got pussies. Easy as that. The same thing. Everyone knows what they're for; everyone can use them to have a good time, make babies and a mess. So anyone can learn to make a noise on an instrument. It's a noise; it is not *music*.' He paused, sipped and raised his eyes skyward for a moment.

'Real pretentiousness alert, baby. Some girls got all the beauty, all the boobs, the ass and all the sweet blue eyes and can play all the notes and even with all that they just do not make any music at all. Other girls got bodies like planks or like balloons and make heaven music like the gods themselves. It's just a thing. It can't be learned. And faking is obvious. Same with an instrument. The most beautiful instrument ever invented is the saxophone. It is golden poetry. In the right hands it can make you want to kill, to kiss, to weep or to wound. In the wrong hands it's just a brassy sludge pump which is impossible to tune.

341

'I'm not a great guitarist. I've known loads of better guitarists. But sometimes it's like the thing plays me. If I let go it just plays itself. Sometimes I start playing a tune I know and it takes my hands and together they do something outrageous. But only sometimes, Jen, mostly I'm just competent. Thing is, that when another musician hears that sometimes solo, they feel what's happening. Sometimes they have those sometimes moments themselves, and if they do their sometimes moment might be at that same time and then you get true blue magic, then time stops and the very gods listen and smile at what they've made. If you believe in them, of course.

'I do talk shit.' He drank a little more. 'But you did ask. I play the same notes in a different way. And the gaps between the notes talk as loudly as the notes themselves. I play bits of chords instead of full chords or single notes; I bend strings, one string, two strings maybe all of them just to prove a point, to make a tune between the tunes; there are notes between the notes. My favourite note is A. A is a great note. The next note up is B flat; a semitone away. But between A and B flat is an infinite number of other unofficial notes, and you get there by bending the string, making A a little bit sharp, a little bit more sharp until it's halfway to B flat. That's a quarter-tone. They don't exist in western music. But they do exist. The quarter-tone is the secret home of the blues. For wind and string instruments only. That is the law. Amen.'

The first officer was rapt, her eyes shone for him. 'And voices.'

'Yeah. Vox. The best and the worst instrument of them all. I can't sing. You met Bili, my lovely, lovely bassist. Did you hear her sing? She can break a heart at a thousand yards. None of this breaking glass nonsense; she breaks entire hearts; rooms-full in a single song. Magic. A goddess. Come and hear her. On dry land.'

'In your club?'

'Yeah. Blue Cube. Yeah.'

'I can take leave from Southampton. Lots due to me.'

'Sweets. I can't. Bad luck and trouble will hunt me down in the UK and I can't bring you into that.' Stoner's eyes were shining. Rage or music . . . she couldn't tell.

'I'll show you something. If Joe's agreeable.' Stoner got to his feet and approached the pianist and the singer and the electric bassist, shared words and returned to their shared table.

'What's the haps, Mr Hand?' Jenny waved away another drink, Stoner caught the waiter's eye and signalled the contrary. A fresh beer appeared before him.

The band's singer waved her fingers at them, and Stoner stood once more, leaned over to Jenny, took her hand and kissed it, whispered 'This. For you.' He walked to the tiny stage and tuned the guitar which had appeared from some secret place. The pianist and bassist played the intro to "Cry Me a River", then the singer sang her song and Stoner played along with her voice and then her voice was quiet and the guitar sang its own sad, blue view of the world and after two complete verses of melodic solo, just when the audience was starting to applaud, Stoner flicked switches on the electric guitar, rose from his three-legged stool to his own two feet and closed his eyes, and the evening soared away from them and he played three more solo verses, each harder, harsher and louder than the one before it and then he was suddenly silent, seated, and the singer sang and clapped to him at the same time, and their tiny audience, an audience of just dozens, clapped and whistled and shouted, and the trio wound up "Cry Me a River" and Stoner ended it solo, one slow note, slow vibrato shifting between sharp and back, then let the note drop and die. And still they applauded.

He rose, clapped to the audience and to the band, bowed and returned to their table.

Jenny stood and applauded him, quietly. Everyone allowed

them their space. Stoner sipped at his beer. Nodded, looked down at the table. Held her hands. Shook his head.

'That's how it goes.' He had tears in his eyes.

Small hours. The hum of the ship surrounding them, a small self-contained world enclosing their own. Still dressed, sitting in Stoner's suite, talking about nothing and everything, a peculiar reluctance to return to sharing a bed. Anticipation tinged with a strange nervousness, perhaps. An electronic shrill interrupted. Jenny pulled a pager from a pocket. Read its silent message, muttered an apology to Stoner, went to the cabin's phone and dialled. Listened. Muttered a confirmation and returned to stand over Stoner, collecting her jacket from the back of a chair and gazing at him with speculation.

'Pirates?' He attempted levity. 'Mutiny? And you say my world interrupts ours.'

'Your world, not mine. Your world interfering again, John. Can't it leave you alone? Just for a while?'

He sat upright from his comfortable slouch. 'My world? At this time of night?'

'This time of morning. That was your greatest fan. The captain. He would be honoured by your company on his bridge, in his office. My company only if you wish it. Which is charming, given that I work here and you don't.'

Stoner stood, frowning as he looked for shoes, socks. 'What's it about? Did he say?'

'A message for you. For you only. For right now. Any ideas, super-spook?'

'None. Nothing good at this time of night. And very few people have any idea where I am, which makes it less likely to be good news of some kind.' He was holding the door for her. 'Come along. If you want.'

'Do you want me along, John? Some woman weeping her eyes out in the middle of the night who's somehow found out where you are and how to get through ship net security?'

'It won't be anything of the sort. You're welcome. Whatever it is.'

'And if I see something really terrible you'll have to kill me?'

'Don't even joke about things like that.' No humour now, they headed for the bridge, encountering a two-man security detail on the way, a detail sent to encourage their presence.

The captain's table, in the captain's cabin. The captain's eyes-only monitor, a decent quality widescreen with an open window containing coding, coding impressive enough to have the captain woken at 03:00 along with his first officer and a passenger. An unusual combination.

'Mr Hand.' The captain shook his guest's hand, rather to the surprise of both parties.

'Apologies for this intrusion, captain.' Stoner radiated confidence and mild confusion. 'I'm supposed to be on holiday, and almost no one knows where I am. Almost no one at all. So what's this?' He gestured at the monitor. 'It's just junk to me, makes no sense.'

The captain pointed at a string of text. 'This is authority from as high as it gets ashore. Someone with high Admiralty clearance – military clearance – has asked for John Hand by name, detailing your cabin details, passport number and date and place of embarkation. Your eyes only. According to the techs, it's a piece of video. Your eyes only. I will honour that, but with some reluctance. Are you connected with the Admiralty, Mr Hand?'

Stoner shook his head. 'Not at all. Civil Service, if anything, but even hardly with them. Security, not military, but I'm not involved in anything meriting this kind of weight. Or urgency. I have no idea what this is. The only person I can think of who comes with the clearance to arrange this kind of thing is recently deceased. I think. Although a lot of guys have been talking about him . . .'

The captain shrugged. 'You want to be alone? I can leave

you with a technician to tell you how to press the start button.'

'No. Your ship. If anything, this is more likely to have relevance to my being aboard rather than to me alone. You need to know whatever it is. I'm not involved with anything that involves the ship. Truth, sir. Who's it from?'

'That's the comedy of it, Mr Hand.' The captain was more relaxed, less uncomfortable at being evicted from his own domain by a passenger. 'Because of the security level, all we see are the authorisations. No names, departments, and in this case no call-back at all. But the Admiralty authorisation is complete and accurate. And it claims to be urgent.'

He waved out the technician, leaving just the first officer and Stoner with him, and hit two keys together on his keyboard. 'Let's see what it is. Then we can get back to bed. We hope.'

The text was replaced by a fresh window containing a sharp, high-definition image of a man. An entirely naked man standing with his arms raised at about forty-five degrees to their shoulders and his legs splayed apart at the same angles, while his head hung down, as though he contemplated the secret meaning of the floor beneath him. He was white, very fit, very well-muscled, considerably tattooed and in a formidable state of arousal.

'Is this a joke?' The captain sounded less angry than might have been expected. 'Do you recognise this man, Mr Hand?'

Stoner nodded. 'I do. I don't think he's alone. I think there's someone behind him. It's not easy to see, but I think there's a second person. And I don't think it's a joke at all. I think . . . Jenny, you might want to leave. Really. Captain, I'm really concerned by this.'

She spoke for the first time since their arrival. 'You've seen this before, then?'

'No. But I know the man, worked with him in tough places for several years, and a joker he is not.'

The naked man raised his face and stared ahead of him.

And he spoke. No sound came from the speakers. Stoner looked a question at the captain.

'The speakers are live, there's no audio, just video.' The captain paused. 'He appears to have something tied around his penis.' He looked embarrassed. 'I'm sorry . . .'

Stoner waved him to silence. 'Shut it. Please. I'm trying to hear what he's saying.'

'There's no sound . . .'

'Watch his face. He's shouting.' Which was true, and as he shouted so the man in the movie snapped out of his cruciform pose and attained a startling military full attention. Legs together, arms straight at his sides, thumbs arrowing down the seams of the trousers he wasn't wearing, cock standing at attention all its own, improbably large and improbably coloured and shining. Both the man and his cock stared straight into the camera as though it were the eyes of an inspecting officer, and the camera moved in towards the face. His change of posture revealed that behind him was another figure, a much darker, more slender figure, a figure still holding the original cruciform attitude.

The man took a single precise step to his left, revealing a black woman, a tall black woman handcuffed to a cross which held her in place. She was as naked as her companion, the black of her skin interrupted only by a skullcap of tight, bright, very short blonde hair; blonde hair echoed at the join between her splayed legs. She glared at the camera, hate in every pore of her expression. Loathing, pure and undiluted. Animal hate.

'Fuck,' exclaimed Stoner, took two steps back and fell into a chair, which rolled away from the image. 'Fuck,' he said again, regaining his balance.

'She's not a stranger, then?' asked Jenny.

'Meet the wife,' muttered Stoner, rolling the chair towards the screen.

'You're married?' the captain and his first officer chorused. Stoner shook his head.

'No. But if I was . . .'

The male lead in the silent drama turned smartly, approached the glowering woman and rammed himself inside her. No pretence at passion, no pretence even at pleasure. He simply rammed it into her and performed like a machine, pumping fast, the tattoos on his back and backside writhing with his efforts and shining with his sweat. A second camera took over from the first, and focused on the penetration; perfect detail and focus. Close up.

'Mr Hand,' the captain wrenched his eyes from the performance. 'Why would someone senior enough to use naval authority one-time codes waste them sending you pornography?'

'Look and learn, captain,' said Stoner. 'Look and learn. And shut the fuck up. I'm trying to work out what they're shouting. There's a reason for the lack of audio. They've got at least two cameras, so it's pro filming . . .' He broke off. 'For Christ's sake, Shard, do it to her, why don't you?'

The pace of the pumping increased, reached its crisis, the buttocks clenched hard. The man grabbed the woman's hips and ground her against him. Pulled himself from her and stepped back, panting, a shining liquid string connecting him to her until it broke. Her hate was unabated. But it wasn't directed at him; she poured loathing at one of the cameras; at one of the operators.

The on-screen release also let loose tensions in the captain's cabin.

'Mr Hand,' began the captain. Stoner propelled himself from the chair, which rolled away beneath him until he caught it, swung it by its arms and flung it across the room, demolishing a water cooler and smashing a picture of the queen of England, who'd been surveying the proceedings without obvious amusement. Before anyone had understood that he

348

had actually moved, Stoner was leaning against the captain, his left forearm pinning that fine officer against the back of the door and cutting off his air. Stoner's right fist slammed into the door maybe an inch from the captain's wide-eyed stare, maybe a little less.

'Another word, and I'll silence you for a week. OK?' Stoner held the position. 'OK?' The captain nodded.

'John,' breathed Jenny.

'You too, miss.' Stoner released the bruised captain into a fit of coughing and turned to the first officer, who shook her head and pointed at the screen.

'It's not over,' she said.

Despite the vigour and intensity of his performance, the silent movie's star was still shouting and his unheard monologue was still accompanied by the presence of a startlingly large erection, huge, shining, dripping wet and as tattooed as most of his body. He shook his head, appearing to be in the process of arguing with himself as he turned away from the cameras and walked stiffly behind the black woman. The woman's gaze never wavered from one of the cameras, or from whoever was behind it.

The male lead, his head shaking from side to side and his expression increasingly anguished, positioned himself behind the crucified woman and rammed himself against her backside. After a moment's resistance – which allowed the second camera to close in on the action – she submitted and he took her in the ass, as hard and as violently as his previous frontal assault. The hate in her expression grew to new levels.

'Oh Christ, John. How can you watch this?' The first officer looked into his eyes. 'Can we just turn it off? He must be really hurting her.'

Stoner shook his head, and his voice was surprisingly gentle. 'She's a whore, Lissa, she's done loads . . . far worse than this. There's a message for me here, Jenny. I just can't see what it is. I've no idea at all why we're seeing this. Look, it's just two guys fucking. Look beyond that.'

'Not just any two guys, is it?' She was insistent. 'It's two people who are – what? – close to you? Important to you?'

He nodded, eyes staying with the screen. 'None closer. Shard's the nearest thing a man like me has to a best friend; Lissa – the dirty blonde, they all call her – is the reason I ran away to sea in the first place.'

'What?' She stared at him.

'Long story. Shut up now – please shut up – and let me try to make some sense from this. I bet we won't be able to see it a second time. I need to understand why Shard was made to fuck her and why serious juice has been used to get the movie of it in front of me. Oh.'

Stoner stopped speaking and stared at the screen.

Shard's right hand reached round in front of the shuddering, glowering woman and appeared to punch her hard in her belly, by her left hip, and then pull across, drawing a rough line below her navel. A seam of blood, dark against the dark skin, followed it. The woman's gaze was torn from its relentless focus of hate and looked down at herself. Blood was running freely and her abdomen bulged weirdly. Her assailant repeated the stab and the slice, all the while continuing with the relentless rape, his face contorted into senseless shapes, his eyes rolling impossibly. And quite suddenly he collapsed, simply fell to the floor, strings cut, entirely still, sweat steaming from him, eyes staring, no longer rolling, simply staring at nothing.

The view pulled back from the prostrate man, the illustrated white man, until it included the black woman, the victim of the violence, hanging from the cross now, not standing, but glaring once again at the camera, panting, drooling, two long cuts across her stomach, blood everywhere, dark on dark, strings of it, dripping and pooling beneath her. The hatred in her stare undiminished. She shuddered, a shining loop of intestine creeping free from her but still she glared at the camera, the hate of an entire black continent in her eyes.

And the video ended as it began. In silence.

'I need to be off the ship.' Stoner was sweating with tension. Pacing. The captain's spacious cabin shrank around him. 'I need to get ashore now. I need to catch a flight and . . .'

'It's not as easy as that.' Jenny and Stoner were alone in her captain's cabin. 'Ships just don't work that way. We're a week from Southampton.' She pulled him down, sitting knee to knee, facing each other. 'Just talk to me. Tell me what we've just seen. It's a message to you. But what? We can't get you ashore, but you can contact – securely – anyone you want. Thinking's all you can do now, John. So think. What's that filth all about?'

'It's a summons, isn't it?' He was fighting himself for calm, face pale and breathing rapid, hands clenching into fists and then releasing themselves again. He stood, suddenly, a clasp knife unfolding, then seated himself again. Pounded his fisted right hand into the palm of his left, so hard that Jenny flinched at the first impact. He reversed hands, slamming his left fist into his right palm. Then switched again, the pace of the impacts slowing. 'It's a summons. A challenge. I can't ignore it.'

The door opened, presenting them with the captain, cool and immaculate in his white uniform. 'We can have you ashore tomorrow in Klaipeda. Or I can call in a medical emergency and get a chopper at first light.' Stoner nodded his thanks. The captain continued, impressively calm. 'You have astonishing clearance for an amateur musician on holiday, Mr Hand. Care to tell me what's going on here? I needed to tell Southampton who the evac was for. Gave them your name, which meant nothing to anyone, then gave them your passport number when they asked for it and all of a sudden you're

Christ down from the Cross, admiral of the fleet, no access restrictions, no service too small, my ship is your ship. Unique. The last time I saw anything like this on a merchant ship was during the Falklands nightmare. So. What is going on? And what do you need?'

Stoner looked up, knives in his eyes, but the sweat had dried as cold condensed around him, and he spoke with growing precision.

'Truth? I don't know. I can make up plenty of theories, but in truth I'm uncertain. And I certainly do not have clout like you describe. Not me. Someone else has set that up.'

'Was it genuine? You said the filming was professional; was the . . . was it real or was it special effects?' The captain's cool was contagious.

'Easier and cheaper if it was real.' Stoner was becoming increasingly matter of fact. He was calming, chilling before their eyes. 'Can't figure out what they'd done to Shard – the guy – to make him behave like that, but it wasn't doing him a lot of good. And Lissa? I think she'd be dead after that, so . . .' He paused. Considered. Several measured breaths. 'So there's no point in me rushing around like an avenging idiot. That's what they'll expect – whoever they are, and I do have an idea about that. A likely candidate. A resurrection. A man back from the dead.

'Thanks for your offer to get me ashore. Sorry about the . . . loss of control. Captain. It's not every day I see something as . . . extreme as that. As personally extreme. But I manhandled you and must apologise for that. Forgive me.' He looked over to the first officer, then looked away, broke the contact between them. 'And thank you – both of you – for helping me think. I'm still thinking. Can you announce that you've put me ashore without actually doing that?'

'Announce to whom?' The captain was puzzled. 'We don't tell anyone who comes and goes from the ship.'

'Oh yes you do, though it's probably not obvious to anyone

352

who's honest.' Stoner's voice was almost calm, his tone remote. Processing. Analysing. Running scenarios. 'Your system will update the passenger manifest. Whoever ashore has the access to send snuff movies through your company's secure comms will certainly be able to read your data files, passport details, probably all your emails, texts and the like, professional and personal, they all use similar systems. Hack one, you've hacked most others on the same servers.'

The captain's surprise was as plain as it was surprising. 'Really?' he managed.

'Welcome to the electric age, captain.' Stoner shook his head gently. 'So I need to officially leave the ship and I need you to do whatever you do to advise your system that I've left. The cabin's paid for until Southampton, so it would help me if I can actually stay here. Is that possible?'

'Why?' The first officer joined in. 'Don't you need to get back to the UK to . . . well . . . sort this out? If the vid's genuine, then don't you want . . . don't you need to see how your friends are? Your . . . what . . . colleagues?' She sounded genuinely puzzled and more than a little concerned. Stoner shook his head slowly again, his surface calm complete and cooling before them.

'If it's real, then they're either dead or in shit so deep I can't do anything about it. If it's a faked-up tribute to the cinematic arts then they're not in trouble and there's nothing to be done. Either way, it starts to look like a crude way of pushing me into doing something predictable, which means that they'd be controlling my actions, which means that they'd be controlling what I do.'

'That's pretty cold, John. Pretty damned cold. Are you OK? You sound . . . different. Are you in shock or something? Two minutes ago you were demanding that we pull the ship into port right now to let you off.'

'I need to be cold, miss. Anything else would be the death of me. This is the old going to war heroism nonsense.' Stoner spoke, the captain nodded his agreement. 'I scream revenge, rush into the plan they've made for me – and they have made a plan, there's no reason for the vid otherwise – and as soon as they know exactly where I am, maybe letting me break a few heads, tip over a couple of tables, make a macho fuss and feel good . . . then something bad will happen. To me. Which must be the purpose of the exercise. They're not doing this for anyone else's benefit.

'They'll expect me to behave all Jason Bourne and go charging around like a movie hero. Three minutes ago that's exactly what I'd have done. But I won't. With your permission' – he acknowledged both captain and first officer – 'I'll just vanish. Maybe get off at Southampton, maybe get off earlier or later, but if I could appear to the system to have left the ship in Klaipeda, that's where they'll look – at routes from Lithuania to the UK. I'm decently slippery, so they won't be surprised when they can't find me, though there can't be many routes available, so they're being smart enough. Captain? Any chance of this happening?'

The captain gazed at his hands.

'Who are you, Mr Hand? Who are you actually? Who do you work for? And what do you do? Are you a risk to my ship and our passengers and crew? I need to ask and you need to answer. Straight up. Do I actually need to put you in a cell and call the police? Despite the word from Southampton, do I need to protect my ship from you? And what you've brought with you?'

Stoner half-laughed, not a comfortable sound. 'You don't need to lock me up, captain. Jen . . . your first officer knows some of it, but knowledge isn't power, knowledge is vulnerability and visibility. People who are not interested in you may take an interest. You've seen the evidence of the kind of people they are. What you genuinely don't know usually doesn't hurt you. If the price you want to permit Plan A – staying here while appearing to do the opposite – is some background, then fine.'

The captain leaned back in his swivel chair, caught his hands together behind his head. 'Convince me, and I'll lie to the company – to Southampton. What you say can't go from this room, because messing around with the ship's security systems would result in my losing my command and Jenny here losing her job. Simple as that. And you're correct. Your plan – Plan A – is the right military way to go. So you're military? I'm a Royal Navy reservist, like a few of my colleagues in the company. Who're you?'

Jenny said nothing, but watched Stoner with close attention as he spoke with deliberate precision.

'OK. Here's me: Stoner, Jean-Jacques. Pleased to meet you,' delivered without a hint of a smile. 'I'm normally employed to locate missing persons, usually by independent arms of the UK government, which is a careful way of telling you that what I do is always politically deniable but almost always official. I served with the infantry in Ireland, Iraq, Afghanistan and the like. For the last maybe ten, twelve years I've been a freelance. A contractor. All the work is security based – national security if you're after a newspaper headline for it. People get damaged, their basic human rights are ripped up before their eyes and electable accountable politicians usually have no idea of the realities of it – apart from some PPS at the Home Office. And maybe COBRA if the shit gets really deep. Is that enough?'

'Who is John Hand, Mr Stoner? There's nothing false about your paperwork. I had it checked. And I think you pulled a stunt before you left us last time.'

'John Hand is a workname. I borrowed it from a dead man.' He stopped, paused. 'A man I believed to be dead.' He shook his head as sudden fury rose along with a heavy flush to his cheeks. 'I'll need to reassess that. The passport itself is genuine HMG issue. Effectively I'm a government employee . . . of the remote sort with no fat pension rights. You have no need to know of any stunts. You have to trust me on that.'

'What do I call you? John Hand or the other one?'

'While I'm aboard this ship you need to call me John Hand.' He paused. 'Mr Hand. I'm a top suite passenger after all. That goes for you too . . . miss. You both need to stay a safe distance away from me, just as Stoner needs to stay in hibernation for a while. Does that mean we can do a deal?'

'For the week or so it takes to return to Southampton? I think so.' That captain stood, beckoned them to the door of his domain. 'And you were right, Mr Hand. We weren't able to copy the video and it won't play again. Someone's very good with IT.'

'You can bet on it. The minute your system tells them I've left the ship, they'll leave you in peace and start checking transport links in Lithuania. I'm banking on their not actually speaking much Lithuanian.' He paused. 'A bigger risk, but one we should be aware of, is that they may have eyes on the ship. It's easy to buy observers and it's easy for them to report ashore in this electric age.'

The captain shook his head. 'I know my crew. I'd vouch for them.'

'You can't. I'm not thinking about your officers, captain. Think about the cabin stewards, cocktail waitresses and cooks. What would they say if they were offered a UK residency and a few thousand dollars untraceable?'

Jenny reached for Stoner's arm, stopped him as he made to leave the cabin. 'Is there anyone you should contact, John? Someone you should warn? Whoever sent the vid – made it – they're plainly insane as well as dangerous.'

Stoner rested his hand on hers, very briefly. Then he lifted her hand from his arm and let it fall. 'Dangerous? Insane? You reckon? They've just taken two of my closest . . . and shown me what they did. No more friends. Sorry, is all. Contact with me's just an invite to them: I'd just be writing their hit list for them.'

'No one who can help you? John?'

356

He paused, considered. 'I'm beaten. That's it. Understand that if nothing else. It's not possible to recover from this. Not here, not now. No one can help me here. Now. And I can't be John for you until this is over. It would kill you. I'm toxic, you've seen it. Stay away. Picture yourself being destroyed by a man like the man in the movie. Maybe worse than that. Don't come near me any more. At all. I have nothing, only horror stories. Forget me. That way you stay alive.

'Same for you, captain. Officially I'm off your ship at the next port. That clears you and your crew. Thank you both . . . for all of it. Now just keep the fuck away from me. Save your souls.' He left, quietly closing the door. Left them in silence. Only silence.

Now read on for an extract from

First Contract,

introducing then-sergeant Stoner in a former life:

Confusion. Instant confusion. Where there should have been order out of the chaos of war there was only chaos and further chaos.

Sudden movements of several bodies disguised the flight of the blade. The sound of the blade's impact was disguised by the grunt of the target as it landed. The source of the blade – the exact source – was disguised by the movement of all the bodies concerned and by the bleeding grunt of the target; all eyes were on him, not seeking the source of the blade.

Blood spurted as the blade sliced a vessel in the target's neck. Either a remarkably skilled and accurate throw, particularly so since the movement had been so effectively disguised, or a singularly lucky throw. The spurt of the blood was stemmed immediately to a restrained flow by prompt action on the part of the soldier standing next to the victim. The transformation from target to victim had been accomplished with exquisite ease; the screech of static from a radio confirmed that the instant call for immediate medical assistance had been acknowledged, so attentions shifted to the source of the attack, a group of five local civilians all wearing the same beards, soft hats and loose clothing, all of the clothing the colour of the scrubby Iraqi desert, no helpful insignia nor useful signs from the heavens above to indicate which if any of them was formal recognisable military or which of them had thrown the knife to such immediate and remarkable effect.

One of the three standing, uniformed and therefore formally identifiable soldiers strode with purpose and plain intent to the group of Iraqis, spread out his opened palms before them and asked them to reveal who had thrown the blade. With a certain inevitability, the same pidgin English which had always been entirely comprehensible for the many non-military transactions of a soldier's life in a faraway land – procuring and negotiating life's little luxuries to ease a tour's burdens and lonelinesses – was now entirely mysterious to the five locals; they rolled their collective eyes in shared anguish at the catastrophe which had befallen the stricken soldier, but plainly considered that the knife's flight was the result of heavenly intervention and that they were all witnesses to a miraculous act, rather than a clever murderous attempt.

The solo soldier, a sergeant, and plainly a senior one, looked back at his stricken comrade. Dressings and pressures had been applied, a medevac chopper promised, but heads were being shaken – heads out of the injured soldier's sightline – and more British blood was leaking pointlessly into the desert sand.

The sergeant repeated his demand for information, speaking gently but with sufficient force for his words to carry to all ears present, to native and invader alike. His tone was one of weariness, resignation, no particular aggression and certainly no violent intent. His words produced only more theatrical incomprehension, much shaking of heads, much shared and plainly sincere regret at the tragic leakage of life before them. The name of Allah was invoked more than once; he was either to blame or was offering comfort and forgiveness, it was difficult to recognise which in the sadness of the moment. Five sets of open palms were paraded before the sergeant; all of them as innocent as the other, was the suggestion.

A single shot interrupted the stage grief; one of the Iraqis sagged from seated to fallen, his dark blood draining from his exploded head into the sands of his native home. The sergeant held his smoking handgun in plain view, spread his arms wide to express his regret, his masculine sorrow. He looked towards his fallen comrade, a friend maybe, certainly a military brother. Heads were shaken. A body was stretched out onto the sands, sunburned British hands reached for weapons; the sergeant shook his own head, turned back to the four remaining prisoners, and spoke once more, revealing his sorrow at the pointless tragedy which had befallen them all, his regret at his poor mortal inability to judge his fellow men, and how he shared the belief of the men before him that their deity was indeed most merciful, most powerful and all forgiving. Particularly the latter; a fine constant in such unpleasant and uncertain times. A comfort in the dark days of this life. He fired again: the nearest prisoner; once in the head, an execution, probably painless, death certainly instant.

Screams of protest arose from the remaining three men, two of whom scrambled to their knees before him, wails of supplication thrown before him for his attention. The third man wailed but he did not kneel. The sergeant once again shot the nearest prisoner to him; more blood, more brain tissue decorated the desert. Shaking his head sadly, he walked to the remaining supplicant, who was gesturing at his seated companion; plainly blame was being allocated and mercies entreated. In decent English. A miracle. The sergeant nodded his understanding and shot the supplicant through his left eye; death was instant, the brain reduced by the bullet's passage into something less than it had previously been. The desert once more reddened around them, and was nourished.

The sergeant stood before the sole survivor, who sat cross-legged and relaxed, holding his gaze with dignity and patience.

No histrionic displays of terror, simply acceptance. 'Salaam,' said the sergeant and shot the prisoner through his left eye, as before, without waiting for a response. He turned to face his comrades, joined them in listening for an approaching helicopter; none was in earshot. No words were necessary; the three men dug five graves, one for each of the native dead. Their own dead companion they wrapped in a bedroll, and they began their trek back to their temporary desert residence. In the distance they could hear the double pulse of a twin-rotor chopper, the unmistakeable call of the Chinook coming to carry them home.

Find out what happens next in the complete short story, *First Contract*. It's available, along with other episodes from the long active life of JJ Stoner, as an ebook at Amazon.co.uk

About the author

Frank Westworth shares several characteristics with JJ Stoner: they both play mean blues guitar and ride Harley-Davidson motorcycles. Unlike Stoner, Frank hasn't deliberately killed anyone. Instead, he edits classic motorcycle magazines and has written extensively for the UK motoring press. Frank lives in Cornwall with his guitars, motorcycles, partners and cat.

Thanks for reading right to the very end. We hope you enjoyed The Corruption Of Chastity. If you did, please take a few moments to review it on Amazon or Goodreads. Your feedback would be very much appreciated.

JJ Stoner will return in the final episode of the Killing Sisters series in the autumn of 2016. If you'd like to stay in touch with JJ in the meanwhile, then you'll find Frank Westworth and info about new Stoner short stories at his website www.murdermayhemandmore.net